Measureless Night

Also by Chris Culver

Stand-alone novels:

Nine Years Gone
Just Run

Ash Rashid novels:

The Abbey
The Outsider
By Any Means
Measureless Night

MEASURELESS NIGHT

CHRIS CULVER

MEASURELESS NIGHT

All Rights Reserved © 2015 Chris Culver

No part of this book may be reproduced or transmitted in any form or by any means, graphic, electronic, or mechanical, including photocopying, recording, taping, or by any information storage or retrieval system, without the written permission of the publisher.

This book is a work of fiction. The names, characters, places, and incidents are products of the writer's imagination or have been used fictitiously and are not to be construed as real. Any resemblance to persons, living or dead, actual events, locale or organizations is entirely coincidental.

Published by Chris Culver

ISBN-13: 9781508924074

Chapter One

Water, the last vestiges of a snow shower earlier that day, slid across salt-encrusted sidewalks to the street before settling and freezing in potholes, forming oily black mirrors in the roadway. The flicker of a television danced through the curtains of an American four-square half a block away, the only sign of life on an otherwise dark night. It was an aberration from what she had seen on the previous seven nights but not enough of one to forestall their plans; likely, the television's owner—an elderly woman who lived alone and whose children rarely visited—had merely fallen asleep with it on.

Inside their vehicle, Carla could still smell the hand lotion she had put on that afternoon, the cheap aftershave Jacob had lathered on that morning, and the stale remnants of coffee in the mug to her side. Rarely did she feel as alive as she did in moments like this, when adrenaline coursed through her body, heightening her senses. Though she had tried every drug her husband had pushed to his less than discriminating clients, adrenaline was Carla's favorite. It reminded her of the power she had inside her, the power of life and death.

Their vehicle was off, had been off for several hours now. Carla preferred to work alone, but she couldn't do the job by herself. She needed help, and Jacob, her stepson, willingly obliged. Michelle Washington, their victim, had light brown skin and hopeful brown eyes that seemed to say nothing bad had ever happened to her. She had the body of a runner, with small breasts, thin hips, and skin stretched taut over the muscles of her arms and legs.

By day, she worked as a social worker for the city, and at night, she slept alone in an antique queen-sized bed with an olive green comforter. She had spent the evening at an Alcoholics Anonymous meeting and had been dropped off by a friend, Detective Ash Rashid, a few minutes ago, only to leave again and walk to her brother's house two blocks away. There, she'd meet her parents and her brother for their weekly Wednesday night supper. Neither Michelle nor Dante nor Ash knew it, but they all had a role to play in the events to come, and they were all dead in theory, if not in fact.

Michelle, the most difficult of the kills Carla had planned, would die first, but she and Jacob had lined the dominos up weeks ago. Now they needed a push.

Carla glanced at Jacob out of the corner of her eye. He stared intently at Michelle's house, just as he had for each of the previous seven nights. They hadn't stayed in the same spot each night, not even on the same street, but she knew the area well. The interstate lay a mere four blocks from the house, the cabin in the Morgan-Monroe State Forest where they planned to extract what they needed from Michelle lay an hour's drive from that, and the dumping ground near the Boy Scout camp on the northeast side of Indianapolis lay a little over an hour from the cabin. They didn't have long to wait, but she still had to find tricks to pass the time without losing her edge.

"Do you ever read, Jacob?" asked Carla, breaking the silence for the first time since their vigil began.

"Like books?"

"Yes, books," she said, casting her gaze out the window. "Novels, maybe. Something for fun, at least."

He looked at her and put his hands on the steering wheel. "No."

She nodded, expecting that answer. "I've been reading some lately. Did you like killing that girl in Kansas?"

The girl in Kansas, twenty-seven-year-old Zoe Dawson, was a newly-engaged single mother who lived in a very cute, historic bungalow near the intersection of Twenty-Fourth Street and Washington Boulevard in the Kansas side of Kansas City. Carla didn't think of herself as cruel, and she wouldn't have chosen Zoe, a woman with so much life to look forward to, had she not fit the profile so well. Twenty-seven years old, five foot four, and a hundred twenty-five pounds, she could have been Michelle Washington's twin. She provided the perfect opportunity to practice, and while her death was unfortunate, the real tragedy was her son, who had woken up at precisely the wrong time and come into the room at precisely the wrong moment.

Carla had lit a candle for both of them in the Cathedral Basilica of St. Louis on the way back to Indianapolis.

"The girl with the kid?" asked Jacob.

"Did you kill anyone else in Kansas City and not tell me?" she asked, smiling sweetly.

"No," said Jacob, quickly.

"It's a simple question, then," said Carla, looking out the window. "Did you like killing her? Was it fun to corner her and see her cry?"

He glanced over but immediately looked back at the house. "What the hell kind of question is that?"

"I'm just curious. I only have my experience to go on, but a couple of the books I've read recently describe it as being an almost sexual experience. I wondered if it was like that for everybody."

Jacob shook his head. "No. It wasn't fun. It was…too wet."

It had been Jacob's first time practicing his knife work, and he hadn't been very sure of himself. As unpleasant as it had been, she needed to make sure he could do the job. Theoretically, she knew anyone who could channel enough force through an ax could cut someone's hand off, but she had never seen it done before. Jacob certainly had the strength, but she didn't know if he had the will. Would he run when their victim screamed? Would he demand they call 911 rather than watch her bleed to death? Before she could move forward, she had needed those questions answered. Thankfully, he had obliged.

Truthfully, Jacob's trepidation had surprised her. It was so unlike his father, her husband. Many of the men she knew—her husband among them—seemed to enjoy killing people. Carla didn't relish the job, but she understood its necessity. Few messages were as effective as those written in blood.

Michelle would be the fifth murder Carla had been involved with. The first had been sixteen years ago, a drug dealer named Reggie Johnson. She had been in high school then, barely through her ugly duckling stage, and she was still trying to find herself.

Reggie specialized in large-quantity deals, so he worked mostly with other dealers, Carla included. She liked the money provided by her illicit career, but more than that, she liked the thrill of it and the control it gave her over others. The day he died, Reggie had worn a black leather jacket, a black turtleneck sweatshirt, and a pair of jeans. It happened in the parking lot of a fast-food joint near I-65, southeast of the city. Supposedly, Carla and her boyfriend had come for a routine resupply of the marijuana Carla sold to her fellow students at George Washington Community High School. David Something-or-other—Carla couldn't remember his actual name now—shot Reggie twice in the chest with a twelve-gauge pump-action shotgun.

She hadn't anticipated it going that way, though she knew David had brought a shotgun with him. Sometimes fate has a way of bringing good things to people who deserve them. Before driving there, she told David that Reggie had sexually assaulted her during a previous drug deal. She explained to him that she couldn't tell the police because they'd demand to know how and why she and Reggie knew each other, nor could she tell another responsible adult. She was on her own, with just her boyfriend to protect her.

In fact, Reggie hadn't touched her at all. Had he merely done that, she could have forgiven him...if given suitable recompense. No, Reggie died because he had asked to die, begged for it really. He called her fat. He had said it aloud to one of his partners, right where she could hear it as she climbed out of her car for a re-up near her high school. *You know Carla. The chubby one.* That's what he had said, explaining who he planned to meet. Reggie's partner looked right at her and nodded. Carla hadn't said anything at the time, not that Reggie would have cared either way, but she couldn't forget it. It was so carelessly cruel.

Carla and David drove out to that Wendy's parking lot on a cold February afternoon to teach Reggie a lesson, but when they showed up, Reggie saw that shotgun and pulled his own weapon, a black revolver, from his pocket and raised it toward her. Despite witnesses, David fired without hesitation, killing Reggie on the spot. Had she known his loyalty ran that deep, she would have slept with him one final time as a thank you.

David didn't try to run after the shooting. He simply put his shotgun on the ground, laced his fingers behind his head, and sat down. Despite an extensive interrogation, and despite being charged with murder, he never mentioned Carla's name. Not once. David Something-or-other, her dashing hero to the end. She really wished she could remember his name; his sacrifice would seem so much nobler that way.

The second murder was both simpler and more complicated. Carla's father was one of the most inept petty criminals in the city and, normally, neither of them cared what the other did. But then in her senior year of high school, her father's drug use increased and he started openly bringing home strays—girls, some the same age as Carla, some of whom she even knew—he picked up in bars around town. The neighbors started talking, raising questions not only about her father's misadventures but also about her. She lost customers, but she could deal with that. Then, her father knocked up one of his girlfriends, which decided his fate.

On an average weekend, her father snorted an eighth of an ounce of cocaine. He bought it from a kid who worked a street corner near his parole officer's office. The product was garbage. Good coke, the kind a quality dealer sells, is roughly seventy-percent pure and won't have any harmful additives. Her dad's coke was probably twenty- to thirty-percent pure and had likely been cut with lidocaine, a commonly available anesthetic that simulated the numbing effect of real cocaine.

Carla, one Friday afternoon, decided to give her dad a taste of the good stuff. She bought a quarter of an ounce of a very good product and purified it further herself with an acetone wash. By the time she finished, she had an eighth of an ounce of extremely refined cocaine, a product somewhere between three and four times the strength her father had grown accustomed to. She swapped his drugs for her own and cheerfully met some friends at the local movie theater. When she came back, she found her father slumped over a cat-scratched coffee table in the living room, dead. The police questioned her about her father's associates and friends, and she happily gave up everyone. The police arrested her father's dealer and convicted him of a number of charges, including involuntary manslaughter. Even though he hadn't harmed her father, he deserved the prison time. Selling the junk he did, he harmed the business for everyone.

As strange as it felt to say, Carla found killing her father to be the most satisfying thing she had ever done. She felt proud of herself for it. She got away with murder, something very few people can say, and she did it for a good reason. She kept her father from knocking up any other unsuspecting idiot girls, and she managed to remove a drug dealer from the streets in the bargain. The world needed people like her, people willing to do the necessary thing at the appropriate time. If that meant she gained something as a result, all for the better.

A car passed their vehicle, its tires hissing on the damp asphalt. In some neighborhoods, that might have been enough for Carla to call the night off. But not here. Not where the homes were so old they had been built with carriage houses too small to hold a modern vehicle. Everyone parked on the street. She and Jacob blended into the shadows and the night itself.

The minutes stretched into an hour, and Jacob's breath grew more and more shallow and rapid. At some point, he started bouncing his foot on the floorboards. Carla understood his nervousness the same way a blind man might have understood the color red. She had read about and heard others talk about their nervous experiences, but the actual feeling was as foreign to her as the landscape of the moon.

Then, Michelle appeared, brandishing the sort of genuine grin that had escaped Carla despite years of practice. It was something in the eyes, she supposed. Michelle's black, thick hair bounced as she walked. A happy young lady returning home from a family get-together, perfectly content and perfectly ignorant of the threat in front of her or the sin that had given rise to it. Lost in her own world, they'd take her easily.

She and Jacob left the car at the same time, pretending to argue. Carla held a map and Jacob scowled. It felt colder than usual that night, and a breeze whistled through the leafless limbs of nearby trees. Jacob had his mother's thin, wiry build. He wouldn't intimidate anyone, but he could take care of himself in a fight. He had proved that in Kansas, removing Zoe's hand with a hatchet while Carla held her down. They carried few supplies between them. A compact semiautomatic firearm for emergencies, polypropylene gloves, a rather expensive cell phone purchased from a convenience store with which they could make anonymous calls. Their primary tools were their brains. Carla preferred it that way.

They caught Michelle as she opened the front door to the house, safety just beyond her grasp.

"Excuse me," called Carla, waving from the sidewalk. "I hate to bother you, but my brother and I are lost."

Michelle huddled behind the storm door as if it were some kind of shield.

"Where are you trying to go?"

Carla folded the map in on itself and strode forward. Jacob followed a few steps behind her.

"We're supposed to meet a friend of mine from college," she said. "I'm in the right neighborhood, I think. This is Irvington, right? My cell's dead, and all I've got is this stupid map I printed from the Internet."

Even though Carla and Jacob kept coming forward, Michelle's face relaxed a little.

"What street are you looking for? I might be able to point you in the right direction, at least."

"Thank you so much," said Carla, smiling and walking the rest of the way to the house. As soon as she reached the stoop, she held out her map with one hand while reaching to the weapon at her waist with the other. "I'm looking for Maple Lane. My map says it should be just up the street, but I can't find it."

"You're fairly close, actually," said Michelle, her voice brightening. "Go to the end of my road and hang a left onto Poplar. It'll intersect Maple in just a block or two."

Carla smiled broadly and let out a sigh of relief. "Thank you so much. I need you to do one more favor for me, and I need you to stay calm. Can you do that?"

Michelle's back stiffened. She seemed to hold her breath, but then she nodded.

"I need you to walk back into your house as if you've just asked us inside," said Carla, moving the map to expose the barrel of her firearm. "If you don't, I will shoot you. We're going to follow you in. If you listen to us, we won't hurt anyone."

Michelle took a step back and swept her arm to the side. "What do you want?"

"You'll find out soon enough."

Chapter Two

In my defense, it didn't start as an unmitigated disaster. By the project's halfway point, though, I'd say I was well on my way toward it. Bits and pieces of my wife's rocking chair—the one her grandmother had rocked her mother in, the one she and I had rocked our kids in every night of the first few months of their lives—lay strewn across my garage floor, while my daughter sat two feet away from me on the other end of my maple workbench, her feet dangling in midair and a curiously understanding expression on her face.

"*Ummi's* going to be mad."

I wiped sawdust and wood glue onto my jeans and stepped back from the products of my labor, marveling at Megan's gift for understatement.

"Yep."

"You should have taken a picture before you took it apart."

I glanced at my daughter and picked up two parts from the floor that looked as if they belonged together. "Where were you two hours ago with that advice?"

She shrugged and kicked her legs. "Probably at school."

I put the pieces on my workbench and leaned forward, resting my forearms on the bench in front of me and looking at the ground. My garage had post-and-beam construction with exposed oak trusses supporting the roof, a poured concrete floor, and thick fiberglass insulation beneath drywall installed one summer just five years ago. It kept me warm even on the coldest December night. I'd probably find that useful when Hannah asked me to sleep in it.

"Your mother is a very kind, forgiving woman. She'll understand."

Megan picked up a juice box and sucked until the straw hit air bubbles. "If you say so."

I glanced at her. "You want to talk about what happened at school?"

"No," she said, kicking her legs harder. "Can we get a Christmas tree this year?"

I bent and picked up a rubber mallet, the inspiration for and source of my current troubles, from the floor. "We're Muslims, so we don't celebrate Christmas. And let's try to stay focused on one topic. I think we should talk about what happened at school."

"Lelia's family had a Christmas tree last year."

I hung the mallet on its hooks on the pegboard wall above my workbench. "We're not Lelia's family."

The glare of the overhead light caught off Megan's black hair so that it almost shimmered as she shook her head. "Mr. Abaza said Christmas isn't religious anymore."

"Mr. Abaza, with all due respect, doesn't know very many Christians, then." Megan started to respond, so I held up a finger. "And even if he was right, we're not celebrating Christmas."

Megan blinked once, and then twice at me, and I could practically see the neurons firing in her brain as she hatched a plan. "Does *Ummi* know you took her chair?"

"Not yet." I turned to my workbench and twisted the orange top of a container of wood glue to close it.

"Sometimes it's better if a husband fixes things before his wife asks. You'll learn that if you get married when you grow up. I'd like to talk about school now. Did you see Sydney today?"

"Of course. I sit beside her."

"Did the other kids make fun of her?"

Megan lowered her chin and raised her eyebrows as if she planned to say something obvious to anyone but the most obtuse. "Not after you kicked Mrs. Mitchell's ass."

Sydney was one of Megan's friends in her second-grade class, and while I didn't know her family well, they lived just a few blocks from us. Yesterday, my wife charged me with picking the two of them up from school, where I found out that Sydney had peed her pants when Mrs. Mitchell refused to let her go to the bathroom without a bathroom pass. After seeing the stain on Sydney's pants and hearing her story, I gave her my suit jacket to wear and escorted the girls to the front office, where I had a discussion with Mrs. Mitchell and their principal. I might have lost my temper and raised my voice slightly.

"I didn't kick anyone's anything," I said, putting my hands on Megan's shoulders. "And that's not a word you should use."

"Which word?"

"You know which word."

She grinned so widely that she nearly had to close her eyes. "Kicked?"

"The next time you use the a-word, I'll put you in time out," I said, turning my attention toward the pile of wood on my garage floor and wondering how the hell I would ever turn it into a functioning rocking chair again. "Did Mrs. Mitchell say anything?"

"She wasn't there. Mr. Raymond said she might not be back for a while."

At least I had accomplished something. "If you ever have a teacher who prevents you from using the bathroom or doing anything else you need, tell me or *Ummi*," I said, feeling my phone buzz in my pocket. "We want to know these things."

"I know."

Megan jumped off the workbench and nearly tripped on two slats of wood as I reached into my pocket. I caught her and glanced at my phone to see who had called. The number belonged to Paul Murphy, a buddy of mine from work. Paul and I had never actually worked together on a case, but I respected him more than I did most detectives. Some guys, they get as many years on the job as Paul and I have, they think they know everything, that they've seen everything, that the world can't possibly toss anything new their way. Paul and I both thought differently. Twice a year—on his own dime—he went to law enforcement conferences to learn about new investigative techniques, new crimes, and new technology. He had a good head on his shoulders and a decent heart. I had liked him from the moment we met.

As I answered my phone, Megan told me she was going inside. I nodded and patted her back, prodding her toward the door.

"Paul," I said, smiling and hoping it was evident in my voice. "Hannah and I are going out tonight, so I can't talk long. What's going on?"

"Cancel your plans. You've got something heading your way. Are you at home right now?"

The smile slipped from my face. "Excuse me?"

"I don't know what's going on," said Paul, his voice a throaty whisper. "But Mike Bowers just tore out of here, and he's heading to your house."

Mike Bowers oversaw the Crimes Against Persons unit at my department. He and I didn't always get along, but he was a good cop, save for rare occasions when he shoved his head so far up his own ass that he couldn't see obvious things right in front of him.

"Why would Mike come to my house?"

Paul paused, but I heard him wheeze as he caught his breath. Even at six feet tall and half again as wide, Paul somehow managed to meet or exceed the department's physical fitness requirements. I have no idea how. In all the years I've known him, I had never seen the man physically exert himself beyond reaching for a pastrami sandwich or a cigarette, one of which he seemed to have every time we met.

"I don't know. Something big. Kent Graham and Nancy Wharton pulled a case this evening. African-American female, mid-twenties, found on Fall Creek Road near the Hamilton County border. It's supposed to be real ugly. They went out to the scene and called us twenty minutes later. Now Bowers is looking for you. That ringing any bells?"

I shook my head and started pacing the length of my garage, stepping over pieces of the chair. "I haven't been up there since July when I taught a gun safety course to the Boy Scouts at Camp Belzer. It was a community relations gig."

"Yeah, well, this is supposed to be a really bad one. Bowers already has a hard-on for you, so you might want to put your lawyer on standby just in case."

Before Paul could say anything else, I saw a blue-and-white light flashing through the blinds on the only window in my garage facing the street. I crossed the room and spread the aluminum slats with my fingers to get a better view. A marked patrol vehicle had pulled to the front of my house, and Captain Mike Bowers and two uniformed patrol officers stepped onto my front lawn.

"Thanks for the heads-up," I said, stepping back from my window. "But I think it might be a little late for that call."

I grabbed my jacket from a stool in the corner of the garage and jogged outside. Despite its being just a little after five, ominous black clouds were draped across the horizon, while a cold early-December wind ripped at the skin of my hands, face, and neck. Bowers and the two uniformed officers who accompanied him stopped walking when they saw me, and I crossed my driveway in five strides, meeting them on the front porch and silently cursing the architect who had designed my house and failed to connect the garage with the main structure. Considering he had likely been dead for the past sixty or seventy years, I doubted he cared.

"Evening, officers," I said, nodding to Captain Bowers and then the two men beside him in turn. "What's going on?"

"I need you to listen, and I need you to be honest," said Bowers, reaching into his pocket for his cell phone. "I've got a picture on my phone, and I need you to tell me if you recognize the woman. It's gruesome."

"How about you tell me what's going on first?"

"We don't know what's going on. That's why we're here," said Bowers, flicking his finger across his phone. "You've been out of town since your hearing, haven't you?"

My "hearing" referred to a disciplinary hearing before a captain's review board the previous week. A couple of months back, Bowers had accused me of conduct unbecoming an officer for pretending to offer a drug user heroin in exchange for information in a human trafficking case. In actuality, I had offered that drug user bundles of brown sugar made up to look like heroin.

That interview and the information it garnered me allowed me to save the lives of almost a dozen young women, but Bowers and the review board seemed to care only about the rules I had broken. The angry part of me hoped they'd fire me so I could wash my hands of the whole department, but the other part of me, a much bigger part, fervently hoped they'd let me keep the one job in the world I wanted to do. I anticipated and dreaded receiving their verdict any day now.

"Yeah. Hannah and I took the kids to St. Louis. Megan wanted to see the Arch. Why?"

Bowers didn't look up from his phone. "Because our victim died two to three days ago. I needed to eliminate you as a suspect."

I crossed my arms. "What victim?"

As if I had said the magic words, Bowers turned his phone to me to show me a picture. A dead woman stared back. I uncrossed my arms and dropped them to my sides. As Paul had said, the victim was a young African-American woman. A jagged gash so deep I could see her vertebrae ran from one side of her neck to the other, while reddish-black blood puddled around her. Pain had twisted her face into an effigy of the kind and intelligent young woman I knew, the young woman whose face adorned a Christmas card in our front hallway. Her eyes, usually a rich, deep brown, stared back at me, dead and glassy. I had to look away before I got sick.

"Do you know this woman?" asked Bowers.

I closed my eyes and whispered a short *du'a*, a prayer, for her, before nodding.

"Her name is Michelle Washington."

"Good. How do you know her?"

I tried to clear my head by shaking it. Bowers repeated the question.

"She's my AA sponsor."

"Alcoholics Anonymous?" asked Bowers.

I nodded. "I just started a few weeks ago. Right after you filed conduct-unbecoming charges against me."

Bowers held up a hand. "Forget about those charges for the moment. What is the extent of your relationship with Ms. Washington?"

I tried to put the image of her out of my head, but I couldn't blink it away. My legs felt weak, so I leaned against the wooden rail that separated my porch from the yard.

"She's a friend," I said once I regained enough composure to speak. "I've called her once or twice when I had a bad day, but that's it." I took a deep breath and exhaled a cloud of frost. "Someone needs to talk to her family. Her brother lives a couple of blocks from her house in Irvington, and her parents live in Ransom Place, I think. I might have their contact information inside."

"We'll get to them," said Bowers, his voice surprisingly calm. "I need you to talk to me now, though. Can you think of anyone who would try to hurt her? A boyfriend, maybe?"

I turned to face him, shaking my head. "I don't think she had a boyfriend, but no one would want to hurt her. She sang in her church choir, and she volunteered for Habitat for Humanity. She was a good person. Everybody liked her."

Bowers ran his finger across his phone and then straightened. "I need you to look at another picture and tell me if it means anything. It might be a little disturbing."

"Okay," I said. He turned his phone so I could see it. The picture was a wide-angle shot of Michelle's body.

Someone had ripped off her shirt and bra. A dark liquid glistened against her brown skin, forming a word from her neck to her navel. I felt sick, but I forced my face to remain impassive, a skill I had picked up from several years working homicides.

"The liquid is probably blood, and it says *slut*," said Bowers. "Someone cut off her hand—before she died, according to Dr. Rodriguez—and then used her fingertips as a brush."

I've been a police officer for a long time, even spending a couple of very good years as a homicide detective. Rarely did I hear things that took me aback, but this did. You've really got to hate somebody to dismember her while she's alive, to hear her scream as the knife strikes bone, and to keep going until the deed is done.

"How'd you connect her to me?"

Bowers glanced up from his phone, but then glanced back at the screen. "She had your card in her purse." He slipped the phone back into his pocket. "And you can't think of any reason why someone would want to hurt her?"

I started to tell him no, but a sick thought hit me. Michelle and I hadn't met by chance. Ten years ago, she and her brother had witnessed a murder. It was one of the first homicides I ever worked, and their testimony helped send a violent and very well-connected gang leader to prison for murder. I didn't often keep up with the criminals I put away, but Santino Ramirez had a special place in my heart. He was the first and only man I ever sent to death row. Unless he won a last-minute appeal, he'd get a needle in the arm in a couple of days. The world would be a better place without him.

I swallowed a lump in my throat and hoped I was wrong about what I was about to say.

"She testified against Santino Ramirez ten years ago," I said. "His old gang might have just called her out."

Chapter Three

At any given time Indiana had maybe a dozen men on death row, so we didn't have many executions. That meant Ramirez was big news, especially after a recent botched execution in Oklahoma. Bowers recognized his name without a reminder.

"Ramirez's gang ever threaten her before?"

I shook my head. "Not that she's ever mentioned, but this close to the big show, we've got to consider it."

Bowers swore under his breath. "I'll have Kent Graham contact the other eyewitnesses who testified against Ramirez. Meantime, I need you to come to the scene with me to see something."

I cared deeply about Michelle, so I wanted to do everything I could for her. But already my hands shook, and I felt a lump growing in my throat. I swallowed it down and hoped my voice wouldn't crack.

"A good friend of mine is dead. I'm not in any shape to go anywhere."

He nodded and looked genuinely sympathetic. "I understand, but there's something at the scene I need you to see. You might be able to help."

"And there's no one else who can do this?" I asked.

"You knew the victim. No one on our team did."

I looked off into the evening sky. The sun had set gloriously half an hour ago, but the stars had yet to make their evening appearances. They would, though; it'd be a pretty night. I wondered what Michelle saw before she died. Hopefully something nice.

"I'll need to tell my wife."

Bowers didn't blink. "I'll wait out here."

I knew my front door was locked, so I went through the side door that led to my kitchen. As soon as I did, my daughter's cat, Garfield, tried to dart out between my legs, so I bent down and picked him up. He hissed at me and pawed at my arms but didn't extend his claws, which I interpreted as a subtle way of saying he loved me and thanked me for protecting him from the cold. As soon as I put him down in the kitchen, he bounded toward the hallway that led to our living room and the rest of the house.

"Somebody needs to feed the cat," I said, scraping my feet on the mat beside the door.

"I already did," said Megan, looking over her shoulder while my wife helped her scrub her hands at the sink. I looked at her and forced a smile to my lips.

"That was very grown-up of you."

She beamed at me, brightening ever so slightly the melancholy mood I could feel myself slipping into. While Megan turned back to my wife, I crossed the kitchen to our breakfast table and tousled my little boy's hair.

"Hi, *Baba*," he said, between bites of a cracker. I knew Kaden would grow up, but he still surprised me almost every day with the new things he did. Recently, he had started telling stories about his about his day and the adventures he went on with his mother. They didn't always make sense, but they did always make me smile. I bent down and kissed his forehead, which he promptly wiped away.

"Garfield's eaten, but the kids haven't," said Hannah, looking directly into my daughter's eyes. "Which means we need to hurry and get ready if we're going to make it to Aunt Yasmine and Uncle Jack's on time." She looked up at me. "They rented a movie for the kids and wanted to watch it before Kaden falls asleep."

My wife had thick black hair that just barely kissed the top of her shoulders and laugh lines around her eyes that showed up every time she smiled. She's the best friend I've ever had. On most nights, I couldn't help but smile when I saw her, even when she was doing something as mundane as helping our daughter wash her hands. Tonight, no smile cracked my lips.

"We need to talk," I said. I glanced at Megan. "Alone."

Hannah kept her hands on our daughter's shoulders, holding her in place.

"What's going on?" she asked, lowering her chin.

"Captain Bowers is on the front porch."

Hannah didn't take her eyes from mine. "Megan, go to your room and pick out an outfit for tomorrow and some pajamas for tonight. And take your brother."

"Can I pick out anything I want?" she asked.

"If it's warm."

She nodded, took Kaden's hand, and then ran—her default mode of transportation—past me and down the hallway to her room.

"What's going on, Ashraf?"

I took a breath. "Michelle Washington is dead. Murdered. It's pretty bad."

Hannah looked confused for a moment, but then I saw a glimmer of recognition in her eyes. "Your sponsor? That Michelle Washington?"

I nodded. "They found my business card in her purse and wanted to know how I knew her. The guy who killed her cut off her hand and wrote *slut* across her chest in blood."

She drew her hand over her mouth and inhaled. "I'm sorry. Are you okay?"

"Not really, but Bowers wants me to see something at the scene."

She nodded and then took another breath. "Are you thinking about having a drink?"

I broke eye contact. It's almost hard to believe now, but I didn't always drink. I started many years ago after arresting a man and woman who had thrown their toddler out of the house so they could have sex without hearing him cry. The boy died of exposure, clinging to garbage in a vain attempt to stay warm. At the time, I didn't have any kids, but I had an eight-year-old niece. Rachel was smart, thoughtful, funny, everything I hoped my kids would one day be. When I saw that boy's body, I thought of my niece and I snapped. I had seen bodies before then, of course, but something inside me broke that day.

Prior to seeing that kid's body laid out on the street, I used to think of myself almost as if I were a chivalrous knight. I locked bad guys up, I kept people safe, and I helped people put the fragmented pieces of their lives back together. I was proud of myself and the badge I put on every morning. Seeing the coroner take that kid away, though, showed me I wasn't a knight at all. I was a garbage man. In the back of my mind, I had known that from the first moment I pinned that badge on my chest, but it took a dead child for me to confront it and admit it. As much as I might have tried to save people, I couldn't. That wasn't my job. I cleaned up messes because, in the real world, the good guys usually lost.

After work that night I went to a bar and had the first drink of my life. It helped. If I had a drink in my hand, I didn't think of that boy. Eventually, I started going out for drinks with my colleagues a couple of times a week. We talked about cases and our families. It was like group therapy, and this, too, was good. Then, I started going out with or without my colleagues. I even thought this was okay. Everybody has bad days. Then my bad days merged with the good, and I stopped needing excuses. My Islamic faith called it a sin, but I drank because life was easier drunk than sober.

"I don't even know what I'm thinking right now."

She stepped towards me and put a hand on my elbow, looking straight in my eyes. "You've been sober for 300 days now, and I don't want you to lose that."

A little knot in my heart kinked. I love my wife, and I want nothing more than to make her proud of me. The older I get and the more I get to know her, the more I realize how lucky I am to have her.

"I don't want to lose that, either, but Captain Bowers is waiting for me. I need to go to work."

She started to say something, but then caught herself. "Do what you need to do. I'll pick up something for dinner. It'll be in the fridge when you get back. If you need to talk, please call me. Or someone else. Just don't do anything you'll regret."

"I won't."

Before leaving, I went into my master bedroom closet and pushed aside a row of suits to expose the steel gray lockbox in which I kept my department-issued firearm, a forty-caliber Glock 22. Unless my evening went spectacularly wrong, I wouldn't need a firearm, but it felt wrong to leave the house without it. I grabbed my holster, felt the tendons in my shoulder snap into place as I secured the leather around my shoulders, and then felt the weight of the loaded weapon against my chest.

Some guys, a gun makes them feel unbreakable, secure in the bubble of their own delusions, but my firearm reminded me how vulnerable I really am. I've been shot twice and I've been shot at maybe half a dozen times in my career. Not once did my gun provide any sort of shelter or protection. I never leave my house without a firearm on my person, but after fourteen years on the job, I have no delusions about its purpose. I carry a gun in case I have to put somebody down. That's it, end of story. My gun doesn't keep me safe; it simply makes me the most dangerous man in the room.

I closed my lockbox and stood, hoping this would be a short trip.

Before leaving the house, I hugged Megan and Kaden, promising that I'd see them as soon as I could. I kissed Hannah last and whispered that I'd be back as quickly as I could. I met Bowers outside, where he had already sent away the two officers he had arrived with.

"You've got single-paned windows in your house," he said, nodding.

"Yeah," I said, drawing the syllable out and wondering why he chose that moment to comment on my home's historic windows. "The house is old. I haven't had time to put the storm windows up for the season yet."

He blinked a couple of times and then cleared his throat. "I didn't mean to, but I heard part of your discussion with your wife."

"Which part?" I asked, my back straightening.

"The part about 300 days. Had I known, I wouldn't have come out here. Staying sober is more important than police work."

I ran my fingers through my hair. "I appreciate your concern, but I'm fine."

He held out a hand. "You know, if you need somebody to talk to, I'm here. Give me a call."

"Thanks. Let's just head out."

Bowers nodded. "Sure. Let's go."

I lost my take-home vehicle to budget cuts a couple of months back, so we got into my wife's old Volkswagen—she had upgraded to a gently used minivan a few weeks back—and I turned on the car. The address Bowers gave me was on the extreme northeastern quadrant of the city. I took the interstate most of the way, but I exited onto Shadeland Avenue and then hung a right onto Fall Creek Road. The street narrowed from four lanes to two, and skeletal, leafless trees replaced the overhead lights of the highway. Darkness smothered the landscape, limiting my visibility to a narrowly defined corridor directly ahead of my vehicle.

"Last I worked a scene like this, I used a portable generator and lights from the training academy on Post Road," I said, glancing at Bowers. "It might be worth calling in."

"If the generator worked, it would be," said Bowers, crossing his arms tightly across his chest. "We've made do the best we can."

Neither of us spoke again for the next few moments. As I neared the address, I saw flickering blue police lights through the trees, and I pulled to a stop on the shoulder behind a gray Chevrolet Crown Victoria, preparing myself for a long night. It was just a little after eight, and according to my dashboard thermometer, it was twenty-nine degrees. I wasn't on duty, but I reached across Captain Bowers anyway and grabbed a fresh notepad from my glove box and wrote down the time, date, and conditions upon my arrival.

I stepped out of my car. My breath turned to frost as I sucked down car exhaust from passing vehicles. Bowers hung back near the car to make some calls while I walked to the scene. Pines and other coniferous trees dotted the woods, limiting my visibility to the right, but there were three police cruisers straight ahead of me and a van from the forensics lab beyond that. Blue and white police lights lit the evening like a nightclub but did little to penetrate the woods to my right. Yellow crime scene tape roped off an area roughly the size of an elementary school classroom around a silver Ford Focus. The car's right wheels dipped into a drainage ditch, while its left wheels just barely touched the asphalt. A young evidence technician knelt at the Ford's side, lifting prints from the door handles.

I walked forward and called out but stayed on the outside of the tape. "You find anything?"

Before the tech could say anything, a uniformed officer stepped out of the nearest cruiser, holding up his hand, palm toward me.

"You need to turn around and leave, sir," he said. "This is a crime scene."

"I realize that," I said, pulling back my jacket to expose the badge on my hip. "I'm Detective Sergeant Ash Rashid. Captain Mike Bowers is just up the road."

The officer took a couple of steps toward me, squinting. He was probably in his mid-twenties, and he had short red hair, bushy eyebrows, and a lopsided smile that created a dimple on one cheek but laugh lines on the other. He looked more like the sort of guy a Hollywood director would cast as the goofy but lovable rookie in a comedy about cops than an actual officer.

"You're *the* Sergeant Rashid?"

"I never considered that there might be more than one of us. Do I know you?"

He walked toward me, his hand extended. I shook it.

"I'm a big fan of yours," he said, pumping my hand up and down. "You came up at the academy a lot. My instructors said you were reckless, but I always supported you."

I dropped my hands to my sides, already dreading the direction of our conversation. "I appreciate that."

"I was really impressed by how you handled your niece's death. You didn't let anybody get in your way. You just took care of the people who killed her."

And that's what I had feared. The legend of Ash Rashid the gunslinger had made its way to the police academy. When my niece died of a drug overdose a couple of years back, the department originally called it an accident, but I knew my niece didn't do drugs. I investigated on my own and found a group of wackos dealing drugs out of a nightclub called The Abbey. It took some work, but I put the ringleader in prison and the rest of her followers in the ground.

"Do you have a log sheet?" I asked.

He fumbled a notepad from his utility belt.

"Sure, here," he said, pressing it toward me. I signed my name and rank.

"Where's the body?" I asked, returning his notepad and pen.

He vaguely pointed to the woods behind him. "Somewhere back there. I haven't seen it. I think the coroner might have taken it. I'd have to call my CO to be sure."

I raised my eyebrows and waited for him to do just that. He seemed confused at first, but then his face lit up and he reached to the radio on his shoulder. "Sergeant Grimes, can you come to the road, please? Sergeant Rashid is here. He wants to see where the body was dumped."

"Thank you," I said, looking at the ground around us while I waited. A thin layer of frost covered the grass. That could have helped us, given that frozen grass held footprints in a way normal grass didn't. But so many people had trampled on the ground near Michelle's car that any footprints we had were gone. I looked up. "Did you get pictures of the ground upon your arrival?"

The officer shook his head. "No, why?"

"Because the number of different footprints might have given us an indication of how many suspects we should look for. You should have roped the scene off and avoided touching anything."

He straightened. "It was grass, so I didn't even think about it."

"Now you know. We all screw up. Get it right next time," I said, looking toward the woods as two men walked towards us. One was Detective Paul Murphy. A lit cigarette dangled from his fingertips and a halo of smoke surrounded his head. Even from that distance, he looked tired. Not that I could blame him. He and his wife had recently started watching their only granddaughter full-time while their daughter went to law school, coincidentally the same law school I had attended. Hopefully she'd put her legal degree to better use than I had put mine.

The second figure, a uniformed sergeant, was in his midforties. Unlike the guy manning the logbook, he actually looked like a cop. After fourteen years in uniform, I can tell quite a bit about my colleagues just by the way they use their eyes, and as this sergeant walked toward me, his eyes never stopped moving, never ceased looking for threats. One look and I knew he had spent his career on the streets.

"Good to see you, Ash," said Paul, holding out his hand. I shook it, and Paul then nodded toward the sergeant. "This is Sergeant Grimes. He found Ms. Washington. I'll show you where."

Before I could suggest we wait for Mike Bowers, Paul turned and walked toward the woods. With just the lights from patrol vehicles to guide me, I couldn't see the small break in a dense row of pine trees until we were almost upon it. Even in the day, I doubted I'd have been able to see it from the road. That meant our killer was familiar with the area. As Paul entered the woods, he held back the limbs of trees so they wouldn't smack me in the face. Once I got past the initial tree line, the vegetation thinned considerably, likely because summer sunlight couldn't penetrate the canopy above my head.

The clearing was maybe thirty feet away. Little light from the street reached that deeply into the woods, but I could still hear cars and smell exhaust.

"Forensics cleared this place yet?" I asked.

As if to answer, Paul tossed his cigarette to the dirt and ground it beneath his heel.

"They have," he said. "Found a ton of stuff, but I doubt any of it will help us. The neighbors say people camp here all the time."

It wasn't a bad spot for that. We were still relatively close to the city, but it felt isolated and private. Not a bad spot to dump a body, either.

"You mind if I take a walk?" I asked.

Paul held out his arm toward the clearing. "Be my guest. We were about to close up here anyway."

Grimes held out a heavy, black Maglite. I took it and thanked him before stepping out into the field. The clearing was about the size of a football field. Trees bounded it on all four sides, but I could see lights from a neighboring home through the woods on the north. Michelle's wounds were so horrific those neighbors would have heard her scream if she had died in that field.

I snapped on my light. I didn't know what to look for, so I just started walking, sweeping the light along the grass. I found some footprints, but other than those, nothing stood out to me until I came to a campsite near the center. It contained a fire pit, a steel trash can similar to the ones in public parks, and benches made from split logs. By the pictures Bowers showed me, I knew patrol officers had found Michelle's body beside the fire pit, but I saw very little blood on the ground. You cut off someone's hand while her heart still beats, you'll have blood everywhere, so that confirmed what I had thought earlier: she hadn't died there.

In addition to the lack of blood, something else about the ground stood out to me, but it wasn't until I squatted down that I saw it. Someone had scratched faint lines in the dirt, making the area around the fire pit look like the sand trap of a golf course. They had raked the ground. Maybe campers would have a reason for doing that, but I doubted it. This was someone covering up his tracks.

I stood, looked at the bloody spot, and felt a lump build in my throat. It was all that remained of my friend.

I had met Michelle and her brother Dante on a case ten years ago. As a detective, I'm not supposed to become involved with the witnesses I interview, but I couldn't help it with Michelle and Dante. They were kids, but unlike almost everyone else in their neighborhood, they had the guts to stand up for a stranger, to point their fingers at a violent gang leader and say, "*He did it. He killed this man, and he deserves to be punished.*" And unlike me, they couldn't leave that neighborhood at the end of the day. They couldn't escape the stares, the threats, the harassment. They took everything that gang threw at them and became stronger for it. Both Michelle and Dante went on to college—they were the only two in their high school class to do so—and they both made something of their lives, she becoming a social worker and he becoming an attorney.

And now she was dead.

I looked around the field and found Paul Murphy, Sergeant Grimes, and a uniformed officer about fifty yards away from me near a pair of beige sheds. They were talking, but as I approached, Paul left the group and met me maybe ten yards from his companions.

"You find anything?" asked Paul.

"You're looking for at least two suspects," I said upon reaching him. "What's up with the sheds and the patrol officer?"

"How do you know we're looking for two suspects?" he asked.

"I'll tell you if you tell me," I said.

Paul looked at the rest of his group and then back at me. "I'll show you the sheds, but I'll warn you first: they're kind of weird."

Chapter Four

I followed Paul around the edge of the clearing until we reached a pair of beige metal outbuildings maybe five feet square each and built on concrete slabs. They'd keep the rain out pretty well by the looks of things, but someone had cut the padlocks on the doors. Sergeant Grimes and a young woman in a patrol officer's navy blue uniform waited for us. She looked straight into my eyes, almost challenging me. The badge on her belt reflected in the moonlight, but I couldn't see it well enough to make out her rank nor did I want to stare, something men probably did to her quite often. One look at her, and I recognized someone strong and confident, maybe even a tad overconfident. I could respect that. Without a word passing between us, I liked her.

I looked at Paul. "I assume the padlock was cut when you arrived."

He nodded to me and then to the woman. "It was. This is Officer Emilia Rios. When we saw the shrine, Sergeant Grimes called her in because he knew she was interested in this stuff."

I raised my eyebrows at the word *shrine* but didn't say anything and instead held out my hand for the officer.

"Ash Rashid," I said, shaking her hand. She had a firm grip. "It's nice to meet you."

"Likewise," she said. "Emilia Rios." She nodded at Sergeant Grimes and answered one of my questions before I got the chance to ask it. "Jim was my FTO two years ago."

Field Training Officer. That explained how the two of them knew each other. She walked to the nearest shed and slid the door to the right, exposing the interior. I knelt beside her to take a look.

Green carpet, like the stuff found on a miniature golf course, covered the slab, and on that rested a pedestal crowned by a skeletal statue of a female grim reaper. The statue had black hair nearly down to her waist, and she wore what looked like a dingy wedding dress. A green robe hung loosely off her shoulders, covering most of her form and most of the dress. In one hand, she carried a scythe wrapped in a twenty-dollar bill, while the other held a miniature globe. To her left, someone had placed a vase full of wilted white roses and four white candles, and to her right, he had placed a nearly empty bottle of tequila. Last, I noticed a black votive candle adorned with a white skull directly behind her.

I stood and looked at Officer Rios. "What am I looking at?"

"*La Santisima Muerte,*" she said. "The Holy Death."

I looked across the field to where Michelle had been dumped and shuddered. "Is this some kind of devil worship, then?"

She shook her head emphatically. "Not at all. The Bony Lady is a saint."

"Tell Detective Rashid what you told us," said Paul.

"I'm not a practitioner," said Emilia, pulling her brown hair into a ponytail behind her head and securing it with a hair tie she had kept around her wrist. "But my dad has a shrine, so I took a picture and sent it to him."

"Go on," I said, nodding.

"First of all," she said, kneeling and then waving her hand over the entire shrine. "There's no such thing as a standard *Santa Muerte* altar, so you can learn a lot about a person by what he includes. The person who set this altar up is interested in justice. That's what the green on her robe and the green carpet means. The guy who owns this could be in legal trouble. He might even be asking the Bony Lady for her help keeping the police away."

Considering we had found the body of a young lady in his field, I'd say we had good reason to think the latter.

"What about the other stuff?" I asked. "The scythe, the tequila, the flowers? What do they tell us?"

Emilia shifted and then pointed to the statue in the center of everything. "My dad said the scythe represents the harvest, but since it's wrapped in a twenty-dollar bill, it means the shrine's owner is trying to harvest money. He's got a business of some kind. The globe in her other hand shows that she has power over everything in the world. He's flattering the Bony Lady so she's more likely to grant him favors."

I nodded, even though I didn't follow everything she had said. "For the sake of those who don't know anything about this stuff, can we just take a step back? Who is the Bony Lady? Is she a real person? Is this a cult? What are we talking about here?"

Emilia looked to the part of the field that had held Michelle's body and made the sign of the cross over her chest. "The Bony Lady is a saint, but the Catholic Church doesn't recognize her. She's from the streets. That's why common people pray to her. They believe that if they pray to her and make her offerings, she'll answer their prayers."

I knew enough about Catholicism to understand to an extent. What I didn't get, I could always research.

"Thank you. That helps," I said, nodding and pausing for a second as I tried to think of an inoffensive way to phrase my next question. "You mentioned your dad is a practitioner, so bear in mind I'm not trying to ask an offensive question. Please don't take it as such." I waited for her to nod, telling me to continue. "Do believers sacrifice things to the Bony Lady?"

"Are you asking if human sacrifice plays a role in my father's faith?"

When put like that, it did sound mildly offensive.

"I wouldn't ask except for the body we already found," I said.

Emilia blinked a few times and looked at the field again. "I've only heard about one instance in Mexico, but the faith's leaders denounced it."

"Did you see Michelle's body?" I asked. Emilia took a breath and then nodded. "Does anything about the body suggest to you that we're dealing with a sacrifice?"

"No," she said, quickly. "For one thing, it's too far away. If the people who killed the vic sacrificed her to *Santa Muerte*, they would have left her near the shrine."

"Good," I said, breathing a little easier. "A human sacrifice would probably ruin my evening."

Both Paul and Sergeant Grimes tittered. I ignored them.

"What about these other objects?" I asked, pointing to the flowers and tequila.

"They're devotional items," she said. I furrowed my brow, confused. "Offerings. If you don't keep making offerings to the Bony Lady, she'll stop giving you blessings."

I pointed to the black candle in back. "What kind of blessing does she give for the black candle with the skull on it?"

Emilia craned her neck to look inside. "I don't think Dad saw that one."

"Do you know what it means?"

She took a step back and blinked her eyes rapidly. "Usually, black is for protection." She looked at Sergeant Grimes. "Can you turn it around?"

Grimes donned a pair of polypropylene gloves from his pockets, and, touching only the candle's rim, turned it, revealing an inscription on the back.

MCME.

I looked at Emilia. "Does that inscription mean something to you?"

"*Muerte contra mis enemigos.*" She paused. "Death to my enemies."

Paul chuckled. "I love a saint who's willing to smite my enemies."

"Please don't disrespect the Bony Lady," said Emilia. "For your own sake. She can get angry."

I raised my eyebrows. "I didn't think you were a believer."

"You don't have to believe in something to respect it."

I couldn't argue with that. I looked up at Paul. "This shrine has a concrete foundation. It's permanent. The property owner hasn't come by yet?"

He shook his head. "No one's come by."

That might have meant he didn't live nearby. Or it meant that he killed Michelle and had fled the area. "Anything in the other shed?"

Paul shrugged. "Barbecue grill and some camping equipment."

"How about a rake?"

Paul looked at Sergeant Grimes and then back to me. "Why do you ask about a rake?"

"Because it looks like somebody raked the dirt near the campground. Might have been trying to conceal footprints. If you find one, print it. You should also pull the tax records for this property from the county assessor's website and track down the owner."

"I *have* done this a time or two," said Paul, humoring me with a smile. "But I appreciate the suggestion. Nancy Wharton is already on the records. I'll take a look at the rake."

"The property owner won't talk to your detective," said Emilia, quickly. "She'll be wasting her time."

Paul started to say something, but I held up a hand, stopping him.

"Why won't he talk to Detective Wharton?" I asked, cocking my head to the side.

She stood and then gestured to the shrine. "Because this is his secret. My dad keeps his shrine in the living room, right where anybody can see it. Everyone else I know who practices does the same. The person who maintains this shrine is hiding it, though, maybe from a spouse. And if I had to guess, there are at least two people with access to it."

Grimes crossed his arms and nodded at her, smiling proudly. "Told you she's the expert and you'd be glad she's here."

I ignored him. "What makes you think two people are using this shrine?"

"Just look at the offerings," she said, pointing to the white flowers. "On the one hand, we've got white flowers and white devotional candles. The white symbolizes purity, holiness. When my cousin got married, my father kept a white candle burning for an entire week afterwards. You put those things in there to say thank you. This other stuff, the money, the black votive candle, they evoke a different side of the Lady. It looks like something a drug dealer would have."

I mulled that over for a moment before nodding. Paul spoke before I could.

"Isn't it possible for one person to want all those things?" he asked.

"Sure, it's possible," she said, nodding toward the statue, her voice even stronger than it had been a moment earlier. "But I've seen a lot of shrines and none of them have looked like this. I'm almost sure that this shrine is maintained by at least two people. The broken padlock corroborates it."

She hadn't convinced me, but Paul would have to follow up anyway. He looked at me.

"You said we should look for two suspects. That conjecture, or do you actually know something?"

"Call it an educated guess. We agree Michelle died elsewhere and was dumped here?"

Paul nodded and then reached into his jacket for a notepad. "That's what Hector Rodriguez from the coroner's office said. Not enough blood to have died here."

I pointed to the north. "And the people who live through those woods would have heard her scream. So we agree she died elsewhere. That meant somebody carried her here. Michelle wasn't a big woman, but she probably weighed a good hundred and thirty pounds. That's a lot of dead weight for one person to handle alone."

Grimes shrugged. "I could probably carry that."

"I might be able to carry her for some of that distance," I said, nodding, "but that kind of weight would get heavy. The campsite has to be three hundred yards from the road, and I didn't see any tracks for a wheelbarrow or cart."

"What else you got?" asked Paul, crossing his arms.

"Just a feeling," I said. "This murder was planned. Our killer is too careful to leave things to chance. He's not going to be out here any longer than he needs to. We're looking at partners." I nodded to the shrine. "How many prints did you find on the shrine?"

Paul sighed and then ran a hand across his face. "None. Someone wiped it and the padlock down. Maybe we'll get lucky with your rake."

Unfortunately, if our killers were smart enough to wipe down the padlock, they were smart enough to wipe down the rake, too. Before I could say anything, Paul looked at Emilia Rios.

"Thank you for your help, Officer. I'm sure Sergeant Grimes can give you a ride back to your duty station."

She nodded, and the two of them left, leaving Paul and me alone by the shrine. He watched her walk away and then turned to me.

"What color underwear do you think she's wearing?"

"I'm pretty sure that's one of those questions we're not supposed to ask. Sexual harassment and all that."

"That's modern women for you. Next thing you know, they'll be asking for library cards and equal protection before the law." He knelt in front of the shrine. "You really think we're looking at two people?"

"I'd call it a strong possibility," I said. "Outdoor scene and a pretty horrific murder. You're going to have your hands full."

"You don't want to help me on this one?"

I looked over the field once more. "Sorry, but you're on your own. Bowers asked me to come by, but Michelle wasn't interested in this shrine stuff. Besides that, I had a disciplinary hearing last Friday, and I'm off until I get the verdict."

Paul straightened and nodded. "I heard about that. I'm sure it'll turn out fine."

I felt pretty confident I'd lose my job, but I appreciated the support. I nodded to him and then turned toward the trail that led to the road. Before I could reach it, Paul cleared his throat, stopping me.

"We found your business card in the vic's purse. How'd you know her?"

A lot of people knew I had a problem with alcohol, but I still tried to keep things quiet. Maybe now was the time to get it out.

"She's my AA sponsor."

Paul tilted his head to the side. "For real?" I nodded, and he took a step forward to pat me on the shoulder. "Good for you. If you need anything, let me know."

"That's not how I met her," I said, quickly. "She testified against Santino Ramirez ten years ago. I worked the case with Keith Holliday."

"The Santino Ramirez on death row?"

"That's the guy," I said, nodding. "You need to talk to somebody in the gang squad about *Barrio Sureño*, his old crew."

Paul took a notepad from his jacket and wrote the name down. "You free tomorrow morning?"

"I could be."

Paul slipped his notepad back into his jacket pocket. "Good. If she died for testifying in a murder trial, I'm going to pull the files and see what I can find. I'd like you to come in and go through them with me. Can you make it in at ten?"

"That'll be fine," I said. "I'm going to head home."

He considered me and then took a step back. "All right, then. Tell your wife hello for me."

I nodded to him and then left, intending to go home for the night, where I could actually grieve for my friend in peace.

I wish it had worked out like that.

Chapter Five

Carla had first met Dante Washington four weeks ago in a Dairy Queen beside Crown Hill Cemetery. It had been warmer then, and she had worn a pair of brown slacks and a cobalt blue three-quarter-length-sleeve shirt. Small diamond studs adorned her ears, while tasteful if minimalist makeup touched up her cheeks and eyes. Normally, Carla preferred skirts, but Jane Rodriguez, the alias she had chosen for the meeting, preferred pants that she could cinch at the waist. Dante had smiled at her eagerly as she walked into the restaurant. He had worn a wool pinstripe suit and black horn-rimmed glasses. It was early in the season to wear wool, but he probably didn't have anything more suitable. A young lawyer, trying to make his mark on the world and willing to take clients from wherever they came. He probably saw himself akin to a character in a John Grisham novel. Quaint.

She walked to his table, catching just the barest hint of her perfume. Bergamot, like a cup of Earl Grey tea, and lavender. The perfume didn't say Carla, but it practically screamed Jane Rodriguez. Before reaching the table, she pulled a pack of cigarettes from her purse, a habit Jane had recently restarted during divorce proceedings from her most recent husband. Again, it was simply part of the story.

"I believe this is a nonsmoking establishment," said Dante, upon her arrival. "The manager will ask you to put that away."

"Of course. I should have known," she said, forcing her hands to tremble as she roughly stuffed the hard pack back into her purse. As she did, she watched Dante out of the corner of her eye. He had a strong jawline and brown eyes perfectly situated in a broad face. Judging by the fill of his suit, he had an athlete's body. The gangly boy who had testified against her husband had turned into a handsome man. Pity that he had to die. "So are you the lawyer?"

At the time of the meeting, Carla hadn't decided how to kill Dante. She had considered meeting him at his office and shooting him in the head, but that didn't send the right message. In the past week alone, she had read about two murders in Chicago performed in just that way. That was too clean, too easy, too…pedestrian. They needed something that would garner media attention.

"I am a lawyer," he said, nodding and grinning, exposing teeth too white to be the result of natural processes. "What can I do for you? You were a little cryptic on the phone."

She smiled obliquely but didn't say anything, having spotted a little girl traipsing toward their table, her fat little fingers wrapped around a straw that protruded from fat little lips. She stared at Carla and sucked her drink. Quickly, the girl's mother came by and ushered the little girl away, whispering apologies to both of them.

Even without consciously willing the thought, Carla found herself imagining how easily she could kill the mom. First, she'd find out what car Mom drove, and then she'd follow her home—she'd never see Carla coming, not with that kid around. Once Carla knew where the family lived, she would wait and stab Mom in the throat with an ice pick that night, maybe while she got something out of the freezer, maybe while she took out the trash. Mom's life would spill on the concrete or on the kitchen tile, and she'd die before she even knew a stranger had opened one of her arteries, all because her child had walked up to the wrong table at the wrong Dairy Queen at the wrong time.

Of course, Carla didn't have reason to kill her or even the time to do it in, so Mom was safe. The thought did make her wonder if people realized how precarious their lives really were.

"The girl remind you of someone?" asked Dante, smiling at her awkward silence.

"My niece," said Carla, lying without hesitation. She tilted her head to the side and watched the little girl and her mother walk back to their table. "My niece is a little thinner, maybe, but they're roughly the same age."

Normally, Carla tried to avoid lying—if she said she had a niece today, she might have to produce that niece next week—but Dante wouldn't live long enough for it to become a problem. She hadn't killed a lawyer before, so she looked forward to it. Being a licensed attorney herself, she knew enough of them, certainly. Most members of the bar saw themselves as powerful or at least beyond violence's reach. A flick of her wrist, a twitch of a finger over a trigger would show Dante the truth. It should be fun to rearrange his worldview. She focused on him again and smiled meekly.

"You're probably wondering why I called you."

He smiled that winning, too-white smile again. "I was, but I'm enjoying the company too much to say anything."

Carla looked away as if her questions were painful. "I'm new to the area, and I don't know many people here yet."

Dante's smile dropped slightly. "How can I be of service?"

Carla looked at her reflection in the window. "Before I ask my questions, I need to know something. Are you a good lawyer or a bad lawyer?"

She looked at him, and he blinked, sizing her up. "Do you have a dollar in your purse?"

"Probably," she said, leaning for her purse.

"Can you give it to me?" he asked. Carla pulled out her wallet and did as he asked. He pocketed the bill. "You are now officially my client. Our conversations are protected, so we can speak freely. I can't be forced to testify against you, and you can't be forced to testify about what you tell me. So go ahead and tell me what's on your mind, Ms. Rodriguez, and I'll tell you what kind of lawyer I am."

Carla wanted to roll her eyes, but she kept them locked on Dante's. He had probably seen the dollar trick in a movie. She wondered if he used it to pick up girls in bars.

"Jane. Call me Jane."

"Okay, Jane," he said, nodding. "The floor's yours."

So Carla told him a story. Like all good stories, it contained half-truths amidst a few outright lies. She told him about a powerless woman whose ex-husband had forced himself on her, who had beat her so badly she miscarried twice, who had held a gun to her head and threatened to kill her if she left him. She claimed she had come to Indianapolis to start a new life for herself. In truth, Carla *had* been pregnant twice, and Tino *had* beaten the child out of her twice. Tino *had* forced himself on her more times than she could count, and he *had* held guns to her head, threatening to kill her if she ever told the police what she knew of him. Unlike Jane Rodriguez, though, Carla had never been powerless. She acted with deadly purpose, always and ever.

"I'm very sorry for what's happened," said Dante, once she finished. "But it sounds like this story has a happy ending. You're free."

Carla shook her head. "No, I'm not. He knows where I am, and I'm scared. I don't know what to do."

"It sounds like you should get a dog, the bigger the better."

"I've thought about that," she said, seriously. "But what if it's not enough? What if he tries to hurt me?"

Dante considered her for a moment, but then pushed himself back from the table. "I'm not sure that I'm the best person to help you. If you feel you're in danger, you should call the police."

"I already did. They told me to get a dog, too."

He held up his hands and smiled. "See? You didn't even have to pay for that advice."

"My husband's in Indianapolis. If he finds me, he's going to kill me."

The smile left Dante's face. "Did you tell the police that?"

She nodded. "Yes. They told me to contact a lawyer to help me file a restraining order." She swallowed. "Do you have any family? A sister maybe? A wife?"

He nodded. "I've got family."

"What advice would you give them in my situation?"

Carla didn't think he would answer, but then his eyes flashed blacker than night itself. Before he spoke, Carla knew how he would die.

"I'd help her apply for a restraining order, and I'd tell her to go to the police if he threatened her."

No, you wouldn't. You'd kill him.

She wanted to say it aloud and to tell him any good sister or brother would do the same. Jane Rodriguez would never say that, though, so Carla simply looked at her hands, becoming meek and humble once more.

"You're probably right. I'm sorry I wasted your time."

"You didn't waste my time. If you'd like, we'll go back to my office and start the paperwork. No charge."

She said she'd have to think about it. As she left, he warned her to think quickly, but she pretended not to hear.

Much had happened in the weeks since that meeting, but Dante had rarely been far from her mind. He played a pivotal role in her plans. Detective Ash Rashid, one of her targets, had somehow befriended a very powerful drug dealer named Konstantin Bukoholov. Though Carla had never met Bukoholov, she had heard the same stories everyone in her business had. That Bukoholov was a former intelligence officer in the Soviet military, that he didn't like competition, that he'd murder not just his rivals but their entire families for multiple generations. Even at the height of his power, her husband had feared him—and with good reason from all Carla had seen. Perhaps one day she and Bukoholov would come to some arrangement, but for now, she couldn't risk provoking him.

Luckily, she didn't have to. Dante would eliminate Rashid for her.

Jacob turned their car onto University Avenue, just two blocks from Michelle's house. Dante lived in a two-story house with office space on the first floor and an apartment on the second. If their plan failed, Carla would have to kill Dante herself, and she'd have to do it in a way that topped Michelle's death. Hopefully it wouldn't come to it, but she had a few ideas. They had cut off Michelle's hand, then slit her throat, but Dante she'd fillet alive. Drug him so he couldn't move and then cleave the muscles and flesh from his bones. Free of his skin, he'd die quickly and in agony, but she could arrange it for him to survive long enough for the first responders to hear him scream.

Because they needed the spectacle, that message in blood.

Of course, none of that mattered if things went according to plan. Dante would kill himself, hopefully taking Detective Rashid with him, saving Carla the trouble.

He lived on a peaceful, quiet street. Jacob braked in front of the house. Some of the homes nearby still needed work, but most of them had resplendent, mature gardens and all the trappings of their historic architecture. Dante owned a two-story Tudor-style home with a brick facade. Evergreen shrubs flanked his front door, while tall phallic-shaped hedges anchored the corners of the building. A wooden sign with the words LAW OFFICE carved into its face pointed to a side door.

Before she could open her door, Jacob looked at her.

"You sure about this?"

"Reasonably," she said, reaching into her purse to ensure she still had her firearm beneath the eyeliner, tissues, and various other accouterments she carried with her. "If I don't think he'll go for the bait, I'll improvise."

"And I'm just supposed to walk away and leave you here to do this alone?"

"Yes," she said, glancing over at him. "I can handle Mr. Washington. He sent your father to prison. He deserves to die. If we don't kill him, you'll look weak."

He fidgeted and removed his hands from the wheel. "I don't like killing people."

She looked in his direction and waited to speak until he looked her in the eye. "Sometimes we have to make sacrifices for the greater good. That's part of what it means to be a member of a family. We are family, aren't we?"

"Yeah," he said, his voice uncertain. "I mean, I guess we are."

Good enough. "And *Barrio Sureño*, your father's family. What about them?"

"They're my family, too," he said, his voice growing stronger, more certain that he had said what she wanted to hear.

"Then treat them like it. Our family has been without its leader for ten years now. We've both seen what's happened, the infighting, the backstabbing. It's time for that to end. It's time for you to stand up and take what's yours."

"And you really think this will help?"

She shook her head as if she were growing annoyed. "Your father will be dead within a week. Are you willing to let the police take his legacy as well? To watch our family tear itself apart? We need a strong leader. We need you to take what's rightfully yours and save our family from itself."

The way she said it, she might have even believed herself. She had her own agenda, though. Jacob played a role, certainly, but she could work around him as well if she needed to get rid of him.

"I didn't mean anything by it," he said. "This is all new for me."

"I know it is," she said, softening her voice. "That's why you've got friends to help you."

He slowly opened his door and started to step out, but Carla put a hand on his arm to stop him. He looked at her and raised his eyebrows.

"You're going to Jockamo's, right?" she asked.

He nodded. It was a pizza place on Washington Street, one of Carla's favorite restaurants in the city.

"Make sure you tell the waitress that you'll have a to-go order in addition to whatever you order. I hate to just show up and ask for another pizza on the way out the door."

"Fine," he said, reaching into his pocket. He handed her the keys. "Anything else?"

"Try to relax," she said. "Put your feet up when you get there and watch a game or something. I'm sure they've got TVs. Work doesn't have to be dreary. I'll call you once I leave here."

He didn't respond and instead just got up and left. She must have said something wrong. She didn't have a lot of experience dealing with teenagers, so Jacob's moodiness surprised her. She'd try to remember that about him.

As he walked away, she stepped out of the car and onto the sidewalk. It was late evening but not quite night yet. Most of the families nearby would be sitting down to eat, not a care in the world. Years ago, when she was still a young girl, she had wished her family would sit down together and eat like that. Television made it seem that a family meeting in the living room could simultaneously cure her mother's depression, her father's alcoholism and drug abuse, and her utter confusion about the volatile emotions of her friends. Now, of course, she knew better.

She walked toward Dante's house, a somber expression on her face in case one of the neighbors saw her. The local newscast had reported Michelle's death, which meant the police had already notified the family. How long Dante would take visiting his parents, Carla didn't know. Ten minutes? An hour? How long do you stay after finding out someone has murdered your sister? It was the sort of question a sociologist should study.

Dante's house didn't have a welcoming front porch like the craftsman homes around it, but he did have a nice, shaded patio with a padded wooden love seat, an espresso-colored coffee table, and a battered, paint-stained glider that had probably come from someone's garage or attic. She sat on the love seat and picked her feet up off the ground, kicking the air nonchalantly while she waited. She had considered stopping by the library on her way to the house for a book, but ultimately decided that sent the wrong message. She needed to appear concerned, thoughtful, and unexpectedly there. A book would say she had planned the night's events.

Since Dante might be a while, she took out her cell phone and began reading a novel someone had recommended to her. Eventually, she became so engrossed in the book that she almost didn't hear Dante's car. He must have seen her, though, because he parked in the driveway, got out, and began walking slowly toward her. By that time, night had overcome evening, throwing darkness on the area like a death shroud.

"Ma'am, I'm sorry, but this isn't a good time," he said. "I'm going to have to ask you to leave."

"Mr. Washington?" she asked, imbuing her voice with a false tremble. "It's Jane Rodriguez. We met a couple of weeks ago."

He sighed. "I didn't recognize you. If you need legal assistance, I'll give you the name of a friend of mine, but I'm not working tonight."

"I'm not here for that," she said, standing and wringing her hands together as if she were nervous. "I know about Michelle."

He looked as if she had just hit him. He held up a hand and shook his head. "This is inappropriate…"

"Just wait," she said, taking a step forward and furrowing her brow in what she hoped was a concerned manner. She had seen someone do something similar once in a movie. "Hear me out. I'm dating a man. He's a police officer."

"And he told you about my sister, and you thought you'd come over here and share your condolences. Well, you've done that, please be on your way."

Carla shook her head but stopped walking forward. "Do you know Detective Ash Rashid?"

Of course he did, Carla knew that before she went over. Dante knew the man very well, and that gave her the opening she needed. She and Dante didn't talk for long, but they didn't need to. She sent him a voice mail containing some of his sister's last words and told him a very special story she had written just for him to help him understand his sister's death. By the time she left, Dante had rage in his eyes to rival anyone she had ever seen. She probably should have been scared, but it excited her. She had found Dante's magic button. That meant the game had begun and the bodies would start dropping in earnest soon.

Carla almost felt like skipping, but she forced herself to maintain a steady pace down the front walkway. Once she reached the car and pulled away from the curb, she called Jacob, who was still at the pizza place.

"Hey. I'm on my way. How about ordering me something with goat cheese?"

Chapter Six

The clock had just struck eight when I reached my house, and I found my wife in the front room, the newest Lee Child novel propped on her chest and a blanket covering her legs. The kids hadn't greeted me, so she must have taken them to her sister's house. I walked into the living room from the hallway, sat on the other end of the couch, and put my hand on Hannah's feet. She wore a pink terry-cloth bathrobe and loose-fitting pajamas. Some of the tension left my chest as soon as I saw her.

"Are you in for the night?" she asked, laying the book on her lap.

I nodded. "Yeah. Were you actually able to get any reading done?"

"A little. I figured I could still have a quiet night at home, so I dropped the kids off at Yasmine and Jack's house."

I held an arm toward her, and she took the hint, scooting toward me to rest her head against my shoulder. She put her hand in mine and squeezed tight, like she had found something great and didn't want to let go. Not for the first time in the last few months, I wondered what she saw that I didn't.

"Thank you," I said, pulling her against my side and inhaling the scent of her perfume. "It's been a long night. I needed a hug."

"What's the news on Michelle?"

I relaxed my arms and then shook my head. "Paul Murphy is working the case, but somebody hurt her pretty bad. I don't want to think about it."

"You want to talk about anything?"

"I just want to sit down for a little while."

She hesitated, but only for a moment. "You want me to get you something?"

She didn't need to say what she meant by *something*. For the past few months I've been seeing a psychiatrist, although realistically, I should have started seeing him a long time ago. Over the years as a homicide detective and then in various other positions in the department, I've seen sides of humanity I wish I didn't know existed. I understand a battered spouse who shoots her abusive husband—I don't condone it, of course, but I understand.

Other crimes, though, make me think people must have a black stain where their souls should be. My doctor had prescribed me antidepressants and had given me some anti-anxiety drugs for those times when things got especially difficult. I was still waiting for them to start working.

"No, thank you."

"The pills are helping though, aren't they?"

"Yeah," I said, nodding and turning my head so I wouldn't have to look her in the eye and lie. "I'm better every day."

She rested her head on my chest again and patted me on the arm. "Even if they're not helping much yet, I know they will. Things will get better."

I gently hugged her and closed my eyes. Hannah and I had been through a lot in our marriage, and for as long as I've known her, she's been my biggest champion, my support when everything else in the world around me fell apart. I wished I could share her optimism.

"I hope so."

"Whatever happens," said Hannah, looking in my eyes, "things will work out. They always do."

She hoped to keep talking, but I didn't know what to say.

"What do you say we sit back and watch a movie? Something I don't have to think about."

She didn't even hesitate. "I think I've got something that will fit the bill."

I kissed her, and she stood and almost ran to the kitchen, where she had a makeshift work station. I didn't know which movie she'd get, but I knew it'd be bad. Probably really bad. Hannah had a blog on which she reviewed bad movies, so she was something of a connoisseur of terrible movies. We watched one together once or twice a week, my schedule permitting. I'd probably have protested, but she sold ads on her blog and made enough money that we might be able to take a real vacation this year, something we hadn't been able to do for quite a while. Hard to complain about that.

When she came back, she put in an action movie called *Samurai Cop* and curled up against my chest. It was among the better bad movies she's put on, which meant we laughed most of the way through. For almost two hours, I didn't think about Michelle or liquor, and it was only after the movie went off that I realized how badly I had needed that.

At a quarter after ten, with the credits playing, Hannah looked up at me and smiled.

"You know, the kids are still gone."

"I guess they are," I said, arching my eyebrows. "You have any ideas about how we can take advantage of this situation?"

She winked and walked her fingers up my chest and then to my chin. "I can think of something."

I wanted to tell her that I'd meet her in the bedroom, but before I could, my cell phone buzzed from the end table. I considered ignoring it, but it might have been Paul Murphy or someone else from my department.

"Can you give me a minute?" I asked, leaning to grab my phone.

"Sure," said Hannah, standing. "I'll get ready. Come in when you can."

She started walking to our bedroom, and I looked at my phone. The call came from a reporter I vaguely knew who worked for the *Indianapolis Star*, our local paper. As I hit the button declining his call, the phone in the kitchen rang. And then Hannah's cell phone rang from our bedroom. I groaned, having a pretty good idea of what had happened.

"What's going on?" asked Hannah.

I looked at my phone to confirm the time. Seven minutes after ten.

"I think someone leaked my name to the press, and the evening news just reported it. Give me a few more minutes. I'll unplug the phone and turn off our cells."

"That sounds like a good idea."

As I walked to the kitchen, I got two more phone calls on my cell phone, both of which I declined. The first came from Sergeant David Lee, a friend of mine who worked narcotics, and the second came from Randy, the lawyer who had represented me at my disciplinary hearing. I probably should have taken the call from Randy, but I had already talked to enough people that evening. If he really needed me, he'd call me the next morning. And if the department really wanted me, they'd send a squad car. I turned my cell off, unplugged the landline, and then met my wife in our bedroom.

I found unlit candles on the end tables on either side of the bed, and maroon fabric strewn over the lamps, dimming the light they cast onto the floor. Red rose petals stood out on the gray of our comforter. She had done the same thing the night we were married. Hannah lay beneath the covers.

"I'm sorry for tonight," I whispered.

"Don't be," she said, shaking her head. "There's something special in the closet. We'll have to try it out some other time."

As I took off my shirt, I rotated my shoulder in a circle, feeling the bones click against one another. Early on in my career, my first partner in homicide, Keith Holliday, and I had come under fire while trying to serve an arrest warrant. The shooter hit Keith in the neck and me in the shoulder. Keith bled out on my suit and died in my arms. I don't know what happened after that except that I passed out and awoke in a hospital bed with Hannah standing over me, crying. I promised her that as soon as I got back on my feet, I'd quit and get a new job, one that would never end with me in the hospital or in an early grave. Before she could say anything, I passed out again, but I remember feeling her tears on my cheeks.

Hannah has never again mentioned that night, but I think it was the first promise to her I ever broke. I didn't quit—if anything, I became more engrossed in my work. It started as a way to make a living, but as I've gotten older, it's become more than that. Certain people are put on this earth to do certain things, and I believe God put me here to help balance the scales, to put the world right. It's not just a religious edict—although justice is a central tenant of my Islamic faith—it's part of who I am. I can't ignore that, and every single time I've tried, I've come to regret it.

"The room looks nice," I said, going into the closet to throw my dirty clothes in the hamper. In the small section reserved for my hanging clothes, Hannah had added a black silk nightgown cut low in the back but otherwise more concealing than revealing. That was her style. She didn't need to flaunt what she had. The nightgown was just revealing enough to be sexy, but not so much that it crossed the line into tawdry. I wished I had been able to see it on her rather than a clothes hanger.

"The gown is nice," I said, pulling on a pair of pajamas. I walked back into the bedroom and then turned off the lights before climbing into bed.

"It is a nice gown," said Hannah. "But I thought it'd just get in the way for now."

I reached over to kiss her goodnight and found that I had come to bed overdressed. Hannah giggled.

"I guess I don't need my pajamas after all," I said, sliding over to her.

We made love and then held each other, enjoying the quiet stillness of the moment. Hannah eventually drifted off to sleep, but slumber couldn't find me. I didn't want it to. I swung my legs off the bed and looked over my shoulder at Hannah.

"I'm going to go for a drive," I said, whispering. "I need to clear my head."

Hannah blinked a few times and then yawned and sat up, the blankets clutched to her chest. "Are you all right?"

"I'm fine, but I just need some alone time to process what happened."

She put a hand flat on my upper arm and looked directly in my eyes. "If you need to talk, we can talk."

"I just need to get out of here for a little while."

"Okay," she said, nodding. "I'll be here when you get back."

I kissed her, and then stood up and dressed as quickly as I could before grabbing my car keys and leaving. The night was cold and dark, but it did little to sap the feeling welling in my stomach. I didn't have a destination in mind, so I simply pulled my car out of the driveway and pressed on the accelerator. In the back of my mind, I knew that I needed to keep moving, that if I stopped, I'd think about Michelle. And if not Michelle, I'd focus on someone else, someone I didn't want to think about. Most police officers with my experience develop coping skills to distance themselves from the things they see at work, but no matter what I do, I can't. My memories follow me home.

Even without making a conscious decision about my destination, I pulled into the parking lot outside a familiar sports bar fifteen minutes after I set out. I had spent a lot of time in that bar over the years. The last time I went there, I went with a buddy after a particularly bad day at work. I don't think I had much to drink—just a beer—but I left feeling better than I had when I entered.

I parked and took my keys out but stayed in the car. If I went in there, I knew I'd have more than a beer. This wasn't just a bad day. This was a day I wanted to forget. In weeks past, I would have called Michelle at that point. She'd say something encouraging, something kind, something that would talk me back from the edge. If I called her now, though, her phone would ring and ring forever. My friend was gone, murdered in one of the most horrific ways I could imagine. I needed a break from that for just an hour or two.

I went in and stayed an hour, long enough to down three shots, two beers, and a basket of pretzels. I had a buzz, but I wouldn't be over the legal limit to drive. Unlike in years past, the liquor didn't make me feel better, but it did make me feel different than when I had arrived. That was good enough for me. After the bar, I drove home, all the while thinking of what I would tell my wife. Already, I could imagine the hurt in her eyes, but she deserved to know. Maybe not tonight, but soon.

I crept inside as quietly as I could, and, just like old times, rinsed with mouthwash before going to the bedroom. Thankfully, Hannah didn't wake up for more than a moment as I crawled into bed.

I don't know how long the two of us slept, but we both woke up at the same time to a creaking sound. We're parents, so we're accustomed to things going bump in the night and to the sound of our floorboards shifting as someone walks around. Our kids weren't home, though, and our floors should have been silent. Hannah sat up first, holding the covers over her chest.

"Was that sound outside or in?" she asked.

"Out, I think," I said, throwing my legs over the side of the bed. My head was a little light, but I couldn't tell if that was from the booze or from a lack of sleep. "Sounded like the front porch. Probably nothing, but I'll check it out."

She nodded, but I could tell I hadn't settled her nerves.

"Do that, and then—"

Hannah stopped mid-sentence. My breath caught in my throat as the creaking noise shifted into a heavy, heart-stopping thump. It sounded almost like a car backfiring, but it shook the entire house. For a moment, I froze.

Then it happened again, rattling the walls.

All at once, my mind caught up with events and the world spun into rapid motion. Someone was trying to kick down my front door. I stood and sprinted toward the closet.

"Call 911," I said, pounding my combination into the lockbox that held my service pistol. The heavy thumping at the front door continued, rhythmically, like a heartbeat.

The front door was solid wood, two inches thick and weighing well over a hundred pounds. Even if the guy had an ax, it'd take him an hour to break through. The frame, though, was comparatively flimsy, so I didn't know how much damage it could take.

Hannah grabbed the cordless and sprinted into the closet after me, throwing on a robe, while I grabbed my weapon, a forty-caliber Glock 22, from the box.

"The safe's open. The Beretta's loaded and ready," I said, slamming a magazine into my weapon and then pulling the receiver back to chamber a round. "You know how to use it. If somebody other than me comes in, shoot him."

She nodded and hunkered down against the wall. I held my weapon at my side and stepped into the hallway that led to our front door. The front door shuddered as the assailant pounded against it.

"I'm an armed police officer. Stop immediately."

He kicked the door again, and the frame splintered with an audible crack. At one time, my hands would have shaken so badly in that situation that I'd be a danger to everyone around me, but as the assailant's foot connected with that door again and that frame finally broke, a calmness came over me and I lost myself in the moment. My hands steadied, and my breath settled into a slow and even rhythm. Despite the five drinks I had consumed that night, I felt as sober as the day I was born.

The door crashed open, slamming into the wall. Hannah shouted, but then she, along with everything else, seemed to disappear and the world felt as if it had stopped moving. Two people existed in that moment: me, and the dark figure who had just kicked in my front door. He held his hands empty at his sides, but he very well could have had a gun in his pocket. I didn't know what he wanted, but he wouldn't have kicked down my door if he had good intentions. Everything about me went cold as my finger slipped from the trigger guard to the trigger.

"Slowly put your hands on top of your head and lie on the ground."

"You killed my sister."

I recognized the voice, but I couldn't place it. My heart thudded hard. Whether I recognized him or not didn't matter; he was a threat.

"Put your hands on top of your head and lie on the ground."

He made no move to comply, but he didn't step forward, either.

"You killed my sister. She was your friend."

Past the anger and the hurt, I knew that voice. I had talked to him just a few days ago. Some of the stiffness left my shoulders. I didn't lower my weapon, but I relaxed a little.

Dante?

"Whatever's going on—"

His right hand shot into his jacket pocket, interrupting me. My shoulders tensed, and I held my breath.

Don't do this.

"Hands in front of you. Now."

He struggled to pull something large out of his pocket. Then I saw it, or a corner. It was black, and even without seeing it, I knew it was a gun.

"Drop it, please."

But he didn't stop, and he didn't drop anything. He jerked his weapon free of his coat, and I fired before he could raise it toward me. Six shots, center of mass. They struck his chest like hammer blows. He fell to his knees and then to his face before he could even raise his arm an inch.

"He's down. I'm okay," I shouted, creeping forward, my gun still held in front of me. As I got closer, my stomach dropped like I had just stepped off the edge of a cliff. Our intruder was definitely Dante Washington, Michelle's brother, and he did have a gun visible, tucked into the back of his pants. But he hadn't gone for that, though. He had tried to pull out his cell phone.

"Damn."

Chapter Seven

When I got back to the closet, I confirmed that I was okay before walking around the exterior of the house to make sure Dante had come alone. That done, I called the police from the front porch. Hannah came out to meet me. She had dressed fully and even thought to bring me a coat and some shoes, both of which I appreciated. Once I had the phone call made, we sat down on the front steps to wait for the police to arrive, giving me time to think.

I had run into Dante by chance a couple of weeks ago when he came to pick his sister up from an AA meeting in the basement of their church. We hadn't seen each other in a couple of years, so we sat and talked for a few minutes around the coffee urn. He had just finished law school and planned to start his own practice out of an office in his house. He even showed me a picture of his girlfriend, a woman he planned to marry when he could afford the ring. Life had turned out well for him and promised to get even better.

And now I had killed him, taking all that away.

This was bad. Even though Dante had broken down my door and screamed at me, he hadn't gone for his gun. I shot an unarmed man. My stomach roiled, and my hands trembled. He was just a stupid kid who made a mistake, and

I shot him for it. Hannah must have sensed how upset I was because she scooted toward me and held my hand in hers.

"That was Dante Washington," I said. "Michelle's brother. I killed him."

"He didn't give you a choice," said Hannah. "You did the right thing."

"No, I didn't," I said. "This was wrong."

She didn't say anything to that, but she squeezed my hand. "It's okay."

Neither of us said anything else until the first uniformed officers arrived approximately five minutes after we had placed the call. I disentangled myself from my wife, and then stood, holding my weapon up in one hand and my badge in the other. The officers confiscated my gun, separated us, secured the scene, and then waited for the cavalry to arrive. Within twenty minutes, we had half a dozen detectives, including two from internal affairs, in my front yard. While the internal affairs detectives interviewed Hannah, one of our forensic technicians swabbed my hands for gunshot residue and a paramedic drew two vials of my blood to test for drugs or alcohol—standard practice for an officer-involved shooting. I didn't feel drunk, but they'd find booze in my system. That certainly wouldn't help the situation.

After the IA detectives finished with Hannah, they asked me to come to their car so they could interview me. I sat in the back while the two detectives—neither of whom I knew—questioned me from the front. They let me tell the story at my own pace, and I told them the truth as well as I could. It was dark, I was scared, and I thought Dante was going for a gun when I shot him. They seemed understanding.

"To clarify," asked the officer in the driver's seat once I finished, "did you recognize the intruder as Dante Washington upon his arrival?"

I shook my head. "Not at first. I thought I recognized his voice, but he was hoarse. I couldn't be sure."

"What did he say?"

I took a breath and then let it out slowly, feeling a tiny bit of the tension in my gut go out with it. "He said I killed his sister. She was murdered. Paul Murphy's working that case."

Both detectives jotted down notes, but then the one on the right glanced up. "We've spoken to Detective Murphy. He's on his way here."

The guy on the left put his pen behind his ear and then narrowed his eyes at me. "I need you to be honest here, because we're going to talk to your neighbors and your friends. Will any of them tell us you and Dante have reason to dislike each other?"

Again, I shook my head. "No. I barely knew him. I talked to him about three weeks ago, and he showed me pictures of his girlfriend. He was saving up to buy her a ring. He was a nice guy."

Both detectives nodded, but I doubted they believed me. The one on the right, the younger detective, spoke next. "During the altercation, are you sure he never reached for his weapon?"

"I thought he was reaching for a gun, but it was his phone. I shot him because I thought my life was in danger."

The two IA detectives looked at each other, and then the one on the left spoke. "Are you *positive* that's how it happened? It would be better if he had reached for his gun."

I furrowed my brow. "What do you mean *better*?"

Both detectives, again, looked at each other before folding up their notepads and looking at me again. The driver, the older of the two, sighed. "I'm not going to lie to you. We can't arrest you for protecting yourself from an intruder, but this is still going to turn into a giant mess. Whether Dante broke into your house or not, you shot an unarmed man. I want to believe you, I really do, but your story doesn't make sense. If he was such a nice guy and you two got along so well, why would he kick down your door and accuse you of murdering his sister? Something's not adding up here. The press gets wind of this, they're going to crucify you. Let us help you. Tell me it's possible that he went for his gun."

At first, I didn't know what to say to that. I leaned back and blinked.

"I'm not going to lie."

"I'm not asking you to lie. I'm asking you to consider the possibility that he reached for his firearm rather than his cell phone. By your own admission, it was dark, it was late, and you were scared. And let me guess, your wife was screaming, right? You didn't know what was going on. All you knew was that someone broke into your house. You wanted to protect yourself and your wife. With all that going on, it's understandable if you were confused by what you saw. It's possible that he was going for his gun and not his cell phone, right? You could have seen that."

I didn't know these detectives, so I didn't know if they were trying to trick me into saying something I shouldn't or if they were genuinely trying to falsify the record.

"What are you guys trying to do?"

"We're trying to understand what happened," said the older detective. "You're not making it easy."

"Fine. I'll make it crystal clear," I said, holding up my hands. "Dante kicked down my door. I held him at gunpoint and told him to lie on the ground. He then reached into his pocket for something. I asked him to take his hands out and put them where I could see them. He then pulled something black out, and I thought it was a gun. I shot him. His firearm, however, was behind him. He didn't reach for it."

The detectives looked at me, nodding. Neither wrote down what I had just said.

"For your own good, you should consider the possibility that you're mistaken," said the older guy. "You're IMPD, and you shot a man. That reflects on all of us, and we're not going to let Indianapolis turn into Ferguson, Missouri. Here, if you shoot an unarmed man who was reaching for his phone, you're going to hang. Do you understand what we're saying?"

The implications of that dawned on me slowly. They didn't want the truth. They wanted a story they could sell to the media. "You can't arrest me for shooting a man who broke into my house."

"No, but we can recommend the chief fire you," said the older detective. "We don't have to protect you from the press, either."

"Do what you think is right," I said. "Since I'm not under arrest, I'm going to get out of this car and I'm going to pretend we never had this conversation. If you need to talk to me again, I'll give you my lawyer's number."

Before they could stop me, I opened my door and left. After talking to those two, I felt like I needed a shower, but they were right: someone would hang for this. This was going to turn ugly. As I walked toward my house, I called Randy Prather, my attorney, and he warned me not to talk to anyone else about the shooting. We made an appointment to talk the next day.

After that, I went back inside, put on a suit and tie, and clipped my badge to my belt. Forensic technicians had taken over most of the house, so I joined Hannah on the front steps. The sun wouldn't rise for a few more hours, but already dark gray had begun to replace black on the horizon. Despite the time, the young couple across the street had put lawn chairs on their front lawn to watch the police work. They had even brought snacks, as if this was some kind of macabre late dinner theater. I waved to them, but really I wanted to cross the street and slap them senseless, to demand to know what had gone so wrong in their lives that they'd get entertainment value out of a young man's death.

My eyes slipped closed without conscious direction, and I found myself praying. Eventually, someone coughed in front of me.

"Ash. Mrs. Rashid."

I recognized the voice even without looking at him.

"Hi, officer," said Hannah, hesitatingly.

"What do you need, Paul?"

He paused and then sighed. "There somewhere we can talk? I've got something I need to show you. Mrs. Rashid can stay here."

I opened my eyes and looked at my wife. She nodded her assent, so I stood up and pointed to the garage. "Unless they've taken it over, we can go there."

Paul followed me to the garage and then whistled when he got inside. "This is a nice place. You can get a lot of projects done here, I bet."

"It's just my garage," I said, sighing. "You heard what happened?"

"Bits and pieces. You really shot an unarmed man?"

I took a couple of minutes and told him my side of things as well as the discussion with the two IA detectives. Paul ran a hand across his face when I finished and then reached into his jacket for a pack of cigarettes. Before lighting up, he held the package out to me.

"You mind?"

Instead of answering, I crossed the room to the recycling bin beside the door and pulled out a Coke can he could use as an ashtray. I put it on the workbench behind him. "Be my guest."

Paul lit up and took a long drag. We both watched the smoke mingle with the rafters above our heads before speaking.

"First thing," said Paul. "Thank your wife for the coffee she made us. It was…interesting."

A lot of people said that about Hannah's coffee.

"The first time I had it," I said, "I thought she was trying to kill me."

Paul looked thoughtful. "I can see why you'd think that." He looked down at the floor. "Sounds like those IA detectives were trying to give you a way out of this."

"By lying."

"A white lie, maybe," said Paul, nodding. "It wouldn't hurt anyone. The kid did come with a gun. Who's to say he wouldn't have tried to kill you if you gave him the chance?"

"But he didn't," I said. "And that's the last I'll hear about it."

"It is going to get ugly, though. You realize that?"

Indiana criminal law gave me a free pass for shooting Dante, but that wouldn't keep the media away. Beside, even with the law on my side, I had done something morally wrong. I didn't plan to lie and defame the very kid I shot to death just to make myself look better.

"I'm not changing my story," I said. "Is that why you wanted to see me?"

"No," said Paul, shaking his head. "I got a call earlier this evening from Anton Boswell in Vice. He knew Dante from church."

"Okay," I said, nodding impatiently.

"He wanted to know if we had an open rape investigation on Michelle."

I felt my shoulders drop a little. "Do we?"

Paul shook his head. "No. Dante had called Boswell and asked him about it. Dante claimed that a credible source told him you raped his sister, and we were covering for you. Might be why he came over here."

It felt as if someone had punched me in the gut. "I'd never hurt Michelle. Dante knew that."

Paul hesitated and then laid his phone on my workbench. "We found a voice mail on Dante's phone you should hear. We think he might have been trying to play it when you shot him."

I swallowed hard and crossed my arms. "Roll it."

He hit a button, and a woman started speaking. I recognized Michelle Washington's voice, but the cadence of her speech and the pitch of her voice were off, making what she said sound stiff and forced, almost as if she were reading something.

"Dante, it's Michelle. I'm calling because I'm a little freaked out right now. He asked me not to tell anyone, but Ash and I have been sleeping together for a few weeks now. I couldn't do it anymore, so I broke it off. For some reason, he thinks I ended it so I could see other guys. I've never seen him this mad. He scared me. He wants me to meet so we can talk, and I don't know what to do. He knows where I live, so I can't just ignore him. I'm going to meet him by that Boy Scout camp off Fall Creek Road. I hate to ask you this, but if I'm not back by six or seven, could you swing by there for me? I don't know what's going on, but I'm really scared."

She may have said something else, but Paul stopped the recording and looked at me, as if expecting me to say something. Unfortunately, I didn't know what to say. A relationship with an AA sponsor requires a lot of trust and even a little intimacy, so most people choose a sponsor of their own sex. I chose Michelle, however, because we grew up in similar neighborhoods and because I knew and respected her. That meant we had to have certain ground rules at the very start to remove any whiff of impropriety.

"Michelle and I never met in private. The guy who leads our group can verify that."

Paul kept his face impassive. "And there was nothing romantic going on between you?"

I shook my head. "No. I'm happily married. I haven't even been in town for the past couple of days. This is why he came here? He wanted me to hear this?"

Paul shook his head. "He wouldn't have brought a gun if he only wanted you to hear something. Dante was there when we did the next-of-kin notification, and he was pretty upset. I think he came home, heard the call, and snapped. I think he came to kill you, but he wanted you to know why first."

I didn't know Dante well, but Michelle's temper could run hot. Her brother's probably did, too, but that didn't explain everything.

"This doesn't mention anything about a rape."

Paul put his phone back in his pocket and cocked his head to the side. "That, I can't answer. His neighbors told us he met someone on his porch before this went down. My guess is that somebody met him, told him you raped Michelle, and then sent the audio file to back up the story. With all the stress, Dante broke."

"Somebody hurt Michelle badly before she died," I said. "They made her say those things."

"Possibly," said Paul, nodding. "But gangbangers don't do things like this."

"You can't believe I hurt Michelle," I said.

Paul put his phone back in his pocket and then sighed. "I don't, but is there anything you're not telling me?"

I turned around and put my hands on top of my head. "I had a couple of drinks tonight."

Paul paused. "I thought you were in AA."

"I am, or at least I was," I said, turning to face him. "My sponsor was shot. I slipped."

"Okay," he said, looking thoughtful. "How many is a couple and what time did you stop?"

"Five drinks total, and I stopped at midnight," I said. I paused and then sighed. "But the bartender has a generous pour. It's one of the reasons I used to go to his bar. It was probably closer to seven drinks."

Paul put his notepad on my workbench and leaned back. He closed his eyes and then sighed. "That's not good."

I didn't have anything to say to that.

"You shot Dante at two, and paramedics drew your blood at a quarter after," said Paul, crossing his arms. "I don't know what your BAC will be, but you're going to have alcohol in your system. Please tell me you've never gotten into a fight with Dante."

"Never," I said, shaking my head. "He was a good man. We weren't friends, but I liked him."

"That's something, at least," said Paul. "Any idea why someone would convince Dante to kill you?"

People have tried to kill me before, and for good or ill, I've put every single one of them in prison or in the ground. I started pacing in front of the garage door.

"I don't think this is about me. I'm an armed police officer with a history that says I will shoot accurately without hesitation. Someone gave Dante that message so he'd come over here and die. This was death-by-cop."

Paul narrowed his eyes and crossed his arms. "How well do you really know Dante and Michelle?"

I shrugged. "I know Michelle well, but Dante I've spoken to maybe five times over the last decade."

Paul took a notepad from the inside pocket of his jacket and scribbled a note. "And you have no connection to Dante other than his sister and the Santino Ramirez trial?"

"None," I said, shaking my head.

"All right, then," said Paul, closing his notepad. "IA's going to look into the shooting. People are going to ask questions about your drinking, so be prepared for that. If the story you're telling holds up, they'll clear you. We're going to find out who left Dante the message and see what's going on. Meantime, you need to stay away from this case for your own good. I'm going to put you in cuffs and take you downtown. It needs to look like we're taking you in for questioning."

I put my hands on my hips and opened my eyes wide. "May I ask why you want to put me in cuffs?"

"Because those IA detectives are going to hurt you for not cooperating with them. That audio file's going to leak and so is the report about your drinking. When the press reports that, the public is going to call for all of our heads. We've got to control this thing while we can still shape the narrative."

"*Shape the narrative,*" I said, repeating him. "When did you become a politician?"

"When a friend of mine shot somebody in his front hallway. That wasn't a request."

Part of me wanted to fight him, but his request made sense. We didn't need the press saying my friends were covering up a murder.

"We can do one better than just taking me downtown. That audio file's going to leak no matter what. Give it to Ken Schiller at the *Star* first. He shoots pretty straight. I don't think he'd try to screw us."

Paul considered for a moment, but then nodded. "If you can make that happen, it might not be a bad idea."

"I think I can," I said. "I'll need my cell phone, though. Somebody took it earlier."

Paul's demeanor perked up just a little, and then he reached into his pocket and pulled out my phone. He tried to keep a straight face, but a smile still crept to his lips. "I meant to give this back to you earlier. Before I do, though, I've got a very serious question. Are you addicted to Islamic pornography? If you are, there are people who can help. The first step is admitting your addiction, though."

"What are you talking about?"

He put a hand on my shoulder and looked straight in my eyes. "I saw the pictures. The women in burqas. It's okay, buddy. We've all been there. I'm not judging."

I took the phone from his outstretched hand. The picture of a young, very attractive woman smiled at me from the screen. Had I not just shot someone, I might have laughed.

"That's a hijab, not a burqa," I said, glancing up at Paul. "A burqa covers the whole body."

"I see," said Paul, nodding. "Since she's not covered as much, would this be considered hardcore Muslim pornography?"

"The woman is a model. I wanted to buy Hannah a new hijab for Susan Mercer's New Year's Eve party, so my sister sent me pictures of hijabs she thought looked nice. I'm sure pornography from the Middle East looks like pornography from anywhere else. You'd recognize it if you saw it."

Paul stood a little straighter. "I didn't get invited to Susan Mercer's party."

"Probably because she doesn't like you," I said. "Can we focus on work?"

"If you're going to be a spoilsport, sure."

"Thank you," I said, already looking through the recently received calls list on my cell phone. I found Ken's number and called him. He answered almost before my phone finished ringing once, and I put him on speakerphone.

"Ken, it's Ash Rashid with IMPD," I said, turning and glancing up at Paul. "I'm here with Detective Sergeant Paul Murphy. I've got something for you if you can get it on your website quickly. You interested?"

Ken had the gravelly voice of a man who had spent his life smoking. "That depends on what you've got."

"Michelle Washington's brother Dante came to my house this morning. I had to shoot him."

"I know. I'm standing behind the police barricade about a block away from your front door."

In my stupor, I hadn't realized the press had already arrived.

"Dante received an audio file last night allegedly recorded by Michelle in which she claimed the two of us had a romantic relationship and that I had set up a meeting with her out on Fall Creek Road."

"Okay," he said, sounding uncertain.

"I never had that kind of relationship with her and wasn't even in town when she died."

I heard Ken's feet shuffle and a car door open and close before he spoke again. "You've never given me a story before, so why are you chatty now?"

I shifted my phone from one ear to the other. "Because someone's going to leak it, and other reporters are selective about the facts. I'd rather get everything out there. If you can't do this, I'll call somebody who can."

I waited for maybe five seconds. "If I run this, I need somebody on record to verify it."

I looked at Paul. He sighed before speaking.

"Use my name. Detective Sergeant Paul Murphy. You can figure out the spelling on your own. I work homicide."

"All right," said Ken, after a moment's pause. "So you're telling me Dante Washington received an audio file. Do you have any idea who sent it?"

"We're still working that end of the investigation," I said. "If we get anything, you'll be the first to know."

Ken paused, probably to write things down. "What's your theory on this?"

I considered lying to him, but Ken would figure things out as soon as he looked our victims up. "Dante and Michelle testified in a murder trial ten years ago. This might be related to their testimony."

Ken paused again, long enough this time that I started wondering what was thinking. "Did you say Michelle and Dante Washington?"

"Yeah," I said, nodding.

"This is the same Michelle and Dante Washington who testified against Santino Ramirez ten years ago?"

I grimaced. "That's them. You recognize them?"

"Yeah, I covered Ramirez's trial. Just to clarify, but when you say these murders might be related to their testimony, do you mean Ramirez's gang may be murdering them in retribution?"

"At this time, we only have facts," I said. "Someone murdered and tortured Michelle. We found her body last night. Also last night, her brother received an audio file in which Michelle claimed to have set up a meeting with me. Dante came to my house and kicked down my door. Believing my life was in danger, I shot him."

I was giving him a big story with an uncertain outcome, and I think Ken sensed that. He sounded almost giddy. "Can I get this audio file?"

I glanced at Paul for confirmation. He nodded. "Sergeant Murphy will email it to you."

Paul went to work on his phone. Within a minute, Ken confirmed receipt.

"I'll get this up as soon as I can," said Ken. "Just FYI, but I just received word that Leonard Wilson wants to speak to the press here."

Leonard was the elected prosecutor. It's rare I meet someone I hold in more contempt.

"He's at my house?" I asked, looking at the floor.

"Well, on your street. He's gathering reporters around him."

Beautiful. Just beautiful.

"Thanks for the heads-up. Get your photographer ready because I'm going to be coming out of my garage in a few minutes, and I'm going to be in handcuffs."

I didn't wait for Ken to say anything before hanging up my phone and slipping it into my pocket. Paul had already begun removing the handcuffs from his belt. I held out my wrists in front of me. If I were an actual arrestee, he would have put them behind my back, but I wanted them free to make some calls.

"Before we go," I said, wiggling my wrists to get used to the cuffs, "I need to see what Leonard has to say before he stabs us in the back."

Chapter Eight

Outside my garage, uniformed officers had erected a perimeter around my yard with yellow crime scene tape. Beyond that, four television cameramen filmed everything that went on, including my perp walk. Ken Schiller nodded when I saw him. He wore a blue-and-gray sweater so hideous he must have lost a bet, and he held a cigarette between lips not much thicker than pencil lines. He jotted notes on a legal pad. Leonard Wilson stood near the cameramen. He wore a navy suit and a politician's thinly veiled insincere smile.

I may break some rules at work, but I'm not crooked. Even at my most recent disciplinary hearing, the review board never questioned my motives. I didn't question theirs, either. We may disagree about the best way to keep our city safe, but we all want the same thing. Leonard Wilson, though...I do question his motives. From all I've seen, he's a genuinely bad man and he has significant power to enact his will. Unfortunately, he also recognizes me as a threat.

"If I could get everyone's attention," said Leonard, waving his arms. "I'd like to make a few announcements on behalf of the prosecutor's office."

The cameras switched from me to him. When all four television cameras and most of the assembled persons faced him, he smiled.

"Good morning. I'd appreciate if everyone came close so I don't have to shout," he said. He waited to speak again until everyone around him was watching. Then he smiled at each of them in turn. "When I got out of bed this morning, I got a very unwelcome surprise phone call from a staffer at the Office of Public Safety telling me about the shooting death of Dante Washington. I came here today to assure the public that the law enforcement community in Marion County is taking this incident very seriously and monitoring events closely. Already, I've received dozens of emails from irate community members demanding I arrest Detective Rashid for shooting an unarmed young man. I'm here to assure the public that justice will be done.

"This is a rapidly evolving situation, and we will not act without the facts. If, however, we discover that Mr. Rashid lured Mr. Washington to his home, as has been suggested, IMPD will react appropriately. If we discover that the weapon found on Mr. Washington's body was, in fact, planted by Mr. Rashid—again, as has been suggested to me dozens of times already—we will react appropriately. I have already been in contact with Mr. Washington's family."

Leonard paused and took a deep breath. When he spoke again, his voice was softer. "Mr. Washington was a fine young man. His death was a tragedy all around."

Leonard kept talking, but I had heard enough. I looked at Paul.

"What do you say we get out of here?"

"Yeah," said Paul, nodding. "That's a good idea."

We walked to his car but not before the cameramen who had focused on Leonard started focusing on me. Their pictures wouldn't help my reputation, but they did send a strong message: nobody's above the law, not even a decorated police officer. Hopefully that would keep the press from pressuring the department's investigation too much. Once we got in the car, Paul looked at me.

"Funny, I hadn't heard any of those allegations Leonard mentioned."

I pulled my seat belt over my shoulder and buckled up. "Now you'll hear them over and over, though. He's wanted to get me fired for a while. It was smart."

"You really think he's that devious?"

I didn't hesitate. "Yes. In politics, perception is reality. He told me that once, right before he ambushed me and made it look like I endorsed him in his last election. He wanted to gain favor with the Islamic community."

Paul put on his seat belt and started driving toward the City-County Building downtown. Leonard had good reason to want me fired, I supposed. A couple of months ago, I had discovered a bed and breakfast in one of the suburbs on the east side of town that offered the services of young women kidnapped overseas and forced to work as prostitutes. I also discovered that Leonard frequented the establishment. Unfortunately, the information came from a gangster who obtained it by murdering the establishment's madam. That made it a little difficult to use in court.

As Paul drove, I looked out the window, watching the few cars around us. The sun hadn't even risen, and yet these early-morning warriors—almost all men—had already begun their daily trek, drinking their coffee, their minds probably already thinking hours ahead to a meeting that morning or an email they needed to write. I wondered if any of them stopped to consider that they would miss their daughter's first smile of the morning, their son's pitter-patter footsteps down the hallway, that special look their wives reserved only for them. Since having children, mornings had become my favorite part of the day. I had missed too many of them for my taste.

We parked in a surface parking lot across the street from the City-County Building. Even though the Indianapolis metropolitan area has almost two million people, most of our government functions still occur in the utilitarian twenty-eight-story office building. The city could probably produce studies showing that a single government building made things more efficient, but I doubted they'd mention how cramped things could get.

As soon as we stepped out of the car, Paul removed my handcuffs. I could see the tiniest sliver of morning on the horizon. In another couple of hours the sun would burn off the nighttime chill, but for now the cold still lingered, sapping me of the heat of my anger. Paul lit a cigarette, and I stamped my feet on the concrete, both to stay warm and to give me something to do so I wouldn't have to think about Dante. In time, Paul's smoking addiction would kill him, but I could see the relief in his eyes as he exhaled. He flicked ash on the ground, and we started toward the building.

"My wife wants me to quit, but nothing in the world makes me feel as good as that first cigarette of the day," he said. "Hard to say no to that."

"Addiction is a pretty powerful motivator," I said, nodding. "Of course, living to fifty has its perks, too."

He looked at me, shook his head, and then tossed his cigarette to the ground. "Next thing I know, you'll be telling me to exercise." I started to say that exercise wouldn't be a bad idea, but he cut me off. "I get enough of that at home. I don't need my friends getting on me, too."

"I wouldn't dream of getting on you. Believe me."

"Good...I think," he said, grinding his cigarette with his heel. "I've got some calls to make, but I had somebody pull the evidence box from your investigation into Santino Ramirez. If you're up for it, I'd still like to go over that."

"That'd be fine."

He nodded and looked left and right on North Alabama Street. Nothing stirred.

"I've been meaning to ask," he said, walking forward. "How'd your disciplinary hearing go?"

"I've still got a badge for now."

He grinned. "So you haven't got the verdict yet?"

I stopped in the middle of the street. Supposedly, the review board kept their deliberations secret, but word still managed to get out more often than not ahead of time. "You've heard something?"

"No, I was making a joke. I didn't mean anything. I'm sure it went well."

"My lawyer said it went as he expected," I said.

Which is to say, it went terribly. Three police captains had grilled me for over two hours, not only about the incident alleged in the original complaint, but also about my acrimonious relationship with Leonard Wilson and my working relationship with Konstantin Bukoholov, a very high-end distributor of narcotics. One day, I hope to put both men in prison for their crimes, but not yet. I've still got too much work to do, and they're still too useful to me. Unfortunately, they probably think the same thing about me.

Upon reaching the building, we took the elevator to Paul's floor. That early on a normal Saturday, Paul's office would be relatively empty, but today five officers, including Captain Mike Bowers and Special Agent Kevin Havelock, the agent in charge of the local FBI field office, met us near the conference room. The last time I had seen Havelock, he tried to convince me to involve myself in a criminal conspiracy to murder a foreign national. He tried to make it seem as if I would be doing my country a service by eliminating a very dangerous man; in actuality, he wanted me on tape incriminating myself so he could arrest me. I put a hand on Paul's shoulder to stop him. He looked back at me, so I nodded to Havelock.

"What are the feds doing here?"

Paul narrowed his eyes at Agent Havelock before turning to me. "I don't know, but I'll find out."

"Be careful around Havelock," I said. "He's ambitious, and he doesn't mind stepping on the little people to get what he wants."

Paul hesitated but then nodded. "Point taken. You go to the conference room. I've got some calls to make. Somebody should bring in the evidence from the Ramirez case shortly."

I thought quickly. If they brought in all the evidence from the Ramirez case, they'd have my original case notepad in it as well. "Give me a few extra minutes. I'm going to have *Fajr*."

"*Fajr*?" asked Paul, furrowing his brow.

"*Salat al-Fajr*," I said. "Dawn prayer. I just need the room and a little privacy."

He nodded. "All right, then. You've got twenty minutes while I work."

I nodded and began closing the conference room's blinds. I didn't actually require privacy for prayer—in fact, I had seen men praying by the roadside once on a trip to Egypt—but I didn't like flaunting my faith, either. As a Muslim, I'm called to prayer five times a day, and perhaps it's hokey and old-fashioned to say, but they're among my favorite times of day. Those times allow me to center myself and refocus on what's most important in my life.

I washed up in the bathroom and then had dawn prayer in the conference room. A couple of minutes after I finished, a uniformed officer deposited a white cardboard banker's box on the conference room table. In many cities, detectives keep "murder books," which act as a written record of an investigation. Usually, they're a three-ring binder that contains the paper trail of the investigation. In Indianapolis, we keep our paperwork and reports in file boxes. If Paul got the right box, I should have transcripts of every interview we conducted in our investigation of Santino Ramirez, the coroner's autopsy summary and report, pictures of the initial crime scene, witness lists, reports from the crime lab—everything we had needed, in fact, to secure a conviction.

I popped the top off the box and felt a wave of nostalgia wash over me when I saw Keith Holliday's handwriting on the case summary, the first document in the box. He had been dead almost nine years now, probably forty years before his time. We never had time to develop the sort of friendship many investigators develop with their partners, but I learned what it meant to be a detective by watching him, by seeing his tenaciousness, by shadowing him as he closed cases others said were hopeless. He was a good man who died too young.

Once my nostalgia passed, I pulled my old case notebook from the box. When we had worked the case, Keith made me do most of the grunt work, including tracking down Ramirez's very uncooperative friends and family. At the time, I thought he was hazing me, giving me some sort of initiation into the homicide unit, but now I see how much utility the work possessed. I had a map of the entire gang, including its hierarchy.

While I certainly couldn't forgive what happened to Michelle, I would have stayed out of the investigation in normal circumstances. Leonard Wilson and Dante changed things, though. Had I been a little slower or had I been out of the house, Dante could have killed my wife. If my kids had been home, a stray shot might have hit them and I'd be burying a child instead of preparing for a meeting. On top of that, Leonard Wilson had now stepped in. I didn't see his game yet, but he'd hurt me if he could. Paul would do a fine job on his investigation, but he'd be slow. I had to end this before anyone else got hurt, and that meant I might have to get my hands a little dirty.

I jotted down as many names at the top of the gang's hierarchy as I could. We had probably put a lot of those guys in prison, and other gangs had probably managed to put a few more of them beneath the dirt, but this was a start. With Paul coming back any moment, I didn't want to push things, so I put my current notebook back in my jacket pocket and started organizing the documents from the box into piles—coroner's report in one pile, interview notes in a second, procedural documents in a third. When Paul returned, he put a cup of coffee beside me on the table.

"Coffee's black," he said. "You want cream or sugar, you're on your own."

"Black is fine," I said, looking up from my stack of documents. "I've tried to arrange things in a logical way. I can walk you through everything, or just those documents you want. What's Havelock doing here?"

Paul sighed. "Just stepping on toes so far. The feds are interested in cartel connections to the local drug trade, so he's going to sit in on our briefings and offer his expertise where he can."

I looked at the door. "Last time I worked with him, he tried to entrap me. Don't trust him. I'm warning you."

"Forgive me for saying so, buddy," said Paul, his lips forming a small smile. "But you rub a lot of people the wrong way. Ever considered that the common denominator in all your poor relationships is you?"

"That's not funny."

Paul tilted his head to the side and then clapped me on the shoulder. "I think it's pretty funny. You keep reading for a few minutes. My team is on the way. You'll brief them."

I grunted and then read through my old case notebook. Over the next five minutes, three additional IMPD officers, as well as Agent Havelock, entered the room. Havelock arrived first. He shook my hand warmly as if we were old friends. The second arrival was Nancy Wharton, a fortyish auburn-haired woman. She had the stern countenance of a nun unhappy that her superiors had assigned her to teach second grade at the local Catholic school. She nodded to me but said nothing and instead sat down beside Paul. The second officer, Kent Graham, I knew relatively well, having attended the Academy with him many years earlier. He had gained a little weight since then, mostly around his midsection, and he wore a suit on shoulders so thin that it hung off him as if on a clothes hanger.

"Lousy circumstances, but good to see you, Ash," he said, smiling and extending his hand toward me. I shook it.

"It's good to see you, too," I said. I glanced at Paul. "Is this everybody?"

"We've got one more," he said, nodding toward the door. "And there she is."

I turned and looked over my shoulder. *She* was Officer Emilia Rios, the *Santa Muerta* expert from the crime scene on Fall Creek Road. Having changed from her uniform into a pair of jeans, a brown leather jacket, and a striped polo shirt, she could have passed for a college student.

"For those who don't know her, this is Officer Emilia Rios. She's here as our subject-matter expert in case we run into more *Santa Muerte* stuff," said Paul, by way of introduction. He then turned to Agent Havelock. "And this is Special Agent Kevin Havelock. He's the agent in charge of the local FBI field office, and he's here to provide support in case we run into any cartel issues. Everybody's going to get a chance to talk, but I want Ash to go first because his report will affect all of us. Then I'm kicking him out. Cool?"

It was more a demand for an acknowledgement that I understood how things would go than a question. Paul had settled into his supervisory role well.

"Yeah, it's cool," I said.

"Good," said Paul, barely acknowledging me as he addressed his team. "Our victims, Dante and Michelle Washington, testified in a case Ash worked ten years ago. The perp in Ash's case was Santino Ramirez, the same Santino Ramirez you've heard about on the news. Barring divine intervention, Ramirez is dead in a few days. My working theory—and I'm open to hearing others—is that his gang, *Barrio Sureño*, is killing our witnesses in revenge. Ash is going to tell us about that case, and then he's going home."

All eyes in the room turned to me. I waited for questions first, but no one spoke.

"Well, like Paul said, I worked the Ramirez investigation, but Keith Holliday, my partner at the time, was the lead detective. Unfortunately, he died a couple of years ago, so you're stuck with me."

I thought they might snicker at the comment, but nothing. Tough room. I cleared my throat.

"The case was open and shut. The victim was a man named Angel Herrera, and his shooter was Santino Ramirez. Ramirez ran a local gang called *Barrio Sureño*. They ran their rivals out of disputed territories by murdering their leaders and their entire families. If I recall, our gang unit thought they had some connections to *Eme*, but we couldn't verify them." I glanced at Agent Havelock. "They boasted of ties to *Los Zetas*, as well, but we never substantiated those."

Paul coughed, clearing his throat and getting my attention. He put a pencil behind his ear. "Just to clarify, by *Eme*, you mean the Mexican Mafia, and by *Los Zetas*, you mean the cartel?"

Primarily, *Eme* was a prison gang, but gang culture being what it was, that gave them a lot of power over a lot of people.

"That's them. *Barrio Sureño* considered themselves real badasses," I said, nodding and looking at Havelock. "But again, we found little to no evidence of ties to national or transnational organizations. They are a *local* street gang."

"In your investigation," said Havelock, speaking for the first time during the briefing. "Did the name Miguel Navarra come up?"

I closed my eyes and shook my head. "The name's not familiar, but it's been quite a while since I investigated this case. Why?"

The special agent shrugged. "Just curious. Tell us about the murder."

He knew something. I wanted to blow him off and look through my original notebook to make sure we hadn't come across the name, but I cleared my throat instead and focused again on my case.

"Angel Hererra, the victim, was a homeless man. Ramirez shot him as he had a late lunch in the soup kitchen beneath the homeless shelter a couple of blocks east of here. From what we discovered, Santino Ramirez believed Angel stole marijuana from a young *Barrio Sureño* member. According to our witnesses, Ramirez walked directly to Angel, pressed a firearm against his forehead, and demanded his marijuana back. Angel said he had already smoked the dope, so Ramirez shot him twice in the chest and then once in the leg, severing his femoral artery."

Paul leaned back in his chair and laced his fingers behind his head. "Tell us about the witnesses."

"Originally, nobody came forward. But then, two days later, we got six people. Five of them volunteered in the kitchen. Dante and Michelle Washington—both of whom are dead now—Brian and Jasmine Alexander, and Valerie Perez. The sixth witness was a homeless man named Xavier Jackson." I glanced at Paul. "You should consider putting the survivors in protective custody as a precaution."

Paul blinked a few times. "Already done that. When I need further advice, you'll be the first person I contact."

He really had settled into his new position well. He had the asshole-swagger down pat.

"What do we know about Ramirez's friends and associates?" asked Nancy, looking at me over the bridge of a pair of bright red horn-rimmed glasses.

I opened my notepad and flipped through a couple of pages.

"He's got a dead brother," I said, upon finding the page. "A second brother serving consecutive life sentences in a California prison for a triple homicide, and a wife named Carla."

"Should the wife concern us?" asked Paul, leaning forward to grab his cup of coffee before looking to me and then Agent Havelock. I waited for Havelock to respond, but he simply smiled at me expectantly. I didn't like how easily he had thrown me off my rhythm, so I coughed to try and hide it before flipping through a few more pages to my interview notes with her.

"Santino used her as a punching bag, so I doubt there's much love lost there. Anything else I have on her is outdated."

Nancy looked across the table at Paul. "We should pick her up anyway and make sure the brother's still in prison."

"We will. Anybody else got questions for Ash?"

They all looked at me and shook their heads politely. Paul stood and patted me on the shoulder. "Enjoy your time off. We'll be in touch."

I would rather have taken my original notebook with me, but I had enough to go on for the moment. As I pushed down on the arms of my chair, I felt my holster bite into my shoulder. Internal Affairs officers had confiscated my primary weapon, leaving me with my backup, a nine-millimeter Beretta 9000. It didn't have the stopping power of my Glock, but it'd put holes in people if needed. It'd do for the time being.

Chapter Nine

It took Carla almost three hours to drive to the Indiana State Prison, located in Michigan City at the very northernmost edge of the state. She knew the route by heart, having made the trip once a month since her husband's murder conviction ten years ago. From the street, the prison could have passed for a private school or even a military installation, but instead of training the young leaders of tomorrow, it warehoused the vilest men Indiana had to offer. A tall chain-link fence ringed the property, but mostly that kept the neighborhood kids from playing on the lawns. The true fences, the ones that separated the inmates from the outside world, had razor wire at their tops and held signs warning of potentially lethal electric shocks if one came too close.

The world needed fences like that, for the men inside that prison had raped and murdered and robbed and done the sorts of things that caused little old ladies to clutch their blankets to their chests as they watched *America's Most Wanted* from bed. Though Carla's husband hadn't murdered Angel Hererra, he fit into the establishment well.

She parked in the visitor's lot and smoothed the wrinkles from her skirt and blouse. She had first met Santino Ramirez thirteen years ago while searching for a steady supplier of marijuana for her growing business at Indiana University. From their very first meeting, she and Tino had gotten along well, and it wasn't just a physical attraction. In those first few weeks, they stayed up night after night together, simply talking. Six months after that first meeting, they married, and for the first few months, life felt almost perfect.

They both went to work—he made the rounds in his neighborhood, while she visited her clients in Bloomington and attended classes as required. Tino had a very good product and connections to get as much of it as she needed, so Carla's reputation and business grew. Meanwhile, her husband controlled his small corner of the city, a neighborhood, nothing more. He seemed content with that, but *she* deserved more. So Carla pushed him where he needed it, whispering into his ear at night. *I heard the police arrested the crew on North Kenwood. You should move in.* And he did move in. Where others vacated due to pressure from church groups or neighborhood organizations, he created a market. Tino had few business skills, but he could squeeze blood from a stone if given the chance. People—other gangs, even—scattered when they saw him coming.

Carla's high heels clicked on the sidewalk as she walked toward the prison's main gate. A line of visitors, women with their bedraggled children mostly, waited outside the reception area to visit their inmate spouses and friends. As a little girl, she and her mother had waited in countless lines like that to visit her father as he rotted in prison. She grew to resent walls and gates and men in uniform. While waiting in a seemingly endless line to see her father on her eleventh birthday, she promised herself she'd never wait in that line again. Her father wasn't worth waiting for.

Ironically, she didn't mind the wait to see her husband. Before she had finished her legal degree, she'd walk into the same lobby she had walked into as a child to see her father, and guards would pat her down just as they had years earlier. She'd wait an hour or two for a fifteen-minute meeting with Tino in a room surrounded by strangers and under the watchful eyes of prison guards. Despite the wasted day, it had been worth it to see him in chains.

She hadn't always hated her husband. In fact, she loved him once. That changed when Miguel Navarra arrived. Miguel worked for *Los Zetas*, one of the more powerful of the Mexican drug cartels, and he taught her husband cruelty that Tino then carried into the streets and their marriage bed. Under Miguel's guidance, Tino expanded his territory by murdering his rivals, he grew his product line by introducing crystal methamphetamine to Indianapolis, and he structured his gang as a paramilitary organization. He also stopped treating Carla as a human being. He sexually assaulted her, beat her so badly she had to go to the emergency room, and gave her venereal diseases he picked up from whores on the street. Carla wanted to kill both men, but she couldn't touch Miguel. He had far too many connections and powerful friends. Her husband, though, would die because of her. Angel Hererra made that happen.

She sidestepped the crowd of visitors, drawing the ire of some of its more vocal occupants, and held up her Indiana Bar Association card to the guard manning the front door. Growing up, she had never thought of becoming a lawyer, mostly because she never knew what a lawyer was. She had wanted to work in a bank. The women behind the counter always looked nice, as if they were going to church, and they seemed happy. Law school only became a consideration after her husband's arrest for murdering Angel Hererra. Now, she led her husband's legal team, which meant they met in private rooms without cameras, guards, or anyone else to overhear their conversations. It made things a lot easier. The guard at the front door nodded to her and opened the door.

"Thank you, Officer," she said, flashing him her brightest smile as she stepped inside. The prison's lobby looked a little like the security checkpoint at the airport but with more families than normal. She showed her Bar ID to the nearest guard, and he escorted her directly to the front of the line. She had been through the security procedures enough to know the do's and don'ts. She hadn't worn a bra with an underwire because they always set off the metal detectors, she had left her cell phone and iPad in the car, she had removed all paper clips and rubber bands from her briefcase, and she had covered up as much exposed skin as she possibly could. Despite her preparation and familiarity with the rules, it took almost twenty minutes to make it through the security checkpoints to the room in which her husband waited for her.

As usual, Tino wore a pair of khaki-colored pants and a white T-shirt. On one arm, he had *The Last Supper* tattooed in black ink, while on the other, he'd had tattooed a rose and a picture of a girl in a bikini. He claimed now that it was Carla, but he had gotten it well before they met. A hair tie held his oily black hair back from his face. His skin, usually a healthy olive color, now appeared slightly jaundiced. He didn't smile when he saw her. Carla looked over her shoulder and nodded for the guard to shut the door. He locked them both in, and almost immediately, Tino reached across the table for her hands.

"Any news?"

Tino hadn't killed Angel, so he assumed he'd win an appeal and either receive a new trial or an outright dismissal of the charges against him. She'd ensured that didn't happen.

"I'm sorry, darling," she said, smiling at him. "We're out of appeals, and the governor's office has refused to hear a clemency hearing."

He took a deep breath. "This is it, then. They're going to kill me."

"Yes," she said.

He dropped her hands and ran his fingers through his hair. Then he pounded on the table. "I'm going to die because a bunch of cops set me up."

"No, Tino," she said, shaking her head. "You're going to die because you're stupid."

He looked at her and screwed up his face. "What?"

"I gave you a chance, you know. I tried to leave you once, but you tracked me down to that little apartment in Bloomington. You threatened to kill me if I ever left you again."

He put his hands flat on the table and sighed. "Don't even start that talk. We gotta talk about our people. You've got to bring Tomas in here."

Carla pretended to think for a moment, but then she stood and shook her head. "I'm not interested in talking business with you. But, just so you know, Tomas has been out of the life for some time now. I've been lying to you for years."

Tino narrowed his eyes at her. She had seen that look before, usually right before he hit her. Now, manacles transformed his rage into impotence, and that made her feel warm inside

"What are you talking about? If Tomas is out, who's leading my business?"

"I am," she said, smiling. "In your name, of course. The guards do a remarkable job of keeping you isolated in here, don't they?"

His eyes bored into her. For the first time in ten years, she didn't look away pretending to be scared. Tino's gaze softened.

"What are you talking about, Carla?"

She rolled her eyes. "I guess if you insist on talking about business, we'll talk about business. I run your business now and have for the last ten years. Our crews believe you're giving the orders, and I'm your mouthpiece, but I haven't relayed a thing you've said since your incarceration began. I do whatever I want to do. Your lieutenants, the men most loyal to you, are dead or in prison or out of the life entirely. I have no rivals."

Tino's lips moved, but he didn't speak. She let his tongue wag without saying a word. This was her moment, the one she had waited for ten years to see, the one where Tino's world came crashing atop him.

"What the hell are you talking about?"

"Forgive me. I guess this is a lot to take in. I'll speak slowly and use small words," she said, unable to keep the merriment out of her voice. "You're done, Tino. Every report I gave you, every story I told you, a lie. All of it. I kept coming back each month because I liked seeing the fresh bruises on your face."

For a split second, his gaze hardened and his eyes flashed black as he reached within himself for rage-fueled strength. And then, like a race car with an empty tank, he slowed and then stopped. The hate left his eyes.

"Why would you do this to me? We love each other."

Carla laughed. "You think you understand what it means to love someone? You don't. You treated me like I was a whore you could just throw away. I would have killed you years ago if I thought I could get away with it. But this is better, seeing you rot in prison, stringing you along with scraps of information about the organization you built and watching as your hopes shatter when you lose appeal after appeal. I don't think I've enjoyed anything so much in my life."

For a moment, it almost looked as if he'd start crying. That would have ruined the moment, though.

"Look at you," said Carla. "I had no idea you were so weak. I could have made you strong. I could have made you into something important, but you were too stupid to understand the gifts I would have given you. You're pathetic."

He balled his hands into fists but refused to look her in the eye.

"You're worse than those goddamn cops who put me in here."

Carla, again, laughed. "This is delightful," she said, smiling. "Those cops didn't put you in here. I did. You always said they must have taken your gun and shot Angel themselves, but they didn't. I did. In all these years in prison, you didn't wonder why I suddenly started volunteering at that soup kitchen? Why I became friendly with that minister and his wife?"

Tino did look at her, then. His eyes had become narrow slits, glassy and black.

"You killed Angel?"

"Yes," she said, nodding. "I took your favorite gun, that big .45, and I spread a rumor that Angel Hererra had stolen some weed from one of your boys to establish your motive. Then I waited until Angel came to the soup kitchen—he came every day at the same time—and I shot him when everyone else left. Twice in the chest and once in the leg, just like you did when you killed somebody. Do you even remember what it feels like to have the freedom to do what you want? If you don't, I assure you that it's exhilarating."

Tino didn't acknowledge the question, but his face grew even redder.

"When I got home after killing Angel," said Carla, "I returned your gun to the coffee table, and I hugged that black jacket you always wore so it'd have gunshot residue on it. Then I went back to the shelter and told Pastor Washington that you had shot Angel Hererra and that you brought Jacob with you. He did the rest, believe it or not. You hurt so many innocent people that even a minister would lie under oath just to get you off the streets."

Tino trembled, his face red. "You dirty cunt."

Carla took a step back from the table. "That's a foul word, so I'd prefer if you didn't use it. But sticks and stones and all that." She took a breath, getting herself back on rhythm. "In a week, the state of Indiana will put a needle in your arm, and you will die. I'll be there to watch. Oh, I'll cry and pretend to be the good wife, but I'll laugh inside as they wheel your corpse out."

"As soon as I get word out," said Tino, shaking his head, "my boys will kill you."

"I don't think so," said Carla. "Your old gang's in a bit of disarray right now, but we're imposing order. They won't follow a woman, but they will follow your son, and your son, believe it or not, looks up to me. He'll do what I ask. If he doesn't, I'll kill him and find someone who will."

Tino licked his lips and shook his head disbelievingly. "Jacob has no part in this life. He didn't grow up here. He doesn't know anything. My boys aren't going to follow him."

Carla leaned back in her chair and slumped down. "Isn't that the truth? You wouldn't believe the things Miguel and I have had to do to build that kid's reputation. Your boys may not follow him yet, but they will once we finish."

Tino's eyes became probes as they passed from her chest to her eyes. "What are you doing, Carla?"

She leaned forward and smiled. "That's my favorite part, so I'm glad you asked. Your son is killing everyone who testified against you in your trial. He thinks he's exacting revenge on those who hurt you, but he has no idea he's killing the only people in the world who could exonerate you. There's something almost poetic about that."

Tino's hands trembled. "You bitch."

She smiled even broader. "You can't hurt me anymore, sweetheart, but I can still hurt you. Just for you, I think I'm going to have Jacob kill Tomas Quesada next. At our wedding, you said he was the best friend you've ever had. How does that make you feel?"

Tino pounded on the table with his index finger. "You can do what you want to me, but my son and my friends stay out of this. Jacob goes to college. He gets the life I never had."

"I'm afraid you don't get a say in this anymore. You punched me, you kicked me, you took off your belt and whipped me with it. I tried my best to leave and give you a way out, but you refused to take it. Now it's my turn to hurt you. I hope you enjoy your last days on earth. I will."

She patted him on the cheek twice and walked to the door for the guard to release her. As Tino started screaming that she was a bitch who deserved to die, she forced tears to her eyes and started sobbing lightly. The guard threw open the door, and she stumbled out.

"I told him he lost his last appeal," she said. "He tried to grab me. I was scared."

The guard glared at Tino and then looked back at Carla, a softer look on his face. "You're all right now. We'll deal with Mr. Ramirez."

Hopefully they'd give him something to remember her last visit by. She nodded and then turned to leave, rubbing the tears off her face. Her husband's bad week had just begun.

Chapter Ten

Paul and his team—including Agent Havelock—got back to work as soon as I left the conference room. Havelock hadn't come down there to merely sit in a briefing, so I couldn't help but feel IMPD wouldn't have that case for long. Ideally, then, I'd find a key piece of evidence that would enable them to break the case wide open in short order, allowing my colleagues to arrest every *Barrio Sureño* member walking the streets. Evidence rarely fell into my lap like that, though, so I needed to go out and make things happen. And with Santino Ramirez in prison, one name on my list of names burned in my memory: Tomas Quesada.

Ten years ago, he had been the gang's de facto treasurer, a relatively high rank. Even if Santino Ramirez still ran the gang from prison, he'd need a leader on the ground with the brainpower to run a major organization and to manage its finances. More than that, he'd need someone he could trust, maybe someone he already had trusted with the thing most precious to him, money. That put Quesada in my crosshairs.

I took the elevator to the lobby and hitched a ride home with a uniformed patrol officer. By the time we arrived at my house, the police had left and Hannah had evidently called in some support. Yassir Wahim, a general contractor who goes to the same mosque as Hannah and I for Friday prayers, stood on my front porch, a tape measure in hand and a pile of two-by-six lumber beside him. Beyond Yassir, I saw a couple of guys in white overalls and green rubber gloves cleaning the blood from the floor. I recognized those uniforms immediately, having seen them at a number of crime scenes; they worked for an industrial cleaning service that specialized in chemical spills and biohazard cleanup.

I waved to Yassir and then took the side door into my kitchen. As soon as I shut the door, I heard soft footsteps coming from the front room, and I turned to see my wife. She wore a green silk hijab, a black turtleneck sweater, and jeans. In two steps, she crossed the kitchen and leaned against my chest. I hugged her tight and felt her tremble against me.

"Is everything okay?" I asked.

She pulled her head back so we could look at each other and nodded, taking a deep breath. "I'm still a little freaked out. Once these guys finish working, I'm going to Yasmine's. I don't want to be here."

It felt like a small prick, nothing more, but as the boy who put his thumb in the dike could attest, even small cracks can have outsized effects. I'm an Arab, and my wife is half Persian and half Turkish. We attend a mosque. My wife wears the hijab. My son and daughter speak Arabic as well as they speak English. Most people treat us warmly, no differently than they would treat other families, but a sizable minority stare at us like we're monsters when we go to the mall, they cross the street when we pass, they clutch their hands to their chests and visibly pale when they see us sitting together on an airplane.

I can tolerate most things, but I can't stand the sneers, the dirty looks, and the occasional insults people hurl at us. They fear and hate us because a group of assholes who claim to believe the same things we do and who happen to look like us blow up buildings and fight to return the world to the twelfth century. This, though, was our home, the one place in the world where we could escape all that and be ourselves. And now my wife didn't want to be here anymore. I felt a flood of cold anger wash over me.

Hannah reached up and put a hand on my cheek. "Your eyes are as black as night. I don't know what you were just thinking, but stop."

I patted her back and extricated myself from her hug. "I'm sorry. I just came by for the car. I've got to go back to work."

"I didn't think you had to go into work again until your lawyer called."

I didn't want to think about my lawyer or my disciplinary hearing, so I nodded to the front door. "This changed things. I'm going to be busy for the next few days."

She looked directly in my eyes, allowing me to see the concern across her face. "Are you doing okay?"

"You're wondering if I'm thinking about having a drink."

She nodded. "I saw the news this morning. People aren't really saying you lured Dante here, are they?"

"If they weren't before, Leonard put the idea in their heads. He's a piece of work."

Her face was drawn as she nodded. "If you need anything, give me a call. You've been through a lot these past couple of days."

As usual, she was right. I cared about Michelle, and while I hadn't known Dante very well, he could have had a long, productive life. Held just beneath the surface of my emotions, I felt a deep, abiding sense of loss and guilt. For the moment, my anger held those feelings in check, but it wouldn't take much to pierce that facade, to burst that dam open. I couldn't deal with those feelings now, though. I didn't have time to grieve.

"I'm fine," I said. "We'll talk in a couple of days. I'll make an appointment to see the department therapist."

"Just as long as you're dealing with things in a healthy manner."

"I'm not going to drink."

Again.

She put a hand on my chest. "I don't want to see you hurt."

"A gang killed my friend and sent somebody to kill us in our sleep. I'm not the one who's going to be hurt."

She turned around and walked to the fridge. "You're already hurt, probably worse than you realize."

"I know, but I don't have time to deal with it."

She turned and looked at me over her shoulder. "Do you want something to eat before you go?"

"Sure."

She made me a sandwich, and I sat down across from her at the breakfast table to eat. Afterwards, I pulled my cell phone from my jacket and called my dispatcher's back line.

"Hey," I said, glancing at my wife and winking. "This is Captain Mike Bowers. I need an address from the BMV database. First name Tomas. Last name Quesada. He's a male, approximately thirty years old."

"What's your badge number, Captain?"

Since he had filed formal charges against me, I had seen Captain Bowers' badge number on reports so often that I had it memorized. I recited it and then repeated it slowly. The dispatcher clicked off for a moment and then gave me an address in a part of the city I didn't expect.

"You sure this is it?"

"It's the address of the only Tomas Quesada we've got in our database. Anything else?"

"That's it," I said, writing the address down on my notepad. "Thank you."

Once I slipped my phone in my pocket, Hannah looked at me and sighed. "Aren't you going to get in trouble for impersonating a superior officer?"

I shook my head and stood up. "Call's logged, but nobody will have a reason to look it up."

She nodded, but I doubted she believed me. I hugged her, though, and told her I'd be safe. Her lips moved as she watched me leave, so I could tell she had started praying. We used to do that together every night. I missed that tradition.

According to my dispatcher, Tomas Quesada lived in Woodruff Place, a historic neighborhood about a mile east of the downtown area. I took my VW over and drove through the neighborhood to get a better feel for the place and to see the exits in case I had to make a run for it. Most of the homes around me had a century of wear on them, but they also had ornate woodwork, mature trees, and a sense of permanence I rarely found elsewhere. These houses had seen wars and peace, rains and droughts, good times and bad and still managed to stand through it all. They embodied the history of our city, and walking amongst them, I felt small and more than a little envious of their owners. If the area had better schools, Hannah, the kids, and I might have ended up there.

Ideally, I would have visited at about four in the morning. People tend to listen a little better at that time of the morning, especially if they see my firearm. If I visited now, he'd be awake and alert, which would make things a lot more difficult. Not that I had much of a choice.

After a few minutes of driving, I parked in front of an American four-square with white clapboard siding, black shutters, and an exposed rubble stone foundation. A red brick walkway led to the front porch, while two posts in front served as hitching points for horses, attesting to the home's age and historic accuracy.

I take on a variety of personas when interviewing people, and which one I choose all depends on the person I'm interviewing. When talking to well-educated people, especially people who think they're smarter than everyone else on the planet, I act a bit like a bumbling detective. Smart people clam up if I come at them too strongly, but they let their guards down around idiots and oftentimes say things without realizing it. Around teenagers and college students, sometimes I act like a parent, while other times I act more like a roommate or a friend.

Gangbangers present unique challenges. The older guys have usually spent considerable amounts of time in police interviews, so they usually clam up and ask for lawyers. The younger guys who are struggling to make their bones in the gang usually try to show the world how tough they are by acting defiantly. I have to give gangsters a reason to talk. That means I usually lie to them.

I followed the bricks to the front porch and then checked my firearm and the badge on my hip. I rang the doorbell twice and then took a step back so he could see me out of the peephole. When he hadn't come within a minute, I rang again and then knocked. Finally, I saw movement through the frosted glass windows beside the door, so I removed my badge from my belt and held it up so Tomas could see it when he opened up. I spoke as soon as he flipped the locks and cracked the door.

"Tomas Quesada?"

"Yeah. Who are you?"

"Detective Sergeant Ash Rashid with IMPD. We spoke a few years back. You free to talk for a few minutes?"

He opened the door about a foot more, allowing me to see him for the first time in almost ten years. He had a trim, athletic build, and we stood roughly the same height. I didn't get to see him move much, but what I saw worried me a little. Occasionally, I run into muscle-bound thugs on the streets or even in my department who try to intimidate people with the size of their biceps or various other bodily appendages. They swagger and talk a lot, but they rarely worry me for one simple fact: most guys with muscles don't know how to use them. They don't need to learn. In just a few steps, though, I saw something different in Tomas Quesada, an economy of movement, the practiced grace of someone who knew how to handle himself. I immediately dropped my right leg back, minimizing the profile I had exposed to him.

Even though we were the same height, he still managed to look down his nose at me. "I remember you. What do you want?"

"Just a few minutes of your time. I need to talk to you about a murder."

"You got the wrong guy, Detective," he said, shaking his head and trying to shut his door. Before he could, I shot my foot forward and into the crack. He looked at it and then frowned. "I left that life a long time ago, right after Tino got pinched."

A lot of well-educated people think the men and women who make a living on the streets are stupid because they're poorly educated or because they don't use proper English. Some are, obviously, but not men like Quesada. He grew up and thrived in one of the roughest neighborhoods our country has to offer. Judging by his house, maybe he had left his old lifestyle and gang behind, but I couldn't take him at his word. That meant I needed to give him a reason to talk.

"Why do you think I'm here?"

He sighed and then crossed his arms. "Because you're an asshole."

That was probably true.

"One of my confidential informants said you were involved in the murder of a young woman named Michelle Washington."

He screwed up his face. "The chick who got killed way out on Fall Creek?"

"The young woman who testified against your former employer and was killed on Fall Creek Road. I see you've heard of her."

He tilted his head up and then looked at me down his nose. "Now I know why you're here, and I'll tell you flat out. I didn't do it. I'm not lying; when you arrested Tino, I got out while I could. Besides, I was out of town when she died."

I reached into my jacket for a notepad. "That's interesting, because we haven't announced her time of death yet. How do you know you were out of town?"

"Because I've been at a retreat with my company for the past week. Got in last night."

If true, that changed things. It'd tell me he really was out of the life and that he truly had no role in Michelle's death. "What kind of retreat was it?"

He tilted his head to the side and pursed his lips distastefully. "The corporate kind. We went to Chicago and sat through lectures about how we could better meet the needs of our clients. I got CPE credit for it."

I pointed my pen at his chest. "What is CPE credit?"

"Continuing Professional Education. I'm an accountant."

I wish I had known that going in, because I would have taken a different tack with him.

"I'm glad to hear you left your old life behind, but I've still got a dead woman and I think you can help me. You make some calls for me and ask around, I'll never bother you again."

He chuckled, but it was more an exasperated noise than a sign of merriment. "You don't get it, man. I don't talk to those people anymore. I don't even know anybody's phone number."

"Oh, come on," I said. "You grew up with those guys. You got to know somebody in that old neighborhood."

"I don't."

I scratched my scalp line with my pen and then looked at my notepad. He was probably telling me the truth, but I couldn't leave without being sure.

"I'll tell you what," I said. "This is a rapidly evolving situation, and I'm not the only person working this case. You help me today, no one will bother you again. If you keep stonewalling me, though, you might get some unexpected visitors at work come Monday morning. It sounds like you're doing pretty well for yourself. You don't want a bunch of homicide detectives coming into your office with questions about you."

By the way his body froze, I'd say I had struck a nerve.

"You know how hard I've worked to get where I am?"

"I have an idea. That's why I want to give you a way out. I don't want to hurt you. Matter of fact, I couldn't be happier that you made something out of your life. I don't get to see too many success stories out of your neighborhood. Help me now."

"You wonder why people hate the police."

"Oh, I don't wonder at all," I said. "I know. And look, I don't want to be here any more than you want me to be here. You answer my questions, and I'll leave. If you're straight with me, I'll be straight with you. That's how this works."

All at once, the hard expression left his eyes and his shoulders dipped a quarter inch as he relaxed his muscles. He dropped his right hand—presumably his punching hand—to his side.

"I don't know anything about your dead girl, but I've heard some rumors. I might know something."

"Anything can help."

He paused for a moment and then focused on some spot above my shoulder. "The boys are split. Tino hasn't named his successor yet."

I narrowed my eyes, a little incredulous. "He's getting a needle in his arm in a week. Why would he not name his successor?"

Quesada's face went red, angry. "Probably because he doesn't think you'll go through with it. That's what they tell you in school, isn't it? Innocent men don't get sent to death row?"

I shook my head. "Ramirez isn't innocent. You're old enough to know that."

"Tino was my best friend. He didn't kill Angel Hererra, and you folks know it. He wasn't even in the country when you guys say Angel died."

"Let's take a step back," I said, holding up my hand in an attempt to calm the situation. "Santino Ramirez is your friend. I'm sympathetic. Tell me about your old gang. They're split."

He hesitated, and then some of the redness left his face. "Yeah, they're split, but they've got common enemies. A man shoots enough of them, might get Tino's attention."

That actually explained a couple of things. Our murder rate had spiked in the past few weeks, odd for this time of year but not odd during a gang war. More than that, it explained why *Barrio Sureño* suddenly had the balls—and stupidity—to send somebody to kill a cop. Maybe the leaders couldn't contain their underlings anymore.

"You got any names?"

"Like I said earlier, I'm out of that life. When you guys set Tino up, I left."

I didn't plan to explain it to Quesada, but we actually had a strong case against Ramirez. In addition to our six eyewitnesses who saw Ramirez shoot Angel, we found the murder weapon in plain sight in Ramirez's home. We then found his prints on the gun and the rounds in the magazine. Not only that, we found gunshot residue on a jacket in his closet and we found out he had a motive for wanting Angel dead. Rarely have I investigated a stronger case.

"Who's leading the rival factions?"

He looked left and right, as if checking to see if any of his old gang buddies had hidden behind the hedges that lined the front of his house. "You'll leave if I tell you?"

I nodded. "Scout's honor."

"Fine, then. Tristan Salazar. He's up at Pendleton. Other boy you're looking at is probably Danny Navarra. I heard he was stirring things up. Lives by the Children's Museum. There are others, too, but they don't have much claim to the throne."

The Pendleton Correctional Facility housed a lot of Indianapolis's more disreputable citizens. The warden once told me I'm not very popular amongst his maximum security population. Danny Navarra's name piqued my interest, too. Agent Havelock had mentioned another Navarra.

"Is Danny Navarra related to Miguel Navarra?"

Quesada tilted his head back and looked at me down his nose. "How do you know Miguel?"

"Are they related or not?"

"Miguel is Danny's uncle."

So Havelock had held back on me. He knew more about *Barrio Sureño* than he let on.

"These two, Salazar and Navarra," I said, nodding, "killing the witnesses in Santino's trial would help them?"

"Oh, yeah," said Tomas, nodding. "No better way to solidify your power base than to neutralize your enemies."

"Could Tristan Salazar order hits from prison?" I asked.

"He's got some soldiers."

"Either of them know the Bony Lady?" I asked, remembering the name Emilia Rios had given the statuette last night.

He narrowed his eyes at me. "Everybody's got to pay the Bony Lady. You caress her face, or you feel her blade. That's how it is."

So either one could have killed Michelle and dumped her at the shrine. I had hoped to eliminate one of the two, but I could work with both. I allowed my jacket to cover my weapon.

"If you're lying to me, I'm coming back and I'm going to be pissed."

"I'm not lying."

I tried to get a read on him, but I couldn't see past the anger in his eyes. Good enough.

"Then thank you for your help."

I turned and walked back to my car. I had at least one more person to see today.

Chapter Eleven

Even without traffic, it'd take me at least forty-five minutes to drive all the way out to Pendleton and then a good hour to get through the security checkpoints to see Salazar. I planned to visit him sometime, but I'd rather pick the low-hanging fruit first and that meant Danny Navarra. As soon as I got in my car, I called the dispatcher for Navarra's address. True to Quesada's word, he lived just a couple of blocks north of the Children's Museum on Kenwood Avenue. The neighborhood had a lot of drugs and gang activity, which, unfortunately, meant it had a lot of violence and poverty as well. Having worked homicide, I knew the area fairly well.

I got onto I-65 at Michigan Street and then drove north, exiting a few minutes later on Twenty-Ninth Street. That took me directly to North Kenwood, a road on which I drove for a few blocks. I saw the street turn from a decent area to one that, even armed, I wouldn't have felt safe traversing at night. In the two-block stretch north of Thirty-Second Street, I passed at least five abandoned homes with plywood sheathing for windows and ivy crawling in and out of the siding, slowly tearing the buildings apart. Tree roots had lifted and broken many of the sidewalks, allowing weeds to grow through the cracks, while potholes marked the streets. Even amidst the poverty, though, I saw occasional bright spots——homes the owners of which obviously took pride in, well-maintained gardens and yards, even a hand-drawn sign on a window that read, "Purdue-bound!"

Navarra lived in a Dutch Colonial with a cinder-block retaining wall out front and concrete steps overgrown with vegetation. Most of the windows were intact and there were lawn chairs on the front porch. Casement windows along the foundation would have allowed some much-needed light into the basement, but weeds had overrun the base of the house so thoroughly I could barely see them. As if daring the police to raid the place, someone had sprayed *Barrio Sureño* in large letters along the garage, letting me know I had come to the right spot.

I parked half a block from the house and took a quick look around. Normally in an urban neighborhood like that, I'd see several cars on the street and I'd probably even hear people talking or kids playing basketball on some far-off court. Here, no one had parked on the street for at least two blocks in either direction, and as I got out of my car, silence greeted me. It felt almost eerie, like I had stepped into one of the bad zombie movies my wife made me watch when the kids went to bed. Maybe, the residents around me had just gone to work or school. Or perhaps more likely, judging by the plywood covering the front doors of at least two of Navarra's neighbors, maybe nobody lived there.

I took the sidewalk north to Navarra's house. The closer I got, the more oppressive the silence became. This late in the season, I didn't expect to hear birds or see squirrels scurrying about, but I thought I'd at least see or hear a few kids. Nothing seemed to move. Odd.

I didn't hurry the rest of the way, but I didn't stop to appreciate the landscape, either. Houses across the street and catty-corner to Navarra's had an unobstructed view of the front door. Thick brush, however, entangled the rusted chain-link fence that separated Navarra's property from his neighbors to the north, while pine trees out back shaded the rear yard and gave it privacy from the neighbors to the west. As with nearly every house on the block, nobody looked home.

I started to walk past the house so I could see if there were any cars around back, but something on the porch drew my eye. The front door hung open. In this weather, I wouldn't have expected anyone to leave the door open. If someone was home, this whole thing would go to hell. I hesitated, and then started across the grass toward the door, feeling the dead lawn crunch under my footsteps. The front porch sagged under my weight, but I didn't stop to wonder whether it would hold me. Instead, I removed my firearm from my holster. The wooden frame around the deadbolt was splintered, likely because someone had kicked the door open. We had a crime scene.

The open door and obvious break-in gave the police cause to perform a protective sweep of the house. That wouldn't give them reason to search through drawers or take drug dogs through, but in court they could introduce what they found in plain sight. I started to take out my cell phone to call Paul Murphy, but I heard something that stopped me cold. At first, it started as a banging noise, like shoes in a washing machine. But then the banging stopped, and I heard a shrill, almost hysterical voice crying out.

Help us.

My heart jumped. Without thinking, I pushed open the front door and swept the entryway with my firearm. All four corners were clear.

The room smelled like urine. At one time, the walls had probably been white, but they had turned yellow with age. Open archways led deeper into the house. Over and above the urine smell, I caught a faint whiff of gasoline. That concerned me, but I had more pressing things to deal with first.

"IMPD. I'm performing a protective sweep of the house. If you can hear my voice, put your hands on you head and come out now."

I didn't have to wait for a response.

"Help us. Please. We're in the basement."

"Come get us."

I heard two voices now, both calling in concert. One belonged to a woman, but the other could have been a child crying. My instincts told me to start throwing open doors so I could find the staircase that led to the basement, but my training and experience told me that even a soccer mom could hide in the corner and shoot me from cover. I readjusted my grip on the firearm and headed toward the hallway that led to the kitchen in the rear of the home, staying close to the wall the whole time.

Time had ravaged the back portion of the house as much as it had the front entryway. I could see water marks near the ceiling in the kitchen, and the floor felt almost spongy, indicating some rather serious structural damage. The cabinets had fared little better. The uppers tilted away from the wall at an angle, making me nervous to even stand near them, while the lower cabinets looked as if an entire youth soccer team had been given free reign to kick everything they wanted. Despite the lack of carpet, it smelled just as bad as the front room. An open doorway near the far wall led down a dark stairway.

If this was an ambush, the trap would have sprung by now. At least I hoped so. I took a cautious step forward and cringed as the floor joists groaned.

"We're down here. Please."

I could hear tears in that voice, and they sounded real.

"Are you alone?"

They both shouted again at the same time, and eventually I heard one of them say yes.

"I'm coming down," I said, stepping onto the first wooden step down. The basement had rough stone walls and a poured concrete floor. Even from the top step, I could smell mold, unsurprising considering the water damage directly above it. Since I didn't want to present a target to somebody any longer than I had to, I ran down the steps and then swept the room with my firearm.

Casement windows near the ceiling allowed a scant bit of light inside, just enough to penetrate the gloom a few feet. Two people, a woman and a young boy, huddled together near a support post in the center of the room. The boy looked older than my daughter but not by a lot. He had blond hair and a thin, narrow face. He wore black glasses. The woman, likely his mother, had a similar petite bone structure, long face, and blonde hair. Neither looked like a threat.

"Is there anybody else in the house?"

The woman cried, but I couldn't understand what she said. The boy put his face between his knees as if he had assumed the crash position in an airplane.

"Are we alone?" I asked.

The woman nodded. "I think so. We've been here for a long time."

I should have probably run to the second floor to clear it, but I didn't think she could lie to me in her state. I holstered my firearm and jogged toward them.

"I'm Detective Ash Rashid with IMPD," I said, kneeling beside them. The boy had a welt on his cheek and his mother had bruises on her forearms and wrists. None of the injuries looked serious, but sometimes the deepest scars form inside. Someone had secured the boy's hands behind his back with black zip ties, the kind I used to secure cables behind my television. I couldn't break them, but even a fairly dull pocketknife could probably cut them. We'd have more difficulty with his mom. Her captors had secured her arms with steel handcuffs. Most handcuffs use a standard key to facilitate prisoner transfer, so normally I'd simply take my key out and untie her. Unfortunately, her captors had filled the keyhole with glue. We'd have to get some tools for her.

"I'm going to call for backup," I said, standing. "Give me just a minute."

I pulled out my phone and called my dispatcher's back line. I told him where I was, and about the people I had found in the basement. He promised to send backup immediately, but since neither of my two captives' injuries appeared life-threatening, an ambulance would be at least ten minutes off. They'd be okay until then. I hung up with him, and then called Paul Murphy. He didn't answer, but I left him a message asking him to get out there ASAP. Once I had finished the calls, I slipped my phone back into my pocket and looked at the two victims.

"I'm going to run upstairs and see if I can find a knife or scissors so I can cut your son's restraints," I said. "We'll get some bolt cutters to get these cuffs off you as quickly as we can. Okay?"

The woman nodded and trembled. I tried to think of something comforting to say before I left, but nothing came to mind. After this, they might need therapy, but they should survive. I smiled at them both and then jogged upstairs, catching the faint whiff of gasoline once more. Normal people didn't keep gallons of gasoline in their houses, and the more I stayed there, the more that worried me. I needed to get this family out of there as quickly as I could before the place went up.

The kitchen was a disaster. I pulled out the top drawer beside the sink only to have a cockroach run across my hand. I jumped involuntarily, throwing it across the room. Aside from cockroach crap, the drawer was empty.

I tried the one beneath it and found nothing again. In the bottom drawer, I found a paring knife, or what may have been a paring knife at one time. The plastic handle had a crack on one side, and the blade had so many nicks and notches that it looked like someone had tried to use it to cut down a tree. Hopefully it'd do.

I carried it downstairs and then knelt beside the boy again. His eyes bulged wide when he saw the knife in my hand, so I hid it behind my back. He had dirt on his face. Had he been Megan or Kaden, I would have licked my thumb and tried to wipe it away. Instead, I gently put my free hand on his shoulder and looked him directly in the eye.

"I'm going to cut your restraints with this knife, so I need your help for a moment. I need you to pull your hands as far apart as you can. You might feel a little bit of a pinch, but if something hurts, let me know. I'll stop and wait for someone to get here with better tools. Is that okay with you?"

He nodded and then shifted his weight forward, exposing his wrists. As he did that, I heard a *thwump* coming from upstairs. My furnace made the same sound when it kicked on, so I didn't think much of it. I started sawing away, but even with such a dull knife, the plastic restraint cut easily. I broke the last little bit, and the boy jumped up. I thought he'd make a break for it, but then he wobbled on his feet and sat down again.

"Are you all right?" I asked.

He didn't respond verbally, but he nodded.

"Did you feel dizzy and lightheaded?" I asked. He nodded again. "You've been sitting down for a while. I bet the blood was rushing to your head. Just take it easy for a minute. We're going to have medical people here to check you out. Okay?"

"Okay," he said, breathless. I turned my attention to his mom.

"The handcuffs holding you to the post have been glued shut, so I can't open them. We're going to get you out of here as soon as we can, but we'll have to wait for backup to do that. In the meantime, I'm going to stay and talk to you. Does that sound okay?"

"Please don't leave me," she said, her voice trembling almost as much as her body.

"I'm not going to," I said, smiling and hoping it would calm her a little. "What's your name?"

"Gail Pennington," she said. "This is my son Mark. Do you have any water? We've been down here for three days."

"I don't," I said, pulling my phone from my pocket. "But I'll tell the officers to bring some when they come. Can you tell me how you two ended up down here?"

Gail started to talk, but then her son interrupted her.

"It smells like smoke."

I hadn't noticed Mark walk to the stairs, but he stood at their foot and looked up toward the kitchen. I walked to where the kid stood. He wasn't lying. I smelled smoke. I should have checked out the second floor when I had the chance.

"We've got to move," I said, putting my hand across the boy's chest and lifting him off the ground. I looked back to his mom. "I'll be right back."

She said something, but I couldn't make out what as I sprinted up the stairs. The smoke smell became stronger, but I couldn't see where the fire was coming from yet. I carried Mark outside and then put him on the grass. He immediately stood up and tried running back into the house, but I caught him and held him there.

"My mom's in there," he said. "Let me go."

"Get across the street. No arguments. I'll get your mom." He kept fighting me, so I pointed across the street. "Get over there right now or I'll tie you to my car."

That got his attention. He cried, but at least he had stopped fighting me to get back into the house. I ran back inside, but now I found smoke traveling downstairs. Gail wailed in the basement.

"Come back. Help me."

I tried to tune her screams out as I ran through the house, to the kitchen and finally back to the basement. Gail writhed against the pole to which her captors had tied her, her eyes squeezed shut.

"Mark's outside. He's fine."

She nodded, but it didn't stop the tears streaming down her face. I didn't get called out to many fires, but I knew a thing or two about older houses. A modern house would have firebreaks between the first and second floor to keep flames from spreading, but this place had to be eighty years old. By now, the second floor would be toast, and the first floor wouldn't be far behind. If the fire reached the trusses in the attic, the weight of the roof would collapse in on itself, taking the house and everything inside it with it.

We needed to move.

"Lean forward," I shouted, hoping to break through Gail's emotional state. She did as I asked, so I pushed on the steel support beam to which she had been tied, hoping it would give a little. I couldn't budge it, so I took a step back and kicked hard. The shock went up my foot and into my knee, almost knocking me down, but the beam didn't move. I looked around the room one more time, hoping I had missed something, a tool that could either cut Gail's cuffs or knock the support beam out, but I couldn't see a thing.

"Please don't leave me. Please don't leave me."

She repeated it over and over, trembling and rocking back and forth. I tried to keep my composure as I bent to look at her cuffs again. When I handcuff a suspect, I typically put them on tight but not so tight that they'll cut someone's circulation or rub against someone's wrists. Gail's had been clamped all the way against her skin.

"Make your hand as small and narrow as you can," I said, holding my hand out and pressing all of my fingertips together in a pyramid shape to demonstrate. "I'm going to pull on the cuff backward, and you're going to pull forward. We'll try to force your hand out."

She nodded but didn't stop the please-don't-leave-me mantra.

I sat on the ground behind her and put my hands on the chain of the handcuffs and my right foot in the crook of her elbow.

"This is going to hurt," I said. "It might even pull your shoulder out of socket."

"Please don't leave me."

Sounded like consent to me. I counted down to three and pulled as hard as I could. Her hand turned red as the hardened steel cuff bit into her skin, bloodying her wrist. Gail grunted, but the handcuff didn't move. I stopped pulling, and in the silence that followed, I heard her sob and saw, for the first time, smoke coming down the stairs and congregating between the joist cavities above our heads. We didn't have any time.

"Are you right- or left-handed?" She didn't stop crying to respond, so I repeated the question forcefully.

"Right-handed," she said between sobs.

"Then put your left hand on the ground."

She did as I asked, tears streaming freely down her face. "Just don't leave me."

"I'm not, but this is really going to hurt. I'm sorry," I said, picking up my foot and then smashing it down as hard as I could on her thumb. Her scream belonged to an animal.

Chapter Twelve

Gail's screams hammered into my skull. In an hour, her hand would swell to the size of a baseball mitt, but for the moment, I had some time to work. I slid her broken thumb down and out of the way, allowing me to remove the handcuff and free her from the post. Smoke billowed through the doorway, threatening to engulf us both. Just as with her son, I didn't give Gail the chance to get her bearings. I simply threw her over my shoulder and ran up the stairs to the kitchen. Black, foul smoke filled the room. I tried to crouch beneath it, but smoke filled every cranny in the room and poured into my lungs like water that no amount of coughing could expel.

I ran without thinking. As the floor transitioned from the kitchen's cracked linoleum to the carpet of the front entryway, the smoke brightened. I emerged from the house coughing, but alive. Gail continued to scream. Heedless of the house we had just run out of, Mark sprinted toward us, crying for his mom. I took her from my shoulder and carried her in my arms, just as I had done with my wife on our wedding day. Gail's cries shifted from pain to relief as she saw her son. I put her on the ground just across the street, and the two of them hugged each other. She cupped his face, so I turned away to give them some privacy.

I pulled out my phone again and called the dispatcher back.

"This is Detective Sergeant Ash Rashid. Situation's changed. I've got a fire with injuries on North Kenwood Avenue. I need EMS, fire and patrol, and I need it right now."

The dispatcher told me we already had units en route, but she alerted the fire department as well. They were approximately ten minutes out. Hopefully the neighboring homes wouldn't go up in that time. I thanked the dispatcher and hung up.

We got off lucky all considered. Gail would have broken bones, and both she and her son would have some very dark memories, but they'd live. The more I thought, the more I could feel something cold spreading inside me. Tomas Quesada claimed to have left *Barrio Sureño* behind, but he had set me up just the same. That house didn't ignite on its own, and I refused to believe Danny Navarra just happened to store gasoline on the second floor in case he needed to light it up and run.

I glanced at the Penningtons. They held each other on the lawn, both still crying, but the tears had changed. They had become survivors. They saw something horrible and made it through. Mark, I think, was supposed to make it. The knife in the kitchen was too convenient, his restraints too easy to remove. Gail, on the other hand, someone wanted to die. She made it because I maimed her. I don't know how many of my colleagues would have done that.

Someone wanted her dead, and he wanted IMPD to watch.

Just a minute or so after I had carried Gail from the house, the first patrol officers arrived. They checked out Gail and Mark, but they left me alone once I flashed them my badge. The fire department took an additional five minutes, and by that time, the house had nearly burned to the foundation. The firemen focused primarily on containing the flames and keeping them from spreading to any of the nearby vegetation or neighboring homes. Mostly, I ignored them, too, and found myself raging inside for the lives very nearly lost today. Captain Bowers came about twenty minutes after the calls went out, just as the ambulances took Mark and Gail to somewhere they could rest in peace. For me, though, there would be no rest until the wicked slept.

Time slipped away from me for a while, and my thoughts became dark as they often do. Eventually, I felt a hand tap me on the shoulder, and I looked up to see Bowers standing in front of me. The fire trucks had left, but the stench of burnt plastic, insulation, and wood hung heavy in the midafternoon air.

"Ash," said Bowers. "I need you to focus."

He reached down, so I grabbed his hand and let me pull him up.

"Sorry. My mind went elsewhere."

He nodded and then gestured toward a squad car about ten feet away. "What do you say we have a conversation in my car?"

I shook my head. "We're fine out here."

Mike sighed and then shook his head. "Why does it always have to be like this with you?"

"You really think now's the time to sit around and talk about our feelings toward each other?"

He reached into his jacket for a pack of cigarettes and then lit up. After taking a long drag, he pointed the burning, red ember toward me. "I'm trying to help you, but it's real hard to help an asshole." He took another drag and then exhaled and coughed. "You saved Gail Pennington's life. I came here to tell you that."

I relaxed a little. "I'm glad." He paused, likely waiting for me to say something else, so I squinted at him. "Those cigarettes are going to kill you. You know that, right?"

"Yeah, I know that," he said. He held his cigarette to his side and looked directly into my eyes. "I don't need to tell you how ugly this is going to get. The lawyers are already trolling her family. They met the ambulance at the hospital."

Of course lawyers met it. I had worked hard to get through law school, and I'm proud of myself for it. I'm proud of most of my colleagues, too. People make jokes about lawyers all the time, but the world needs us. At our best, we're advocates, not just for our clients, but for justice, too. As in all professions, a certain percentage of us fall short of our loftier goals.

"Aside from her name, what do we know about her?" I asked.

"She is a stay-at-home mom from Carmel. Her husband is a cardiologist at the IU Health Center. Mark is her son."

I blinked, trying to make sense of that. "Why would a doctor's wife be in a gangbanger's basement?"

Bowers coughed and then looked off into the distance. A crime scene technician had started taking pictures of the remnants of the house.

"Eleven years ago, she was a 911 dispatcher who took a call about a murder in a soup kitchen." He paused and then sighed. "She testified in the Santino Ramirez trial."

I felt something in me, something important, crumble.

"So Michelle and Dante definitely died because they testified against Ramirez," I said. "They died because they did the right thing."

"We don't know that definitively yet," said Bowers. "We're still working this case. Speaking of which," he said, nodding toward the still-smoking rubble of Danny Navarra's house, "how'd you happen to stumble across this place?"

He said it casually, but the question held more import than his tone reflected. If I answered honestly, he could arrest me for obstruction of justice, a felony. At the same time, I didn't want to lie to him. Bowers and I hadn't always gotten along, but I understood him, I think. It had taken me a long time to see it, but unlike a lot of my supervisors, he didn't play games with his subordinates, he didn't play politics with his superiors, and he didn't try to screw people over just to improve his own position within the department. He did what he thought was right, and a guy like that deserved my respect.

"*Barrio Sureño* killed a friend of mine, and then they came after my family," I said.

Bowers nodded. "I know that, and I'm very sorry for what happened."

He hadn't arrested me for a near admission, so that was a good sign.

"I need to work this case."

Bowers crossed his arms and looked directly into my eyes. "Why?"

I started to say something about their deaths being an extension of my original investigation into Angel Hererra, but that was a lie. Truthfully, I didn't have a good answer. My wife reads a lot of crime novels and likes to talk about them with me. The guys in her books, they'd tell Bowers right away why they wanted to work the case. One guy believes homicide work is a mission, a calling rooted deep in who he is. Another guy views it almost as a game, a chance to match wits with an opponent willing to do anything to win. A third guy she reads views himself as a sort of knight in a world shrouded by darkness.

I'm not like those guys. I applied to the police academy after college because the job came with great benefits, it paid well, and I'd have an option for early retirement after twenty years of service. For a guy with a degree in philosophy, I didn't think I could do better. Once I went through the academy and put on the badge, I started buying into the life. I started to believe that I was called to police work, that it was *my* mission, and that God had put me on earth to help put things right.

I don't know anymore. A couple of years ago, Detective Sergeant Michael Davidson from aggravated assault came across a car stuck in the middle of an intersection in the middle of a nasty winter storm. The driver kept spinning his wheels, but he didn't have traction on the ice. With the storm in full force, visibility must have been a couple dozen feet at best. Davidson pushed the car out of the way, but before he could get back to his cruiser, a snow plow operated by a slightly intoxicated driver came through the intersection at thirty miles an hour. Killed Davidson on the spot. Guy had twenty years on the job, two kids in high school, a wife, a home. As soon as he put his kids through college, he planned to retire. And he died for nothing.

I'd like to think there's some grandeouse plan for us all, but the older I get, the more I doubt that. We are who we choose to be, and I chose to be a cop. Santino Ramirez chose to murder Angel Hererra. Sergeant Davidson chose to help a stranded motorist. I'm going to lose my job in a couple of days—I'm resigned to that fate—but I don't have to like it. I enjoy being a detective and putting bad guys in prison. I'm going to miss that, but I'm not done until they take my badge from me. Until then, I refuse to stop working.

"I'm really good at this," I said. "You know that."

"You are quite good at ruining my day," said Bowers, nodding without a trace of a smile on his face.

I tilted my head to the side and raised my eyebrows. "I saved two lives. If that ruined yoru day, maybe you should reconsider your priorities."

"Maybe, but Paul Murphy's very good at his job, too, and this is his case."

"Paul won't be fired in a few days. I will be. This is my last shot. I'm not asking for much. Just stay out of my way. That's it. I'll coordinate with Paul and make sure he gets the credit for anything I do."

Bowers blinked and then took a step back, softening his posture. "The board may not fire you."

"I appreciate the encouragement, but I'm gone in a few days. We both know that."

Bowers took a deep breath as if he were thinking. Then he looked around. "Officially, I have to say you're on leave until you get a verdict from your disciplinary hearing and IA clears you from the shooting this morning."

"How about unofficially?"

Bowers looked down at the grass beneath his feet. "Try to stay out of trouble and try not to hurt anybody."

"Thank you." I paused for just a second. "For what it's worth, the house is owned by a guy named Danny Navarra. You should put out an APB for him and see what he knows."

"No need," said Bowers. "Our gang intelligence unit gave us the house this morning, but you beat us to it. Danny Navarra is sitting in jail right now on a B and E charge. Picked him up two weeks ago, and he couldn't make bail."

"So he didn't set the fire?" I asked.

Bowers shook his head. "No. Mitch Kelly from the Fire Investigations Division at IFD came out with some of the first responders. Place is too hot to get in, but he said it was probably remotely triggered. They've seen a couple of those this year. Arsonists will go into a high-end hobby shop and buy a remote-activated launch system as well as a couple of engines for a model rocket and put them on top of a bucket full of gasoline. You hide, hit a button, and the rockets blast, igniting the gas vapors. Costs some money, but it's a lot easier and safer than running a fuse."

"So anybody can do this?"

Bowers nodded. "I sent Nancy Wharton by the local hobby stores that sell this kind of system, but I'm not hopeful. If our arsonist was smart, he bought it on the Internet."

"Sounds like you've got this under control."

"We do for now," said Bowers.

"Then I'm going to leave you to it. I've got some stuff to do."

"Good luck, and stay out of trouble."

I nodded and then walked the remaining half block to my car. With my department's unofficial approval, Tomas Quesada would pay for this "tip."

Chapter Thirteen

The sun had started to set by the time I got back to my car. On a normal night, my wife and I would be feeding the kids right about now. I drove a couple of blocks away to the parking lot of a CVS on the corner of North Kenwood and Thirty-Eighth Street and called Hannah's cell phone. When she answered, I could hear Kaden saying something in the background, which made me smile.

"Hey, sweetheart," I said. "I just wanted to call and say I'm going to be a little while. I've got a project at work. It's going to be a big one."

"I thought you might," she said, her voice soft. It wasn't until she spoke that I realized how much I had needed to hear her voice. People at our mosque look at us and see a decorated police officer and his nurse wife and kids and automatically think I'm the head of the household, the backbone of the family. They have no idea that every ounce of strength I have comes from my wife. "The kids and I are staying at Jack and Yasmine's. You're welcome to come, too."

I wondered how welcome I would be if she knew I had gone out drinking before I shot Dante.

"I'd like that," I said. "Is there somewhere we can talk there?"

"Of course," she said, her voice sounding surprised. "Are you okay?"

"I'm fine, but we should probably talk later."

"Of course, sure," she said, concern edging out her surprise. "I'm going to put Kaden to bed soon, but Megan will be up until nine or so, and I know she'd like to see you. We can talk after that."

"I'll do my best," I said. "I'm working, though, so I've got to get going. Hug the kids for me."

"I will. I love you."

Despite everything that had happened to me, I found myself smiling. "I love you, too."

After hanging up, I forced the warm feelings I had for my family as deep into my mind as I could. I lived in two worlds. In one, my family was my greatest strength, the wellspring of everything good in my life. In the other, I couldn't afford sentimentality. It clouded my judgment, kept me from doing the things I needed to do. Tomas Quesada had sent me to Danny Navarra's house so I could watch a woman die. Even if he had just passed a message and location along, somebody had pulled his strings. Whether he wanted to talk to me or not, he would give me that name and then he'd go downtown to talk to my department about everything else he knew.

As I turned into Quesada's neighborhood, I found kids playing an evening game of basketball in the light cast by floodlights on nearby houses, with hoops they had wheeled into the street. When they saw my car, they shouted "Game off!" and jumped to the sidewalks and wheeled their hoops to the nearest driveways.

Attending an elementary school in central Indiana, I had grown up with basketball. We played it every time we had gym class, and I eventually got fairly good at it. Despite my being a decent player, the other kids rarely invited me to those sort of neighborhood pickup games, partly because

I was a smartass, but partly because the other kids didn't understand why I had to periodically go home in the middle of a game for prayers, or why I couldn't have hot dogs at neighborhood barbecues that seemed to pop up every weekend when the weather was warm, or why my mother and sister covered their heads, even in the heat of the summer. The kids in my neighborhood let me see their world, but they never let me forget that I existed outside it. Looking back, I should have thanked them for that. They made me stronger than I could ever have been on my own.

I waved to the boys as I drove past. A few reciprocated, but most simply started shouting "Game on!" and grabbed the hoops to start up again. In the day-to-day grind, I forget why I do the job I do, but neighborhoods like that, places where kids can play without being threatened by gang members or drug dealers, serve as a reminder of the importance of my job. I do what I do so those kids don't have to live in fear. That doesn't make the missed family events any easier, but it does make it seem worthwhile.

I parked directly in front of Quesada's house and checked my firearm to ensure I had a full magazine, including a round in the chamber. The temperature had probably dropped ten degrees since the sun went down, and the rhythmic thump of a basketball striking concrete carried on a cold north wind. As I stepped out of the car, I pulled my jacket tight around me to conceal the firearm on my shoulder.

Quesada's house looked little changed from earlier that day. A light over the porch illuminated the front walkway and door, and I caught the flicker of a television from one of the bedrooms upstairs. Like my own house's, the driveway on the left side led to the detached garage and backyard. I doubted he'd be too open to seeing me again, so I didn't bother knocking on the front door. Instead, I walked past the house and down the driveway as if I were an invited guest. None of the boys playing basketball up the street seemed to notice me.

The rear of the house had a pair of French doors that opened onto a brick patio. None of the lights were on back there, but one of the doors had swung open. With the temperature in the thirties, I doubted Quesada had done that on his own. And if he had, he would have shut it immediately. Something was off. I reached into my jacket, pulled out my firearm, and chambered a round before crossing the yard to the door. I paused at the threshold, listening intently as I looked into the kitchen. Quesada had simple white cabinets, marble countertops, and stainless steel appliances. Not even a single coffee cup cluttered his counters. Despite the open door, I couldn't hear movement.

I crept inside. A hallway directly in front of the French doors stretched to the home's main entrance on Middle Drive and two doors, both of which were painted white to match the cabinets, led from the kitchen. The first led to a powder room—empty—while the second led down into an unfinished cellar. I couldn't hear anyone down there, so I closed the door softly and left the kitchen, being careful to stay near the walls in the hallway to prevent the floor from creaking. A staircase in the entryway led to the second floor, while open archways on the left and right led to a living room on one side and a dining room on the other. Again, both appeared empty.

I stopped and smelled the air. No gasoline this time. The first floor appeared clear. I had put one foot on the bottom step when someone flicked off the overhead lights.

I vaulted into the living room and felt the floorboards sag beneath my weight. The room had two couches, neither of which afforded me much of a hiding spot, and a marble fireplace. A black candle burned in a *Santa Muerte* shrine in the fireplace. I gritted my teeth and pressed my back against the wall beside the arched opening to the entryway. Almost as soon as I did that, I heard the floorboards creak upstairs. The way Quesada had moved earlier, I would have expected his footsteps to be quick and light, but these were heavy.

The wall behind me vibrated as the guy came down. I held my breath and pointed my firearm directly at the archway in case Quesada's guest decided to go into the living room. The floorboards at the base of the steps creaked as he hit the bottom, but he didn't linger at all. He simply turned right and headed to the kitchen. This very well could be the man telling Quesada what to do. I couldn't let him leave, not without finding out who he was, at the least. I stepped out into the entryway in time to see a figure silhouetted in the moonlight in the hallway. He carried something big, like a basketball, tucked under his right arm and what I could only describe as a sword in the left.

"IMPD. Stop where you are and drop your weapon right now."

The figure in front of me stopped as I had asked, but instead of dropping his sword, he slowly turned. In the dim light, I couldn't get a glimpse of his face, but it was clearly a man. I'd say somewhere between five foot ten and six feet, with average build and dark skin. No facial hair, at least that I could see. I didn't know how long his knife was, but I should be out of arm's reach.

"IMPD," I said, repeating myself. "Stay where you are and drop the weapon. Now."

He started to bend down, reaching toward the ground with his right hand as if he were going to comply, but then he stood suddenly and overhanded whatever he held in his left hand straight at me. It hit me in the arm, almost knocking me back, before striking the floor with a hollow, meaty sound. The figure stood still, and then he sprinted out the back door. I took chase, but my first footfall hit something slick, something that hadn't been there a moment before. I caught myself along the wall and regained my footing and ran after him. I'm in pretty good shape, and I can outrun most people, but this guy flew. As I reached the back door, he had already crossed the backyard and started vaulting over the fence that separated Quesada's house from the neighbor to his south. His weapon lay on the patio, its edge glinting in the moonlight.

I hit the patio at a dead run and thankfully, my feet found sure purchase on the bricks. I didn't bother trying to vault over the fence as my quarry had. Instead, I put my hands on top and jumped so that I could see over. Straight in front of me, I saw a man dive into a dark four-door vehicle and drive off. He was gone. I let myself fall back to the ground, where I took a breath for the first time since shouting. Whoever he was, I had chased somebody fast and athletic. Much more so than me. Sweat began to drip down my brow and into my eyes, so I started to wipe it away and found I was leaving something on my forehead, something sticky. I looked down at my hands. In the moonlight, my right hand was black, although I had the feeling it would look red in better lighting.

I crossed the patio. He hadn't dropped a sword, after all, but a wickedly sharp machete, probably the same one that had cut Michelle. The coroner's office would tell for sure. Realistically, I should have stayed outside and called in the troops, but I needed to confirm something before I did. I walked back into that house, through the kitchen and front hallway to the object the man I had chased had thrown at me. As my eyes adjusted to the gloom, I gradually began to make it out. First, I saw the general shape, and then the hair, and then the eyes and the nose and the mouth. He had thrown Tomas Quesada's head at me.

I backed off slowly, trying not to disturb the pools of blood on the ground.

"This is messed up."

Chapter Fourteen

Jacob dove through the Chevy's open front window, and Carla floored the accelerator, causing the vehicle's tires to chirp as they bit into the asphalt. The car shot forward just in time for Carla to look over her shoulder and see a head pop over Tomas Quesada's fence. At that distance and that time of night, she couldn't recognize him, but he had still seen their car. He couldn't have seen the license plate, but if he was a cop, they'd put out an APB on all similar vehicles, which meant she'd have to ditch the car and get another. Just one more thing to worry about on a day of endless worry. Despite their early success with Dante and Michelle Washington, Carla's plans had stalled today. She didn't need this on top of everything else.

"Are you hurt?" she asked, glancing at the blood covering Jacob's shirt and arms as he shimmied inside the vehicle. Miguel reached over and clapped him on the shoulder.

"Did you do it?" he asked.

Jacob looked back at him and nodded before looking to her. His breath came to him gradually. "I'm fine. He didn't touch me."

"Where's the head?" asked Miguel.

Carla turned right onto Michigan Street and whipped her head around to look at Jacob. They had entered an old part of town, and historic brick homes and office businesses surrounded them, but she had no interest in staying to appreciate the architecture. In a couple of blocks, they'd hit I-65 north. She'd feel more comfortable on the interstate, an anonymous rusted Chevrolet amidst cars from all corners of the area. Until then, though, she felt exposed on the surface streets. She didn't know who had chased Jacob out of Tomas's house, and for all she knew, he could have been following them at that moment.

Tomas Quesada needed to die, but they shouldn't have hit his house tonight. They should have waited until he let his guard down and until the police no longer had an interest in him. They could have hidden half a block away and shot him from a tree. But instead, they had gone tonight, the same day the police had ruined another operation. Why Miguel demanded they go tonight of all nights, she didn't know, but he should have known better.

"What head?" she asked, tearing her gaze off the road long enough to look at her stepson.

Jacob hesitated and looked back to Miguel. "Quesada's."

She pounded the steering wheel. "That's what took you so long? You tried to take his goddamn head with you?"

A crooked smile formed on his lips as he looked toward the backseat, toward Miguel. "I didn't just try. I had it, for a moment. Then some guy came in."

"Good boy," said Miguel, tousling Jacob's hair from the backseat. Carla glanced at him in her rearview mirror. She didn't want to work with Miguel, but he had resources beyond anything she could gather on her own. One phone call, and he could have professional hitters fly up from Mexico to take out whomever she needed and then disappear, never to be seen again. Not only that, Tino's men knew and respected him. Sure, they'd listen to her, but they'd ignore her just as often as they'd do what she said.

With her, every order became a chance to argue, to bicker and think of another way. With Miguel, they simply shut up and acted. One word whispered from his lips to the wrong person could ruin everything she had planned, so she had to bring him in, but she didn't trust him. Poor, stupid, naive Jacob, though, believed everything Miguel said. Not only that, Miguel seemed to trust him; he seemed to believe he had found a student in Jacob. This could end very badly for her unless she figured something out.

"Not a good boy," she said, shaking her head. "You took so long in there somebody showed up. Who was he?"

"Just some cop," he said. "And I'm fine. He couldn't see me in the dark."

But it hadn't been dark in the house. She had seen the lights go out. They needed to back off now and think this through. The state would still execute Tino, nothing would change that, but they couldn't risk confronting the police. Not with so much left to do.

"We've got to ditch this car," she said, starting to breathe a little easier as she thought through the situation. "We'll find another and take this one to the long-term parking lot at the airport. The police won't find it for weeks."

"Nobody saw the car, Carla," said Miguel. "It was dark."

She looked in the rearview mirror. Miguel had such dark skin that she couldn't see anything but the whites of his eyes. "Jacob's mystery cop popped over the fence. He knows what we're driving."

In her peripheral vision, she caught Miguel waving the suggestion off. Jacob looked concerned at first, but then he stared out the window.

"See, Jacob," said Miguel from the backseat. "This is why we've never had a woman president. They don't have any balls."

He laughed and Jacob tittered a little as well, but Carla could tell he didn't put his heart into it. He saw the stupidity of continuing in that Chevy even if Miguel didn't.

As she turned north onto I-65 a moment later, she breathed a little easier. The operation had ended poorly, but they still accomplished their mission. With Tomas Quesada dead, they had one less rival for *Barrio Sureño's* throne. She slipped into one of the center lanes and set the cruise control to five miles over the speed limit. To any police officers driving by, they'd look like a family going home for the evening. Jacob might have screwed up, but he hadn't screwed up so badly they had no return. This could still work. She glanced at her stepson.

"How'd you do it?"

He turned so that his back faced his door and glanced at her and then to Miguel. "I knocked on his door and said I had a message from Dad."

"Attaboy," said Miguel, covering Jacob's forearm with his hand. "What'd you tell him?"

"Nothing," said Jacob. "As soon as I got in, I showed him the gun and told him to go upstairs. He tried to tell me Dad wouldn't want this, but what would he know, right? He helped send him to prison in the first place. We should have killed him years ago."

"How'd you do it, boy?" asked Miguel, his voice excited. Had Carla seen his pants, it wouldn't have surprised her to see an erection.

"I just stabbed him in the gut, like you said to do," he said. "He started bleeding everywhere. That's when I did what I had to do."

He couldn't even bring himself to say he cut off Quesada's head. Jacob, as much as he believed otherwise, wasn't ready for what lay ahead. He played too important a role in her future plans to die now.

"You made a mistake," said Carla, glancing over at him. "I see the symbolism in what you did, but it took too much time, and in a job like this, time matters. You had a gun, and you should have used it. Shoot him and get out. Your survival is your first goal."

"I would have used the gun, but—"

"Shut up," said Miguel. "You're not this boy's mom, so you don't get to talk to him like that."

For a split second, she looked in the rearview mirror. The whites of Miguel's eyes flashed back at her.

"I didn't mean it like that," said Carla, trying to make her voice sound conciliatory when she truly wanted to turn and shoot him. "But I don't want him to get hurt. I'm his stepmother. I still have to look out for him, don't I?"

Miguel laughed. "Typical woman. Always thinking with her heart instead of her head."

Jacob chuckled, too, but again, Carla could tell he didn't put his heart into it. That gave her hope. "Typical woman."

"Tell her why you took Quesada's head," said Miguel. "Tell her who told you to take it."

Jacob hesitated, looking almost embarrassed. He had spent part of his summers with her every year since he turned ten, so she knew him well by now. He didn't want to say, so she lowered her voice.

"Go ahead," she said. "Tell me."

"*Nuestra Señora de la Santa Muerte,*" he said, looking straight ahead to avoid looking her in the eye. "Our Holy Lady of Death."

"Did you hear that?" asked Miguel, his voice growing louder. She saw a flash and heard the slosh of liquid in his flask as he took a drink. "The Bony Lady's talking to him in his dreams. The boy's got the gift."

Jacob's only gift was an ability to read people and tell them what they wanted to hear. Miguel impressed him, and Jacob wanted to please him. Nothing more.

"I don't believe in *Santa Muerte*," said Carla, looking straight ahead.

"She believes in you," said Miguel, seriously. She wondered if he had seen that on a bumper sticker. "Jacob had to take Quesada's head. Whether you believe it or not, she's watching over us right now, guiding us and protecting us from our enemies. We stop showing our appreciation for that protection, it's over."

Miguel believed that, too, which meant pressing Jacob on the act's stupidity wouldn't get her anywhere. She let the matter of Quesada's head drop and settled into the drive. As soon as she could, she exited onto I-70 east and then onto I-465 south, circumnavigating the city to come to their house in the Bates-Hendricks neighborhood. Carla didn't own this house, but she knew the lawyer handling its previous owner's estate. No one would meet them there anytime soon.

She parked about half a block away, already planning to ditch the car as soon as she could, despite Miguel's dismissal of her nervousness. Meanwhile, Miguel and Jacob walked arm in arm toward their house as if they were old school buddies. When they got inside, the two men immediately walked to the *Santa Muerte* altar in the living room. She, however, went upstairs to the room in which they made their plans. As soon as she had procured that house, Carla had driven to the nearest interstate rest area and picked up maps of the entire region. She knew precisely where each of their future victims lived and had even taken surveillance photos of some of their workplaces. Despite the setbacks, they had the abilities and resources to do this.

The plan could still work. With some improvisation, it *would* still work. She went downstairs and saw Jacob and Miguel kneel before the *Santa Muerte* altar in the fireplace. She had seen the ritual often enough to know what would happen, and she had refused to participate often enough that they no longer invited her.

"Saint Michael the Archangel," began Miguel. "Defend us in battle. Be our defense against the wickedness and snares of the Devil. May God rebuke him, we humbly pray, and do thou, O Prince of the heavenly hosts, by the power of God, thrust into hell Satan, and all the evil spirits, who prowl about the world seeking the ruin of souls. Amen."

Miguel leaned into the shrine and then lit a red candle. Miguel had something big planned tonight. According to believers, *Santa Muerte* was the embodiment of death herself, a very powerful being indeed, so she could overwhelm even the most faithful of servants. To temper that influence, people like Miguel first called on another saint for protection. Miguel looked at Jacob.

"Do you have coins?"

This, Carla hadn't seen before. Jacob reached into his pocket and pulled out a number of quarters. Miguel then dropped each of them into a clay pot.

"I pour this for you, *Santisma Muerte,* my beloved," he said, pouring the contents of the pot on the ground. The liquid had a viscous texture and looked almost black in the candlelight. Blood, human if she had to guess. "Please accept it from your servant."

After pouring the blood, Miguel reached into his pocket and pulled out a small glass vial. He poured a small amount of cocaine into his palm and then blew it over the statue.

"Holy death, dearest of my heart. Do not abandon or forsake me in my hour of need. Protect me, but do not let my enemies experience peace. Keep them bound and restless, bothered always with the thought of me."

Jacob had never exhibited a religious side as far as Carla knew, but he began reciting an Our Father. As Jacob prayed, Miguel poured another small measure of cocaine on his palm and once again blew it on the statue.

"Holy death, my great treasure, never leave me. You are the powerful owner of the dark heart of life and Empress of night. Please pour favors upon me. May my enemies be at my feet, humiliated and repentant for their sins. Make them never leave my side until I receive what was promised to me."

Miguel did it again and again, nine different verses in total, each time asking for the death or torment of his enemies and requesting that the Bony Lady make her will known to them so that they might act. Until that moment, Carla hadn't understood the depth of his belief, but Miguel truly believed *Santa Muerta* protected him and spoke to Jacob. Carla had studied enough history to know that the world had been shaped by men and women who believed a deity talked to them, and while they all came from different eras and cultural milieus, they all had one thing in common: they didn't take orders from anyone but their god. After the ritual, Miguel hugged Jacob, and Carla knew she had made her first big mistake. She had misunderstood Miguel and believed money could induce him to her will, but that wouldn't do. He was a believer. She hadn't taken that into account, but she could still use it.

She leaned her back against the nearest wall and slid down so that she sat Indian style on the floor, rocking back and forth. Her movements started slow and small, but gradually she built momentum.

"*Quiero que mates Gail y Mark Pennington.*"

She rocked back and forth, whispering the phrase over and over. Jacob noticed her first, but then Miguel turned and watched as well.

"What's she saying?" asked Miguel.

Jacob knelt at her side and held his ear close to her lips. He looked at Miguel.

"She wants us to kill Gail and Mark Pennington, but she's speaking Spanish."

Miguel crossed the room and nudged her feet with his boot. "What are you getting at, woman?"

"*Quiero que mates Gail y Mark Pennington.*"

Carla continued rocking, ignoring the others in the room. If they needed an order from God, they would get an order from God. Miguel nudged her again, this time a little harder.

"Come on. Nobody's buying this, Carla."

Jacob looked up at him. "She doesn't speak Spanish, dude. This isn't Carla talking."

Carla did speak Spanish, in fact, quite well. She had taken several classes after law school, but she hadn't bothered telling her husband or Jacob, nor had she ever spoken it to Miguel, who considered Spanish a higher form of communication than English. He considered her for a moment, and then took a step back and made the sign of the cross over his chest.

"She's listening," he said, his voice barely above a whisper as he looked to the ceiling. Carla continued rocking and reciting the phrase, trying not to roll her eyes. It didn't matter who the orders came from, but Gail and Mark Pennington had to die. Miguel and Jacob had supposedly worn ski masks every time they met the pair, but as long as the Penningtons drew breath, they threatened her and made them all look weak. They had to go, one way or another.

Jacob looked at the altar in the fireplace. "We'll do it. We'll kill them."

"They'll die by our hands," said Miguel.

Carla stopped the chant but continued rocking. Inside, she smiled, but outside, she kept her expression somber. After a few minutes, she slowed her rocking and then came to a stop. After that, she looked around the floor as if opening her eyes for the first time.

"How'd I get on the floor?" she asked.

Miguel reached his hand down and pulled her to her feet. "Come. We have work to do. *Santa Muerte* has given us her protection and a mission."

Chapter Fifteen

Before leaving the house, I checked the second floor to make sure we didn't have any other victims. I didn't find any, but I did find Quesada's body in one of the bedrooms. In addition to his decapitation, he appeared to have puncture wounds to his abdomen and chest. I've been to a lot of grisly murder scenes, but rarely do I hear of someone cutting off another person's head. There are better, easier ways to kill people. Guns work pretty well. You cut off someone's head, though, you do it for a reason.

I went back downstairs and left the house to call in backup. The dispatcher would call in the troops, but I requested she place an additional call to Paul Murphy. He'd need to see this. The first officers should arrive within a few minutes, so, once securing the scene as well as I could, I walked to my car and sat on the hood. Normally, I would have gone up to the kids playing basketball up the street and asked them to get their parents so I could warn them that police officers would be arriving shortly, but since I had blood all over me, I didn't think that'd be the best thing to do.

I held up my badge as the first patrol vehicle arrived. Unfortunately, the lights and sirens drew the kids. They didn't recoil when they saw the blood on my hands and face, but it did dampen their enthusiasm some. After introducing myself, I led one of the officers to the backyard while the other entertained the boys. Paul—or whoever was given the case—would need to talk to those kids, so establishing a rapport now could go a long way toward securing their cooperation in the future. I showed the beat cop the machete, the back door, and the spot on the rear fence where our killer had jumped over, but neither of us wanted to go back into the house to see the body. He did flash his light through the French doors, though. Quesada's head sat where I had left it. Both of us agreed that we didn't need to check his pulse to ensure we weren't dealing with someone who modern medical science could save. I went back to my car to wait for the detectives assigned to the case.

Paul Murphy and Captain Mike Bowers arrived at roughly the same time fifteen minutes later. Bowers wore a brown sport coat, white shirt, and a mustard-colored tie, while Paul wore a pair of jeans and an Indianapolis Colts sweatshirt. Both men had bloodshot eyes, haggard faces, and several days' worth of facial hair on their chins. Homicide detectives routinely work twenty-four or even thirty-six hours straight after getting a case, and if I had to guess, Paul and Bowers were probably pretty close to that.

"Head's in the front hallway," I said. "Body's upstairs. Aside from me, no one has gone inside the house." I pointed toward the patrol vehicle around which the boys huddled. "Those boys were playing in the street when I drove up, so there's a chance they might have seen something." I pointed toward the patrolman leaning against his car in front of the home. "That officer—I don't know his name—is manning the log book, so you'll want to sign in with him."

Paul yawned and nodded before looking around. "We ID'd the victim yet?"

"Tomas Quesada. He's a member of *Barrio Sureño*, or at least he was ten years ago."

Bowers crossed his arms and then looked at Paul Murphy. "Could you excuse us for a moment, Sergeant?"

Paul looked at Bowers and then at me. He mouthed *good luck* and then nodded to Captain Bowers. "I'll be by my car."

Once Paul had walked a sufficient distance away that he wouldn't hear our conversation, Bowers looked at me and shook his head, sighing. "I thought I asked you to stay out of trouble."

"I tried. It found me."

Bowers rubbed his eyes and then reached into his jacket for a hard pack of cigarettes. He lit one up. "Tell me what's going on. Honestly. Who was this guy?"

"Ten years ago, he was *Barrio Sureño*'s treasurer. I visited him this morning hoping he could shed some light on the people who killed Michelle and sent Dante to kill me. He told me to check out Danny Navarra, whose house burned earlier, almost taking Gail and Mark Pennington with it."

Bowers took a long drag on his cigarette and looked to the growing crowd of children around the patrol officers' cruisers. "I assume your conversation with Mr. Quesada was polite and reflected well on our department."

I tilted my head to the side. "I was as gentle as the situation merited."

Bowers nodded and then took a long drag on his cigarette. "After that fire, you naturally thought you'd, what, come back and have tea with him?"

I shook my head. "I had hoped to have a sensible conversation about his partners, after which I would have placed him in custody and driven him to your station for further interrogation."

Bowers looked over his shoulder and waved for Paul Murphy to return.

"I appreciate that you include IMPD in the investigation. It's sweet of you," said Bowers. He waited until Paul Murphy arrived to continue his questions. "Can you tell us how you got the blood on you?"

I waited for Paul to take a notepad from his pocket before I spoke. "I went to the house, and upon arrival, I found the back door open. Fearing the worst, I went inside to perform a resident safety check. I announced myself and found a man carrying what I thought was a sword. In fact, it was a machete. It was on the back patio, but I imagine somebody picked it up by now. The assailant threw Tomas Quesada's head at me and ran. I gave chase, but I couldn't catch him. He dove into a car a street away."

Paul wrote a few things down and then looked at me. "Just so you know, the official record will state that you came to this house and got a little head from an unnamed dude. Wanted to let you know in case you hear rumors around the station."

Bowers shook his head, but I actually smiled a little. "Classy. Thank you for that, buddy."

Bowers crossed his arms. "What'd your assailant look like?"

I thought back to the hallway. "It was pretty dark, so I didn't get a look at his face. He's a little shorter than me, maybe six feet. I'd say two hundred pounds tops, but probably closer to one-eighty. He's fast and athletic. Skin tone in the darker shades. By the gang involved, I'd say he's probably Hispanic. Took off Quesada's head, so he's got some upper-body strength. I don't particularly want to run into him again."

Paul wrote that down and nodded. "Anything in the house stand out to you?"

"I cleared it quickly, so I didn't get much of a look at the place. I saw a *Santa Muerte* shrine in the fireplace in the living room, but I didn't get much of a look. You'll have to bring in Officer Rios. She might know something."

"Anything else you want to tell us?" asked Bowers.

I looked at the house and shook my head. "I'm having a bad day. How's your investigation going?"

Bowers looked at Paul.

"Not as well as yours, evidently," said the sergeant. "What's your next move?"

I looked at Bowers. He nodded, so I looked at Paul and spoke. "I plan to visit a *Barrio Sureño* associate at Pendleton and see if he's heard any rumors lately. You want to come along?"

"You've given me and my team enough work here," said Paul, glancing up from his notepad. "We're going to be busy cleaning up this mess."

Beneath Paul's jovial facade, I could tell I had pissed him off. "I apologize for giving you a mess, but I didn't kill Quesada. I didn't want or expect this to happen."

Paul hesitated for a moment, but then he sighed and I saw his shoulders relax a little as he looked at Captain Bowers. "I know. If Captain Bowers wants you involved, I guess you're involved."

"It's nothing personal, Paul," said Bowers. "We've got people dying, so we need whatever help we can get and Ash knows this case. We'll use him as needed, but if he gets in the way, tell me and he's gone."

Paul looked at me out of the corner of his eye. "No. He's not in the way. I just kind of wish he'd stop finding bodies."

"Me, too," I said. "But unless you guys need me, I'm going to head out. Considering that I shot Dante Washington yesterday, I'm not sure that I should be here when the media arrives."

"Then get out of here," said Paul. "I've got your number if I need you."

"And, Ash," said Bowers. "Don't watch the news tonight."

"You're censoring my TV now, boss?"

"No," said Bowers, shaking his head. "Dante and Michelle Washington's family held a candlelight vigil at their church. A couple of newspeople attended, and the family didn't say too many nice things about you."

I exhaled slowly. On my reports and in conversation with my colleagues, I referred to Dante and Michelle as the victims. They weren't the only ones, though. Their parents had lost two children in one night. I couldn't even imagine that kind of pain.

"Thank you for the warning."

"Good luck out there," said Paul.

I nodded to them both before heading back to my car.

It had been a long day, so after my conversation with Mike Bowers and Paul Murphy, I could practically feel weights attached to my eyelids. I wanted to join Hannah and the kids at her sister's house, but I needed some clothes first. After twenty minutes of driving, I turned into my neighborhood and found a black-and-white patrol vehicle parked in front of my house. I parked on the street behind the cruiser and got out of my car. Even from the street, I could see that somebody had broken one of my front windows.

I brought my hand to my jaw and swore under my breath. A heavyset patrolman stepped out of the cruiser and nodded to me.

"Detective Rashid?"

I nodded. "Yeah. I assume you're here about the window."

The patrolman looked at my house and then back to me, nodding. "Yeah. After that riot tonight, we've been trying to go by your house every half hour to make sure you're okay."

I furrowed my brow. "What riot?"

"You haven't heard? There was some kind of march down Shadeland Avenue. It was just people holding signs, so it wasn't a big deal. Then somebody brought out some booze, and the troublemakers got all riled up. They decided to torch the porno store on Massachusetts Avenue."

I ran my hands through my hair. "Captain Bowers told me it was just a candlelight vigil."

"There *was* a candlelight vigil, but they weren't a problem. It was the people outside." The patrolman paused, looked around, and then drew a breath. "My partner chased down the guy who broke your window. He's bringing him back now."

"Good," I said, nodding. "I'm going to go inside and see the damage."

The patrolman said something, but I was lost in my own thoughts. When I got inside, I found a brick in my living room. Someone had written FUCK YOU on it with a black permanent marker. The glass would take a while to clean, but the damage was cosmetic mostly. I closed my eyes and thanked God that my kids weren't there.

When I got back outside, the patrolman's partner had come back, and he held a familiar squirming young man.

Daniel Robinson. He was a high school senior, and he lived a block and a half away. His dad was my plumber, and the boy mowed one of my neighbor's lawns. In the summers, Megan would sit at the window and watch him, but whenever he glanced toward our house, she would duck behind the couch. She denied it, but I'm pretty sure she had a crush on him. He seemed like a nice kid. Seeing him there, squirming against a police officer's side, I felt a profound sense of loss that I couldn't quite explain.

"Hey, Daniel," I said. "You throw the brick through my window?"

"Fuck you."

I've been a police officer for a long time, and people scream at me all the time. Words don't hurt, but other things do. Daniel practically spit, he was so animated. In years past, that kind of screaming would have drawn everyone on the street out of their homes to make sure their neighbors were okay. Tonight, though, those doors remained shut and window blinds remained drawn. I realized in that moment what I had lost. Hannah and I might have owned this house, but we weren't welcome on that street anymore.

The patrolman holding Daniel nodded to me. "I caught him about three blocks north of here. He didn't have any weapons on him, but he did have a black marker in his pocket. You want us to take him in?"

As mad as I was at him, I understood where Daniel came from—at least to some degree. I got into trouble as a teenager, but I never thought the police would shoot me if they showed up. Daniel likely did—and he had good reason. I've got colleagues who would call him a thug simply because of his skin color. They'd judge him a threat and a criminal and treat him accordingly before they knew the first thing about him. Had I been in Daniel's position with his experiences, I would have been pissed, too. I might have thrown that same brick. I didn't think I deserved his anger, but it had merit and foundation.

At the same time, I'm not in his position. I've had at least half a dozen kids his age pull guns on me in my career. So far, I've been able to talk them down, but that's not always going to be the case. In some of those instances, I probably had justification to shoot. Many of my colleagues wouldn't have had the same restraint, and I couldn't blame them. If we don't shoot first, we might not make it home.

Contrary to what seems like popular belief, this isn't a problem politicians can solve by shouting at each other on television. We've got too many guns on the street, too many young men without any hope for legitimate employment at all, and too many officers willing to shoot young men of color with or without provocation. I don't know how to fix that. I don't even know how to start. My only hope is that people smarter than me start caring about our young people and our communities enough to stop pointing fingers at each other and start thinking about real solutions.

I held Daniel's hate-filled gaze, and for a moment I thought he would spit on me. I shook my head. "No. I'm not pressing charges."

"You sure about that?" asked the heavyset patrolman.

I nodded. "Yeah. Drive him home and tell his dad what he did. I'm not going to send a kid to jail for doing something stupid."

"But you'd shoot one for knocking on your door," said Daniel, straining against the patrolman's grip.

"Knock it off," said the heavyset patrolman. "The detective's doing you a favor."

I wished I could think of something to say, something that would help Daniel understand my perspective. But I couldn't. We came from different worlds entirely, and the collisions between those two worlds were rarely peaceful or sensible.

"Just make sure he gets home safe," I said.

The patrolman holding Daniel nodded to my house. "You need any help with the window? My brother's a contractor. Might be able to help you out."

"Thanks, but no. I've got some plywood in the garage. I'll tack it up and worry about the window later."

The patrolman holding Daniel began guiding him toward the waiting cruiser, while the heavyset patrolman stayed and looked at me. "Just to let you know, the guys in the northwest district support you and what you did. Even the black guys. We all agree: guy breaks into any of our houses, we're taking him down, too."

I almost grimaced. I didn't shoot Dante because he broke into my house, and I certainly didn't shoot him because he was black. I shot him because I thought he had a gun. And even that didn't make it right. I've, unfortunately, killed a number of people in my career, and I can say with some authority that it's deeply and profoundly wrong, even when justified. How I could make people understand that, I didn't know, but now didn't seem the time to argue.

"I appreciate your support. And thank you for watching out for my house. I'm lucky to have so many friends."

The patrolman nodded his agreement and got back into his car. As they drove away, I felt as if someone had just reached into my gut and pulled everything out, leaving me empty inside and completely numb. My tools and plywood were in the garage, so I walked over. Back when I drank, I used to stash bottles of bourbon all over my house in places I didn't think Hannah would look. I'd gotten rid of all of them but one in that garage. I don't even remember buying it, it had been so long ago, but I'd find it, unopened and perfect, behind my pegboard tool organizer above my workbench. All I'd have to do was stand on the workbench and reach behind.

I feel like I wake up every morning only to find someone staring at me from the dark. Wherever I go, he follows me, watching for those times I'm weakest. When I stumble, he pushes me down. When I struggle, he laughs. When I succeed, he tells me about the times I've failed. Every time there's a reason to have a drink, he reminds me of it. I do whatever I can to ignore him, and I usually succeed. It's not always going to be like that. I now know that whenever an alcoholic says he takes things one day at a time, that's what he means. I don't know what will happen tomorrow or the day after that. Maybe that dark figure will win, maybe he won't. All I know for certain is that I'm going to have to fight him every single day for the rest of my life.

As I grabbed a sheet of plywood from the stack near my workbench, I thought of that bottle, of how it would feel in my hand and how its contents would taste and what it would do for me. Then I thought of how it'd make my wife feel. If I closed my eyes, I could see her face crumple, I could see her pain, her anger. I could also see the disappointment. I'd already given in once this week. I couldn't do it again. One day, I knew I'd break into that bottle, but not tonight. Not with what I hold dear so close.

I walked inside the house, knowing I'd soon see them again.

Chapter Sixteen

I screwed the plywood into the lumber that framed the interior of my window, securing the house for the night before driving to my sister-in-law's place. I told Hannah about our broken window, but I didn't think I had the strength to tell her about my trip to the bar the night I shot Dante. Tomorrow. My wife and I slept in the same bed that night, which was nice. Sometimes just that little contact can make the world seem okay.

At nine the next morning, I drove to the City-County Building. Paul and his team probably hadn't even made it home from Tomas Quesada's house. While I wondered if they had come up with anything, I still had leads to chase down. As soon as I had something they could use, Paul would be the first call I made. Until then, I didn't want to lose the momentum I had.

I took the elevator to the floor that housed the homicide unit, and browsed the desks until I found the one with a picture of Paul's wife, Becky, on it. He had left his computer running, so I sat down to search the Department of Corrections' database. Before his demise, Tomas Quesada had given us two names; the first owned a home that hid two captives, while the second, according to the DOC's database, lived in the Pendleton Correctional Institute where he was serving a fifteen-year sentence for armed robbery.

Before this most recent conviction, IMPD had arrested him multiple times on drug charges and still considered him a suspect in several open unsolved violent crimes. Based on his file, he very well could have had soldiers on the outside.

Realistically, Paul or someone else from my department should have called Pendleton and set up an appointment, but I had friends in the administration there. I called the assistant warden at home and caught him before he went to church. With a little prodding, he agreed to set up an interview with Salazar at noon, which meant I needed to move quickly to make it on time.

I turned the computer off, and took the elevator to the ground level and then walked to the parking lot. The drive to Pendleton took just under an hour in morning traffic, and I spent most of that listening to a jazz CD my wife had purchased for me. She thought I needed to broaden my horizons and add some depth to my character, apparently having gotten the idea after falling in love with a series of mystery novels about an LA detective who listens to jazz. Try as I might, I couldn't get into it. I don't think I'm cool enough.

I arrived at the main administration building at Pendleton at a little after eleven to begin the check-in process. Reluctantly, I surrendered my firearm and cell phone as part of that. I knew the justification behind it—not even corrections officers carried firearms if they were going to meet with inmates—but it always made me feel uncomfortable. After that, I went through half a dozen locked checkpoints and nodded hello to almost a dozen guards. By the time I made it to the interview room, over an hour had passed since my arrival.

The room looked purposefully designed to depress everyone who stepped inside it. A stainless steel table and matching seats were bolted to the center of the floor, while a video camera hung in the corner of the room. A large red panic button adorned the wall beside the door. I'm sure an enterprising inmate given sufficient time could manufacture something in that room into a weapon, but I should be safer there than just about anywhere else in the building.

I sat down facing the door, waiting while the guards brought Tristan in. He had a shaved head and tattooed flames where his hair should have been. Restraints secured his hands near his waist, while leg irons kept him from running. He looked at me, and I saw the sort of cool, dispassionate anger in his eyes that I had seen on more faces than I care to recount.

"I don't know you," he said, shuffling toward the table.

"No," I said. I looked to the guard. "You can go." I then looked at the seat opposite me. "Sit down."

The inmate wriggled the chains that bound his wrists and grabbed his crotch. "How about you crawl under this table and suck my dick?"

He probably thought that would shock me or maybe even intimidate me. I didn't blink. "All these years in prison, we both know who in this room likes to suck dick, and it's not me. Now why don't you sit down before we give the guards watching us something else to laugh at?"

Salazar turned around and glowered at the still open door. "That *concha's* not going to say anything to anybody, is he?"

He had just called the guard—a man—a quite vulgar name for part of the female anatomy.

"That's not going to win you too many friends," I said. "Now sit down and shut up."

He didn't sit down so much as slither into his seat. The guard shut and locked the door finally. "They told me you're Ash Rashid."

"You can call me Detective Rashid," I said, reaching into my jacket for a pen in case he said something worth writing down. I glanced to the video camera in the corner of the room. "You know the drill. Cameras aren't on, but you tell me something, I can use it against you in court. You can have a lawyer here if you want." I paused and shrugged. "You know the rest by now, I'm sure."

"I know my rights," he said, lacing his fingers together on the steel table. "You going to tell me why you wanted to talk to me?"

I shrugged and looked around the room. "To be honest, I really don't care about anything you have to say. I came because I wanted somebody to search your cell, and I figured since I drove all the way out here, I might as well say hello."

He tilted his chin up at me so he could look at me down his nose. "What do you think you're going to find in my cell?"

"Cell phone. I've heard a rumor that you're ordering murders on the outside. Care to substantiate that?"

He leaned forward and then reached beneath the table. "Care to substantiate my ball sack?"

I opened my mouth to respond and then realized that I didn't know what to say. "That doesn't even mean anything."

He merely smirked and then slouched down in his chair. I crossed my arms.

"Let's start over," I said. "I came here to talk about two murders. Two individuals who testified against Santino Ramirez have been murdered. So was Tomas Quesada. You remember him?"

Tristan crossed his arms. "You lie on the stand, you die in the streets. It's called justice. As for Quesada—if someone took him out, he deserved it."

I shook my head. "Our witnesses didn't lie."

"Tino wasn't even in town when Angel went down."

Quesada had said something similar. I didn't believe him, and I sure didn't believe Tristan, but it wouldn't hurt to hear what he had to say.

"If Tino wasn't in town, where was he?"

Tristan leaned forward and rested his elbows on the table. "It's none of your goddamn business."

"What was he doing?"

"Working."

I raised my eyebrows. "What kind of work?"

He refused to look me in the eye. "The kind that needed to be done."

Probably killing someone, then. If so, that would explain why Ramirez hadn't brought it up during trial as an alibi.

"Regardless of what Santino Ramirez did or didn't do, a lot of people in Indianapolis are pointing fingers at you."

"Is that right?" he asked. He leaned forward, held up his hands, and jiggled the chains. "They tell you how I killed anybody while I'm sitting here?"

"Let's not play stupid," I said, shaking my head. "We both know how this works. One phone call from you, and somebody in my city drops. I'm asking man-to-man if you've been making those calls. I'll even tell your homeboys all about it to make sure you get the credit."

He leaned back and looked almost as if he wanted to put his feet up. "My boys know when to give credit when it's due."

"The way I hear it, your boys couldn't find an asshole at an asshole convention right now. You sure they even remember your name?"

"What's that supposed to mean?"

I shrugged. "Just that I've heard they're moving on. Santino Ramirez is going to die in just a couple of days, and his gang is going to need a leader. I hear Danny Navarra's stepping up."

He waved me off. "Danny's a stupid kid. Nobody's going to follow him."

"What about his Uncle Miguel?"

That shut him up for a moment. "Miguel's got his own thing."

I waited for him to elaborate, but he didn't say anything else.

"I'd suggest you start talking. I'm building a case against the people killing my witnesses, and one way or another, you're going to be involved. You don't work with me, the next time you get out of this building, you'll be in a coffin."

He turned away, snickering. "You can't do shit to me because you don't have shit on me."

I put my hands on the table and leaned close to him. "You'd be surprised at what I can do to you."

"You want to waste your time, you go right ahead, Detective."

"I'm going to give you some time to think this through. I'll be back in a couple of days."

Before Tristan could say anything, I walked to the door and motioned for the guard to open it up.

"Hey, Detective," say Tristan, smiling from the table. "Can I ask you something?"

The guard unlocked the door and stepped inside. I gestured for him to wait near the exit while I walked back to the table. Normally prisoners take a day or two to stew before contacting me.

"Yes?" I asked, drawing the syllable out.

He gestured for me to come closer. I kept my eyes on his hands and then leaned in another inch or two.

"Your wife still wear that tablecloth on her head when she goes outside?"

My body went cold. He shouldn't have known that Hannah wore the hijab. Not unless he had seen a picture of her. I looked over my shoulder at the guard. "Did you hear what he just asked?"

The guard nodded, and Tristan gave me a toothy grin. For most of my adult life, I've stood across metal tables just like this one, staring at men and women just like Tristan Salazar. Almost every time, I've felt something inside me, something very dark, try to claw its way out. It begs me to lash out, to hurt those people who would hurt others. At one time, I would have given in. I would have punched Salazar from across the table and broken his nose. I'd probably even call it justice and argue that he deserved it for threatening my family.

But that's not justice, and it never made me feel better anyway. I put my hands on the table and leaned forward so I could look Salazar in the eye. I had read his police jacket before coming over. He was thirty-three, and we'd arrested him multiple times for nonviolent felonies, most recently for auto theft. Most of the people we arrest for nonviolent felonies aren't bad. They grew up in poor neighborhoods with terrible schools, few employment opportunities, and little chance to make something of themselves. Had I seen Salazar's arrest record without knowing anything else about him, I might have recommended him for an alternative program, one that taught job and life skills, rather than locking him up. Salazar, though, had a mean streak and a violent temper. I had no doubt that he had left a string of bodies in his wake; we simply hadn't caught him yet.

"You may not know me, but I know you. You're in for auto theft, and you've got a year left on your sentence."

"That's right," he said, crossing his arms.

"I'm also pretty sure you were murdering someone with Santino Ramirez the day Angel Hererra died."

He pursed his lips but didn't say anything.

"You looking forward to getting out next year?" I asked.

"I got some plans."

I smiled, but I refused to allow any goodwill into it. "Then you had better hope nothing happens to my wife or anyone else I care about. On the street, threatening people probably makes you sound cool or scary. Here, it implicates you in a conspiracy to commit murder. If anyone so much as lays a finger on her, they'll bury you here."

I didn't give him the chance to say anything before leaving the room. On the way out, I asked the guard to put him in isolation so he couldn't contact any of his friends on the outside.

If he had threatened me, I could let it go. But Hannah was a civilian. He wouldn't get the chance to hurt her.

Chapter Seventeen

Nobody could hurry the steps required to leave a prison, so it took me almost forty-five minutes to reach the lobby and pick up my stuff. By that time, the guards had finished searching Salazar's cell. They found and confiscated a couple of pornographic pictures, but no cell phone or other contraband. That disappointed me, but I still had leads to follow. I checked my voice mail as soon as I got my phone back. Paul Murphy had left me three messages, his voice growing increasingly urgent with each message. The first message simply asked me to meet him at a crime scene. The second asked for my location, while the third said that if I didn't call him back within the hour, he'd put patrol on notice for my car.

As soon as the messages finished playing, I called him back.

"Paul, it's Ash. What's going on?"

"I had your wife and kids picked up, and I've got people looking for you now. You okay?"

"I was going to ask you to pick them up, so thank you. And I'm fine," I said, crossing the asphalt toward my car. "I've been visiting a prisoner at Pendleton. What's going on?"

"We found our killer's safe house. They know where you live, they know what you drive, and they've got the weaponry to kill you before you even see them coming. We found AK-47s, AR-15s, and enough ammunition here to stock a small army."

I held my phone to my ear with my right hand and looked at the landscape around me. I was alone, so no one could overhear me.

"Slow down. Where are you?"

"A house in the Bates-Hendricks area. The place should be empty, but people have been staying here for the past few days. One of the neighbors let us in. We found a *Santa Muerte* shrine covered in human blood on the first floor, maps and surveillance photos on the second floor, and a clean room in one of the bathrooms. We ran a bomb-sniffing dog through. We think they had explosives, but they're gone now."

I arrived at my car but didn't open the door yet. "Tell me about the surveillance photos. Who are they of?"

"Your family, for one thing. That's why I had them picked up. They've also got pictures of the judge who presided over Santino Ramirez's trial and everybody else who worked the case."

I nodded and let my mind process that for a moment. From Paul's description, the people who had stayed in that house had surrounded themselves with the implements of war. Heavy weapons, surveillance photos, maps, explosive devices, and a room in which to make more. There was no telling if this was even the only safe house they had. This gang could hit us where we didn't expect it and then slink back to the darkness before we ever got the chance to stop them.

I ran my hand through my hair. "This just got a whole lot bigger than a couple of murders. Have you talked to Special Agent Havelock since that first briefing?"

"No," said Paul, his tone a little softer. "What would Havelock have to do with this?"

"I don't know yet," I said, opening my car door. "Are you still in the house?" I asked. He said he was. "Describe the room you're in."

"Why?"

"Just humor me," I said.

He grumbled, but I could hear the floorboards creak as he turned around. "I'm in a bedroom. There's a camp stove near the window, a pair of sleeping bags in the center of the floor, and surveillance photos and maps tacked to the walls. There are three AR-15 rifles in the corner and three boxes of ammunition beside them."

"And there's a clean room down the hall," I said.

"Yeah."

"You ever heard of gangbangers engaging in that level of planning?"

"Not usually."

"Have you ever seen it?" I asked.

Paul paused for a moment. "You think we're dealing with domestic terrorists?"

"I don't know yet, but Agent Havelock came to your initial briefing for a reason. He mentioned the name Miguel Navarra. He's come up at least twice so far in my investigation. I think we need to find out everything Havelock knows."

"I'll give him a call, then," said Paul.

Even though we were fifty miles apart, I shook my head. "Havelock and I go back a ways. Let me handle him. You work your case."

"I'm getting tired of being kept in the dark, Ash."

"I don't mean to keep you in it," I said, quickly. "As soon as I find something, you and Mike Bowers will be the first two people I call."

He told me that had better be the case and then hung up. Special Agent Kevin Havelock and I had worked a case together a couple of months back, so I had his cell number in my call history. I sat down in the driver's seat of my VW and called. Unfortunately, his phone went straight to voice mail.

"Agent Havelock, this is Detective Ash Rashid with IMPD. We need to talk off the record about *Barrio Sureño*. I think you know something, and I think you're holding back on us. We've got enough victims as is. If you can help us close our case, I would be very grateful. Please call me back."

As soon as I hung up, I waited, half hoping he'd call me back immediately. That didn't happen, but I didn't expect it to and I had other calls to make. So far, I had resisted calling on my network of informants, but I had one in particular who could probably help me out a lot. He'd want something in exchange, though, something expensive. Given our present situation, I couldn't see any other option but to pay. I slipped my phone back in my pocket and then drove northeast to a Speedway gas station a couple of blocks away, out of eyesight of any of law enforcement officials.

Truthfully, the informant I planned to call was probably the most dangerous man in Indianapolis. He had professional hitters at his beck and call, and I knew of several murders in which he played an active role. He's a bad man, no doubt about it, but because of him, I've taken out a human trafficking ring that sold children for sexual exploitation, I've arrested one of the Midwest's largest distributors of cocaine, and I've stopped a group of rogue police officers from murdering innocent people to cover up their crimes. Every single tip Konstantin Bukoholov has ever given me, in fact, has paid off, but every single tip has also given him something important, something he couldn't have achieved but through my help. He uses me, and I use him.

I make no excuses for the things I've done. Bukoholov is a murderer, and in an ideal world, I'd arrest him as soon as I could. I don't live in an ideal world, though. In my world and in my experience, justice is a compromise, the least bad choice in an array of bad choices. In a world like that, one where you deal with true and radical evil, sometimes you've got to deal with the devil behind the backs of the saints.

Once I was sure none of the drivers around me were paying attention, I got out and popped the trunk on my car and then lifted the fabric trunk liner to expose the cavity that held my spare tire. Beneath that tire, I kept a prepaid cell phone. I grabbed it and entered the only number in its call history.

"Mr. Bukoholov, it's Ash Rashid," I said, closing my trunk.

"It's good to hear from you, Detective Rashid. I heard about your friend Michelle. I'm very sorry."

Michelle's death had obviously made the news, but my relationship with her hadn't. The fact that he had heard confidential information about a case didn't even take me aback anymore. The man had resources the federal government would have envied.

"I appreciate that. I'm calling to ask if you've ever heard of a gang called *Barrio Sureño*."

He paused, but for just a second, and I walked around my car to sit on the front seat. "Up-and-coming Hispanic gang run by an ambitious young woman named Carla Ramirez."

I lowered my chin. "Carla? You're sure about that?"

"I wouldn't have mentioned her if I wasn't sure. I maintain an interest in certain industries, and I watch the men and women who run them."

And by that, he meant he watched his competitors closely, probably so he could kill them or recruit them when needed. I hadn't considered Santino Ramirez's wife in our murders yet, but I should have. Santino beat her so often and so soundly that she likely knew the physicians at the ER on a first-name basis, but she still stayed at his side, even through his trial and death sentence. Maybe she still loved him, or maybe he had some other hold on her. Either way, if she ran the gang now, I needed to find her.

"That gang is killing people around town. I'm going to take them out, top to bottom, and you're going to help me."

"Why would I do that?"

I didn't always like the world I lived in, but I couldn't escape it. A lot of well-meaning people believed that if we just rounded up the drug dealers from bad neighborhoods and sent them to prison for the rest of their lives, we'd make the streets safer, we'd get rid of the drugs, and we'd turn our urban neighborhoods into peaceful, wonderful places to live. The real world doesn't work like that. In my world, if I take one drug dealer down, five more will stand up to take his spot. Sometimes that transfer of power and territory occurs without violence, but not often, and usually the innocent suffer the greatest number of casualties.

I grimaced before I even spoke.

"Because you're going to take over their territory. You do that, we both win. The streets will be safer, and you'll expand your reach into new areas without firing a shot."

Bukoholov paused, presumably thinking the situation through. I wouldn't say we trusted each other, but we hadn't tried to screw each other over, either, and I needed him to bite on this.

"No."

I opened my mouth, surprised and uncertain what to say. "What do you mean, no? If I do this, you get his territory. This isn't a scam, and this isn't a trap. I'm asking for your help and proposing more than adequate consideration."

"Respectfully," said Bukoholov, speaking slowly. "I know my limitations. You should as well."

Again, I didn't know what to say. I had only known Bukoholov for a few years, but I had heard stories about him and the things he had done. He kept old-world gangsters from New York, Chicago, and Cleveland out of Indianapolis with just a whispered threat, and he had a reach that extended into countries I barely knew existed. He could make a phone call, and I'd be dead within the hour. Never once had I ever heard of him backing down from a threat or a challenge.

"Who are you scared of?" I asked, my voice barely above a whisper.

"I'm too old for anyone to scare me," said Bukoholov. "*Barrio Sureño* unnerves me. Their leaders partner with some extraordinarily dangerous people."

"Like who?"

Bukoholov took a deep, raspy breath. "Miguel Navarra. He represents and manages the interests of the *Zetas* cartel in the midwestern United States. As your friend, I'm warning you now. If you endanger his business interests, he will murder your entire family without hesitation or remorse. I can't protect you from him, and I will not act against him."

I hadn't asked for protection, but I appreciated the warning. It also told me something important: Agent Havelock definitely knew more about *Barrio Sureño* and its business dealings than he let on.

"What's Miguel's relationship to *Barrio Sureño*?"

"From what I hear, he supplies them methamphetamine and weapons. I have little interest in either trade, so I know little about it. That's really all I know."

That explained the guns Paul had found, at least. My department could take on most any manner of crime, but only if we had time to prepare.

"They've threatened my family," I said. "They already sent somebody to kill me."

Bukoholov paused, but I could hear him breathe. "Then get them out of town. In light of the business we've conducted together, I might be able to make a phone call to at least get your wife and children off their list. That's the only help I can provide in this matter."

"Is *Barrio Sureño* really that dangerous?"

"My business thrives because I don't find out. I advise you to adopt a similar attitude. Is there anything else?"

I shook my head and sighed. "If you can't help, I guess not."

"Then the next time we speak, I expect to hear a little deference in your voice. For your services, I am willing to give you wide latitude, but never presume to give me orders again. Is that clear?"

Even though it was just a simple phone call, I could actually feel myself shrink back.

"Yes."

He hung up, and I sat still, my hands trembling ever so slightly. Bukoholov with his veins full of ice water may have been too old for anyone to scare him, but that old man scared me. I didn't know what could unnerve him, but I didn't want to find out. I took a few deep breaths, and once I had regained my composure, I slipped my throwaway phone into my pocket and pulled out my regular phone to call Agent Havelock once again. Like before, my call went to voice mail.

"It's Ash Rashid again. You haven't called me, but I would very much like to get in touch with you. I know you're holding back on us, and the more I learn, the more nervous I get. I know Miguel Navarra is a member of *Los Zetas*, and I know he is in business with Carla Ramirez and *Barrio Sureño*. What do you say you call me back before more people die? We both know it's going to happen unless you help me."

I didn't know if I had just lied to him or not, but I at least sounded as if I knew what I was talking about. After that, I put my phone in my pocket, turned on my car, and headed back to Indianapolis. When I arrived at the City-County Building about an hour later, I took the elevator to the homicide unit's floor and took over the first vacant desk I could find. I wanted to take Bukoholov's advice to heart, but I couldn't back off now, not with a threat to so many people still out there. Besides that, the old man had given me a lead. Carla Ramirez. Maybe if we could get to her, we could shut this down before the situation escalated.

I started by looking her up on the state's criminal record database and the FBI's National Criminal Information Center's database. She was thirty-five years old and had never been arrested as an adult, but she had a long juvenile record, including multiple arrests for possession, two assaults, and three counts of public intoxication. She had even witnessed a murder when her boyfriend, David Acosta, had shot and killed a man named Reggie Johnson. I vaguely remembered her record from my investigation ten years ago, but we had such a strong case against her husband that I never considered her a suspect. Perhaps I should have.

I ran my fingers through my hair and then behind my neck. Nothing in her record frightened me, but Bukoholov's warning did. At the very least, it told me I shouldn't try to confront her without more information. I looked up David Acosta, her murderous boyfriend, next. The Department of Corrections had released him six years ago after serving a six-year sentence for manslaughter, and according to his parole information, he currently lived in Avon, a suburb west of town. That didn't sound like the typical *Barrio Sureño* member, but if he had committed a murder with Carla, he might have kept in touch with her. I called the number listed as his cell phone and waited through three rings for him to pick up.

"This is Detective Sergeant Ash Rashid with IMPD. Are you free for a few minutes?"

He hesitated and lowered his voice before speaking. "I'm at work."

Not what I expected from a gangbanger. I leaned back in my chair, hoping to sound relaxed. "Oh, yeah? What kind of work do you do?"

"I build kitchen cabinets."

Again, not what I expected from a gangbanger, especially one who spent time in prison. For many men who went to prison, even a six-year stretch turned into a veritable life sentence. Every employment application in the world asks if the applicant has ever been convicted of a crime, so no matter how smart he is or how well an ex-convict fits a position, he rarely gets the job.

"You work for a company or on your own?" I asked.

He again hesitated. "For a company. Look, I'm not supposed to be on the phone. Can I call you back?"

Normally, I work around a source's schedule, but I needed information and didn't have time to wait.

"That's not how this works," I said. "Can you meet me somewhere in about twenty minutes?"

"I'm at work, man. I can't lose this job."

I tried to make my voice sound understanding. "Don't worry about it. That's fine. How about I get the name of the company you work for from your parole officer and come by tomorrow morning? Your boss does know you have a parole officer, doesn't he?"

I could hear the tremble in his voice now. "And you have to meet me now?"

"I'm working a time-sensitive case. If you help me out, I'll minimize the inconvenience. I'll even write your supervisor a note telling him you had to take off because a detective needed your help in a murder."

"Don't do that," he said without hesitation. "I'll just tell him that I'm not feeling good."

I grabbed a notepad out of my pocket. "That's fine with me. Tell him whatever you need to tell him. Now where can I meet you?"

"You know Highway 36 in Avon? There's a sports bar called Opening Day. It's in a shopping center."

I didn't know it, but I could look it up. "Can you be there in twenty minutes?"

"Yeah," he said.

"Good. See you then."

I hung up and tossed my phone onto the seat beside me and put my notepad back into my jacket. I had come on a little strong on the phone, but the call had clearly terrified the man. I tapped my foot on the floor and then rubbed my eye sockets with the palms of my hands. He would have brushed me off if he was the big, badass murderer I originally thought, but he could still shed some light on my case and Carla Ramirez. God knew I was getting tired of sitting in the dark.

Chapter Eighteen

I left the office immediately and arrived at the bar within twenty-five minutes. As David had said, it sat in the middle of a strip mall beside Highway 36. I parked in the lot out front and checked my badge to ensure I still had it on my belt. The bar's interior matched the sporting theme quite well. The ceilings stretched high above my head, and somebody had painted the walls a deep green. Projectors played ESPN on two screens on the west wall, and maybe a dozen people sat around the bar and nearby tables talking and drinking. Walking inside, I heard the clink of glasses and sucked great lungfuls of the familiar alcoholic smell that permeated every bar I've ever stepped foot inside, and I felt almost like I had just stepped into an old friend's house. It felt comfortable, far more comfortable than it should.

I put my hands in my pockets and felt the leather keychain in my right pocket. If anybody in the world saw that keychain, they'd think nothing of it. Objectively, I knew it was just a strip of leather cut out and stamped with the word *Baba*. My daughter had made it for me in some kind of summer program at the YMCA. Feeling it between my fingers reminded me, though, why I didn't drink. Since going to AA meetings, I've met a lot of people who lost their families because of their addiction. I couldn't let that happen to me. My kids and my wife are all I've ever wanted in the world.

More than the meetings, more than any number of steps, they keep me sober and made my sobriety worth the fight.

I pulled out a chair from one of the pub tables near the bar and sat down. A young woman in black jeans and a white T-shirt came over almost immediately to take my order.

"Can I get a Coke, please?" I asked, looking around. The girl nodded.

"Is that it?"

"Yeah," I said. "I'm meeting a guy named David Acosta. He might be a regular. You know him by chance?"

She nodded again and smiled. "Sure, I know David. If I see him, I'll let him know you're here."

I watched TV until the waitress came with my soda. David Acosta—I recognized him from his license picture—came very shortly after that. He had a rounded face, spiked black hair, and sawdust on his jeans and T-shirt. At first glance, he looked like the kind of guy I'd suspect of being the class clown in high school, but something about his movements changed my perception. His eyes darted around the room, and he walked on the balls of his feet. Whenever he walked past someone, he made sure to stay well out of arm's reach. Those habits had probably kept him alive and well in prison, but they marked him to those who knew the signs as a man who had spent time behind bars.

He walked directly to the bar and then looked around nervously before my waitress directed him to my table. I nodded to him as he walked up.

"Thank you for coming. I'm Detective Ash Rashid."

"The news says you murdered that Dante Washington guy."

Wasn't exactly how I wanted to start our conversation. "I shot him while defending myself. I didn't murder him."

He nodded but his expression didn't change.

"Do I sit down, or what do I do?"

"Sit down," I said. "Have a drink if you want one."

He pulled out a seat across from mine and sat down before nodding at my drink. "What are you having?"

"A soda. I don't drink anymore. You want something, order it. It's on me."

He nodded to our waitress and ordered a beer. When she left, he looked at me again.

"What do you want?"

"I'm here for background information on a murder suspect. If you tell me you committed a crime, I can use that in court, but I'm not here to bust your balls. I just need information on Carla Ramirez."

He started to say something, but I held up a hand to shush him, having noticed our waitress walking toward the table, a bottle of beer in her hand. She set the drink in front of him, and he nodded to her before grabbing the bottle and taking a quick pull.

"I don't know how much I can help you," he said, tilting his beer bottle on end and rolling it in a circle pattern on our table. "I haven't seen Carla in like fifteen years, since we were in high school."

He didn't look away when he said that. Maybe he wasn't lying.

"That's okay," I said, nodding and clipping my badge back to my belt. "Her name's come up in a murder investigation."

He furrowed his brow. "Not her dad, is it? Because I didn't have anything to do with that. I was in Pendleton then."

I hadn't come about her father, but any background information could help. "Tell me what you know about her dad."

He looked down at his drink and mumbled something. I asked him to speak up.

"He knocked up a girl who went to our high school. I think he paid her for the sex. It was gross."

Middle-aged men having sex with high school girls was gross. And illegal.

"He ever get caught?"

David hesitated. "Not by the police."

I waited for him to say something else, but he didn't. "What happened to him?"

He quickly looked down at his beer. "He OD'd. He did a lot of drugs, but I heard Carla switched his stash with something stronger."

Carla had several juvenile arrests for possession, so she had clearly had access to drugs, and if he had slept with her friends, she could have had motive to kill him. "She'd do that?"

He nodded and took a deep pull on his beer, his brow growing red. I've been a cop long enough to know the look. David had a burden on his soul, something he wanted to free.

"Tell me about her."

He started talking and didn't stop for half an hour, telling me a story about a far different young woman than the one I had met ten years ago. In his narrative, Carla had a void where her heart should have been. David had loved her, and he believed she loved him, but now he knew otherwise. She dealt drugs and used David as her muscle to ensure people paid her. One day, she told him her supplier, a man named Reggie Johnson, had sexually assaulted her during a routine drug buy. David killed the guy for it. He committed murder, plain and simple, but because Reggie had a gun on him, the prosecutor let David plea-bargain to manslaughter. Carla never visited, never called, never sent a letter, never answered the letters he sent her. Years later, after his release, one of Carla's high school friends confided in him that Reggie had never touched Carla. David killed a man and went to prison because a drug dealer had called his girlfriend fat.

"She took six years of my life," said David. "I've got an okay job now, but what happens if my boss finds out I'm on parole? I lose my job, I lose my apartment, I lose everything I've earned." He paused and took a long pull on his beer. "I wanted kids, you know? A house, a wife. Now I share an apartment with a convicted child molester."

I wanted to say something comforting to the guy, but I held back. As much as he thought otherwise, he wasn't the innocent victim here. Whether or not Carla manipulated him, he had murdered a man. You do that, you deserve to pay in this life or the next.

"I'm sorry for what's happened, but thank you for meeting me. It's been a big help."

"You're not going to tell my boss about me, are you?" he asked.

I shook my head and stood up to leave. "No. You've paid enough."

"Thank you."

I nodded to him, and as I did, I saw the bartender pour a shot of bourbon into a two-ounce whiskey glass. I shouldn't have been able to smell it from where I stood, but my brain seemed to believe it had superhuman powers at the moment. If I closed my eyes, I could practically feel the alcohol bite into my throat and slide down my chest.

Even with one slip up this week, I thought I'd be okay going into a bar again, but I wasn't. I needed to go back to my station and research Carla Ramirez further, but I needed out of that bar even more. So I pulled my phone from my pocket and called my wife to tell her I was on my way to Yasmine and Jack's, giving me a reason to leave immediately and to avoid going to another bar or liquor store on the way home. Hannah, unbeknownst to her, did me a favor by asking me to pick up Megan from a friend's house on the way.

I could use a friendly face after the afternoon I had just had.

I had difficulty with the first steps out of the bar, but they got easier after that. By the time I reached Sydney's house, I hardly even wanted a drink anymore, and by the time I saw my daughter's face light up when she saw me, my urge had gone completely.

As soon as Sydney's mom opened the door and called for my daughter, she sprinted toward me and gave me a hug, filling me with a contentment alcohol could never match. Megan talked nonstop on the drive to her aunt and uncle's house, filling me in on both the schoolyard gossip and the scuttlebutt about our neighborhood. When we passed the grocery store, she stopped speaking and practically squealed.

"*Baba*, I almost forgot. We need to go by the grocery store and get some ice cream. *Ummi* wanted some."

I smiled. "Did *Ummi* want some, or did you want some?"

She rumpled up her face as if I had gravely insulted her, but then she smiled again as some new thought entered her mind. "Did you know Detective Paul picked us up today?"

"I did know that," I said, nodding as I turned into Jack and Yasmine's driveway. "He was there to keep you guys safe."

"You can never be too safe."

I wondered who had told her that. Before I turned off the car, I nodded down the street to a small neighborhood park we had passed on the way in.

"You want to go to the playground in a few minutes?" I asked. "I'll push you on the swing."

"Really?" asked Megan, a smile breaking across her face. I nodded. "You mean I don't have to do my homework?"

"You still have to do your homework, but we'll go to the park first."

"Okay," she said, throwing open her door and jumping out. I didn't know where she got the energy. I unbuckled my seat belt and opened my own door in time to see Megan walk through the front door and announce to anyone listening that the two of us were going to the playground, but Kaden had to stay with *Ummi*. I didn't remember the latter stipulation, but it worked out for the best because Hannah had just put Kaden down for a nap.

While Megan put on some warmer clothes, I kissed my wife hello and then walked down the hallway to the guest bedroom my son slept in. I stopped at the door and watched the sheets rise and fall with his breath, hoping I'd get to hug him at least once before the night was through.

About ten minutes after we arrived at Jack and Yasmine's, my daughter emerged from the bedroom she had taken over wearing a bright yellow sweater and blue corduroy pants. Hannah must have laid the clothes out earlier because rarely did my daughter choose to wear anything but pink. I helped her put on a coat, and then we began walking to the playground. Megan talked and laughed and giggled the entire time, reminding me why I do the work I do. Mark Pennington, the boy I had found tied in Danny Navarra's basement, could play on a swing tonight because I had gotten him out of there before the house collapsed. No matter what else happened in the case or in my career, I still had that, and I thought it'd be enough.

The temperature drove us home pretty quickly from the playground, but we both had fun for about fifteen minutes. I held her hand as we walked to my in-law's' house; I think she liked that. When we got to Jack and Yasmine's, Hannah and my sister-in-law had just started making dinner. I told Megan to wash her hands in the bathroom, and Yasmine excused herself from the room, giving me a private moment to greet my wife. I put my arms around her back, and she slipped her hands behind my neck.

"Are you here for the night?" asked Hannah, smiling directly in my eyes.

"In fact, I am home for the night," I said, leaning forward to whisper in her ear. "I am also open to your sexual advances and dirty talk at any time. Just letting you know."

She smiled and then lowered her voice. "I don't know if that's appropriate in my sister's house."

I pulled my head back and raised my eyebrows. "Inappropriate or not, doesn't it sound like fun?"

"We'll talk later."

We had a nice evening. Megan stayed up for another forty minutes, and then the adults sat down to a board game. I didn't usually like board games, but I liked the company. For the entire time I was there, nobody mentioned the news, nobody mentioned Dante Washington, nobody called me a murderer. I appreciated that. About halfway through the evening, I felt my phone buzz in my pocket, so I excused myself and glanced at the screen. The caller had a phone number from the block reserved by IMPD, but no name came up. I walked to the kitchen and then answered.

"This is Ash Rashid."

"I'm so glad to talk to you, Detective Rashid."

The caller's speech sounded gravelly and very slow. It was probably too low to belong to a human being. My wife and kids had surprised me with a similar phone call once, having purchased an app online to distort their voices.

"Who is this?" I asked, leaning against the counter.

"You'll find out soon enough," said the caller. "I just left Gail Pennington's house. I've left a little surprise for you in the basement."

"I don't think so," I said, shaking my head. "If you were at the Penningtons' place, you would be under arrest right now."

"I'm afraid Officer Dennison and Officer Osbourne are a little the worse for wear right now. They won't be arresting anyone anytime soon."

My heart jumped a beat. "Excuse me?"

"There I go ruining part of the surprise. Check out the basement for the rest of it."

The caller hung up. For a moment, I just stood there, staring at my phone, trying to figure out what had just happened. Then I heard Hannah and Jack and Yasmine laugh from the front room, which brought the world back into focus. My hands shook ever so slightly. Whether that came from adrenaline or something else, I didn't know. I left the house through the kitchen door and walked into the backyard. Not a single cloud obscured my view of the stars, but I couldn't focus on the view. I dialed the dispatcher and tried to swallow back my increasing sense of unease.

"This is Detective Sergeant Ash Rashid. I need a status check on officers assigned to watch Gail and Mark Pennington."

The dispatcher asked me to hold on, so I paced the length of the porch for the next few minutes, trying not to overreact but wondering what the hell had happened. Every time I stopped and turned, I felt my heart beat a little harder.

Finally, I heard a click on the line, indicating the dispatcher had returned.

"I can't raise them on their radio or cell phones. They're probably in a poor reception area."

I closed my eyes, feeling as if someone had just hit me with a hammer.

"It's not a poor reception area," I said. "I need Gail Pennington's address, and I need backup to meet me at the house. We've got officers down."

Chapter Nineteen

I didn't have lights or sirens on my VW, but I drove as fast as I could anyway, flashing my brights at anyone who got in my way. The Penningtons lived on the northwest side of town, directly south of the Woodstock Country Club, in a neighborhood called Golden Hill. Night had cloaked the area in shadow by the time I arrived. Two patrol vehicles met me on the side of the road a block from the Penningtons' house. Trees and dense vegetation surrounded us, lending the area homes a bit of privacy but also blocking most of the moonlight. I parked, stepped out of my car, and met three uniformed officers near my hood. I had hoped for more people, but I'd take whomever I could get. The first two officers looked young, maybe mid-twenties to early thirties, while the third could have probably retired at any time. He had a swagger and confidence about him that I saw on a lot of older officers, a look that said *"I've seen everything, so don't try to pull anything on me."* That attitude got people shot.

"The dispatcher tell you what's going on?" I asked, walking around my car to the trunk. I pulled out a tactical vest and a flashlight. All three officers stopped walking.

"We were just told a detective needed assistance before searching a house," said the old-timer.

"You were told wrong, then," I said, putting my arms through the vest as if I were putting on a sweater. I rarely wore that vest, so the Kevlar-impregnated fabric felt stiff and almost unyielding. That'd take some getting used to. "Gail Pennington and her son, our homeowners, were abducted several days ago and found in the basement of a home on the north side of town. After their rescue, Officers Kimberly Dennison and Doug Osbourne were assigned to guard them. I just received a phone call telling me Kim and Doug are dead and that we've got a surprise in the basement. Since then, our dispatcher has been unable to raise anyone on the radio. Get your tactical vests and get a shotgun if you're rated for one. We're going in."

The two younger officers jogged back to their cruiser, but the old-timer stepped a little closer. "Shouldn't we call the Violent Crimes Unit for this? They're better equipped than us."

"I'd love to call them in," I said, flashing my light at the ground to make sure it worked. "But we don't have time. We might have live victims in there, so we're going in. Get a vest. If you're not comfortable with that, you can hang out by the back door and make sure no one can get out."

Almost as soon as I finished speaking, a pair of bright headlights turned down the road. As the vehicle came closer, I saw that the headlights belonged to a full-sized van with an extendable antenna for live broadcasts. The media had already arrived, which likely meant somebody—maybe even our killer—had tipped them off. I swore under my breath.

"Belay that last order. Your job is to keep these assholes busy."

"That I can do," said the old-timer, holding up his hands for the van to stop. I left him to his devices and joined my younger colleagues beside their cruiser. One held a shotgun, while the second carried an M4 tactical rifle. A lot of US soldiers carried M4 rifles during the wars in Iraq and

Afghanistan, and since our department recruited vets heavily, many of our younger officers had a deep familiarity with the weapon. It seemed like overkill for most jobs, but if we got into a firefight, I'd be grateful to have it nearby.

"We'll sweep the perimeter. If we find a threat, we'll back off and call in SWAT. If we don't, we're going to clear the house and detain everyone we see inside. Our officers, if they are still here, will be in uniform. Questions?"

Neither of them had any, so I took a breath and led them toward the house. The Penningtons had a red-brick Tudor-style home, set back from the road and partially hidden by mature trees. A brick walkway led from the street to their front door, while a thick, waist-high stone fence surrounded the property. It'd offer protection as well as concealment in case someone started shooting, so I nodded toward my officer with the M4 rifle.

"Stay behind the fence and cover us."

"You really think someone's waiting to shoot us?"

I wanted to snap at him, but I held my tongue and counted to five. "I don't know. That's why you're going to stay back there. That's not a suggestion."

I turned, and the officer with the shotgun and I crouched in the shadows cast by an oak tree as we crept along the home's exterior. Lights illuminated several of the rooms, but nothing stirred inside as far as I could tell and none of the windows looked broken. The side of the house had vegetation along the fence line so dense that I couldn't see the road.

As I squinted, hoping my eyes would adjust to the dark, a breeze kicked up, carrying with it the faint, almost coppery scent of fresh blood. I flicked on my light and sucked in a sharp, surprised breath. Officer Dennison lay on her back about ten feet from us, her eyes still open and her hands empty. She wore a navy uniform and a puffy department-issue jacket with a badge over the right breast. Someone had slit her throat.

"Oh, Christ," said the officer behind me.

My heart started to pound and I could feel my adrenaline spiking off the charts.

"Keep it together," I said, forcing a measure of calm and strength I didn't feel into my voice. "But get on your radio and call this in. We've got an officer down."

My partner jogged back the way we had come, and I squeezed the grip of my firearm hard before creeping forward again to round the back of the house. The night air had frozen the moisture on the lawn, leaving it slick. Unlike in the side yard, the home's designer had installed floodlights to illuminate the back. Evergreen hedges cordoned the yard from the street, giving the homeowner privacy for a cedar play set in the far corner and a red-brick patio directly off the rear of the home. Even though the neighbors lived just a hundred yards away, I felt completely isolated from them.

With the floodlights on, I presented a clear target to anyone in the house, but no one started shooting or came running. I had the feeling the people who had killed Officer Dennison had long since left. Doug Osbourne wouldn't have let his partner die alone, so I knew we'd find his body here somewhere, too. Maybe the Penningtons had gotten out, though.

I rejoined my team behind the stone fence in front of the home. I couldn't see their faces in the dark, but I could hear their ragged breaths. The one with the shotgun whispered frantically into his radio, and while he did that, I looked at the guy with the rifle.

"We've got to find Officer Osbourne and the Penningtons."

He hesitated. "Shouldn't we wait for backup?"

"Not if people are inside dying. Let's move."

He adjusted his grip on the rifle, but I didn't give him a chance to hesitate before walking up the path toward the home. Like before, nothing stirred in the windows. The front door looked like heavy, solid wood with a black wrought-iron knocker tacked to the center. I directed my new partner to stand on one side of the door, while I stood to the other and tried the knob. The door swung open with a creak, exposing the wood-paneled interior. Doug Osbourne lay on the floor, his mouth open wide in a surprised O. He hadn't worn a vest. Someone had shot him twice in the chest, likely with a low-caliber weapon judging by the size of the entry wounds.

"Keep it together," I said, carefully stepping inside before the man behind me could say anything. "We need to find the Penningtons."

Of course, I already knew where I'd find them. My caller had left us a surprise in the basement.

I followed the smell of gasoline through the front hallway, to the kitchen, and finally to a nondescript six-panel door beside a walk-in pantry. I turned the brass doorknob, and my partner gagged almost immediately. Over the years, I've been to a lot of death scenes, four of which involved incinerated bodies. I've never forgotten that smell, and even though I couldn't see Mark and Gail, I knew what waited for me at the bottom of those stairs. My caller had finished the job he had started in Danny Navarra's house, only this time, I hadn't been around to pull them out before the fire reached them.

I turned and looked at my partner. "Wait up here."

He nodded, gratefully it seemed, and I took the steps down, slowly, reverently, knowing I had entered a tomb. The Penningtons had left the basement unfinished, but they had installed fluorescent lights on the ceiling. A smoky haze hung in the air, and as I reached the bottom step, I recited a prayer for the family before me. Gail and Mark lay on the ground. Black, charred skin covered their faces and chests, but the flames had been so intense on their lower extremities that the flesh had rendered off completely, exposing blackened bones. Mark had clung to his mother, and she had held him against her breast, the cast still on her arm and wrist from where I had broken her hand. I hoped that final hug had given them some measure of peace, for they had clearly died in agony.

Chapter Twenty

One look at Mark and Gail and I knew why *Barrio Sureño* unnerved Konstantin Bukoholov. The old man might have been willing to kill his enemies, but he wouldn't touch children. The people who could burn one alive...I didn't know what to think of them. My chest felt tight, and I wanted to vomit, but I had work to do and it didn't involve me brooding. I took the stairs to the first floor. My young partner waited for me in the kitchen, his face ashen.

"Did you find the homeowners?"

I nodded and tried to say something, but my throat felt thick. I swallowed hard and then coughed to clear my throat.

"Yeah, I found them." My voice threatened to crack, so I coughed again, hoping it would lend me strength. "They're dead. We need to clear the second floor."

He nodded and followed me through the kitchen and then upstairs. As we walked on that plush carpet in the hallway, I felt like I was floating, like the world moved around me while I stood still. We went through each of the rooms on the second floor, checking the closets, beneath the beds, in cabinets, everywhere someone could hide, to make sure the house was empty. Throughout the search, my mind stayed in the basement, on those I had left behind. After searching the last bedroom, I walked to the top of the steps.

I heard it, then. A tapping noise and a pair of soft footsteps that could have belonged to a child. Or to someone attempting to ambush us.

The hackles on the back of my neck rose, and I slowly removed my firearm from its holster.

"Downstairs," I mouthed. My young partner nodded and positioned himself behind me on the steps. I appreciated the carpet because it'd muffle our footsteps, but I didn't like our position. In a firefight, the second floor would give us a tactical advantage, but I didn't plan to shoot anybody if I could help it. If we had found our killer, I wanted to take him alive.

I took the first three steps and then crouched and pivoted so I could see the entryway, my weapon held in front of me. I found a small Asian woman with a cell phone staring back from the front hallway. Kristen Tanaka, a reporter with one of the local television stations.

"Who are the bodies in the basement, Detective?"

I didn't lower my firearm. "Drop the cell phone and slowly put your hands on your head."

Instead of dropping anything, she held the phone toward me and hit a button, presumably snapping a picture. She turned the phone toward herself and then touched the screen. "My producer knows I'm here, and now my Twitter followers know you're pointing a gun at me. Are you really going to shoot a second unarmed person in a week?"

I put my weapon back in its holster. Reporters were tricky. Even if I had cause to arrest her—and I did have cause here—the amount of ill will she could create would overshadow any good it did. There were better ways to deal with her.

"You're illegally trespassing at the scene of a quadruple homicide."

She titled her head to the side. "Who are the bodies, Detective Rashid?"

"That's none of your business," I said, taking the stairs down to look her directly in the eye. "Give me the phone."

"I push one button, and photos of your victims go straight to my Twitter feed and the six o'clock news. Come on, Ash. We can help each other out here. I'm just doing my job. Whose house is this? I've already got a researcher looking it up."

Tanaka and I had run up against each other before. She was pushy, which I could respect, but her moral compass left much to be desired.

"If you refuse to put your phone down, I will Tase you."

She tilted her head down and smiled, blinking rapidly. "That doesn't look like a Taser."

"How about the one behind you?"

She turned to look over her shoulder, and in that time, I stepped forward and wrenched the phone from her hand, causing her to stamp her foot like a child.

"Give me my phone back."

I ignored her and looked at the screen. She had already posted the pictures to Twitter and her station's Facebook page under the caption "Breaking News. Caution: gruesome." I jerked my head up to look at her.

"Do you have any idea what you just did?" I asked.

"I broke a major story, a quadruple homicide involving two police officers."

"No," I said, shaking my head. "You just posted pictures of four dead human beings—one of whom was a child—before we could even tell their families."

She crossed her arms and stuck her chin out at me. "I'm doing my job. Cut the self-righteous act."

I held out the phone. "Take your phone and get scarce."

She snatched the phone from my hand. "Is this where you threaten me?"

My hands started to tremble. "Get out of here before I arrest you for trespassing and interfering with my investigation."

She hesitated, and I gritted my teeth.

"Get out. Now."

She practically sprinted out the door. I balled my hands into fists and exhaled through clenched teeth. I looked at my partner. "Follow her out and make sure she gets back to her truck. Then find out how she got in."

He nodded and jogged out after her. My entire body trembled. If I stayed in that house, I knew I'd do something—punch a wall, slam a door—that would potentially contaminate the crime scene, so I walked to the front lawn and pulled off my tactical vest. The cold air hit my throat, opening it up slightly. We sorted out the Kristen Tanaka mess easily; her cameraman and the producer she had brought with her had made such a scene that the old-timer I had asked to deal with the media needed help. He called my officer stationed near the front door, and while those two dealt with that situation, Kristen climbed through the hedges from two houses down to infiltrate the Penningtons' home.

I put the old-timer on the logbook and asked the other two officers to deal with crowd control until backup arrived. After that, things settled into a familiar, easy routine. As always happens when an officer goes down, police officers came by the dozen in civilian vehicles and in patrol cars. I used some to work the scene and sent the others home. Paul Murphy arrived maybe twenty minutes later to take over. His face was ashen and somber, his brow red. No smile met my gaze and no jokes seemed forthcoming.

"You heard?"

He nodded. "Yeah, I heard. The whole city's heard. I know Tanaka's done some awful things before, but this..." His voice trailed off, and he took a breath and then shook his head. "Doug Osbourne's wife found out he died by watching the six o'clock news. That's not right."

I wanted to scream and shout, but I couldn't. Paul and I were the two most senior officers in sight, which meant we both needed to appear cool and collected so that the officers under our command knew what to do. All the while, beneath the surface, my temper simmered and my grief for families I barely knew grew. Mark Pennington was eight years old, just a few years older than my daughter. When I closed my eyes, I still saw him wrapped around his mother's body, and it tore me up inside. But I swallowed it down because our team needed a professional in charge.

"It's not right," I said. "And we'll deal with her when we can. In the meantime, you need anything else from me?"

His eyes focused on me. "Your statement about what happened, but that can wait."

"I'll make myself available. Meantime, I've got some stuff to do."

Paul nodded and then turned and started directing officers working the scene. While he did that, I called Mike Bowers on his cell phone. He answered on the fifth ring.

"It's Ash. Have you been watching the news?" I asked, looking around to make sure none of the reporters had managed to sneak through the police barricade.

"Yeah."

"I think Detective Murphy needs some assistance out here. This could get real ugly if our officers' families arrive."

Bowers sighed. "I'm already on my way. Meantime, we need to talk. You didn't handle Kristen Tanaka well. She was clearly in the wrong, but that's going to come back on you. I can guarantee that."

"Then this will really piss her off. You should subpoena her phone records."

Bowers actually chuckled. "Say again?"

"We need her phone records. She got here the same time I did. No one had even called 911 yet, so I'm guessing the person who called me called her, too."

He paused. "If you're serious, her station's going to fight you with all they've got. The way she uses social media, she'll have us looking like thugs out to crush free speech."

"We've got four bodies, including two police officers and a child. If you don't go after her, you'll have a revolt from the rank-and-file."

I counted to five before Bowers said anything. "I'll talk to the Sylvia and the prosecutors. Maybe we can work out something with Tanaka's station."

"Good. Get on that."

I hung up before Bowers could respond, already planning my next step. Kristen Tanaka wasn't the only person willing to manipulate public opinion through the media. We needed to play some offense. I walked to the police barricade. The cameramen congregated around me immediately, jockeying and shoving each other aside for the best shot, their bright lights blasting my face. I squinted and held up my hand, waiting for my eyes to adjust. When they did, I saw a number of familiar faces, the ones I saw every time I turned on the evening news. I had given interviews to a couple of them, so I knew they were mostly good people. Others, though, were opportunistic assholes.

"Detective Rashid, can you tell us what happened tonight?" asked a reporter.

"First of all, I didn't come out here to speak as Detective Rashid. I'm coming here to talk to you as a father, and a human being. Four people, four very good people, lost their lives tonight. None of them and none of their families deserve what happened to them. None of them deserved what one of you did tonight, either."

One cameraman started to lower his camera, but the others stayed riveted on me. They probably hoped I'd start screaming at them, threatening them. A video like that posted to the Internet could get their stations national attention.

"I understand yours is a competitive business in which seconds count. I also believe there are lines you don't cross, no matter the competitive advantage it may give you. At least one of you spoke to a killer tonight. You were given this address, and you arrived well before anyone called us. You took pictures of our victims, and you broadcast them before we could notify their families. You hurt people needlessly to benefit yourself."

I searched for one reporter in the crowd. "Ms. Tanaka, you crossed a line that shouldn't have been crossed. I just want you to know how deeply ashamed I am of you. Our officers gave their lives protecting two innocent victims. A mom and her eight-year-old son lost their lives tonight. The least you can do is respect their deaths."

I took a breath and then a step back, feigning resignation when more than anything in the world I wanted to shout at her. "That's all I've got. The department's public relations team will give an official statement later."

The lights of the cameras dimmed. One of the uniformed officers manning the barricade clapped. A second officer joined, but it didn't go beyond those two. I appreciated their support, but I hadn't spoken for their benefit.

One short speech wouldn't make the public turn on Kristen Tanaka, but we needed to put her on the defensive. It might be the only thing that kept her from screwing us in the future.

That done, I walked back to my car and called Special Agent Havelock. His phone actually rang this time, and he picked up after two rings.

"Detective Rashid," he said. "That was quite a moving speech. Channel 7 ran it live."

"Yeah. We need to talk. If you refuse, I'm going to the press with everything I know about Miguel Navarra."

Which was precisely nothing. Hopefully he wouldn't call me on the bluff.

"You remember the Hardee's we met at a couple of months ago?" asked Havelock. "Meet me there in half an hour. I've got to get something out of my office."

"See you then."

Chapter Twenty-One

I left the crime scene and took I-70 east across town and then I-465 north to Castleton. My meeting was in a restaurant parking lot beside a strip mall on the corner of Eighty-Sixth Street and Allisonville Road, just a couple of blocks from the FBI field office. Even with little traffic, it took me almost twenty-five minutes to get there. The stores around me had closed hours earlier, but the fast-food workers still toiled away, likely cleaning the place for the night. I doubted they'd want to see me this late in the evening, so I stayed in my car and waited. Havelock arrived in a black SUV approximately fifteen minutes later. The last few times I had seen him, he had the preened look of a man who took his appearance very seriously. Now, though, he wore an Indianapolis Colts sweatshirt and a harried expression on his face.

We both rolled our windows down at the same time. Before I could tell him anything, he waved me over to his car.

"Get in. It's too cold to sit outside, and I'd rather not yell from car to car."

His car did look a little more comfortable than mine, so I stepped out and climbed into the passenger seat of his SUV. Almost immediately, he reached to the seat behind us and handed me a thick stack of papers. After that, he put his car into gear and began reversing out of his parking spot.

"Before we talk, I need you to sign that document," he said. "There's a pen in the glove box."

I shook my head. "I'm not signing anything until I get some answers."

"And you're not going to get any answers until you sign that. This is a sensitive topic, and that's a non-disclosure agreement." He pulled out of the parking lot and onto Eight-Sixth Street. "If you don't want to sign it, I'll drop you off right here."

As an attorney, I've seen a lot of non-disclosure agreements, but rarely have I seen one that went over five pages. This had to go on for fifty.

"This is a lot more than a non-disclosure agreement."

Havelock pulled to a stop at a light on the corner of Allisonville Road and Eigthy-Sixth street. "That's the same document my agents sign when earning their commission. The federal government needs a guarantee that we can trust you."

I flipped through it to see if anything immediately stood out for me. The agreement looked fairly standard except that a violation of it could result in the Department of Justice filing treason charges against me. If I needed to, I was sure I could find a way around it. I signed with a pen from my jacket pocket and looked at Havelock.

"I've signed it. Now what else do you want?"

"What makes you think I want anything else?"

I threw the agreement onto the seat behind me. "Because you finally agreed to meet me. You think I can give you something. What?"

I didn't know if he'd answer me at first, but then he drew a deep breath and squinted while looking at me. "You like living in Indianapolis, don't you?"

"It's home," I said, nodding.

"Well," said Havelock, shrugging, "my home is Washington, DC. When the bureau promoted me, I thought this would be a temporary assignment, but I've been here for five years now. I'm three years from retirement, and I'd like to spend those at home doing something worthwhile. You're going to help me get there."

I had a feeling I knew what he wanted, but I wanted to hear him say it. "Oh, good. I thought you wanted something difficult. You get the truck, I'll help you pack it up. No problem."

Havelock didn't even smile. "I want Leonard Wilson, and I want you to help me bring him down."

Leonard was the prosecuting attorney. I knew he had done some illegal and despicable things in his life, and I knew he had received money from questionable sources for his most recent election, but I hadn't expected the FBI to have an interest in him.

"Should I be insulted?" I asked. "You used to want me."

He tilted his head to the side. "That was before I got to know you. Over the last couple of months, our forensic accountants combed through your finances pretty well, but we couldn't find any irregularities that would indicate you're on anyone's payroll but the city of Indianapolis. You got a steal on your house, by the way."

I sunk back into my seat a little. "I'm so glad your illegal search of my finances cleared me of wrongdoing."

Havelock clucked his tongue and shook his head. "It wasn't an illegal search. You give to Islamic charities. It's not hard to find a judge who believes that gives us cause to search through your finances to make sure you're not funding terrorism. I'd offer to show you the warrant, but it was sealed."

That should have disgusted me, but I've heard similar stories enough that I've grown inured to them.

"What's Leonard doing that interests the FBI?"

"We've heard rumors that he picked up where Jack Whittler left off. You prove those rumors right, I'll arrest Leonard on federal corruption charges, and my superiors will take note of my good work and whisk me out of this wonderful town."

Jack Whittler was the prosecutor a couple of years back, and under his supervision, justice had come with a price. He did everything his job required of him—he prosecuted the bad guys, ran the office, kissed the appropriate asses of the appropriate judges—but he'd overlook a lot of transgressions and refuse to prosecute strong cases if given the right price. He also wasn't afraid to harass the enemies of his largest campaign donors. I caught him rubbing elbows with a gangster a couple of years ago and tipped off the FBI. They arrested him, and last I heard, he spent most days in the library of a minimum-security federal prison camp in South Dakota.

Considering IMPD would likely fire me in the next few days, I didn't have much to lose by saying yes. "Sure. Where are we going?"

"We're just out for a drive," he said. "I don't like staying in one spot too long. Civilians tend to get a little curious."

A little justifiable paranoia probably wouldn't hurt any of us.

"I've talked to a couple of *Barrio Sureño* members these past few days," I said. "Miguel Navarra has come up in every conversation. Who is he?"

"Understand that you cannot tell anyone what I'm about to tell you." He took his eyes off the road long enough to see me nod. "He was *Fuerzas Especiales* and retired as a light colonel eight years ago."

Mexican Special Forces. That was another of the many unintended consequences of the war on drugs. While the world's private security forces could only hire so many former soldiers, the world's drug lords had a need for manpower and the seemingly bottomless coffers to hire whomever they wanted. So not only did *Barrio Sureño* have ties to a cartel, they had ties to a man who had hunted and killed other men and women for a living.

"Do you have any idea how many people have died in this past week alone because of *Barrio Sureño*?" I asked, trying and probably failing to keep the anger out of my voice. "Do you have any clue?"

"I have watched the news."

I leaned my head back and looked at the vehicle's headliner. "Then you should have told us. We thought we were going up against a street gang. If we had known that *Barrio Sureño* had ties to men like Miguel, we would have taken precautions. We sure as hell wouldn't have let two police officers guard the Penningtons on their own. These deaths are on you."

I waited, hoping he'd say something, but he didn't. Then I looked over at him. The muscles beneath Havelock's cheeks flexed as he clenched his teeth. "I don't like this any more than you do, but I'm bound by that same document you signed. I couldn't tell you about Miguel."

I wanted to kick something or vent my anger in some way, but all I could do was clench my hands tightly into fists. "You didn't have to tell us about Miguel. All you had to say was that we were dealing with someone especially dangerous, someone we should watch out for. That's it. A little warning that we were going up against a man who could kill our officers before we even knew he was in the room. I don't think that's too much to ask."

Havelock clenched his jaw once again, and then tilted his head down and to the side. "We didn't know if Miguel was involved. We knew he had ties to your street gang, but I had no idea he would involve himself in their internal politics. For what it's worth, I'm sorry."

I looked out the window. "I'll be sure to relay your apology to the families of the men and women he's murdered." Neither of us said anything until I sat up straighter about a minute later. "So Miguel is a drug smuggler. What else do you know about him?"

Havelock drew in a breath and then another, and I knew before his lips moved that he planned to tell me something I didn't want to hear. "He's not a drug smuggler. He ran the *Zeta's* assassination squads. He's admitted to forty-eight murders, but I think we can safely say he's been involved in at least a hundred. Again, though, I didn't expect him to become involved in your street gang. He's strictly a cartel hitter."

I squeezed the door handle to my right to keep from hitting him. "You son of a bitch. You knew we would come into contact with this man, and you did nothing. Two cops are dead because of you. They had families, kids, spouses. This didn't have to happen."

Havelock sighed and looked down at the steering wheel. "I understand how you feel, but now isn't the time to berate me or my employers. I'm here to help you prevent any future deaths. Before we get to that, there's something else you should probably know."

I crossed my arms. "What?"

Havelock turned the SUV into a residential neighborhood and then glanced at me. "Santino Ramirez didn't murder Angel Hererra. On the day Mr. Hererra died, Santino Ramirez and Tristan Salazar were in Nogales, Mexico on Miguel Navarra's orders murdering the deputy chief of police. Our sources indicate that Tristan drove a pickup truck while Santino rode in the back and shot the chief's vehicle with an automatic weapon."

I threw up my hands. "That's just terrific. We sent a man to death row for a murder he didn't commit, and you could have stopped it with a phone call. Thank you very much."

Havelock didn't say anything as he drove deeper into the neighborhood. After turning down two streets, he pulled to a stop in front of a Garrison colonial and turned the vehicle's lights off but kept the engine running.

"Miguel Navarra is the highest-ranking member of *Los Zetas* that we've ever turned. Because of him, we've interdicted two tons of methamphetamine before it reached our streets this year alone. I understand that you've lost people, but do you know how many lives we've saved because of Miguel's tips?"

I shook my head. "That doesn't matter."

"It does matter. You go to the border towns in Mexico or even in the United States, you'll find the war on drugs is a very real war being waged by men armed to the teeth and willing to kill so they can keep selling poison on our streets. My superiors decided that we couldn't risk losing a very valuable asset to save the life of a murderer."

I held up my hands. "I don't care about Ramirez right now. I've got four bodies on the ground tonight and two earlier this week. What can you do to help me with them?"

The FBI agent sighed again. "I didn't make the decision to use Navarra. That was way over my head. If I could, I'd send him to prison. Since I can't, I'll give you everything else I can. Manpower, intelligence, whatever you need, but I can't touch Miguel Navarra or this gang."

Havelock's voice held anger, sure, but also real regret. I leaned back and took a breath, giving myself a moment to think that through. "When you came in and met us after Dante died, you gave us Navarra's name purposefully. You wanted us to take him out. You've wanted that since we found Michelle's body."

"I've wanted that for a long time, but that's not the reason I mentioned him. He's dangerous, and I didn't want you walking in with nothing. Giving you his name was the least I could do."

I looked out my window. "At least you got that right. Giving us his name was the least you could do. Take me back to my car, please."

Havelock waited a moment, but then he put his car in gear and drove back to the Hardee's parking lot. Before I got out of the car, Havelock cleared his throat to get my attention. I looked at him and crossed my arms.

"This where you apologize?"

He shook his head. "No. I did the only thing I could to help you out. Now close your case before it blows up any further."

I opened my door but didn't get out right away. I wanted to say something, but I realized before I opened my mouth that I didn't have anything to say. Instead, I merely nodded at him and got out of the car. He drove off, leaving me to smell his exhaust. Had our positions been reversed, I like to think I would have done more, but I don't know. And that's what bothered me the most. Some days, I don't even know what right and wrong are anymore. I climbed into my car and texted Hannah to let her know I planned to stay at our house tonight instead of at Jack and Yasmine's. With luck, no one would shoot me in the night.

By the time I pulled into the driveway, I could feel a need building in my gut. In years past, I would come home in the middle of the night like this and pull a bottle of bourbon from my glove box. I'd drink until I felt better. Some days, I'd only need a little, but other days, the things I saw at work refused to leave until I drank them into oblivion. I'd then go inside, brush my teeth, rinse with mouthwash, and pretend I felt fine. I didn't want to bring the despair, the anger, the hopelessness that I experienced at work home with me. I thought that made me a good father and husband. In reality, it made me a fool who very nearly lost everything important to him.

I turned off my car and stepped out into the cold night, feeling the chill sap my anger, leaving a dull emptiness inside me. I didn't want to see Gail and Mark Pennington when I closed my eyes, but they wouldn't leave. Mark wasn't the first child I had seen die, and I knew he wouldn't be the last, but that didn't make it easier. I sat down on the hood of my car. My text to Hannah said I didn't want to wake anyone up by going to Yasmine and Jack's this late, but I had another reason entirely for going home.

As much as I loved my family, I didn't want to see them right now. I wanted to go to a bar. People in bars didn't need me or ask things of me. They see a man sitting alone with a double shot of Jack in front of him, they figure he wants to be alone. As long as I had a shot in front of me, I didn't have to process the things I'd seen.

As I sat there, staring at my shoes of all things, the kitchen door opened. My wife stepped out, her chest rising and falling and her breath coming out in puffs of frost. She wore a thick pink bathrobe and slippers. Even at one in the morning with no one around, she covered her head with a scarf. At first, her eyes bore into mine, but then they softened and I found myself drawing strength from her.

"I saw the news tonight," she said. "I saw what happened."

I looked away. "And you came here thinking I was drunk, didn't you?"

"I know you're not drunk."

"No, I'm not," I said, looking at the ground. "That is why I came here, though. That's the loser you married."

"We'll go inside and we'll talk." She held out an arm for me to go inside, but I stayed in the driveway. She pulled her robe tighter. "What's wrong?"

I couldn't look at her. "After I found out Michelle died, I went out to a bar. I had five drinks. It was the first time in three hundred and however-many days."

Hannah's posture didn't change, but she blinked rapidly. A tear fell down her face. "I don't know what to say."

"I'm sorry. I thought you should know."

She took a deep breath and nodded, rubbing her arms for warmth. "I saw the pictures on the news tonight."

I started to speak, but my voice cracked and caught in my throat. I swallowed the lump that threatened to form. "Mark Pennington was just a couple of years older than Megan."

"I know," said Hannah, nodding. "You saved him once, but you can't be everywhere."

"They killed his mom because I sent Santino Ramirez to prison."

"No, they didn't," she said, not a hint of hesitation in her voice. "Come inside, Ashraf. It's too cold to stay outside."

I didn't try to argue with her. I simply stood and walked inside. We sat down on the sofa in the living room without saying a word. Thankfully, she had left the kids at her sister's house. For all of my life, I've thought of myself as strong, able, fit to take on the world, but I'm not. After seeing Gail and Mark and more similar scenes than I can remember, I'm broken. I'm lucky to have someone willing to help me pick up the pieces.

Chapter Twenty-Two

The next day came quicker than I wanted with a 7:00 a.m. phone call. I rolled over and picked up the handset from the end table beside me. It was Ken Schiller, a reporter from the *Indianapolis Star*.

"Who is it?" asked Hannah, draping a hand across my shoulder and snuggling up behind me.

"It's a reporter," I said, putting the phone to my ear and swinging my legs off the bed. Our frigid hardwood floor sent a chill up my spine. "I owe him a favor."

Hannah started to sit up. "I'll put on some coffee. It's time to get up and get the kids anyway."

I didn't shudder at mention of her coffee, but I came close. A couple of years ago, I had a cup, and I swear, my entire left side went numb. I've built up a tolerance to it since then, so it rarely makes me feel as if I've had a stroke, but that doesn't make it stop burning as it travels down my esophagus.

"Coffee would be great," I said, hitting the talk button on the phone. Hannah leaned over to kiss my forehead, and I tried but failed to avoid ogling her chest as I answered the phone. She saw and winked and mouthed *later*. At least I had something to look forward to.

"Ken, it's Ash Rashid," I said, refocusing on my work. "What do you need?"

"Kristen Tanaka is going on the Channel 9 morning show in an hour, and I've heard she plans to talk about Santino Ramirez. You know what she's going to say?"

I blinked and rubbed my eye sockets to wake myself up. "Probably that Ramirez didn't kill Angel Hererra. Don't quote me on that."

"Are you serious?"

I couldn't think of a way to tell Ken anything without violating the NDA Havelock had made me sign, so I simply sighed.

"It's a very strong possibility."

Ken paused, probably to write something down.

"I'm hearing that she's none too pleased with her handling last night."

"You hear a lot of rumors at this time of morning?"

"Occasionally," he said, his voice scratchy. He paused another second and then sighed. "If you can give me some details about Ramirez, we might be able to get ahead of this."

And by that, he meant he didn't have enough to write a story and scoop her.

"If I had anything I could give you, I would."

"All right, then," he said, his voice sounding more than a little crestfallen. "I'll see what I can find without your assistance. Can I call you back for a quote if I find anything?"

"Sure."

I thanked him, hung up, and then met my wife in the kitchen, where she immediately poured me a cup of coffee.

"Everything okay?" she asked.

"For now," I said. "A reporter is going to unveil some big story on an old case I worked. I have the feeling it's not going to paint me in a pleasant light."

"At least you know what to expect," she said, walking to the fridge. "You want some breakfast?"

My sister had recently given Hannah my mother's recipe for *ful medemes*, an Egyptian dish made from slowly cooked fava beans, garlic, olive oil, and other spices. When we were kids, my mom had always topped it off with a hardboiled egg for extra protein to carry us through the day, but Hannah usually put fried eggs on top. Working men in Cairo, my parents' hometown, ate it for breakfast all the time. The way my mother talked about it, you could walk down certain streets in the city and smell the garlic, the cumin, and the oil coming from every open window you passed. Growing up, I had it almost every single morning, not because I wanted it but because my mother kept making it, day after day. I think it reminded her of simpler times before my father died.

I sipped the coffee and shook my head. As usual, my throat almost closed up, preventing me from swallowing. I forced it down somehow and smiled, hoping it wouldn't look too much like a grimace. Hannah furrowed her brow.

"Is the coffee okay?"

"Just hot," I said, standing and taking my mug with me. "I'm going to turn on the news. And thank you, but no to the breakfast." I held up my mug. "I'm good with this."

She smiled and nodded. "I'm going to take a shower. For a brief while, I'll be naked. You should consider joining me."

I looked at my cup of coffee, and then I looked at my wife. "You know, I think the morning news can wait."

I followed my wife to our bedroom. Before the kids came along, Hannah and I had made love almost every morning. I liked revisiting the tradition. As my wife showered afterwards, I walked into the living room and turned on the television. Generally, I'm not a fan of morning shows, local or national. Too much fluff, not enough substance. That morning promised to be different. After two of the hosts made French toast with a local chef, and then a round of commercials, the camera panned to a pair of lounge chairs. One sat empty, but the other held Kristen Tanaka. She wore a form-fitting navy dress that landed on her midthigh and a white, probably silk, shirt to cover her cleavage. She looked dignified and elegant, and she had a somber expression on her face to match the somber news she would likely deliver. She didn't smile, even as the camera zoomed in on her face.

"Good morning. I'm not ordinarily on the morning show, so for those who don't know me, I'm Kristen Tanaka and I'm an investigative journalist for this station. We try to keep our morning program light, but a very serious situation has recently come to this station's attention. Our producers felt the public deserved to know as quickly as possible."

]Outside of work, I'm sure Kristen was a fine person, but at work, I doubted her supposedly altruistic motives.

"I'm here," she continued, "to talk about a man named Santino Ramirez. If you've watched the news lately, you've likely heard of him. If you've not heard his name, he was tried and convicted for the 2002 murder of Angel Hererra and is set to become the first man executed by the state of Indiana since December of 2009." She paused, closed her eyes as if she were nervous, and then drew in a deep breath. "Due to the nature of his crime and his upcoming execution, our station felt that we had to get this information out as quickly as possible. Hopefully it's not too late to prevent a tragedy." She took another deep breath. "Forgive me, but I'm a little nervous. This is probably the most important story I've ever reported. Mr. Ramirez is innocent of the crime for which the state sentenced him. My sources indicate that he was set up by the very police officers who should have protected him."

She paused for dramatic effect and reached to the table beside her for a computer printout.

"A source recently sent me this surveillance photo taken by a camera on the US–Mexico border at 11:14 a.m. on the day Mr. Ramirez allegedly shot Angel Hererra."

A grainy, black-and-white surveillance picture replaced Kristen on the screen. I couldn't see many details, but the image showed two men in a truck. They could have been Ramirez and Salazar crossing into the US after murdering the deputy chief of police in Nogales, but they also could have been two random strangers. In the end, it probably didn't matter. In TV news, perception becomes reality nine times out of ten, the truth be damned.

"That is Mr. Ramirez in the driver's seat and a friend in the passenger's seat. They are crossing out of Mexico after visiting Mr. Ramirez's elderly mother in Nogales."

The picture shifted from a surveillance photo to a road map of the United States with the route from Nogales, Arizona to Indianapolis highlighted in yellow.

"This is a trip of almost two thousand miles and takes over twenty-four hours to drive," she said, continuing. "Even if he had flown, Mr. Ramirez could not have committed this crime."

The picture shifted back to a live shot of Kristen staring directly into the camera, an impassioned look on her face.

"My own researchers uncovered this photo with little difficulty, so it's unclear how the arresting officers missed it. Detective Keith Holliday, the primary detective on the case, gave his life while on duty, but his partner, Detective Sergeant Ashraf Rashid, continues to work with the department."

The picture once again shifted to a still image, this time to a picture of an older African-American couple holding a candle. "This picture was taken two nights ago at a candlelight vigil to remember Dante and Michelle Washington. As viewers may recall, Detective Sergeant Rashid shot Dante Washington in cold blood. This morning, the prosecutor's office released information pertinent to that case. Vials of blood taken from Detective Sergeant Rashid shortly after the incident show that he had an elevated blood alcohol level at the time of the shooting."

Kristen paused. "In other words, he was drunk. The investigation into that shooting is still ongoing."

I stood and turned around, running my hands through my hair.

"It's time for the news media to stand up. In all my dealings with IMPD, I've met good men and women, individuals who come to work every day to do what's right. As a journalist, I report facts and try to keep my opinion out of the story. I apologize for my demeanor this morning, but as the victim of police violence, I can't stay quiet any longer. As a city, we have to say 'no more.' We deserve better than men like Detective Rashid, men who would think it nothing to point a gun at a reporter to scare her off a story."

I balled my hands into fists and started pacing. The phone rang in the kitchen, but I barely registered it.

"Alone," said Kristen, looking past the camera before focusing on it again, "perhaps I can't do much. Detective Rashid is a powerful man with powerful benefactors. There are days I feel like a lone voice crying out in the wilderness."

A humble voice, too. I didn't know Christian theology beyond what I had studied in college, but she had just compared himself to John the Baptist, one of the preeminent figures of the New Testament. Kristen waved someone forward.

"But today, I don't stand alone. I brought somebody into the studio today to amplify my voice." She waved past the camera again. "Carla, if you don't mind, could you step up here, please?"

I stopped pacing and stared at the TV, my hands on my hips. Hannah must have answered the phone; I could hear her speaking.

"You've got to be kidding me," I said, dreading what I expected to happen. I hadn't seen Carla Ramirez in years, but little had changed. She wore a ruffled gray skirt and she stepped diffidently, almost awkwardly, in front of the camera.

"This is Carla Ramirez, Santino Ramirez's wife," said Kristen, standing to greet the new guest. "She has been without her husband for ten years because of Detective Rashid and those who enable him. Ms. Ramirez is a wonderful person, stronger than I can imagine, but she's just a lone voice. I have heard her story, and I think it's time the rest of the city did as well. It's time for us to draw a line beyond which we will not budge. It's time for men who would do our city harm for their own gain to leave."

"Honey," said Hannah, speaking from the hallway outside our living room. I glanced at her. She held the phone in her right hand. "Mike Bowers is on the phone. He said it's important. Everything all right?"

"No," I said, shaking my head and walking and grabbing the remote from the coffee table. Carla started to say something, but I muted the sound. "We just got our asses handed to us on live TV."

Hannah raised her eyebrows and handed me the phone. "That's bad, I take it?"

"Yeah, that's bad," I said, nodding. "And thank you for the phone."

She gave me a faint smile and mouthed *good luck*. I put the phone to my ear. "Mike. Have you been watching TV?"

"Yeah. So has Sylvia Lombardo. She just called and wants to know if we should have a strategy meeting to discuss our response."

That is what a politically savvy person would do.

"If you want to have a meeting, you have a meeting. We've got other things to worry about."

"And that is?" asked Bowers.

I looked at the TV again. The camera had zeroed in on Carla's face. Tears streamed down her cheeks, and even without hearing her voice, I knew how believable she would have sounded.

"Carla Ramirez is killing our witnesses."

Chapter Twenty-Three

Bowers didn't respond for at least a five count. "Say that again?"

"Carla Ramirez is killing our witnesses," I said. "I think she killed Angel Hererra, too."

And the more I thought about it, the more convinced I became. Aside from the eyewitness testimony, we had had solid evidence against Santino Ramirez. We found the murder weapon in his house with his prints all over it. Not only that, we found gunshot residue on his hands and clothes. That wasn't just his house, though. Carla lived there, too. And we hadn't found just Santino's prints on the gun. We found hers as well. And Santino's weren't the only clothes with gunshot residue on them. We assumed Carla had gotten her prints on the gun simply by handling it while it was in the house, and we assumed the GSR on her clothes was the result of physical contact with her husband, but I had a whole different picture now.

Bowers paused. "She looks like a woman grieving her husband's wrongful incarceration to me."

"That's what she wants you to think," I said, shaking my head. "Carla is not who she lets on to be. She's got a pretty heavy record. Look it up."

Bowers had been a cop for a long time, so he should have understood what I meant. He paused.

"If you're right and she killed Angel Hererra, we put an innocent man on death row."

I shook my head and began pacing. "Santino Ramirez is far from innocent, but I know he didn't kill Angel. He was in Mexico at the time of the shooting."

"You couldn't even see the pictures on TV. For all we know, they're selfies somebody took with his camera phone and printed out at CVS."

Wishful thinking wouldn't get us anywhere. Kristen Tanaka might use unscrupulous methods to gain information, but she wouldn't risk herself by going on TV and shouting nonsense.

"I'm not basing this on the pictures. Just trust me. I know he was in Mexico."

I counted to three before Bowers spoke. "How do you know?"

"I can't tell you."

"Tell me you didn't beat it out of a suspect."

"No," I said. "I can't tell you because if I told you, I would violate a non-disclosure agreement I recently signed, committing treason in the process. My source is impeccable. Trust me. This is way above both our pay grades. I stumbled on it, and I wish I hadn't."

Bowers started to say something, but then he lowered his voice. "You're serious about this?"

"Yes. Don't ask me to talk about this. All I can say is that Santino Ramirez didn't kill Angel Hererra. He's a murderer, and he deserves to be in prison, but not for the crime we convicted him of."

"What do we do, then?"

I shrugged. "Let the system work. His lawyers will file an appeal, and the attorney general's office will do their job. That's irrelevant for us because Ramirez isn't killing our witnesses. We should pick Carla up before she kills somebody else."

"Do you have classified information on her, too?"

"No," I said, my mind already moving several steps ahead of me. "But I know her."

Bowers paused, and I could hear him muttering something. "Kristen Tanaka really put us up against the wall. If we pick Carla up now, it'll look like we're harassing a grieving widow. I'll put her under surveillance, but I'm not going to bring her in without something solid." He paused again. "And you need to stick around your phone today. You'll have some news coming in about your disciplinary hearing."

Meaning we had a verdict, so I shouldn't get too involved considering I was about to lose my job. "I wasn't drunk when I shot Dante. You should know that, at least, before you shut me out of everything."

Bowers' voice softened. "I know you weren't drunk. You had a BAC of .03. It's like having a beer. And I'm not going to shut you out of anything," he said, quickly. "Just stay by your phone this morning. We'll watch Carla. If you're right, she's not going to hurt anybody. You'll get news shortly. Okay? Just stay by the phone."

He didn't wait for me to say no before he hung up. I stayed still and rubbed my eyes. I didn't need this right now, not with everything else I had to do. I glanced at the clock on our TV. Half after seven. We had had six witnesses testify that they saw Santino Ramirez murder Angel Hererra. That meant we had six people swear to God to tell the truth and then lie. One of those witnesses was a Baptist minister, and I doubted he made a habit out of lying. I had a lot of questions, and I intended to get some answers while I still could.

I walked into the kitchen, where I found Hannah eating breakfast at the coffee table and reading the news on her laptop. As soon as I saw her, some of the anger I had felt earlier disappeared.

"I need to get to work. If somebody calls, tell them I went out and that you don't know where I am."

She looked up from her laptop. "That's an odd request."

"It's an odd kind of day."

She shrugged and looked back to her computer. "If that's what you want me to do, that's what I'll do."

"I love you."

She looked up and smiled again. "I love you, too. Now go catch some bad guys."

Brian Alexander ran a shelter and soup kitchen for homeless persons just a couple of blocks from the City-County Building, and while I hadn't been there for a while, I had a general idea of its location. I drove downtown and parked in the surface lot beside my building, and then took Market Street east until I came to a gray building with a cross embossed on its side.

When I see homeless people on TV, nine times out of ten, they're drug users who haven't seen a washcloth in years and who simply exist moment to moment, waiting for their next fix. The reality is much more complicated than that. The city has its fair share of drug users, but most of the men and women who visited that shelter had never touched illegal drugs in their lives. They had simply taken a wrong turn somewhere. Maybe they lost a job, maybe their spouse had left them, maybe they had mental health issues. No matter what had happened, they needed help, and Brian Alexander and his wife spent their lives providing it. That made my job that morning even harder.

When I reached the shelter, I found the front doors locked, but someone had propped open the back door, the one that led down into the dining room. I heard a low murmur of conversation wafting out from inside, and I could smell chili, probably that afternoon's lunch. Despite providing services for those down on their luck, the shelter and the area around it appeared clean and well tended. None of the walls had graffiti, someone had freshly swept the concrete steps, and the linoleum floors inside practically gleamed. Someone took justifiable pride in this operation. Our city was lucky to have it.

Since I didn't know the proper protocol for entering at off hours, I put my badge in the front pocket of my jacket and stepped inside. Black-and-white linoleum tile led into the dining room with the kitchen just beyond that. I counted eight people inside, sitting around a white Formica table. Two of them turned and smiled when I walked in. Both were men, and both wore the white collar of a Christian clergyman. The one nearest, an older black man with flecks of white coloring his goatee, waved me forward.

"Come on in. You've got a couple of hours before lunch, but something tells me you're not here to eat."

"I'm not," I said, taking a quick look around the room. It looked just as it had ten years ago. "I'm Ash Rashid, and I'm looking for Brian Alexander."

"Brian's doing the dishes right now," said the minister who had spoken before. "Why don't you have a seat, Officer Rashid? You've had a rough morning. You deserve a break."

Evidently, even clergymen watched TV. The others around the table tittered, but not in a malicious way. I walked forward, and one of the men immediately offered me his seat. It was only as he stood up that I saw his collar as well.

"Are you all ministers?" I asked, looking at the men and women assembled around me. They laughed, as if I had walked into the room in the middle of a joke.

"Most of us are," said the man who had spoken earlier. "I'm Martin." He held his hand out to the woman beside him. "This is my wife, Connie. We tend a church on Capital Avenue. Just so you know, I baptized Dante and Michelle Washington. Their parents are members of my congregation."

I felt the hackles at the back of my neck rise. I took a step back. "I didn't realize. I'm just here to talk to Brian Alexander."

"Doesn't matter who you came to see. You're here," said Martin, gesturing to the lone empty seat at the table. "Have a seat. We should talk."

I really didn't know what to say, honestly. The ministers around town were doing their best to keep the protests against Dante's death from spiraling out of control, but they were standing over a tinderbox ready to ignite at any moment. I sat. Martin started to say something, but I held up a hand to stop him.

"I know what you're going to say, and I'm sorry. I know you don't believe that, but I am. I liked Dante. He was a nice man. If I thought I had a choice, I wouldn't have shot him."

"I know you're sorry," said Martin. "The Washingtons know, too. They're hurt beyond anything I can imagine, and they are both having a real hard time not hating you, but they don't blame you. They know Dante broke into your house with a gun. They want to know why."

I had expected him to come at me guns blazing, so I hesitated before speaking.

"If I could take that night back, I would."

Martin leaned back from the table. "Would you switch places with him?"

I considered lying, but then shook my head. "No."

Martin took a deep breath and then ran a hand across his face. "Thank you for your honesty and courtesy. I'll do my best to extend the same courtesy."

As Martin finished speaking, the other men and women gathered around the table introduced themselves, but I couldn't keep track of everyone's name. In addition to two ministers and their spouses, I met one Catholic priest, two monks from the Order of St. Benedict, and a Jesuit priest. I didn't know what distinguished a Jesuit priest from a run-of-the-mill Catholic priest, but from his serious demeanor, I didn't think he wanted me to know, either.

"So why are you here?" asked Martin. "Unless, of course, you want to help with the lunch service. We can always use volunteers."

"Some other time," I said, shaking my head. "I need to talk to Brian Alexander."

Martin nodded his head and closed his eyes. "And why do you need to talk to our illustrious dishwasher?"

"You know about my morning, so you've been watching the news," I said.

Martin, once again, nodded. "I did see the news." He looked at his fellow ministers. "For those who like to sleep in, Detective Rashid had a few choice words for Kristen Tanaka very early this morning, and in return, she pilloried him on the morning show." He looked back at me. "Anyone with a brain in his head would understand that it was tit for tat."

Several of the men and women around the table grunted their assent, and one, the Jesuit, looked as if he had to stop himself from spitting on the floor.

"I take it you guys don't care for Ms. Tanaka," I said.

"She's a cancer," said the Jesuit. "I hope she gets hit by a truck."

The comment obviously made some of them look uncomfortable, but nobody disagreed.

"Gabriel may have a touch for the melodramatic," said Martin. "And I think he'd be the first to say he doesn't actually wish harm on anyone, but Ms. Tanaka's reporting has occasionally made things difficult in our neighborhoods. She has a tendency to inflame some of our more hotheaded residents."

That summed up my experience with her as well. A couple of months back I had worked a very tough, very high-profile case that required a team I led to sweep a neighborhood for men and women with outstanding warrants. For the most part, the sweep worked out fine and we managed to bring in a number of suspected felons. Unfortunately, we ran into a problem with one house in which the homeowner came at my team members and tried to pick a fight with them. To protect them, my team leader shot the homeowner with a Taser. When Tanaka reported it, she failed to mention that the man our officer Tased had recently beaten his parole officer—a very nice, middle-aged woman—with a lead pipe or that he had come after my team and tried to hurt them. I guess the context got in the way of her story.

"If it makes you feel better, she's not been well received by the department, either."

"I'm afraid that doesn't make me feel better," said Martin. "I, for one, will continue praying for her and hoping for a change of heart." He straightened. "Tell me why, again, you need to talk to Brian."

"For one," I said, tilting my head to the side, "I wanted to make sure he was okay. We've lost some men and women who testified in Santino Ramirez's trial."

"Brian's a tough man," said Martin, smiling. "I wouldn't worry about him too much."

"Do you have the opportunity to minister to gang members?" I asked.

"We all know gang members," said Gabriel, the Jesuit. He crossed his arms above the table. "But I cannot and will not tell you anything we speak about. The private conversations we conduct with our parishioners are our own."

"I wouldn't ask you to violate anyone's privacy," I said, speaking in what I hoped was a calm, commanding voice. "If you see members of a gang called *Barrio Sureño*, could you give them my card and ask them to call me? I want this violence to end, and I want Santino Ramirez to receive the justice he deserves. No one else has to get hurt."

Gabriel considered and then nodded, so I reached into my jacket and pulled out a stack of cards. I only had five or six left, and each of the ministers took at least one.

"Thank you, everyone, for talking to me," I said, standing. "I'm going to see if Mr. Alexander is available."

Before I could leave, Martin put his hand on my forearm, stopping me. He looked directly in my eyes. "Brian Alexander is as good of a man as I've ever met, and I've known a lot of good men. All have sinned and fall short of the glory of God. Remember that before you judge him."

I nodded. "I will."

"I believe that," said Martin, removing his hand from my arm. I nodded to him and then the rest of the table before walking toward the double swinging doors that led to the kitchen. As I passed through those doors, I heard water running and Brian singing, his voice so deep I could practically feel it rumble in my chest from across the kitchen. Two enormous pots of chili simmered on a commercial range on the right side of the room, while a stainless steel walk-in freezer dominated the left. Four stainless steel islands, like desks in a classroom, sat in the center of the floor.

"Brian," I called out. "It's Ash Rashid from IMPD."

Brian turned around. He didn't recognize me at first, but then a smile cracked his chapped lips and he threw me the towel he had on his shoulder.

"We've got aprons in the supply closet," he said. "If you can give me a hand drying, I'd appreciate it."

I considered telling him I hadn't come to volunteer, but he had a pile of dirty dishes on the counter to his left, a pile of clean ones on the counter to his right, and little time before the lunch rush probably began. He could use some help, and I could use some goodwill. I removed my jacket, rolled up my sleeves, and got to work. Since I didn't know where anything went, I dried things as well as I could and then stacked them in what seemed like logical piles on one of the center isles. Despite what seemed like a lot of work, the two of us washed everything in about fifteen minutes, after which Brian wiped his hands on his apron and turned to me.

"Most of the time when police officers come here, they want to arrest one of our guests. It's good to see that's not all you people do."

"I'm not here to arrest anyone," I said, leaning against the nearest island. It must have been bolted to the floor because it took my weight without budging. "I'm here to talk."

Brian reached into the murky water of the right sink and pulled out the drain. When he removed his arm, water ran to his elbow. I threw him one of the towels I had been using.

"Much obliged," he said, nodding. "And I assume you're here to talk to me."

"I am."

Brian nodded and threw the towel into a dirty-clothes hamper near the sink. "How's the drinking?"

I furrowed my brow. "Excuse me?"

"I'm a man of God, Mr. Rashid. You and I may not be of the same faith, but we are of the same flesh. I know its temptations, and I know Michelle was your AA sponsor."

It took me a moment to respond. Brian didn't know me, but he seemed to genuinely care. Martin was correct. This was a good man, and that changed how I needed to approach this. No tricks, no games, no threats. Just questions.

"I appreciate that," I said. "I think you know why I'm here."

"Do I?"

"Santino Ramirez," I said. "You lied on the stand. So did your wife, Dante Washington, Michelle Washington, Valerie Perez, and Xavier Jackson. We haven't been able to find Xavier to warn him of what's going on, so if you could help us locate him, it'd be much appreciated."

Brian smiled. "The X-man is one of our projects that turned out okay. After testifying, he moved to St. Louis to live with his sister and her family. Jasmine and I visited him a couple of years back. He took us to a Cardinals game."

I wrote the information down.

"Ten years ago, you told me you witnessed Santino Ramirez shoot Angel Hererra in the dining room. Where were you really when he got shot?"

He didn't hesitate. He simply flicked his eyes upward. "In my office with Dante and Xavier. Valerie and Michelle were with my wife in our conference room. We were preparing to deliver some meals to our less ambulatory guests. Back in those days, we didn't have GPS on our phones, so we were going over maps. We wanted to make a game out of it, boys versus girls, to see who could deliver their meals first and get back to the Mission."

"When you heard the shots, what'd you do?"

Brian gestured to the pile of dishes behind me. I nodded, and he grabbed a pair of dry, large cutting boards and lugged them to a cabinet beside the stove.

"Same thing I do every time I hear shots. I ducked."

I smiled a little. "What'd you do after that?"

"When nobody shot back, I called the police. Uniformed officers came, swept the building, and then your partner showed up."

I didn't want to get hostile, but he had held back. I shook my head to let him know I didn't plan to let him get away with that. "You've skipped a few steps. Did you talk to those uniformed officers?"

Brian smiled indulgently, patiently. "We've had a few shootings in the area, so I knew we'd have detectives come shortly. I didn't want to have to repeat my story, so I cut out the middleman and told the officers I would only speak to the supervisory detective assigned to the case."

"And that was Keith Holliday," I said.

Brian nodded and then picked up a large sauté pan from the pile I had dried. He ran his hand across the interior and then grabbed a reasonably dry towel. "You missed the handle. You put a dish away like this, it's going to attract ants."

"I apologize," I said. "Did you tell Keith this story about Santino Ramirez doing the shooting?"

"Wasn't a story," said Brian, glaring at me as he ran a cloth over the handle of the sauté pan. He held the pan toward me. "See that? That's how you dry a pan."

"Let's try to stay focused, if you don't mind. You were upstairs when somebody shot Angel Hererra, but you testified that you were in the kitchen with a clear view."

Brian nodded and hung the pan by its handle on a rack above the stove. How ants would reach that, I didn't know.

"I did, and to the detriment of my soul, I convinced the others as well. Your partner understood."

I blinked, sure that I had misheard him. "You told Keith the truth?"

"Yes, I did," he said, taking a clean spoon from a drawer beside the sink and walking to one of his vats of chili. He tasted it and leaned back. "This is going to be just right in a few hours."

"Let's go back to my partner. What exactly did you tell him?"

"The same thing I'm telling you right now."

My mouth almost fell open. "And how did he react?"

"Little less surprised than you are. He simply asked me one question: why?"

I waited for him to continue. He didn't. "Okay. Help me understand like you helped Keith. Why'd you lie on the stand?"

Brian stopped walking a few feet from me. "Somebody had to." Before I could say anything, he held up a hand, interrupting me. "Let me tell you a story about a runaway I met a couple of years back. He never told me how old he was but couldn't have been more than sixteen. Kids on the street called him Noodles because he liked spaghetti so much," said Brian, smiling to himself and leaning against the stainless steel island beside mine. "He'd tell stories like you wouldn't believe. You'd hear him, and you'd laugh so much your belly would ache. You want to know what Santino Ramirez did to him?"

I shifted and looked down to my feet. "Killed him?"

"Nah," said Brian, pausing until I looked him in the eye. "He gave him a gun. Noodles was lost when I met him, but he was a good kid. Now, when I see him, I look in his eyes and I see night without measure. No stars, no moon, no dawn, just cold black. I don't scare easily, but he scares me."

I knew the look, and it scared me, too, although probably for different reasons. In my case, I feared one day I'd find it staring back at me from the mirror.

"The world would be better off without Santino Ramirez, but that didn't give you the right to lie about what you saw, nor did it give you the right to convince others to lie, either."

"I know, and that is something I will have to atone for at the end of my days. Santino Ramirez murdered Angel Hererra. Everybody knew it, but nobody stepped forward. His own wife told me it was going to happen two days before it did. I called the police, but they said they couldn't post someone here indefinitely."

I furrowed my brow. "Carla Ramirez told you her husband planned to shoot Angel?"

"Yeah. She was one of our regular volunteers. Twice a week, rain or shine, she'd come on her lunch break and serve our less fortunate men and women. When she had time, she even stuck around after the lunch rush to help me with the dishes. She was a nice woman who didn't deserve her husband."

During our investigation ten years ago, I saw photos taken from the emergency room documenting some of the beatings he gave her. Murderer or not, he deserved whatever he got in prison.

"So you lied because Carla asked you to?"

"No, Detective Rashid," said Brian, shaking his head. "I lied because I found out Santino Ramirez wasn't alone that day."

I cocked my head at him. "Who was with him?"

"His son, Jacob. Kid was about eight years old. Carla told me he spent winters with his mom in Dayton, but summers in Indy with his dad. I had already seen Santino Ramirez ruin one life, so I drew a line in the sand and said no more.

I told a lie and convinced others to do the same. If that damns me to Hell, that damns me to Hell. Is that what you wanted to hear?"

"No," I said, softly. "But it might tell me who murdered Michelle."

Chapter Twenty-Four

Carla hadn't expected the early morning phone call from Kristen Tanaka's office, but she agreed to stand beside her on the morning show without hesitation. Even though the reporter had no idea what Carla did for a living, she'd owe her a favor and in Carla's business, favors made the world go round. Before the show had begun, Tanaka showed her the picture of Tino crossing the border into the United States on the day he supposedly shot Angel Hererra. She didn't know where Tanaka had gotten the picture or why she chose to produce it now, but Carla doubted it had anything to do with justice. The rich and powerful played by slightly different rules than the common folk, but they played the same game she did. Tanaka expected to get something out of that picture

No matter what happened because of that picture, it didn't matter. Even if the state of Indiana dropped the murder charges against Tino, she had enough information about her husband squirreled away to send him to prison for ten lifetimes. Over the years, he had killed almost a dozen people and buried them on a quarter-mile stretch of Sugar Creek, just north of Turkey Run State Park. Having canoed that same creek, Carla knew that campers oftentimes pitched their tents and drank themselves silly there, having no idea that two entire families decomposed just six feet beneath them. One of those families belonged to the imprisoned leader of an African-American street gang. Had his gang enjoyed ties to a national organization, Tino would have left them alone; since they didn't, their territory had become an acquisition target, one they refused to give up freely. The second family belonged to a man and woman who had organized neighborhood watch groups in an area Tino intended to annex. They, too, refused to give up freely, and they, too, died for their misjudgment.

If the police exhumed the bodies, they'd find bullet fragments they could tie to the very same gun she had used to murder Angel Hererra, only this time, Tino wouldn't weasel out of the charges. This time, he had no alibi. This time, he'd rot for good. She'd make sure of that.

As she hurried out of the television station, salt spread on the sidewalks to keep them from frosting overnight crunched under her heels. She had worn flats, a sensible choice considering she didn't know how much time she would have on her feet that morning. Events had progressed quickly after invoking *Santa Muerte* and murdering Gail and Mark Pennington. Tino's old crews didn't suddenly accept her, but they had begun accepting Jacob, especially when Miguel stood near him. The crew boys had stopped fighting each other and focused on their common enemies, namely the police and the men and women who had put Tino in prison. They wouldn't move without Jacob or Miguel's say-so, but she could rally at least fifteen members of Tino's old crews to their cause. Every day brought new recruits.

Chaos and infighting made things difficult, true, but they also made change possible. Like a forest fire, Tino's execution would wipe the ground clean. She had another week, she guessed, to shape *Barrio Sureño* into the lean, strong organization it should have always been, and that meant she had little time to cull the chaff from the wheat, starting with some of her husband's more questionable business enterprises.

When Miguel Navarra had come into her life, she and Tino controlled a small area and moved perhaps half a million dollars of various products a year. They did reasonably well for themselves, but that success made them vulnerable. They needed partners to expand their territory and to preserve what they had. Miguel provided everything they needed. In those first few weeks, Tino used to stay up at night telling her about the things Miguel had done, about the men and women he had killed, about the business he had secured. Her husband had an infatuation with the man, that much she saw immediately, and she couldn't blame him. A former colonel in the Mexican Army, Miguel had a swagger about him that left women whispering to one another about his availability when he left the room.

He taught her husband how to better utilize his resources, how to instill loyalty in his recruits, how to develop the skills he had inherent in him. For a time, business went well and everyone profited. Then, Miguel began coming to Tino with other ideas. With their trucks and their connections at the border, Miguel and his business partners had an easy time bringing not just drugs but people across the border, and sometimes, Miguel needed help with those people in Indianapolis. Tino stepped in without hesitation, providing manpower where needed.

Each week, Miguel brought twenty to thirty people across the border, across the Great Plains, and into Indianapolis. Carla didn't know how much he charged them, but Tino received two hundred dollars for every person he helped usher into their new life in the US. At first, Tino and his crews didn't have to do much. They stopped the occasional fight, they babysat, and they contacted families to pick up their loved ones. It became a supplemental income, but a quite important supplemental income. Then, Miguel and his handlers became greedy. They realized that some of their smuggled clients could afford far more than whatever they charged in Mexico, so Tino set up a network of stash houses across the city in which they would put migrants after their long journey. Miguel or someone from his organization would then contact the client's family and request more money, sometimes five or ten thousand dollars. Miguel never threatened anyone the first time he made contact, but most people understood the situation and paid.

Those who didn't pay received a body part in the mail, usually a finger but occasionally a toe or an ear if it had an identifying mark. Everyone paid eventually, or their loved ones died. Carla hated the business. She didn't mind killing people when needed, but this had far too much risk and not nearly enough reward. If one person—just one single person out of the hundreds they brought into the US each year—escaped and made his or her way to the police, the soldiers of *Barrio Sureño* would fill death row to capacity. No one should have to operate with that hanging over their heads, and now that she had her opportunity to rid herself of it, she would.

She headed southwest. *Barrio Sureño* rented and maintained a network of warehouses and homes for their illicit trade, but Miguel used one warehouse in particular to stash his more valuable assets, VIP immigrants among them. She drove until she left the city behind and entered an industrial area. Miguel counted a freight company amongst his neighbors, so Carla knew she had come to the right area when she came across a semi carrying a load of what looked like hundreds of wooden pallets on the back of a flatbed. Two more turns, and she saw Miguel's warehouse, a red-brick, two-story building at the end of a rutted lane. She parked beside Miguel's truck and watched as a young man emerged from the nearest door. He had a buzz cut and a sour expression on his face. Her husband would have known his name, where he came from, and the names of the women he had slept with most recently. Tino had a gift for that sort of thing. Carla remembered seeing him once or twice, but she didn't know who he was affiliated with. She'd have to rectify that in the future.

She grabbed her iPad and stepped out of her car and nodded to him. "Excuse me. I'm looking for Miguel. Is he in?"

"You his old lady or something?" he asked, squinting at her and reaching into his jacket with his left hand.

"No," she said, closing her car door and stepping forward. "My name is Carla Ramirez. Miguel and my husband are friends."

He looked at her from her feet to her face, paying special attention to her chest. "You're Tino's bitch? I didn't recognize you."

"I'm Tino's *wife*," she said. "If you call me anything but Mrs. Ramirez, it will be the last thing you call anyone."

He stood a little straighter and then looked around, as if for help. When he found himself alone, he looked back at Carla, but he looked as if he had shrunk two or three inches. "I didn't mean offense. I'm just saying, you're Tino's girl, right?"

He waited, as if for her to say something, but she merely stared at him, unblinking.

"Seriously, I'm sorry, Mrs. Ramirez," he said. "I'll tell Miguel you're here." He started toward the door, but stopped before opening it. "And I'm sorry about Tino. He was a good dude. He was like my hero growing up."

She forced a small smile to her lips. "Tino's not dead yet. Please don't talk about him as if he was."

He nodded and then pounded a fist to his chest before stepping inside. She couldn't hear him through the warehouse's brick facade, but he emerged a moment later, holding the door for her. "Miguel's in his office. He said go right in."

She walked inside. Carla didn't know what its original designers had intended that warehouse to hold, but it now held five shipping containers against the far wall, their doors thrown open and people freely milling about and talking in hushed tones while men from *Barrio Sureño* stood guard. Each container held four or five cots for individuals Miguel had smuggled across the border into the United States. He treated them relatively well as far as these things went—never beating them, never allowing his men to sexually assault the women, even feeding them three times a day—but no one left that warehouse without Miguel's leave. For a select few of those people whose relatives and loved ones refused to pay the ransom, they'd never see the sun rise again.

Carla ignored that scene and crossed the concrete floor to a small enclosed office on the other side of the room. Someone had closed the door but he hadn't bothered drawing the window blinds shut, allowing her to see inside. The room had a desk, a couch, and a television on a wooden stand. Miguel sat at the desk, his hands behind his head and his feet up, while a Spanish-language soap opera blared from the television. As soon as she opened the door, he waved her in.

"Come in, *chica*. You here to make sure we're still treating the product well?"

Carla walked to the nearest window and closed the blinds. "You've always handled this end of the business well, but we need to talk." Once she had closed all the windows and doors, she handed him the iPad. "Someone sent me a link to a blog you should check out."

He glanced at her and then the iPad before reaching into his desk for a pair of reading glasses and tapping the home button to wake the device up. He thumbed through the document she had open for him, but then looked at her.

"What is this?"

"It's a blog written by a journalist from Mexico City who's hired coyotes to bring her from Nogales to the United States. She's writing about her experiences along the way and submitting them via a cell phone."

In fact, Carla had written the blog the night before and had then edited the time stamps to make it look as if the posts had come in over a one-week period.

"What's she saying?" asked Miguel, leaning back.

"Everything. She documents how your partners recruit clients in Mexico, how you bring them across the border in trucks, what happens to them along the way. It's not good, Miguel. She's one of yours." Carla picked up the iPad, browsed until she found the posting she wanted, and began reading. *"Their leader is a former soldier named Miguel. He has the blackest eyes I've ever seen and a hateful mouth."* She turned the screen toward him and pointed at him. "She's talking about you."

"I can see that," he said. He paused for a moment and then exhaled hard and long before nodding toward the nearest window. "Has she talked about this?"

Carla shook her head. "She had to dump her phone before she could, but you know she's going to. Her family's going to buy her out, and she's going to tell the world what we're doing. This is going to hurt business, but worse than that, this is going to bring the federal government down on us. We can't afford that right now."

Miguel tilted his head to the side and shrugged. "Then we'll kill her. Who is she?"

"If I knew who she was, I would have killed her myself. The fact is, we don't even know if it's a woman. Her first post, she says she has to conceal her identity. She might be a man pretending to be a woman." She started pacing the small room. "We get FBI agents in here, we all go down. I told you this would happen."

He held up his hands, palms toward her. "Relax. I'll deal with it."

She turned toward him. "How?"

"We'll ask around. People will talk, I'm sure."

Carla shook her head and then pounded her finger on the desk. "Not good enough, Miguel, not when our lives are on the line. You ever picked apples?"

"When I was young."

"Then you know," said Carla, nodding. "One bad apple ruins the whole bushel."

Miguel looked toward the window and then ran his hand across his face. "We've got almost a hundred people around the city right now. That's a lot of meat to get rid of."

"Then throw a barbecue."

Miguel shook his head again and then took a deep breath. "I'll take care of it."

Carla straightened and grabbed her iPad from the desk and then pointed toward the window in the direction of the shipping containers. "These people jeopardize our business. It's over. Never again. Do you understand me?"

His eyes narrowed. "Do you talk to your husband like this?"

"No, but in a couple of days, my husband will be dead. I'm not going to join him. Clean this mess up."

Miguel agreed, and Carla left the building. More than likely, he'd try to weasel his way out of his responsibility, but it didn't matter. As soon as she secured *Barrio Sureño*, Miguel would die.

Chapter Twenty-Five

I left Brian in the basement of that soup kitchen, unsure what to do. Not only had Santino Ramirez not committed the crime we had convicted him of, my partner had known the eyewitnesses had lied. At the very least, Keith should have told me. We might have disagreed, and we might have fought over it, but partners don't hold this sort of thing back from each other. Had he been alive, I think I would have found him and punched him. Of course, nothing changed what I needed to do.

A cold wind ripped at my cheeks as I stepped back onto the sidewalk, but I ignored it and took out my phone to call Paul Murphy. His phone immediately went to voice mail, which meant he had either run out of battery, entered a low-service area, or had turned it off completely. Any way I looked at it, he wouldn't call me back anytime soon. I left him a message to let him know Xavier Jackson was in St. Louis and that he should try to track him down, when he could, to make sure he was still alive. I called Captain Bowers next, and he answered on the first ring.

"Ash. You're not at home."

"Yeah, I stepped out for breakfast."

I could practically feel him grinding his teeth. "Your lawyer's been trying to get ahold of you. Lot of people need to see you."

"Forget about that for a moment," I said, walking west on Market Street. "First thing: Carla Ramirez definitely killed Angel Hererra. If you look at the evidence, you'll see that we found her prints on the murder weapon and GSR on her clothes. We found the gun on a coffee table in her house, so we just assumed she had touched it. We also assumed she had the GSR on her due to contact with her husband. With Santino in Mexico at the time of the shooting, she's our only viable suspect. Not only that, she told Brian Alexander that Santino would kill somebody in the basement of the soup kitchen two days before it happened. She knew because she planned to do it herself."

I could hear Bowers breathe, but he didn't say anything. Indianapolis had gone through a lot of changes since my childhood, including a major revitalization of the downtown area. Unfortunately, that gentrification hadn't spread much beyond the central core, leaving the landscape even a few blocks to the east and west mostly devoid of industry or life. I had parking lots to my left and right and a parking garage about a block ahead of me. Aside from the homeless shelter, no churches, stores, restaurants, or other businesses lined the streets. The wind whistled through the streets like an Old West ghost town.

"Our surveillance team is still trying to track her down. When they find her, I'll just have them pick her up and bring her in. We'll see what she has to say."

I shook my head and kept walking, hoping I could shake off the chill. "She wouldn't have gone on TV to protest her husband's innocence without some plan to deal with us. We pick her up now, she'll pin it on somebody else. Besides that, she's not doing this on her own. She's got at least one partner. I say we follow her and see where she goes."

"It's a risk. I'll think it over. What else do you have to tell me?"

"Santino Ramirez has a son named Jacob."

"What do we know about him?"

I reached the parking garage and ducked inside the stairwell that led to the second floor to get out of the wind. "Not a lot. Keith and I crawled pretty far into Ramirez's life when we investigated him for the murder of Angel Hererra, but we never found the kid. He was eight when Angel was shot, so Jacob would be eighteen or nineteen now. Carla Ramirez is too young to have an eighteen-year-old kid, so he's not hers. I don't know if he's involved, but we should track him down. If nothing else, he might have heard some rumors."

"I'll put Emilia Rios on that. She has contacts in *Barrio Sureño*'s neighborhood. Anything else?"

"We need to start thinking about how we can keep Santino in prison. He gets out on the streets, he'll be in the wind before the day is done and we'll have bodies from here to Mexico."

"Okay," said Bowers, drawing the word out, clearly growing tired of the conversation. "Anything else?"

I looked at the concrete around me, debating whether to tell him about Keith's subterfuge. If Bowers actually pushed this case, he'd find out Keith had known our witnesses had lied. I didn't know how to handle it, and I was still too pissed off to figure it out.

"That's it."

"Good," said Bowers. "Get over to your lawyer's office. We'll talk later. All right?"

I started to say sure, but he hung up before I did. My heart sort of flip-flopped in my chest. One way or another, calling Randy, my lawyer, would change my life wholly and completely. Seven days had passed since my hearing, seven days since I tried to explain a judgment call, made in the midst of one of the most stressful situations of my life, to three police captains who hadn't been there, who hadn't studied the briefings, who hadn't actually worked a case in a decade or more. It was a lot of power to give three political hacks—everyone that high in the department's hierarchy was more politician than police officer—but that's how the system worked. Those without a whit of understanding passed judgment, while those of us in the trenches, those of us with our arms elbow-deep in filth, were second-guessed at every opportunity.

I didn't want to talk to him, but I couldn't avoid it any longer. I called his office and got his assistant.

"This is Ash Rashid. I'm returning Randy Prather's phone call."

She sucked in a breath. "We hoped you'd call. Randy is entertaining some guests right now. He wants you to come down here ASAP."

Entertaining some guests. How nice for him. He had company.

"You can't interrupt him so we can do this on the phone?"

She hesitated. "You need to come down here, Mr. Rashid."

So now even the office assistant could order me around. Maybe that's what life held for me in the future. I sighed.

"All right. Tell Randy I'm on my way."

I hung up. Randy rented an office in a building on Ohio Street, just a couple of blocks north of me. On the plus side, I knew of a liquor store just a block away from his building, so I could go out and get sloshed in the parking garage if the worst came to pass. I left the parking garage and headed north on New Jersey Street and then west on Ohio.

With the case going on, I had almost forgotten the heavy weight above my head. Now I felt it pressing down on me.

I had passed the bar and I did have a license to practice law in Indiana, so theoretically, I could start applying at law firms. Of course, few corporate law firms would even look at the résumé of a thirty-five-year-old guy without prior legal experience. I could get a job at a criminal defense firm, but that'd feel an awful lot like I was betraying my old colleagues. I'd have to figure something out.

Randy's building had its own garage, and since I didn't know how to get to his office except through the elevator in the garage, I walked inside, passing several cars along the way. A couple in a minivan argued loudly enough that I could hear them even with their doors shut and their windows up, making me hope they had come to see the marriage counselor who rented the other half of Randy's floor. They—and I have no idea who "they" are—say that married couples argue about money more than any other topic. I wondered if Hannah and I would start arguing like that if the department fired me. Hopefully, if we did, we'd find a better place to do it than a parking garage.

I took the elevator to Randy's floor, steeling myself for bad news. I had only met her once, but the receptionist greeted me by name as soon as I stepped into the lobby. She said Randy would be right out, so I sat on an upholstered wooden chair and leaned forward, feeling my nervousness rise. With its stark white walls and gray Berber carpet, the office felt like the waiting room of a hospital, and I felt like a man awaiting the results of a cancer screen.

When Randy came out, he gestured for me to follow him back to his office.

"Good news or bad?" I asked, standing.

"More unorthodox than anything else," he said. "Let's go to my office and talk. There are a couple of people here who need to see you."

Calling the ruling unorthodox did little to assuage my nerves. Like the lobby, the corridor that led to Randy's office had white walls, gray carpet, and white acoustical tiles on the ceiling. I couldn't imagine a more banal decorating scheme. Randy's office, while similarly decorated, had a wall of windows overlooking Ohio Street and a wooden desk and lightly stained bookshelves. As he had said, we weren't alone. Leonard Wilson, the prosecutor, stood beside the window, looking down at the city that had recently elected him, while Sylvia Lombardo, the recently appointed director of public safety, sat in a chair facing the desk.

"Ashraf," said Leonard. "It's good to see you."

I looked at Randy. "Why is this asshole in the room?"

Leonard actually chuckled. In my life, I've met a handful of truly despicable people, people the world would be better off without. Leonard landed somewhere in the middle of that list.

"Don't hold back now, Ash," said Leonard. "Tell me how you really feel about me."

I looked at him. "How about we catch up later? We'll pick up some underage prostitutes. I hear you're into that sort of thing."

He smiled and laughed again.

"Ash, let's just stay calm for a minute," said Randy, in a low, throaty tone. "Everyone is here because we have a difficult situation to deal with."

"And what situation is that? Am I fired or not? Or maybe Leonard wants to accuse me of a crime?"

Sylvia Lombardo stood and turned to face me. "No, you are not fired. Early this morning, Mike Bowers rescinded the charges against you."

I furrowed my brow, confused. "Why?"

"We're not here to talk about the why," said Lombardo. She folded her hands together in front of her sky-blue pencil skirt. "But we do need to talk about your future. You've put us in a tough spot. You're an asset to this department, but your media profile is a little too high for most of our units."

I nodded and crossed my arms. "And by that, you mean I pointed a gun at Kristen Tanaka while she had a camera in her hands."

Leonard laughed. "Your phrasing leaves a bit to be desired," he said, his laugh turning into a smile that translated into his voice. "But you got the gist. That's why we put our heads together trying to find somewhere for you. Sylvia even suggested the prosecutor's office."

I had worked as an investigator in the prosecutor's office for a number of years and knew most of the staff, so it was a good suggestion.

"You didn't want that, though," I said, glancing at Leonard and forcing myself to smile. "Who needs a watchdog?"

Leonard formed one of his hands into a gun and shot me in the head. "Especially when I don't know who's holding the leash." He smiled and glanced at Lombardo. "IMPD has received some bad press lately, some deserved, some not. Sylvia and I have gone back and forth on this all morning. We even butted heads a time or two. We both agreed that we need more than a good PR team. We need to get better, prove to the people who elected us—elected me, at least—that we're taking crime in this city seriously. Together, Sylvia and I decided that we need a unit laser-focused on those cases that might prove too burdensome for our more inexperienced investigators. We need a dedicated major case squad composed of the best officers in the city. You, *Lieutenant* Rashid, are its inaugural commanding officer. Congratulations."

He held out a hand and shot me a knowing smile. There were certain power brokers in the city who wanted me to work in Leonard's office to keep him in line. This was evidently his plan to keep me at bay. It was so transparent, I was almost a little disappointed.

"You going to stop accusing me of things on TV now?" I asked.

"I'll never stop fighting for the people of Indianapolis, if that's what you mean," said Leonard, smirking.

"How about cases of political corruption, then? Will I have authority to handle them?"

His smile never wavered. "We'll have to see about the extent of your authority as time progresses. For now, you don't have a lot of resources. If you want a case, you'll run it through Ms. Lombardo's office. She and I will decide if it's an investigation worthy of your squad's time."

Which put Leonard in a position to deny everything I wanted, leaving me with a do-nothing job without resources, a staff, or any power of my own.

"What if I refuse?"

Leonard shrugged. "Then maybe IMPD doesn't need you." He stood and shook his head at me. "I don't think you're going to refuse, though. And whatever you do, don't screw up. People are watching, and you've got nowhere to go from here but down."

He looked at Sylvia and then to Randy. "Now that I've said my piece, I feel that I should be leaving." He looked at me. "Good luck, Lieutenant."

I watched him leave the room, unsure of what to think. After a moment, I stuck my head into the hall. I couldn't see Leonard, so I went back in the room and shut the door.

"What the hell just happened?"

"The only thing that could happen," said Sylvia, looking at the door. "I don't trust him, though."

"You shouldn't," I said. "He's a snake. He wants me out of the department because I know who and what he is."

She shook her head and reached into her purse. "These are powerful men you play with, Mr. Rashid," she said, pulling out a new lieutenant's badge. She tossed it to me. "You'd better be careful, or you're likely to get burned."

I held up the badge. "What if I don't want this?"

"You care about this department?"

I didn't hesitate. "Of course."

"Then you'll take it." Her voice and face softened. "IA cleared you in the shooting death of Dante Washington, by the way. We'll hold a press conference this afternoon to announce that along with our findings. Kristen Tanaka wants you—and by extension, our department—on trial in the court of public opinion. We're going to make sure the public has all the facts before rushing to judgment."

She looked at my lawyer and then back to me before plastering a huge politician's smile on her face. "Now if you'll both excuse me, I have other meetings to attend." She looked at me. "You should probably discuss with Captain Bowers the next step in your case."

She left the same way Leonard did. I looked at the badge. I had always envisioned myself climbing the department's hierarchy, but this felt wrong.

"What just happened?" I asked, looking at my new badge.

"A miracle as far as I can tell," said Randy, reaching to his desk to pick up a thick envelope. "This is yours, too. It's your new orders and a key to your office. And before you ask, I had no idea what was going to happen until Leonard Wilson showed up. From what I gather, this plan came together pretty quickly. You're not going to get much free advice from a lawyer, but I'm going to give you some: take the job."

I hesitated and then slipped the badge into my pocket and took the envelope from his outstretched hands. "I'll think about it. Meantime, I've got work to do."

Chapter Twenty-Six

I sat in the reception area outside Randy's office to read through my new orders. IMPD has five divisions—Operations, Investigations, Administration, Training, and Homeland Security—and every sworn officer, more or less, fits somewhere within those divisions. Our professional standards unit—Internal Affairs—reports directly to the chief of police, but even they have a place within IMPD's clear-cut hierarchy. According to my orders, I didn't. I reported directly to Sylvia Lombardo, the civilian director of public safety, so unless I went out of my way, I could likely go through an entire week without talking to another officer.

I read through the rest of the paperwork to see if I could find a loophole or some explanation of what my new assignment would entail. I didn't find any of that, but I did discover that I now had an office. Unfortunately, IMPD didn't have an open space, so they had borrowed one from the prosecutor's office. As of now, I worked out of the building on Alabama Street. Objectively, I should have been happy. The prosecutors had a newer building and fresher coffee, and my coworkers would likely be less surly at eight in the morning. Of course, that'd take me even further from actual police work.

I dropped my paperwork on my lap and brought my hands to my face. I had told Randy I had work to do, but I didn't, really. Paul had everything he needed to wrap this case up. With what we had, we had a reasonable shot of proving that Carla had murdered Angel Hererra and framed her husband. She, and perhaps Jacob, had very likely killed our other witnesses as well. Paul had a ways to go to prove that, but once we had Carla and Jacob in custody, we'd match them to prints or hair or other fiber evidence found at the crime scenes, and then the prosecutors would agree to refrain from seeking the death penalty in exchange for the two of them rolling over on the rest of their gang. We had them; they just didn't realize it yet.

And that gave me time to think, the last thing I wanted to do at the moment. I needed a distraction, and luckily, I had a new office to check out. I walked to the building on Ohio Street and took the elevator up. Like IMPD, the floor had a cubicle maze in the center with private offices around the perimeter. Two lawyers sat at desks, watching me, so I held up my badge and nodded to them.

"You know where 1504 is?" I asked.

One lawyer looked to the other and then back to me. "The storage room?"

"I guess that's it."

He pointed to the other side of the room. "It's the one by Jackie Kaminski's office. Good luck."

That didn't bode well for me. I zigzagged my way through the cubicles to the other side of the room and then stopped at a locked door marked 1504 and fished my keys from my pocket. My new home away from home.

I unlocked the door, stepped inside, and almost instantly sneezed. The room had a window facing a brick wall. Little light filtered inside, but it didn't take much light to see that my new office was a shithole. There were filing cabinets stacked two high along one wall and a low-slung wooden desk beneath the window. Aside from the computer someone had set up for me, a thick layer of dust covered nearly every flat surface. Curiously, there was a bottle in a brown paper bag on that desk, and as I crossed the room toward it, I found a note beside it, almost embedded in dust.

Congratulations. - Susan

I pulled the bottle from the bag. Perrier—seltzer water. Susan and I had known each other for a couple of years now, and while we didn't always get along, I couldn't have asked for a more supportive supervisor or friend. She had called me out for my excessive drinking several years ago, something none of my other friends or colleagues had ever done. At the time, I resented her for it and thought she had overreacted, but now, with hindsight, I could see she took a risk to help a friend in need. For that, I respected her more than almost anyone within the city's law enforcement community. I made a mental note to stop by her office on Monday to thank her.

After that, I sat down on my new chair and spun around. When I had gone to law school five years ago, I had hoped to become a prosecuting attorney. I could still do that, I guess. I wouldn't work for Leonard Wilson, but I was licensed to practice law anywhere in Indiana, so I could move to Evansville or Fort Wayne or one of the other smaller cities around the state. I wouldn't be a cop, but I'd have a job that mattered. And that was all I really wanted. It'd be easy to take this lieutenant's position, to coast for the rest of my life and retire in comfort, but that's not who I was. At the end of my days, I wanted to be able to say I had led a life that mattered, that I had helped people, that I had made the world a better place. That was all I wanted.

Maybe this was what I deserved, though. The department couldn't fire me for shooting Dante, at the risk of admitting fault before the inevitable lawsuit his family filed. And they couldn't keep me in a public position, either, for risk of pissing off our community. So they just put me on a shelf.

I stood up from my chair, knowing that if I stayed in one place, I'd just get more upset. At first, I simply walked aimlessly, but then I found myself heading toward the Indianapolis Artsgarden, a glass and steel atrium suspended above the intersection of Washington and Illinois Streets. I bought a paper and immediately flipped to the obituaries section. Both Michelle and Dante had a listing, but the Penningtons and our two officers hadn't made it in yet. The Washington family planned to bury their children on the same day in a dual ceremony. As the guy who had shot Dante dead, I had no business going, so I made note of the cemetery. I'd visit on my own time and pay my last respects to Michelle, my friend.

After that, I tried to read the rest of the paper, but I couldn't focus. I simply sat and watched the cars drive past, thinking. I sat there for maybe an hour before my phone buzzed. The caller had a 314 exchange, which meant it came from outside Indianapolis. I probably should have ignored it considering my mood, but very few people knew my number and those who called usually had a reason. I answered after a couple of buzzes.

"This is Ash Rashid."

"And you have an interest in Xavier Jackson?"

The speaker had a smooth, low voice, one I didn't recognize.

"I do," I said, looking around me quickly to make sure no one had gotten close enough to eavesdrop on my conversation. As befitted such a large-scale atrium, the Artsgarden's designers had installed trees in pots near the exterior windows as well as smaller plants throughout the space. Shoppers from the nearby Circle Center mall hustled through the area, but few stayed long enough to draw my attention. By all appearances, I was alone. "Who am I talking to?"

"Detective Josh White with the St. Louis Metro Police Department. I got a call earlier from Detective Sergeant Paul Murphy. I couldn't get in touch with him, but he left your number as a backup. You work with Detective Murphy?"

"Yeah," I said, glancing down to the badge clipped to my belt. "If you need a name and rank for your records, I'm Lieutenant Ashraf Rashid. You've probably seen me on CNN lately."

He passed for a moment, presumably writing down what I told him. "You're that guy, huh? The one who shot the home invader?"

"That's the one."

"Well, look, for what it's worth—black, white, purple, orange, whatever his skin color—I would have shot the guy, too. If it makes you feel any better."

A lot of people had said that to me lately, but then none of them had been in my position. It's a lot easier to justify something after it's done than to do it yourself and live with the consequences.

"I appreciate that," I said. "You mentioned Xavier Jackson?"

"I did. Why are you asking about him?"

I had never liked these get-to-know-you conversations, although I understood why my fellow officers insisted we go through them. As far as I knew, Detective White had no reason for hostility toward me or my department, but few police officers trusted lightly. We existed in a world of lies. Sometimes we perpetuated those lies, but most of the time, we heard them passed off as truth by men and women who lied as freely as they breathed. In our world, trust came slowly and only with good reason.

"About ten years ago, he witnessed a murder I investigated," I said, settling into my seat. "I've heard he moved to St. Louis and cleaned himself up."

Detective White drew in a breath. "Soooo," he said, holding the syllable out. "This is a personal call?"

"No. Someone has been murdering witnesses from the case, and I want to make sure Mr. Jackson's all right. If he'd agree to it, I'll put him in protective custody."

I counted to five, waiting for him to respond. "Your call's a little late. Mr. Jackson's dead."

My mind refused to hear that, so I asked him to repeat his answer. White, again, told me Jackson had died. The second time, it sunk in, and I slumped down on my bench and rubbed my eyes. I asked my next question hopefully. That'd make it easier to take.

"He get back into drugs?"

"No," said White. "Not that I know of, at least. I ran the X-man as a confidential informant. He ministered to the local homeless community and helped them get into shelters. I know at least five guys who got clean thanks to him. Our working theory is that one of our illustrious drug dealers got tired of Xavier meddling with his customer base and decided to take him out. Anything you can tell me about him?"

I glanced up and ran my hand through my hair.

I just need one break, God. Just one break, please.

"I don't think so," I said. "I don't know any drug dealers in St. Louis. They shoot him or what?"

"I wish," said White. He paused, and I heard a metallic clank followed by a soft sucking sound. I had hung around with enough smokers to know he had just lit up. "They poured gasoline on him and then lit him on fire."

It felt like someone had just hammered a bolt through my spine. My posture shot straight up, and I covered my mouth. Anyone watching probably thought something had bitten me. I didn't care, but I lowered my voice anyway.

"Tell me he's the only murder you've got with that signature."

"He's our only one. What are you telling me?"

I closed my eyes. We were too late. *I* was too late.

"You still there, Detective?" asked White.

"Yeah," I said, hoping my voice didn't sound too crestfallen. "Somebody killed Xavier Jackson because he testified here. We had a very similar murder recently. A 911 dispatcher who testified in the same trial Xavier testified in ten years ago. Your coroner determine when Xavier died?"

"Medical examiner says four weeks ago."

I closed my eyes. Even if we closed it today, too many people had died because of this case. "I'm going to have Sergeant Murphy call you. He's spearheading this investigation, so he'll likely send somebody out to St. Louis to share information."

"I look forward to his call, then."

"Yeah."

I hung up the phone, not knowing what else to say. Seven people dead now—one of whom was a child—because I sent the wrong man to prison. Part of me wanted to find somebody doing something wrong and punch him out, but another part of me wanted to find a bottle of something and crawl into it for a week or two. I leaned forward and rested my elbows on my knees. I could have wept, but instead, I balled my hands into fists.

"God damn it."

I said it loud enough that several people around me stopped mid-step and stared. When I looked up, they hurried off. In normal circumstances, I probably would have felt guilty about that, but now I didn't know what I felt. I called Paul Murphy, but his phone went to voice mail.

"Paul, answer your goddamn phone next time I call."

Again, I attracted the attention of several people around me. None of them had kids, so I couldn't have cared less. They had heard worse. I stood and began pacing in front of the bank of windows overlooking Illinois Street, waiting for Paul to call me back. Evidently, my swearing had received more attention than I thought because approximately two minutes later, a uniformed security guard began walking toward me. A lot of uniformed officers took second jobs as armed security guards, so there was a fair chance the guy walking toward me played for the same team I did. When he got near enough, I pushed back my jacket to expose both my firearm and the badge—now a lieutenant's badge—at my hip. Paul chose that moment to call me back.

"You got something to say, buddy?" I asked the guard.

He held up his hands and took a step back. "We're closing soon. I just thought I'd come over and tell you in case you didn't hear the announcement."

"Why are you closing? It's the middle of the afternoon."

He shook his head and took another step back. "I don't make the calls, sir. I just do what I'm told. And can you try to keep the swearing down?"

"Yeah, I will," I said, reaching into my jacket for my phone. I had no business snapping at a man doing his job, so I softened my voice. "Sorry. It won't happen again."

He nodded and then slowly backed away. I watched him until I didn't think he could hear me and then answered my phone.

"Thanks for calling me back."

"You sounded pissed. I was afraid you'd slash my tires if I didn't."

I put my elbow on the glass overlooking the street and then leaned my forehead against my forearm. The cars below me zipped by as if their drivers didn't have a care in the world. On most winter days, I wouldn't expect to see many people on those sidewalks, but now they were as crowded as the day after Thanksgiving.

"I'm not in the mood for jokes, so just stow that for now."

"All right," he said, his voice serious. "By your tone, I'm guessing you found something and you don't like it."

I looked down at my feet and then pressed off from the glass to resume my pacing. "Yeah, I found something. Xavier Jackson's dead. Doused in gasoline and lit on fire in St. Louis at least four weeks ago."

"You're kidding," said Paul.

"I wish I were," I said, feeling my exasperation rise to the surface and fuel my temper. "He turned his life around after the shooting. The guy became like a community organizer, tried to get homeless men off drugs. And now he's dead, and it's our fault."

"You said this happened at least four weeks ago. It'd be a hell of a coincidence, but we don't know if his death is connected to anybody else's."

I looked around me to make sure the security guards and mall walkers kept their distance from me. Evidently, my body language was hostile enough to create a ring of solitude in an otherwise crowded atrium. I lowered my voice anyway.

"Don't even try to go there. Xavier is dead because we screwed up."

Paul hesitated. "Did you brief St. Louis about our situation?"

He couldn't see me, but I nodded anyway and switched the phone from one ear to the other. "Didn't tell him everything, but yeah. I said you'd call. You should send somebody over there to share information."

Paul muttered something I couldn't understand, but then his voice became stronger. "I'll send Nancy Wharton. She went to college near St. Louis, so she'll know the area. Meantime, where are you?"

"Downtown."

"Good," he said, breathing a little easier. "Come on in. I'm a little out of the loop working this case, but something's going on. Mike Bowers is calling in the troops."

Whatever the reason, I doubted it'd help us any.

"Fine," I said, nodding. "Before you get off, I need to tell you something and I only want to say it once. I got a verdict in my disciplinary hearing."

"Okay," said Paul. "What's the story? You still got a badge?"

"It's complicated."

He grunted. "They didn't put you on probation, did they?"

"No," I said, straightening. "They offered me a promotion."

The word hung in the air for a moment. Out of the corner of my eye, I noticed a young boy carrying a balloon as he stared out the window and walked crookedly toward me. I stepped to the side and tried to smile at his mother as she took his hand and directed him toward the center of the room. Evidently, I was only partially successful, because she hurried back to her husband, clutching her kid like I was some kind of monster.

"So you're Lieutenant Rashid now? How do you go into a disciplinary hearing and leave with a promotion?"

"Like I said, it's complicated," I said, shaking my head. "I don't even know if I'm going to take it. I wanted to tell you before you heard the rumors."

"What rumors?"

"The inevitable ones," I said. "You're going to hear that I'm on the take, that I've got incriminating evidence against somebody important, or that a gangster made all this happen."

"Any of those true?"

I held the phone against my ear with my shoulder and buttoned my coat, pretending not to have heard the question. He repeated it.

"I've never taken a bribe in my life."

Paul whistled. "But the other two?"

"Just drop it, buddy. I'm on Washington Street, so I'll see you in about ten minutes. Try to think of some way we can close this case before somebody else dies."

"Is that an order, Lieutenant?"

"Yes, it is," I said.

Chapter Twenty-Seven

I hung up my phone and slipped it back into my pocket. As soon as I did, I looked around and caught the crowd's vibe for the first time. The Artsgarden connects directly to Circle Center mall, and normally, people leave there reasonably happy. Today, though, people moved a little too fast, and curiously, they seemed to be giving me an even wider berth than normal. Outside as well, I saw two marked police cruisers beneath the awning of the Conrad Hotel and another two parked at the intersection of Illinois and Market Streets. I followed the crowd down the nearest set of steps to Washington Street and then jogged east. The City-County Building was only four blocks away, and by the time I arrived, four news vans had parked in spots out front. All four had their antennas up to broadcast a live feed. A crowd had begun to form on the front pedestrian area.

I skipped the crowd out front and walked to the Alabama Street entrance. Four uniformed officers stood out front, blocking entrance to anyone but authorized personnel. I flashed my badge, walked inside, and took the stairs to the homicide unit's floor rather than wait for the elevator. Bowers must have called in everybody from every shift, because I found twenty or thirty detectives there and more were arriving every few minutes. Paul sat on his desk with

Emilia Rios beside him. I walked through the crowd and joined them.

"What's going on?" I asked.

Paul shook his head. "I've been digging through public records all morning, so I haven't got a clue." He nodded toward Officer Rios. "Emilia says we've got fires all over town."

I looked at her and furrowed my brow. "What kind of fires?"

"The kind with—"

A booming voice from the door nearest the exit interrupted whatever Emilia had planned to say next.

"I need everybody's attention."

The voice belonged to Mike Bowers. He wore a navy pinstriped suit, light blue shirt, and coordinated blue tie. He looked as if he had shaved as well. Normally, Bowers didn't care about his appearance, so whatever had happened, he planned to go on TV.

"I assume most of you have heard rumors about what's going on. For those who haven't, calls started flooding in approximately eighteen minutes ago about a significant quantity of gunfire in the Broadripple Village area. After that, we received news of an explosion on the east side of town and major residential fires at four separate locations around town. We now know that we have six mass-casualty situations involving somewhere between sixty and seventy victims. We expect that number to rise."

He paused to let that sink in. In an average year, Indianapolis had between a hundred and a hundred twenty murders. If these numbers kept going up, we could come dangerously close to meeting that in a single day.

"We don't know what's going on, and we don't know if these events are connected, but we are not taking chances.

Word's coming down from the mayor's office that we are locking the city down. The State Emergency Operations Center is already up and running and coordinating with appropriate agencies, federal and local. We are calling in every single officer we have, including reserves. Once I receive orders, I will share them with your lieutenants and sergeants who will alert you to your assignments, but we are all going to hit the streets shortly. I stress that we don't know what's happening, but I don't think I need to tell you how dangerous this situation could become. There are going to be a lot of frightened people out there, and frightened people do stupid things. Everyone use your heads, use good judgment, and stay safe out there."

When Bowers stopped speaking, the room erupted into conversation, and I felt my heart sink. I closed my eyes.

God, don't let this be a Muslim terrorist.

I'm sure every Muslim who had heard the story shared the same thought, and I hated that. I hated that my kids would have to grow up in a world that demanded they apologize for their beliefs and explain constantly that they didn't believe the same things as the Taliban or *al-Qaeda* or whatever other extremist self-proclaimed Islamic groups were in vogue. I hated everything about it, but I also knew my hate wouldn't solve a thing. If I wanted the world to be a better place, it started at home and in my heart. I had to teach my kids to respect everyone—even those who believed differently than they did—and to stand up when they saw ignorant thugs teaching hate in the name of God. I also had to have the courage to do the same.

Already, I could feel eyes upon me and see the men and women around me edging away. Most of them probably meant nothing by it, but I could see anger in others. The room felt smaller than it had just a moment earlier.

I leaned closer to Paul Murphy so he could hear me over the ruckus.

"I think I need to get out of here."

Paul looked around us and nodded, catching the vibe. "I'll run interference. Take Emilia and meet me in the men's room by the elevator."

Normally, I would have questioned his choice of meeting place, but I didn't think it mattered now. I nodded to him and then turned, apologizing as I forced my way through the crowd. I had almost made it to the door before a young detective stepped in front of me. He had dirty blond hair that had just begun graying at the roots, a cragged, pitted face, and the pitiless eyes of a man staring at something he despised. He started to say something, but then I felt a rough, strong hand prod me to the side. I looked over in time to see Paul Murphy push past me, heading directly toward the detective in front of me.

"Hey, Silverman," said Paul, patting me on the back as he pushed past me. "How's your sister feel about sleeping with big men? I hear she's a wildcat in bed."

I took the hint and hurried past as Paul distracted Detective Silverman. More than likely, Silverman would simply say something stupid and bigoted, but I had enough going on at the moment. We didn't need to add a fight to it. With Paul blocking, I left the office and then opened the men's room door near the elevators. Empty. Good.

"In here," I said, holding open the door. Emilia hesitated and pointed to her chest.

"You want me to go into the men's room with you?"

"Yes," I said, motioning her forward. "Come on."

The bathroom had gray-tiled walls, a rough-textured tile floor, and a white ceiling. The chrome fixtures where I could see them gleamed, and I could smell the cleanser the janitorial staff used to clean the toilets. Paul Murphy stepped through the door a moment later and then twisted the deadbolt, locking the rest of my department out and giving us some privacy.

"Lot less impressive than the ladies' room, isn't it?" asked Paul, raising his eyebrows as he turned to Emilia.

"Cleaner than I expected, though," said Emilia. "Growing up, my little brother could barely hit the bowl. Your aim must get better as you get older."

"Actually," said Paul, puffing out his chest. "Some of us just get bigger—"

"Let's stop right there," I said, interrupting him. "That guy in the office need something?"

Paul waved me off. "He's fine. Just wanted to get something rude off his chest. You don't need to worry about him."

"Anybody else I should worry about?"

Paul took a moment to think, but then shook his head. "No. Those of us who know you and your family have your back. Others are terrified that you'll shot them in their sleep. I wouldn't be surprised if somebody talks to you seriously about radicalism amongst Indianapolis's Muslim community, though."

That'd be a short conversation, at least. Maybe we do have Muslims in the area willing to take up arms and abandon the basic tenets of their faith to murder other people, but I don't know them. I don't want to know them.

"Thank you. I appreciate the heads-up and the help," I said, nodding to him. "We've got to keep working. Xavier Jackson is dead. How do we move forward?"

Emilia looked at me, and then back to Paul, and then to me again. "I thought you were on leave."

"He *was* on leave," said Paul before I could say anything. "But he's back, and now he outranks everyone on this floor but Captain Bowers. It's a rarified world of palace intrigue that Ash inhabits."

"I'm impressed you know what the word rarified means," I said, glancing at Paul. Before he could respond, I started talking again. "Let's talk about the case. Did you ever find Santino Ramirez's kid?"

Paul looked at Emilia and gestured for her to speak. She blinked a few times and then sighed. "I asked around. One of my grandmother's friends said his name is probably Jacob Valdez. His mom ran around with Santino Ramirez in high school, but her parents shipped her off to live with her cousins in Cleveland after he got her pregnant."

I almost closed my eyes and exhaled in relief. "That's good work. We know anything else about him?"

She looked at Paul again, evidently unsure about answering my questions. Hopefully her diffidence would wear off soon because Paul, once again, nodded.

"I heard a rumor that he's been staying in a house in Beech Grove. Nobody seemed to know exactly where in Beech Grove, though."

I didn't know that part of the county well, which meant we didn't get too many serious crimes out there. That told me something interesting, though. I had read a book a couple of years back about Eastern European organized crime in the New York area. I expected the gangsters to hang out in bars or social clubs all day. Some of them did that, but others looked and acted just like normal immigrants. They bought homes on Staten Island or in New Jersey and commuted to the city to do whatever the hell they did. They shopped at Whole Foods. They walked dogs. They bought health insurance for their employees. It shouldn't have surprised me to see organized criminals in Indianapolis move to middle-class neighborhoods, but it still felt wrong.

"Before you get too excited, he hasn't been back to that house for a while and we haven't been able to track him down," said Paul.

"If he lives there, he will be back," I said, settling down a little. "What about Carla? Did you find her?"

"Oh, yeah," he said, nodding. "Our surveillance team found her at a gym she owns. She had her receptionist send out bottles of water and a note that said they were welcome to use the locker rooms if they needed to use the restroom."

If she knew we had guys watching her, hopefully that would keep her from doing anything.

"Good. Call your surveillance team and tell them to pick her up for the ten-year-old murder of Angel Hererra. We'll use that as leverage to get her to roll on whoever she's working with now."

Paul squinted. "You run this by the prosecutor's office yet? Because if we pick her up for Angel Hererra's murder, Santino Ramirez's lawyers are going to raise a shit storm."

"I suspect they're raising a shit storm anyway," I said. "This isn't going to change that."

"It's your call, Lieutenant," he said, already turning away. "I'll call my team and have her brought in. You got somewhere you want to take her? Because we're kind of busy here."

"We'll find somewhere."

Paul nodded and then started his call. I leaned against the sink and looked down at my feet. It didn't take Paul long to start swearing. Both Emilia and I looked at him at the same time. His face had gone red, and a vein throbbed in his forehead.

"Please don't tell me we've got another body," I said.

He tilted his head to the side. "No. The brass pulled everybody in for this fire thing, including our surveillance team. They left her twenty minutes ago. She's in the wind."

"Didn't they say they were on an assignment?" I asked.

"Deputy chief himself called their lieutenant and said to bring in everybody unless they're currently making an arrest. Our surveillance teams are now patrolling as part of the show of force."

My hold on my temper began to fray, so I took a couple of deep breaths to calm myself down and give me a moment to think. "Okay. You two, go do whatever you need to do with this fire business, but stay near a phone. I might need some help."

Paul stood a little straighter. "And what are you going to do, Lieutenant?"

"I'm going to find Carla Ramirez, and it'd be best if you guys didn't see how."

Chapter Twenty-Eight

I left the bathroom with my cell phone already pressed to my ear. In a normal case, I'd call up a detective from the gang squad or a confidential informant and ask him or her to set up a meeting with a *Barrio Sureño* member who might know Carla's location, but I didn't need to do that today. We already had a member in lockup, just waiting to talk to us: Danny Navarra. He might not know exactly where Carla was, but he'd know about the gang's safe houses. Finding them would at least give us somewhere to search.

I called a buddy of mine with the sheriff's department and arranged for a meeting. My buddy couldn't guarantee that Danny would talk, but I'd have him in an interrogation room to myself as soon as I reached the jail.

I walked south on Alabama Street for a couple of blocks until I arrived at the jail. Security wasn't quite as tight as it would be at a maximum-security facility, so it only took me ten minutes from my arrival to the time I walked into the interrogation room. Danny Navarra met me inside, wearing an orange jail-issue jumpsuit. He had closely cropped hair, light brown skin, and bright, almost chipper green eyes. The tattoo of a woman adorned his right forearm, and three teardrops in green ink seemed poised to slide from his left eye and down his cheek.

I had seen that teardrop tattoo on a lot of gangbangers, and it had a number of different meanings. Some guys tattooed them on as a symbol of the men they'd killed, while others put one on for each year they spent in prison. I had read Navarra's jacket, so I knew he hadn't ever been convicted of a serious crime. He had spent time behind bars, usually in two- to three-month increments. I thought he intended the teardrops to show his toughness, but in my experience, the really tough guys didn't need to tell anybody anything. One look at any of them, and you knew you didn't want to mess with that guy. Navarra, on the other hand, probably needed all the help he could get.

I wanted to get in there, throw him against a wall, and demand he tell me everything he knew. A TV cop would have done it, but in real life, that wouldn't get me anywhere. It's easy to earn an inmate's fear, but I needed trust, and that meant sucking up my anger and frustration.

"How you doing?" I said, sitting across the table from the prisoner. "I don't think we know each other. I'm Ash Rashid, and you're Danny Navarra, right?"

He looked me up and down and then smirked. "You don't look so tough."

"You're the only tough guy here, I assure you," I said. "I'm just a guy here to talk to you."

He leaned back and crossed his arms. "I hear you talked to Tristan Salazar at Pendleton."

So word was getting around about me. I could use that. "He and I had a conversation, yeah. What's it to you?"

Navarra uncrossed his arms and leaned forward. "You try to entrap me, I'm gonna mess you up. How's that sound?"

He might have heard of my encounter with Tristan Salazar, but evidently he hadn't learned the right lesson. Threatening a police officer is a bad idea.

"I'm just here to talk, kid," I said. "You're in here for what, B and E?"

He looked at me again and shrugged, trying to look cool but barely able to maintain eye contact. "That's what the cops say, but you can't trust Five-O. Ass holes are always after us."

I took a notepad from my inner jacket pocket and laid it in front of me. "I know. We're horrible human beings for arresting you. I appreciate the dignity you bring to your situation, though. I came here to talk to you about your future."

"Whatever you got to offer, I'm not interested."

I leaned back. "I wouldn't be so sure. We both know what's going on with your gang. Santino Ramirez hasn't named a successor, and *Barrio Sureño* is tearing itself apart."

He put his hands on the table. They trembled ever so slightly. The guy was obviously nervous about something, and normally, I would have let him sit in jail for a few days to think things through. Time mattered here, though. I needed to find Carla before she killed anyone else.

"*Barrio Sureño* is fine," he said.

'We both know that's not true," I said, shaking my head. "It's also why I'm here. I hear you're an important man in your gang, one of its leaders."

"I do what I got to do," he said, leaning back. "What's it to you?"

"Then as a smart guy, you understand Carla Ramirez and your uncle Miguel are screwing you, right?"

He shrank just a little, and the bravado I saw in him earlier subsided just the tiniest bit. That told me I was going in the right direction.

"They're killing witnesses who spoke against Santino Ramirez. Everybody in your gang knows it, so they're getting all the credit with your friends. But they're putting these murders on you. You understand what I'm saying? When they're done with you, you're never getting out of here."

He shook his head and pushed back from the table as if he could get away from me. He had nowhere to go, though, and he knew it.

"You're just talking shit now," he said, looking half at the floor and half at the table in front of him.

"I'm telling you how it is," I said. "I'm the only friend you've got right now. Whether you believe me or not, your name is on top of every report I write. Carla, your uncle Miguel, Jacob, they're all pointing fingers at you."

He looked left and right, cocking his head. "I'm in jail. How can I kill anybody?"

"You wouldn't be the first guy to set up hits from jail. Maybe you didn't pull the trigger, but you're going down just the same unless you help me."

"I'm not going to help a cop. I do that, I'm as good as dead."

And that was probably true. Danny Navarra lived in a brutal world, one in which even an accident as benign as spilling your drink on the wrong person in a nightclub could earn you the death penalty. I didn't know Danny well, but ten minutes in a cage with him, and I could already tell he didn't fit into that scene. He had some felonies on his record, but he was young enough that he could still make something of himself.

"How about if I offer you protection?" I asked. "Would you talk then? We'll put you in protective custody, and then, once this is all over, we'll help you move. You can go to school if you want. You can learn a trade. I know a lot of former gang members. You don't have to live like this."

"Like what?"

"Like a guy who's terrified of his own shadow. You tell me what I want to know, and I'll make the calls. You'll be safe."

He didn't even hesitate before responding. "I'm not going to turn on my uncle. He's family."

If he didn't want to go the easy way, I could push him down the hard road just as easily. I have a reputation on the streets. I don't like it, but I can certainly use it. Without taking my eyes from Navarra's, I nodded my head toward the camera suspended from the ceiling.

"We're alone and the cameras are off, so we can talk freely. That first offer was from a cop. This one's not. *Barrio Sureño* and a man I represent have some common business interests. At the moment my employer is sitting on an excess of certain products, and we'd like to utilize *Barrio Sureño's* network to move them. We don't want to work with Carla or Miguel, though. We don't think we can trust them."

His eyes darted from my eyes to my side, where I would normally keep a weapon, and then back to my face. All the while, he ran a tongue across the inside of his teeth, creating a bulge beneath the skin. The comment had taken him out of his element, robbed him of some of the confident swagger he thought he possessed.

"I've heard some things about you," he said, almost haltingly. "I didn't know you did business."

I bored my eyes into his. "If you've heard things about me, then you know who I work for."

His Adam's apple bobbed as he swallowed. "You're a cop."

I shook my head. People called me Mr. 187 because they thought I had become some kind of vigilante in the employ of a gangster.

"You heard who I really work for?"

Navarra's tremble passed through his arms and into his face, causing a blood vessel to twitch beneath his left eye.

"Carla said you work for some Russian guy. Supposed to be like Keyser Söze. That's why she didn't kill you herself. She didn't want to provoke a war."

Keyser Söze is a shadowy, all-powerful gangster in the movie *The Usual Suspects*. From what I knew of Konstantin Bukoholov, the movie's writer could have used the old Russian for a model. Good to know Carla still feared something.

"Close enough. Tino's going to die, and there's no way around that," I said. "In the aftermath, your organization is going to need some help. They need a leader to step up. My boss wanted Tomas Quesada, but he's dead now. We're not going to work with your uncle or Carla. That leaves us with two options: we either kill everybody, or we throw our weight behind you. It's your choice."

Navarra tapped both of his index fingers on the table in front of him. He fidgeted like my daughter when she had to go to the bathroom.

"Are you offering to give me *Barrio Sureño?*"

I shook my head. "We're not giving you *Barrio Sureño*. We're giving you an opportunity to take *Barrio Sureño*. You just have to have the balls and the will. We can get you guns when you need them, and we might even be able to get you a hitter or two. A pro. In exchange, we want a partner. You sell my boss's product, and you cut off anybody else you're buying from. We can get you anything you want in whatever quantities you need."

He considered and then furrowed his brow while leaning forward. "And your boss sent you here?"

"I wouldn't be here otherwise." Sensing that I had started to lose him, I stood. "Look, I don't want to work with you or *Barrio Sureño*, but I don't get to make that call. If it were up to me, I'd find out where you and your friends live, slit your throats in your sleep, and take over your territory. As a sign of respect, my boss is giving you an opportunity. You don't want it, we've got other options."

As I started for the door, Navarra called out. "You don't need to go. We've still got business to discuss. What do you need me to do?"

"First things first," I said, turning so I could face him. "We need things to settle down. I don't care about the civilians, but two cops died last night, and you'd better believe IMPD is looking to take revenge. Who killed them?"

"Why do you need to know?"

I rolled my eyes and crossed my arms. "Tell me you're kidding. Tell me you're not really stupid enough to ask me that question."

"Take it easy, man," he said, holding up his hands. "I ain't going to turn on my man without good reason. That's all."

I walked back to the table and rested my hands on the edge opposite Navarra and leaned forward, getting right in his face.

"You've got good reason. Someone's going down for killing two cops yesterday. You don't give me a fall guy, I'll put it on your Uncle Miguel and say you coughed up his name."

Navarra pulled his face back from mine, his skin growing a little pale. "Hey, hey, hey, man. You do that, I'm dead."

I gave him the iciest stare I could, one that would have scared even me had I seen it on someone else. "Then give me a name."

He wiped his mouth with the back of his hand and then looked at the door. "Who died?"

"Two cops. That's all you need to know."

"No," he said, shaking his head and looking at me. "Other than the cops. Who died?"

"A family. A woman who testified in Santino Ramirez's murder trial."

"Your girl Carla did that," he said, leaning back. "She's got this bug up her ass to kill everybody who testified against Tino. I bet Jacob's with her."

That confirmed what I had thought, but I needed more than the word of an inmate. I needed physical evidence, corroboration.

"Not good enough," I said, shaking my head and pulling my chair close to Navarra's. I sat down beside him and put my hand on the back of his neck, squeezing hard. "Carla's too high profile. I go after her, nothing's going to stick. Tell me about Jacob."

Navarra started to respond, but then he shrugged. "I never knew him. He didn't grow up in the neighborhood."

"What do you know about him?"

"Somebody told me he's from Cleveland. That's all I know."

That jibed with what Emilia had heard. Good. We very likely had the right guy. "What about Carla? Where's she staying?"

"My house."

"If you're going to lie to me, at least make it believable," I said, standing once again. I smacked him on the back of the head. "Carla burned your house to the ground."

"Nah, man," he said, waving me off. "That wasn't my house she burned. I stayed there some, but my house is nice. It's out in the 'burbs. Tino gave it to me."

My heart rate ticked up just a hair.

Keep talking.

"Why would Santino Ramirez give you a house?"

Navarra hesitated and then tilted his head to the side, like he didn't know how to answer.

"It...it ain't technically mine. Technically, it's got some stuff growing in it, but I live there. Technically."

I had seen that arrangement before. Ramirez gave him a marijuana grow house, probably in exchange for tending the plants. We didn't find it in Indianapolis often, but in communities further south with larger migrant populations, drug dealers would buy distressed properties, upgrade the electrical systems for the future power drain, and then install grow lights in the basement and attic. They'd then find a poor family and promise them the house free and clear if they watched over the plants inside and kept their mouths shut. The system worked out well for the drug dealer, but not so much for the family. When the police raided the place, the dealer would be long gone, leaving them alone to take the fall.

"Where's your house? I've got to find her."

He looked at me and squinted again. "You're sure Tino's gonna die? Because he ain't gonna be too happy if I give up his wife."

"You want some advice? Man to man?" I asked, leaning forward. I didn't wait for him to acknowledge the question. "Grow some balls and stop worrying about Tino. He's in prison, and he's not getting out. You want to be his bitch the rest of your life, go ahead and be his bitch. But if you want to make something of yourself, you've got take what you want when you want it."

"All right, all right," he said. He gave me the address of a home in Beech Grove, a suburb to our southeast but still within Marion County.

"I'm going to check your house out. If I find her, I'll do everything I can to get you out of here."

Of course, Navarra had admitted to involvement in at least half a dozen felonies in our conversation so far, so I probably wouldn't be able to do much for him.

"Keep on trucking," said Navarra, holding out his fist.

"Do what you got to do in here," I said, hitting his knuckles with my own as if we were old friends. "I'll take care of the rest."

I left him in that room, and once the guard shut the door behind me, I took out my cell phone to call Paul Murphy. He answered on the first ring.

"I've got a lead on Carla Ramirez. She's about to have a real bad day."

Chapter Twenty-Nine

With the entirety of my department working on the events around town, I wouldn't get a lot of help no matter what happened. Captain Bowers had co-opted Paul to work a tip line, but I still had Emilia. I met her beside my car in the parking lot nearest the City-County Building. She wore a tactical vest beneath an IMPD jacket and had pulled her hair away from her face with a hair tie. She wore her weapon on her hip and kept her jacket pushed back so anyone around could see the gun. She looked like she meant business. I grabbed my own bullet-resistant vest from my trunk just in case.

"How quickly can you get us to Beech Grove?" I asked, taking off my suit coat and then putting on my vest.

"That depends on what you had for lunch, sir."

"All right, then," I said. "You drive. Where's your car?"

We took a marked patrol vehicle, and before I could even put on my seat belt, we sped off, heading east on Washington Street toward I-65 south. Once we hit the interstate, she flashed the lights, turned on the sirens, and floored it. The car roared, the front end lifted with the acceleration, and I felt the back of my head start to embed itself into the vinyl seat. Evidently, I had picked the right driver. With the mayor's office having locked the city down earlier, we met little traffic on the road and those few cars we did see got out of our way quickly. Normally when I had somebody else drive me on a case like this, I found myself urging the driver to go faster. Here, I actually found myself praying that we'd make it alive.

By the time we pulled off the interstate onto Emerson Avenue, I had difficulty forcing my clenched fists to open.

"That was some spirited driving, Officer Rios," I said, hoping my voice wouldn't crack.

"You can call me Emilia," she said, glancing over at me. I pointed to the road in front of us, directing her gaze to oncoming traffic. "Sir."

"You can call me whatever you want as long as you don't kill me."

We pulled into a working-class neighborhood called Farhill Downs seven minutes after we left the jail. Even with my lights and siren blaring, that same drive would have taken me at least ten minutes. Impressive, and a little nuts. Farhill Downs had wide streets, clear sidewalks, and homes with well-kept lawns. Judging by the architecture, it had probably gone up sometime in the late seventies to early eighties, but it looked well maintained. I wouldn't have been surprised to see a colleague or two live there. We followed the main road as it curved to the left. The address Danny Navarra had given me belonged to a single-story brick home with a privacy fence in the backyard and a front-facing garage. He—or maybe Carla Ramirez—had put a family of stone geese beside the front door. It didn't stand out from the other homes in the neighborhood at all save for one addition: solar panels covered nearly the entire roof.

I pointed them out to Emilia as we drove past.

"They're smarter than we thought. Power company knows to monitor houses that use too much electricity," I said. "Solar panels make them harder to catch. Bet Carla even got a tax break on that."

Emilia nodded and parked half a block up. "Maybe we'll get her for tax evasion, too."

"Maybe," I said, reaching into my jacket for my firearm. I never carry my weapon around without a full magazine, but I checked anyway to make sure. I looked at Emilia and watched as she did something similar. "You ready?"

I looked at the house again. *Barrio Sureño* had done their due diligence on this house. It blended in with everyone around it. They could probably even park a van in the garage, close the door, and load up their dope without its ever seeing the light of day. A house like that, if I had to guess, had surveillance as well. She'd see us coming, but maybe we could use that.

"You have a Taser in here?"

She tilted her head to the back. "In the trunk. You comfortable using one here?"

Despite their low lethality, Tasers have become somewhat controversial in law enforcement circles. They incapacitate a subject by shooting him with a pair of electrodes, which then deliver a 50,000-volt shock that overwhelms his nervous system, forcing every muscle in his body to contract at once. A member of our SWAT team once shot me with one a couple of years ago, and I can safely call it one of the most physically painful experiences of my life.

I nodded. "Yeah. I tried running someone down earlier. Didn't work out for me. She takes off, I'm shooting her."

"How do you want to handle this?"

I pointed to a dense thicket of pine trees that separated Carla's home from the one beside it. "I'm going to get out here and hide out in those trees in the neighbor's yard. You're going to drive up the street and give me two minutes.

After that, blast your lights and siren and go tearing toward her house like your hair is on fire. I want everybody on the block—including Carla—to know you're here. Carla doesn't want to die, so she's not going to open fire on you. If she does, stay behind the car for cover and call in backup. More than likely, she's going to take off out the back door as soon as she sees your car. I'll subdue her in the backyard."

Emilia nodded. "Sounds easy enough."

I almost told her that nothing in this job came easily, but she'd have to learn that lesson on her own.

I opened my door. "Pop the trunk, would you?"

As I stepped out, she nodded and then reached beneath her dash for the trunk release. I walked around the car and pushed aside the jumper cables in the trunk so I could pull out a plastic box similar to the one that held my power drill. This one held an M26 Taser and five cartridges. I pulled the Taser out of the box and checked the mechanical sights and the charge. The maker did a remarkably good job of mimicking the feel of a handgun, so I felt comfortable with the weapon despite my minimal experience with it. In a real emergency, nothing beat an actual firearm, but this would bring most people down without a problem.

I slipped a cartridge into the weapon and then put the whole assembly in my pocket before shutting the trunk. As per our plan, Emilia drove off quietly, only to turn around about three blocks up. That meant I had two minutes to get into Carla's backyard. I turned directly down the driveway of the nearest home. Had it been dark, I might have tried to conceal myself in shadows, but the sun shone down like a spotlight from Heaven itself, illuminating both sinner and saint. I hoped to look casual, like an invited guest or maybe the gas meter reader, so I didn't hurry. Once I reached the backyard, I walked on the edge of the lawn and then turned toward Carla's house. Her neighbor directly to her east obviously had small children, because they had a wooden playset in the backyard and a sandbox beside the home. If she started shooting, I'd try to remember that, but hopefully the family would have enough common sense to stay inside.

I reached the tree line and privacy fence separating Carla's house from the neighbor's, without incident or notice. From what I could see of Carla's backyard, she had a sliding glass back door that opened onto a concrete patio. Carla—or whoever owned the house—didn't have furniture or anything else to obstruct her exit. That didn't leave me with a lot of hiding places, but hopefully she'd be so busy trying to escape that she wouldn't look around too well.

I hopped the fence and then immediately crouched and jogged toward the house. As per the plan, I heard Emilia's siren kick on about a minute later. It sounded distant at first, but she closed that distance remarkably quickly and then slammed on her brakes, causing her tires to bite into the concrete. I held my breath, waiting.

Then I heard it.

The back door slid open. I reached for my Taser, took a breath, and then stepped out into the lawn. For a brief moment, my eyes locked with Carla's. She looked surprised, but then she smiled slightly and I heard a deep, guttural noise and I realized she hadn't come to the door alone. A dog the size of a miniature pony trotted out of the house. He had a black snout, a fine chestnut-colored coat, and clearly defined muscles.

"Oh, shit."

The dog snarled and sprinted toward me, while Carla sprinted toward the back fence. I could probably hit her with the Taser from where I stood, but I only had one shot. Some of my colleagues might have used that one shot on the dog, but I didn't even consider it. Instead, I just turned and sprinted back toward the fence. I cleared it, but just barely before the dog slammed into the wood. The slats shuddered, and for a moment, I thought he'd break right through. Thankfully, it held.

"Carla's heading south," I shouted, hoping Emilia had gotten out of her car. I sprinted along the property line, feeling the branches of fir trees hit me in the face. When I emerged into the clearing of another neighbor's backyard, I could see Carla running. She wore gray sweats, a white shirt, and black tennis shoes. Several dogs around us barked, and I took off running. The houses around me blurred. I exercise regularly, and I can do pretty well for short bursts, but long distances kill me, and as I ran and as the landscapes and yards around me blended into one another, I felt my lungs start to burn. I passed swing sets and barbecue pits and more patio furniture than I usually saw outside a home center, but after fifteen or twenty houses, I could feel my feet already slowing.

Carla hadn't even lost a step.

I jumped over one last fence—a six-footer with slats nailed close to give the owner privacy—and found myself in the last yard before the end of the street. It was a corner ranch house with a storage shed in the backyard. A car waited on the road, maybe ten feet from Carla and seventy from me. I wasn't going to make it. She looked over her shoulder, and I could almost see the smug look on her face. I dug into my gut and pushed as hard as I could, but it wasn't enough. I barely made it halfway through the yard before Carla dove inside the car, and I barely made it five steps beyond that before I heard the engine turn over and the tires squeal as she floored the accelerator.

I pounded to a stop at the end of the lawn and could only watch as Carla turned, looked over her shoulder, and gave me the finger.

But then I saw her face shift. She put her hand down slowly and braced herself for an impact. I felt the wind whip past me almost before I heard the car. Emilia's cruiser slammed into the rear quarter panel of Carla's vehicle, causing it to spin like a top. The car crashed into a light pole with a wrenching sound of metal crunching on metal and moved no more. I sprinted once more toward the now crashed vehicle. Carla's head lay back against the headrest, but she blinked slowly. I threw open the passenger door and shoved my Taser right at her.

"Put your hands on the steering wheel where I can see them right now."

Carla blinked several more times and then looked at me. Slowly, recognition sprouted on her face as her wits came back to her, and she shot her hand to the seat beside her, presumably for a weapon.

"Wrong move," I said, squeezing the trigger on the Taser. Two electrodes shot out, hitting Carla in the neck. I squeezed the trigger again and her entire body went rigid as 50,000 volts coursed through her. I hate to say it, but I found it a little satisfying.

After the first jolt with the Taser, she got out of the car willingly, and Emilia immediately cuffed her and threw her in the back of the cruiser.

"I've got backup on the way," she said, shutting Carla inside the vehicle. "Should be here within a minute or two."

"Good. Tell them to bring somebody from the Humane Society for a dog. I'm going to go back to the house and check it out."

Emilia nodded and then climbed back into her car to place the call. I walked five or so blocks back to Carla's house. The dog was still in the backyard. The neighbors wouldn't like it, but I found a rubber kid's ball on their grass and threw it over the fence. Immediately, Carla's dog gave chase, picked the ball up, and then brought it back to the fence. He didn't growl this time. Instead, he just dropped the ball and wagged his tail, patiently. Maybe the guy just needed a friend. I walked to the gate at the side of the house and let myself in. The dog looked at me and then nosed the ball. I could appreciate a single-minded fellow. I threw the ball to him twice more, and by that time, he lost interest in me, allowing me to go into the house unmolested. Just the same, I shut the glass sliding door behind me and stepped into the kitchen.

The room smelled almost overpoweringly of incense and raw marijuana. Danny Navarra hadn't lied to me. This gave us more than enough to hold Carla—and him. I didn't open any of the kitchen cabinets, but I doubted I'd find much interesting in them. Too obvious. The front room had beige carpet and faux oak paneling. Carla had layered blankets on the floor near the front window, creating somewhere soft to sleep. I saw no other furniture at all. I cleared the rest of the first floor and found nothing.

With the house secure, I took the basement stairs down and found grow lights in rows on the ceiling, and so many plants that I might have stepped into the greenhouse at the botanical gardens. Not only did I find marijuana plants, though, I found six burlap sacks full of it as well. I kicked one, and it barely moved. If they weighed fifty kilograms—a common weight for burlap sacks full of marijuana—they'd go for a good hundred grand each on the street. Next, I accessed the attic via a folding ladder in the main hallway and found rows of grow lights and a couple dozen plants. All told, it promised to be one of the bigger drug busts the department has had this year, but I hadn't come for drugs. It did give us some leverage, though, and I liked that.

I started to exit the house a few minutes later, but I paused at the threshold, listening for the sound of sirens. They sounded distant still, but they grew stronger the longer I paused. We'd have help soon. I pulled the door shut behind me and walked back to the scene of Carla's accident. Emilia walked toward me, glancing back at her cruiser, where Carla sat on the back seat.

"What'd you find?" she asked.

"Enough marijuana to supply every college campus in the state for a week or two," I said, nodding toward the cruiser. "She say anything?"

"No."

I looked at the cruiser and saw Carla through the window. Despite being handcuffed in the back of our cruiser, she had the same smug look on her face as she had had when she gave me the finger. We had a good case against her for murder and an even better case for the marijuana, and she didn't seem the least bit concerned. She had something planned, something that would hurt. I had a bad feeling growing in my gut.

"As soon as patrol arrives, we'll get her downtown, then."

Chapter Thirty

Getting downtown took a little longer than expected because Emilia had flattened one of her cruiser's tires when she hit Carla's car; but once we got that sorted out, we drove to my building on Alabama Street. Along the way, I called Paul Murphy and asked him to meet us. With everything else going on, even the prosecutor's office had shut down for the day, leaving the floor virtually abandoned. Paul met us outside the storage room the department called my office, a dour expression on his face that brightened only somewhat when he saw us lead Carla ahead of us in cuffs.

"I commandeered the conference room," he said. "It's got video, so we can interview her in there on the record."

I nodded to Emilia, and she began leading the suspect to the open door. Paul, then, stepped closer to me.

"We haven't found Jacob Valdez. Not that anyone's been looking."

I nodded, having learned early in my career that I couldn't rely on lucky breaks. "I'm betting Carla knows where he is, and even if she doesn't, I bet she's got a way to contact him."

Paul looked over his shoulder at the conference room. "You think she'd be willing to help us?"

"Not without some pressure," I said, walking past him toward the open door. "But she's planning something. Let's keep the cameras off for this one until we can figure out what she wants."

Paul hurried to walk beside me. "If that's how you want to play it, that's how we'll play it."

The conference room had a wall of windows overlooking Alabama Street and the parking lot of AAA Bail Bonds. Sunlight filtered through black blinds, lending the room a bright, almost cheery feel. Had we conducted this interview in the City-County Building, we would've used an interrogation room barely bigger than the interior of an SUV, and we'd have secured Carla's hands to the wall via a steel ring screwed directly into the concrete. I liked the rooms over there because they reminded inmates that I controlled their fate, at least for a time. It let me manipulate most suspects, but I doubted it'd do much for Carla. She seemed a little slick for simple tricks.

I smiled at her when I walked in. She still had her hands secured behind her back, so she had to sit toward the end of her chair, her back straight. She wore the same sweatpants and shirt she had worn earlier and no makeup. I could see defiance in her eyes, but also something else, something far colder. I would have shuddered had I not seen similar eyes so often on the men and women I had put in prison.

"Mrs. Ramirez," I said, upon entering the room. "I apologize for what happened earlier. We don't normally Tase suspects while bringing them in."

Despite her hands being pulled behind her back, she shrugged nonchalantly. "I would have shot you had you not Tased me first. Hope you don't harbor hard feelings."

I looked down at her restraints. "Considering the circumstances, not at all. Has anyone advised you of your rights?"

She pushed her chair back from the table with her feet and stood up. Emilia started toward her, but I shook my head, wanting to see what Carla had planned. She walked straight toward the bank of windows and looked out as if she were an office worker in the midst of a particularly insufferable meeting. In my experience, men and women facing the kind of charges Carla faced did one of two things: they broke down and cried, or they shut up and asked for a lawyer. Her obvious confidence worried me.

"I'm an attorney, Mr. Rashid. Like yourself. I know my rights."

I hadn't known that, but I pretended as if I did. "Then you know you have the right to remain silent, but if you choose to speak to us, we can use what you tell us in court. If you want, we can bring in an attorney. That's your right, too. We can even stop this discussion right now if you want that. Bearing all that in mind, would you mind talking to us?"

She turned around and smiled at me. The fading sunlight caught off her skin, almost making her appear to glow. Funny how often the most beautiful things in nature turned out to be the deadliest.

"The colloquial Miranda warning. That's cute. For the time being, I choose to waive my rights."

"Good," I said, taking a seat at a black leather chair a little more comfortable than the ones IMPD usually supplied. "You want those cuffs off?"

She nodded, so Emilia undid them. Carla pulled out a chair across from me at the table, folding her hands together. I've sat across from a lot of suspects in situations like this. Men and women who make their living on the street think they're tough, but you slap some cuffs on them and threaten them with a life sentence, they usually break. Carla, though, had the cool, calm, and collected demeanor of someone who knew she'd walk right out at any moment. She should have been terrified.

"I assume you know why you're here," I said.

"Because I killed Michelle, and Gail, and Mark, and those two police officers. I never learned their names." Emilia tensed and brought her hand to her waist, near her weapon. She didn't draw it, but she looked as if she wanted to. Carla looked at her and smiled. "I'd feel a lot more comfortable if you took your hand away from your sidearm."

I would have felt more comfortable too, so I coughed to clear my throat. "Officer Rios, would you mind getting us some water? My throat's dry."

"Lieutenant?" she asked.

"Water," I said. "I can handle Mrs. Ramirez on my own."

Emilia hesitated before leaving the room.

"You're a guy who can take charge," said Carla. "I like that. Congratulations on the promotion to lieutenant, too. This morning, Kristen Tanaka called you a lowly sergeant. The promotion must be exciting."

"Yeah, I'm ecstatic," I said. "I noticed you didn't mention Tomas Quesada."

"No," said Carla, nodding. "I didn't mention Tomas. Jacob killed him. I drove the car."

That explained why he outran me so easily. He was a kid. "It's unfortunate he's not here. You know how I can get in touch with him?"

Her smile could have charmed Oscar the Grouch. "I do know how to get in touch with him, as a matter of fact. In fact, I know where he is right now. He's entertaining a pregnant young woman named Valerie Perez."

I sat up straighter and blinked. She was one of our eyewitnesses. "Excuse me?"

She rolled her eyes and sighed as if she were exasperated. "I told him not to take her, but you know how kids are. They get something in their minds, nothing will get it out."

I looked at Paul and tried not to express my sudden worry. "You mind checking up on this?"

"I'm on it," he said, nodding, his voice uncertain.

"Don't bother checking her house," said Carla. "She's long gone."

"If you'll indulge us just the same," I said. "He'll be back in a minute." I looked at Paul. "And have Emilia check the hospitals. If Valerie's pregnant, she may be in the hospital."

Paul inhaled and nodded, looking from me to Carla and back. Carla waved at him.

"Good luck," she said, smiling broadly. Paul left the room without a word, leaving me with just Carla. Thankfully, she didn't say anything for the next few minutes until Paul stuck his head back in the room. He motioned me out, so I stood and followed him into the hallway, joining Emilia.

"I called Valerie's cell phone, but she didn't answer. We had a black and white a couple of blocks from her house, so I had him swing by. Somebody kicked in the back door."

"She's not in the hospitals, either," said Emilia. "She's gone."

I brought my hand to my mouth and sighed. "Damn."

"Yeah," said Emilia, nodding.

I took another breath and then sighed. "Carla knows where she is. We're going to make a deal, and it's not going to be pretty. If you guys aren't up for that, stay in the hallway."

Paul looked at Emilia. "We're good, I think."

She nodded again, so the three of us walked back into the room. Now I knew why she smiled so smugly. She thought she had us.

"What do you want?" I asked. "I can't guarantee you immunity, but if you talk to us now, I'll put in a good word with the prosecutors."

She shook her head. "As much as I love helping other people out, I'm not interested in being prosecuted. I'd rather you let me go right now. I think it's in your best interest, too."

I crossed my arms. "Okay. I'll play along. What would we get?"

"You'd save twenty-three lives." She tilted her head to the side. "Twenty-four if Valerie gives birth."

I blinked. "Whose lives are these?"

Carla stood up again and once again walked toward the window. She motioned me over. Emilia had patted her down for weapons earlier, and she hadn't grabbed anything, so she didn't pose a threat. I joined her at the window.

"Do you see the smoke?" she asked.

I nodded. "Yeah. We've had a number of incidents around town."

She chuckled. "Incidents? That's what you call them?" She shook her head, allowing her hair to brush against her shoulder. "The word incident is so clinical. I'd say you've got what, a hundred dead so far? I'd call that a massacre."

That did feel like a better word. "What about it?"

"Your victims are all illegal immigrants smuggled from Nogales, Mexico to here in semitrailers. Sometimes Miguel puts forty of them in one truck with one bucket for a toilet. Winter's not so bad with that many people because they can huddle together for warmth. Summers are rough, though. In August, a couple of them die on the way usually, but I guess it's like carrying produce. You've just got to expect some rot."

She wanted to shock me. I breathed out through my nose and nodded as if comparing human beings to apples made sense. "So you know Miguel Navarra."

"Yes," she said, turning to me. "I assume you're acquainted?"

"I know of him. I didn't realize he smuggled people. I heard he just killed people for the *Zetas*."

"He does what his employer needs," she said, shrugging. "He used to just bring people up and let them go, but he keeps some now. The prize fish, he calls them. When they arrive, they call their families, and those who can pay a little extra are released. Those who can't, he holds until their families pay. Sometimes he has to send them a finger or two in the mail, but they all pay in the end."

"Who's killing them now?"

"Miguel and several members of my husband's gang," she said, nodding. "I told him a journalist from Mexico City had hitched a ride in one of his trucks and planned to write a story about her experiences. He didn't think that'd be good for business."

I exhaled heavily through my nose. "So rather than get a bad review, he's killing all his customers."

"Yes," she said. "I guess he tried shooting them at first but found that was too much work. Burning them is so much easier. Miguel hasn't hit all his warehouses, though. You can still stop him."

So she wanted a trade. "And I bet you'll only tell me the location of his remaining warehouses if I release you."

She shook her head and continued to focus on the window. "He only has one warehouse left, and I'll tell you its location for free. No strings attached."

"Why?"

"Because it's in my interest." She took her gaze from the city and then looked at me. "The second piece of information, that's the one you pay for." She smiled and chuckled a little. "First one's free, and then you start charging. I feel like I'm slinging crack."

I ignored the quip and crossed my arms. "Lay it on us, then. Where's this warehouse?"

"Howard Street, maybe half a mile south of I-70. I don't remember the address, but it's a red-brick warehouse building. There's a freight company nearby. You'll know you're in the area when you see a parking lot full of shipping pallets."

I didn't know the street, but we could find it easily enough. "Why hasn't he torched this warehouse yet?"

"Because he's a weasel and he puts his most valuable customers there. These people have families in the US already, so they can pay the most. He's probably going to try to unload as many of them as he can. The rest, he'll kill. He also stores methamphetamine there, so he'd want to load up as much of that as he could."

I'm sure Carla could lie convincingly about any topic in the world, but she had no reason here. If this tip didn't pan out, we'd ignore anything else she had to say. "Give me five minutes. I need to call somebody."

"Sure," she said, smiling.

Paul and Emilia stayed in the room while I stepped out into the hallway. Bowers answered his cell phone on the third ring, but I had difficulty hearing him over the clamor in the background.

"Mike, it's Ash. The victims in these mass casualty situations. Are they all Hispanic?"

"Hold on," he said. I waited thirty seconds or so while he got somewhere quieter. "So far. What do you know?"

"They're illegal immigrants smuggled into the US by a man named Miguel Navarra. I've got a credible CI who says he's got one more warehouse that he hasn't lit up yet."

"Where?"

I described the warehouse's location.

"I'll get units en route," said Bowers. "If this pans out, I'll need access to your CI."

"I've got her in custody, so she'll be around. Good luck."

Bowers thanked me and then hung up. I dialed a second number. Special Agent Kevin Havelock picked up shortly thereafter.

"I'm afraid I don't have time to talk, Lieutenant," said Havelock.

"I know," I said. "I've got a CI who says Miguel Navarra is our fire starter. He's murdering men and women he smuggled into the US."

Havelock paused. "Who's your CI?"

"Carla Ramirez. She's the wife of Santino Ramirez."

"She with you now?"

"Yeah. Red building on Ohio Street. Fifteenth floor."

Havelock didn't say anything; he simply hung up, and I walked to the nearest vending machine, where I purchased four bottles of water. When I got back to the conference room, I put them on the center of the table.

"You're a dear," said Carla, reaching for one of the bottles. "I don't suppose you'll give me my cell phone while we wait? It might be a good time to check my email."

"I don't think so," I said.

"Just checking," she said, after taking a long pull on her water. She turned her chair to look out the window. The conference room faced east, so we didn't have a view of the sunset, but we could still see streaks of purple, orange, and red in the sky. It looked to be a glorious night. Special Agent

Kevin Havelock knocked on the door about fifteen minutes later. Paul Murphy and I met him in the hallway.

"IMPD has dispatched the SWAT team to the warehouse," said Havelock. "I've got a couple of agents there as well. We'll hit the building shortly." He looked at the door that led to the conference room and then to me. "That Carla Ramirez in there?"

"That's her," I said.

"She said anything else about Navarra?" he asked, glancing at Paul Murphy.

"Nothing pertinent, but I thought I'd call you in just in case you wanted to talk to her."

"I appreciate that," he said, nodding. He looked at Paul again. "What does your support staff know?"

I shook my head. "Nothing."

"I am right here, guys," said Paul. "I can hear you, and I kind of feel like I'm out of the loop."

Havelock looked at him and then clapped him on the shoulder. "It's nothing personal, but if you'll excuse us for a moment, I'd appreciate it."

Paul looked at me. "It's a rarified world you live in, my friend."

"Unintentionally so," I said. I waited for Paul to go into the conference room again before looking to Havelock and speaking. "I know Navarra is your informant, but if he's at that warehouse, he's going down. No way IMPD can keep it quiet."

"If Miguel is at that warehouse, he's going to go down shooting. I already told our teams."

That's what I feared. I allowed my eyes to settle on Havelock. He and I lived in different worlds, but we fought the same fight and employed some of the same tactics. I should have known he planned to use me when he showed up at our briefing the night after I shot Dante, but I hadn't been seeing straight. Now that I was, I don't know if I blamed him for the deception or not.

"When you gave me Miguel Navarra's name, did you have any idea about this side business?"

Havelock took a step back and then tilted his head to the side. "You think I gave you Miguel Navarra's name?"

"I don't think," I said, shaking my head. "I'm pretty positive. Miguel's a problem for you, so you mentioned his name knowing I would eventually investigate him and bring him down."

For a moment, the FBI agent simply blinked and stared at me. Then, he smiled just a little.

"Whether I mentioned him intentionally or whether it was an accidental outburst, I had no idea of his involvement in these fires. If I had known, I assure you that he'd be in prison right now."

His eyes never wavered as he looked into mine. He was telling the truth.

"Good," I said, turning toward the conference room door. I stopped before reaching it. "Just for future reference, if you ever use me to take out your garbage again, I'll burn you to the ground. Clear?"

"We'll see."

I wanted to say something snappy back to him, but instead, I simply walked back to the conference room. Havelock followed a moment after me, and for the next hour, we sat and watched the city skyline as afternoon changed to night. Periodically, Paul or Emilia or Agent Havelock would stand up and stretch or go to the restroom or just walk around, but no one spoke. And then, Havelock's phone rang. I don't remember why he had put it on the conference table, but we stared at it as if it were some artifact from a future we knew nothing about. When Havelock answered, he spoke in a low, hushed tone. He sighed twice, but I had no idea what that meant. Eventually, he looked at me and shook his head, but again, I had no idea what that meant. By the time he hung up, his face had gone red. He looked at each of the officers in the room in turn.

"IMPD's SWAT team hit the warehouse and came under heavy fire immediately. Three officers went down. At least two are gone, while the third officer is in surgery now." He looked at Carla. She stared at him with unblinking green eyes. "They took down all five men guarding the facility and found twenty-two people inside. They also found six fifty-five gallon drums full of crystal meth."

Carla smiled.

"That was the free tip," she said, looking at me. "Remember, Valerie Perez is still out there. I can give her to you."

I wanted to strangle her, but instead, I looked her directly in the eye. "Why would Jacob and Miguel kidnap Valerie?"

"They wanted to kill every eyewitness who testified against Tino," she said, shrugging. "They believed that would help solidify *Barrio Sureño* around them."

I could see that, I guess, but it left one pretty big question. "Why is she still alive, then?"

To that, Carla actually tittered. "Because they're Catholic, and Valerie is pregnant. Seems like a silly stipulation to me, but they won't kill the unborn. As soon as Valerie pops, she's dead."

My jaw dropped open just a bit. I looked at Paul and Emilia. They looked as dumbfounded as I felt. "Okay, sure," I said, nodding as if that made sense. "I assume you're going to want some guarantee that I won't arrest you as soon as we find her."

"Oh, you're not going to have the chance," she said, shaking her head. "By the time you find her, I'll be long gone."

"How's this going to work then?" I asked.

Carla paused. "This is the part you're not going to like."

Chapter Thirty-One

"Go on," I said, crossing my arms. "Tell me what I'm not going to like."

"Well," said Carla, looking from me to Emilia to Paul Murphy and then to Havelock. "I hope you all forgive me for saying so, but I don't trust any of you." She settled her gaze on Emilia. "Here's what I propose: this officer and I get into an unmarked, civilian vehicle. We drive to a location I specify—a safe place—and I drop her off. At that point, I will tell her where Jacob is holding Valerie. I take the car and go. I'll even drop it off somewhere she can pick it up. This officer will then walk until she can get cell reception—and it's not that far, half a mile at most. You'll rescue Valerie, and you'll never see me again. Everyone wins."

She hadn't lied, at least—I didn't like it.

"How long have you been planning this?" I asked.

She took her gaze from Emilia and settled on me. "I'm improvising, believe it or not."

I leaned forward, resting my elbows on the table. Carla matched my posture.

"Why should we trust you?"

She blinked and then smiled wickedly. "Because you don't have a choice." I started to shake my head and stand, but she held up a hand. "I have no reason to hurt anyone else. My husband is going to die for the crimes he's committed. Miguel and Jacob deserve to die, too, I suppose. But not me. I'm getting out, and you're going to watch me walk away."

The room went quiet. I could practically feel Emilia's eyes burn into Carla before she told her, "You killed seven innocent people. You don't get to walk away."

Carla narrowed her eyes at Emilia. "The adults are talking, sweetheart. Please shut up."

For a moment, I thought Emilia would slap her. Thankfully, Havelock spoke before she could. "Can you give us Miguel Navarra?"

"And who are you again in this?" asked Carla, narrowing her gaze at Agent Havelock.

"Nobody important," he responded.

"Well, nobody important," she said, raising her eyebrows. "I haven't seen Miguel since he and my stepson decided they no longer needed me. However, I don't imagine he's left Jacob. The two of them believe they're on a mission from God."

I waited for Havelock or Carla to say something else. When neither did, I looked at Emilia and then to Paul and then to the FBI agent. "Let's go talk about this outside." I looked at Carla. "Stay there. You stand up, I'll tie you to that chair."

"I'll stay."

The three officers and I left the conference room and shut the door behind us.

"What do you guys think?" I asked.

"I think she's cuckoo for Cocoa Puffs," said Paul.

"She didn't lie to you about the warehouse," said Havelock, quickly. "Crazy or not, she's in the middle of this."

"Then I'll go with her," said Emilia. "I guarantee I can get her to talk."

"Bad idea," said Havelock, almost immediately. I nodded, concurring.

"Did you know Kim Dennison or Doug Osbourne?" I asked. Emilia started to say something, and I could tell that she was going to lie to me. I shook my head to stop her. "We all saw your reaction when Carla mentioned killing those two. I doubt you knew the civilians, so I'm guessing you knew one of our fallen officers."

Emilia's face reddened, and she took a deep breath through her nose. "Kim, all right? She was my friend, and she didn't deserve what that bitch did to her."

"No," I said. "She certainly didn't, but there's no way I'm leaving you and Carla alone together. I'm going."

Paul sighed. "You sure about this?"

I looked back at the door and shook my head. "No, but it's our best shot to get Valerie back."

"You're seriously just going to let her go?" asked Emilia, crossing her arms.

"Oh, no," I said, turning to face her. "Carla knows that, too. She's probably going to try to kill me as soon as we get to wherever we're going. I don't plan to let her."

"What's your plan, then?" asked Emilia.

"We're going to follow him," said Havelock before I could say anything. He reached into his jacket pocket for his cell phone. "I need twenty minutes. I'll put a GPS tracker on your car and have a team five minutes out wherever you are."

I nodded to him, and he left our group, his cell phone already pressed against his ear. I stepped in closer to my team and lowered my voice. "I want you two following me, and I want you less than five minutes out. I'd rather not die if I can help it. See if you can get some night vision goggles from the tactical team so you can drive with the lights out."

"Any thoughts on how you will prevent Carla from killing you?" asked Paul.

"I'll figure that out when I come to it." I raised my eyebrows and looked at my two partners. "Other thoughts?"

"You're as nuts as she is," said Emilia. "Other than that, it sounds fine."

I looked at Paul. "You got anything?"

"I concur with her," he said, looking to Emilia. "Try not to die."

"All right," I said, turning to go back into the conference room. Carla perked up at our entrance. "You're on, but you're not going with Officer Rios. You're going with me."

She wiggled her nose and then squinted at me before brightening. "That's acceptable. Where's your car?"

"You'll see in just a bit. I've got stuff to do first."

"And whatever you have to do is more important than Valerie Perez's life?"

I blinked and crossed my arms. "How about I put it like this: if Valerie Perez dies, all deals are off. We will hunt you down and kill you. Clear?"

"Direct and clear," she said.

I took a step back and then looked at Paul. "Watch her. I'm going to call my wife and have *Maghrib*."

"That another prayer?" he asked.

"The one just before sunset. If I die tonight, I figure I'll need to get in as many prayers as I can."

Paul shook his head. "That's not funny, but go and do what you need to do."

I called Hannah from my office. She sounded okay—tired, but okay. I didn't tell her what I had planned, but I said we had a lot of work to do and that I'd be back as soon as I could. I talked to Megan and Kaden a little bit as well. Both of them told me they loved me and promised to be good for their mother. I could have stayed on the phone with them all night and been happy, but talking to them reminded me of something very important. Valerie Perez was a daughter, too, and her parents were probably crying or even praying about her right now. I'd seen too many corpses because of Carla and Jacob; we needed to finish this soon.

After hanging up, I had evening prayer and then recited an additional *dua*, a short prayer, asking God for protection and guidance. I met Paul, Emilia, and Agent Havelock outside the conference room after that.

"We're set," said Havelock. "You're taking your wife's VW, right?"

I nodded.

"Good," he said. "We put a GPS transmitter in the right rear wheel well and an emergency transmitter in the storage compartment on the driver side door. The transmitter's shaped like a garage door opener, so if you come under fire, press the button like you're opening your garage and we'll come running. I anticipate that Mrs. Ramirez will ask you to go unarmed, so we also wedged a Beretta M9 beside your seat. It's got a fifteen-round magazine, so use it wisely."

"How'd you get that in my car?" I asked. "I'm pretty sure I locked the doors last time I used it."

"We've got a few guys on staff with experience breaking into cars," said Havelock. "Remember, you hit that button, we're still at least five minutes away. Try to anticipate when you'll need us."

I nodded to him and then looked to the rest of my team. "You guys squared away?"

Emilia and Paul nodded. Hopefully they weren't lying. I nodded to each of them before rejoining Carla in the conference room.

"You ready?" I asked, looking at our prisoner.

"Almost," she said. "I'm not going if you're carrying a weapon."

Just as Havelock had said. I nodded and took off my jacket. Havelock pretended to look alarmed. "Are you sure that's wise, Lieutenant?"

I doubted the wisdom in anything we had planned, but I nodded anyway and slipped my arms through my shoulder holster. A dull pain spread from my shoulder joint and into my chest as I rotated my arm, but I tried not to grimace.

"Bum shoulder?" asked Carla.

"Asshole shot me a couple of years back," I said, nodding and handing my weapon and holster to Paul. "Good enough?"

She looked down at my legs. "Do you have a backup firearm?"

I nodded to the weapon Paul held. "That is my backup piece. Detectives from Internal Affairs confiscated my primary weapon after I shot Dante. They haven't returned it."

"All the same," she said. "Can you step around the table and lift up your pant legs so I can see if you're wearing an ankle holster?"

"This is ridiculous," said Emilia.

"Her tip, her rules," I said, walking around the table. Once Carla could see my lower torso, I lifted my pant legs halfway up my calves. I looked at her. "Satisfied?"

"Rarely, but that's not your fault. Let's go."

Carla and I left the building and then crossed the street to the surface lot that serviced the City-County Building. Neither Emilia nor Paul followed us out, but I could practically feel their eyes on us. When we reached my Volkswagen, Carla paused and tilted her head to the side, looking at it the same way someone at a used car lot might have. I half expected her to walk around it and kick the tires, but then she sighed and looked up at me.

"I guess this will do. When I drop you off, I can lose it for you if you'd like. You could tell your insurance company that somebody stole it."

"I like my car a lot more than I like you," I said, inserting my keys into the lock on the passenger side. "I'd watch what you say."

"I'll try to remember that," she said, climbing inside. I walked around the car but kept an eye on her most of that time. She folded her hands in her lap and simply sat there. I still didn't know what she had planned, but I could feel my adrenaline rising.

God, let this be a good idea.

Chapter Thirty-Two

As I put the key in the ignition cylinder, the dashboard illuminated with its familiar blue light and I looked at Carla. "I've got about half a tank of gas. That cool with you?"

"How many miles can you drive on that?"

"Two hundred or so," I said, shrugging. "Give or take."

"Plenty, then," said Carla, nodding. "Do you know how to get to Martinsville from here?"

Martinsville was a small town of about 12,000, forty miles southwest of the city. Driving through, I'd seen churches on almost every corner, and small mom-and-pop stores around the courthouse. The KKK no longer held rallies there, but I have minority friends who still call it a sundown town, meaning they don't feel comfortable there after dark. The town has cleaned itself up over the years, and I know the vast majority of men and women in that town are good, honest folk. I also know that I, as an Arab, would never feel safe walking through it at night, even today.

"What's in Martinsville?"

"We're not going to Martinsville, but head in that direction."

Since I rarely traveled that way, I only knew one way to go. I drove south on Pennsylvania and then west on Morris Street until I hit Harding, a street I knew would turn into Indiana 37. Thirty miles on that should take me right to

Martinsville. Oddly enough, considering the company in my car, I found myself settling into the drive easily. As soon as she could, Carla would try something, but I hadn't come completely defenseless. I had a firearm beside my seat and backup behind me. We could handle this.

I drove until I left the city buildings behind. Comparatively few cars joined us on that lonely stretch of road, but I could see a few in my rearview mirror. Hopefully they included Paul and Emilia.

"If we're not going to Martinsville, where are we going?" I asked.

"Why do you need to know?"

I drummed my fingers on the steering wheel. "I'm driving. Sometimes it's nice to know where I'm going."

"Tonight, you'll just have to live in suspense, then."

That's what I had thought. I drove for another half hour before reaching the outskirts of town. At first, the businesses and churches we passed sat on large plots of land. They sold plumbing fixtures, off-road vehicles, four-wheelers—the kind of things people would go out of their way to purchase. Then, as we approached the town, we passed convenience stores, chain restaurants, and other businesses that relied on foot traffic and impulse shoppers. Traffic picked up, and I could see streetlights in the distance, bright and almost garish as they overpowered the light of the stars.

"We're in Martinsville," I said. "You care to tell me where we're going now?"

"No," she said, staring out the window. "Keep driving straight."

We drove most of the way through town until we approached an intersection with a Walgreen's on one corner, a heavy equipment yard on the second, and a gas station on the third. Mahalasville Road.

"Hang a left," said Carla.

I nodded and slowed at the light before doing as she asked. Mahalasville felt tight and cramped after Indiana 37. It had two lanes with a double line down the center, and I knew as soon as I turned on it that we'd shortly be leaving civilization behind. I glanced in my rearview mirror. If Emilia and Paul turned off here, she'd notice. Hopefully they'd hang back some. At that time in the evening, blackness enveloped us quickly as we left the town behind. The road swooped left, and we passed what might have been a field full of winter wheat, but I couldn't tell in the dark. I could feel myself growing a little worried. Out there alone with a crazy woman, I felt awfully isolated.

"You've got to tell me where we're going," I said.

She sighed. "You're like a child. It's not far. Just keep driving."

We passed an elementary school, and the road swooped to the right. My headlights swept across a landscape as lonely as the moon. Plants, hills, trees. Not a single house in sight. Far behind us, I could just make out two pinpricks of light. Headlights, hopefully my backup. We drove on and on, into that blackness, and I found myself sinking deeper and deeper into that measureless night at the core of every man's soul when he truly looks at himself and knows that he is alone in the world.

"Our turn is up there," said Carla, pointing ahead of me. I slowed the car and searched out the side of the road until I saw it. A small break in the asphalt, nothing more. It looked like a driveway. Low Gap Road, the sign said. I turned and found myself, once more, on a dark road to nowhere.

"I used to come out here when I was young to escape my family," said Carla. "I used to hope they'd change when I came back. They never did, though."

"People don't change, not who they are," I said, surprised that I found myself agreeing with her. "We get older, and then we die. That's it."

I could see her cock her head at me in the glow of the dashboard lights. "You and I aren't really all that different. I wish I had met you under other circumstances. We could have been friends."

"I don't think so," I said, shaking my head. "I don't befriend murderers."

"I guess I am a murderer," she said, turning her eyes toward the road in front of us once again. "But you've killed people, too. Lots of people, from what I've seen."

"I have," I said.

"We've both done what's necessary to protect others and to punish the wicked. The only difference between us is that I'm not afraid to look in the mirror at the end of the day."

Part of me shuddered inside because part of me agreed with her. "I'm not like you."

She looked out of the window again. "You fight monsters long enough, you'll become one, Mr. Rashid. If you're not there yet, you will be one day soon. Turn up here."

I turned as she asked and flicked on my bright lights. Deep woods bounded the road on the right side, blocking my view, while an open field to my left allowed me to see the moon and stars. I turned once more at her direction onto Rosenbaum, a strip of asphalt no wider than a school bus. I passed a couple of houses, two of which had no-trespassing signs out front, and then the woods pressed in on me once again as I left the fields. As I drove, the road seemed to narrow even further, forcing me to slow to a virtual crawl. Then I saw a break in the tree line and a shaft of moonlight on the asphalt, maybe half a mile up.

"Kill your headlights and pull up to that driveway."

"Whose house is it?"

She didn't take her eyes from the road in front of us. "Mine. I bought it to escape my husband before he went to prison."

"Who's in it now?"

She didn't answer. I turned off my headlights and continued driving at maybe ten miles an hour, my engine barely idling. When I came to a stop, I found a two-story farmhouse in front of me. It had light-colored shutters and peeling paint that allowed me to see the underlying wood, like liver spots on an elderly man's hands. No lights sprung on and no one came out to greet me. I heard nothing in the cold, still night.

"What now?" I asked.

"You'll put your arms to your side," said Carla. I did as she asked, not because she asked but so I could reach the firearm beside my seat. As soon as my palm touched the textured grip, I used my thumb to disengage the safety. "Miguel and Jacob are inside the house, but I imagine they have other men with them. Miguel keeps a loaded AR-15 beside him at all times and a loaded pistol on a belt holster within reach wherever he goes. On either side of the door, he's installed a half-inch thick metal plate that you will not be able to shoot through. I thought it only fair to tell you that. It'll even the odds."

"Is Valerie in there, too?" I asked.

"If she's still alive," said Carla, staring straight ahead at the house. She had something planned, but I couldn't see it yet. Carla blinked but didn't say anything.

"Is this where you plan to take my car and leave?"

"No," she said, turning her head toward me. "This is where we both run."

Before I could stop her, she lunged toward me. My instincts and training told me to protect my firearm, so I held my left hand at my side and shoved her forward and into the center console with my right. I realized only too late that I had done exactly what she wanted. Her hand went right to the horn. The sound cut through the night, echoing off the woods around us.

"What the hell did you just do?" I asked.

"Bye, Detective Rashid," she said, throwing open her door. I would have tried to stop her, but the home's front door opened a crack and a figure appeared. I couldn't see him well in the moonlight, but he carried a long gun, which he pointed right at my car.

"Damn," I said, ducking beneath the console. A modern vehicle feels solid, but it's not at all. The aluminum sheeting on the outside might withstand birdshot or BBs, but even a .22 would go right through it. The engine block, though, gave me some cover, at least for a time. The man on the porch—Miguel, I guessed—fired. The weapon had the kind of low and loud report most people only heard in war movies or on video games, and when those rounds struck the radiator and front end of my car, they rocked the entire thing on its chassis. Glass hit me in the back of the neck as shots ripped through the front window and thumped onto the seats behind me.

And then, silence.

I held my breath, my hand gripping my weapon tight. In that dark night, I heard the shooter's feet clamber down the wooden steps and onto the gravel driveway. I crept to my right, slithering across vinyl seats toward the door Carla had left open. If my shooter knew the first thing about tactics in a firefight—and Miguel Navarra certainly did—he'd never give me the chance to lie in wait and ambush him as he came to the car. If it were me, I'd walk about halfway down the driveway and start firing again. That meant my best chance to survive lay in getting the hell out of there now.

I dove through the open door, twisting so that my back landed on the gravel outside. It bit into my shoulders and neck, but I barely noticed. Before my eyes could adjust to the scene in front of me, I reached under the door with my firearm and squeezed the trigger four times, hoping to stop my assailant from coming any closer. He immediately jumped back and retreated toward the house, giving me some breathing room and time to turn onto my stomach and pull myself out of the car completely. The woods to my right looked deep and dark enough for my purposes, so I fired toward the house two more times and sprinted across the gravel driveway toward the tree line. With just nine rounds remaining, I didn't have the firepower or knowledge of the surrounding property to win this fight on my own. My goal shifted from saving Valerie to surviving long enough for backup to arrive.

The night seemed to darken as soon as my foot left the driveway and touched the hard-packed, frozen soil. I ran maybe ten yards into the woods and then ducked behind a tree with a trunk big enough to conceal me. My breath came out as a cloud of frost. As much as I wanted to hunker down and wait, I couldn't. Miguel had hunted men for a living as a special forces soldier in the Mexican Army, and I didn't even know how many friends he had with him or what kind of equipment they had. If I stopped moving, they'd shoot me before I could even see them.

I took one final breath against that tree and started running again, but I only got a few feet before a powerful spotlight swept the woods around me. Before I could second-guess myself, I dove to the ground. Gunfire shattered the night silence, and bark and wood fragments rained down on me as rounds thwacked into nearby trees. I tried to turn and fire back, but the shooting stopped and the light went out. If he had even half a brain, the shooter would be on the move, and I didn't have ammunition to waste on return shots with such a low probability of hitting a target.

I pushed myself to a crouched posture and scurried deeper into the woods, putting as many trees as I could between me and the shooter. After maybe a dozen yards, I pressed my back into a tree and peered around. Even as dark as the woods were, I could still see movement. There were two figures about a hundred feet away, and they both moved with the practiced confidence of men accustomed to the woods. As I watched, their hands flashed signals to each other, and one of them broke off his pursuit and hunkered down behind the trunk of a fallen tree. The other kept moving toward me at an oblique angle, trying to flank me and force me to a spot where they could both fire at me without fear of hitting each other. A kill box.

Unless I took one of them out now, I wouldn't survive long enough for my backup to arrive.

I looked at the woods around me. Five or six feet away, a small, dry creek bed—a depression in the dirt maybe a foot deep and two feet wide—ran to the northwest. Tree roots popped through the soil, but it'd give me a little cover. I crouched low and stepped toward it lightly, hoping my footsteps wouldn't carry in the cold night air.

A shot rang out and a round thwacked into a tree to my left.

I dove flat and felt my breath leave me in a rush. I didn't know which of the shooters that had come from, but it didn't matter. I needed cover. I crawled toward the creek on my belly and heard another shot ring out. This time, the round hit a tree maybe two feet from my head. They were zeroing in on their target.

I rolled into the ditch and lay on my back. The depression in the earth gave some cover for the time being, but I couldn't defend myself from that position.

"Come out, come out," shouted the stationary shooter. He had a heavy Spanish accent. "I know you're there."

I didn't dare raise my head to see if the second shooter had changed his direction of attack. Instead, I rolled to my stomach and started crawling, hoping they couldn't see me. Another shot rang out, this time hitting the creek bank to my right, spraying dirt across my face.

"You still breathing, cop?"

Barely.

As I looked ahead of me I could see movement. The second shooter, and he had a clear line of sight right at me. I was outgunned and out of options. I would have given anything to hug my kids one more time.

Chapter Thirty-Three

I expected to feel a bullet rip into me at any moment, but before one did, I heard a deep, almost guttural blast to my left. The bark of the tree nearest the mobile shooter, the one who I thought would kill me at any moment, exploded.

"Police. Drop your weapon and lie on the ground."

It was Paul Murphy. My backup had arrived. Paul racked another round into his shotgun, while the mobile shooter began to raise his rifle. Before he could fire, three staccato shots rang out and three rounds slammed into a second tree near him. Emilia must have had a rifle with her. I could have kissed both of them.

After that initial volley, the two groups opened up their arsenals and fired freely, seemingly forgetting about me. Rounds whizzed above my head, and in that controlled chaos, I saw my chance. I crawled forward, much faster now than I would have dared a moment ago. I could see Paul on the move to my ten o'clock, running from tree to tree and drawing the mobile shooter's fire as he retreated. The mobile shooter pressed forward, crossing the ditch in which I hid. Emilia drew his partner's fire from my six o'clock.

I pushed up to a crouch and then to a kneeling position, tracking the mobile shooter's back until I had a shot free of impeding trees or limbs. And then, as he took an ill-advised step to his left, I had it. I whistled, and he whirled around. With my backup in position, I didn't bother trying to conserve ammo. I shot him six times in the chest. He fell straight down, his shirt looking as if his heart had erupted.

"One down," I said, crouching as I hurried toward the body. I stuck my handgun inside my right jacket pocket and then picked up his rifle, an AR-15 with a pretty decent scope. "Paul, you okay?"

"Fine," said Paul, still behind a tree. "You?"

"Alive," I said, turning to the last position from which I had heard Officer Rios shoot. "Emilia?"

"Still here, but he's got me pinned behind a tree."

As if to emphasize the point, the stationary shooter, the one I hadn't paid much attention to recently, popped up, fired four shots at her, and then ducked behind a log. I didn't have a firing solution on him yet, but we had a numbers advantage now. Still crouched low, I ran to a walnut tree near to the tree behind which Paul hid.

"How many shells you have left?" I asked, my voice barely above a whisper.

Paul felt the outside of his jacket pocket. "Seven shells and twenty rounds for my .45."

I wished we could coordinate with Emilia, but that should be plenty of ammunition for our purposes.

"Our shooter's dug in there pretty well, so I'm going to sweep around and try to get to his side. If that's Miguel Navarra, he's a former special forces soldier, so he's going to see this coming and try to intercept me. You see him move, you move straight toward him and fire at his back. That will free Emilia, and hopefully she'll follow. We should be able to flush him to open ground where we can take him down."

Paul looked toward the shooter's stationary position. "You sure this is a good idea?"

"No, but it's all I've got."

He nodded and then took a deep breath. "It's been nice knowing you."

"Yeah, you, too."

Paul fired at Miguel's position and I ran to a maple tree to my nine o'clock. We waited a moment, and then Paul fired again, giving me cover as I ran to yet another tree, this time about a dozen yards away. Emilia must have sensed what we were doing because she fired as well in the interim, pinning the stationary shooter down. For the first time, I thought this could work.

And then it all went wrong.

The shooter popped up and threw something at Emilia's position. Our department receives bulletins every day from law enforcement agencies around the world warning of particularly dangerous threats. One recently mentioned that Border Patrol agents had reported confiscating a box containing fifty-five hand grenades, surplus from civil wars in El Salvador and Nicaragua, from a drug runner near the US–Mexico border outside of Douglas, Arizona. The cartels purchased them in bulk for a couple hundred dollars each.

I should have expected Miguel to have some.

The grenade thumped against a tree a couple of feet from Emila's position before coming to rest on the ground.

"Get down," I shouted. She dove away from the device, shielding herself with the trunk of a maple tree. The grenade blew like a firework on the Fourth of July, and just like the fireworks, the sound reverberated through the woods. The shooter turned and sprinted. Paul started to give chase, but I waved him off and pointed to Emilia.

"Check her."

I held my breath and waited long enough to see Emilia move before sprinting after the shooter. He had probably twenty yards on me, and he hit the tree line at a dead run. Even with the distance, I heard his feet bite into the gravel.

I couldn't let him get to the house. If he carried a grenade on him, I didn't even want to speculate what he had inside.

As soon as I reached the tree line, I sprinted toward my car to use the hood to steady my shot. If he hit the house, he'd dive behind the steel plate Carla mentioned he had built beside the door, knowing I couldn't shoot through it. Then this would turn into a siege, and with a pregnant hostage potentially in the house, that wouldn't end well. Too many innocent people had already died because of this case.

I lined up the shot. As the shooter's foot hit the stairs at the base of the porch, I squeezed the trigger. The rifle jerked against my shoulder but not as much as I expected. I fired again, and then again, and then again. Four rounds total, each of which hit the shooter in the back. He fell straight to the ground and didn't move. I held my rifle in front of me in case I had to lay down covering fire, and sprinted towards his corpse. As I reached down to feel his throat and make sure I had killed him, a firearm roared from deep inside the house and the left side of the doorframe exploded. Wooden shrapnel hit my arms, ripping my coat sleeve in several spots. A piece of wood hit me in the chin, almost knocking me back. I could taste blood in my mouth.

Before the shooter could get another shot off, I dove onto the porch and crawled as fast as I could toward the front door. That steel plate inside wouldn't just protect the shooter, it'd also protect me. I pressed my back into it. The second blast hit that plate with an almost deafening thud, causing the entire house to shudder. The shooter had tracked me via the sound, and by the damage he had caused, I'd say he had a shotgun loaded with lead slugs. At this distance, even had I been in full body armor, those slugs would rip right through me as easily as they'd go through paper. Even with my rifle, he had me outgunned at such close quarters.

I grabbed the largest chunk of wood I could find and tossed it to my left. Two more shots rang out, splintering the home's exterior where the wood hit the ground. Most of the shotguns I've fired have a 4+1 capacity, meaning they can hold four shells in the magazine tube and one in the barrel, but I know of several that hold eight rounds or even more if someone's modified them. I wouldn't win this by going toe-to-toe with him. Worse than that, I had maybe twenty yards of open space between me and my vehicle. If I made a run for it, he'd pick me off. I needed a plan.

My lip had started bleeding heavily, and I could feel the coppery blood begin to travel down my chin, so I spit onto the porch. The liquid glimmered black in the moonlight and that gave me my idea. Hansel and Gretel. I looked at the door and bit my lip hard enough to tear open the wound a little more. What had been a trickle turned into a flow. I spit again, forming an even bigger mark on the porch. Next, I spit into my hand and laid it on the ground, forming a print. I glanced at the door, half expecting to see somebody coming out. For this to work, I needed to move now.

I pressed my back against the house and crept to the far corner of the porch, periodically leaving a new mark in blood in my wake. Once I reached the corner, I slipped off the porch but kept my back to the house. I dropped the rifle and took my handgun out of my pocket, and there, in the shadow thrown by the eaves, I waited.

I could hear the shooter as he walked inside the house, presumably searching for me through the windows. His footsteps faded a moment later, but then I heard them again, this time unfiltered by the home's walls. He had stepped onto the porch. The night stopped dead. I held my breath, my body tensing.

Come on. Follow the trail.

The steps came toward me, lighter than I would have expected, and then they stopped altogether. I slowly inhaled. His footsteps started again, haltingly. He couldn't have been more than five feet away now. I could hear his heavy breathing.

And then his breath stopped, and in that moment, I knew he planned to move. I was ready.

He whipped around the corner faster than I would have given him credit for, but not fast enough. Instead of stepping back and drawing my weapon on him as he probably expected, I stepped toward him before he could bring the shotgun around, stopping him from leveling it at my chest. I hooked my left arm over the heavy weapon, pinning the barrel against my side. He pulled hard on the shotgun with both arms. In the moonlight, I caught sight of a teenager's acne-scarred face.

I brought my pistol up to his chin. His body instantly tensed.

"Your partners are dead. I don't want to kill you, but I will."

He snarled and then yanked hard on his gun. Even though I probably had forty pounds on him, I knew I couldn't hold him off with one hand. I closed my eyes and squeezed the trigger.

It was over.

Chapter Thirty-Four

While Paul tended to Emilia in the woods, I cleared the house and found Valerie Perez gagged and tied up in a second-floor bathroom. She'd go to the hospital, but she looked physically okay to my eyes. I helped her stand and then took her to the front porch.

"Paul, it's clear."

He didn't say anything, but I saw him carry Emilia from the woods a moment later. Blood had seeped through one of her pant legs, but her head swiveled left and right, telling me she was still alert. He set her on the steps and then took a deep breath.

"I've got to stop smoking," he said, his lungs wheezing as he breathed.

"You okay, Emilia?" I asked, kneeling beside her. She nodded.

"Shrapnel wound, I think. It's not bad. Bleeding's mostly stopped. Everything copacetic here?"

I nodded. "Yeah. We're safe."

Valerie started sobbing as soon as I said the word safe. I would have put my arm around her, but Emilia beat me to it. Since none of us had a cell phone signal, I went to the gunshot-ridden wreck that was my car and hit the emergency button Agent Havelock had given me. The four of us sat in silence beside Miguel Navarra's corpse until four black

SUVs skidded to a stop with anticlimactic flurry. Four black-clad FBI agents jumped out of each vehicle, their weapons drawn. They spread out, looking for threats. Special Agent Havelock climbed out of the driver's seat of the lead vehicle gingerly. I stood and waved him over to the body.

"Everybody's dead but Carla. I have no idea where she went."

"I see you shot Miguel Navarra," he said, focusing on the body at my feet.

"I guess I did," I said, glancing at the corpse.

"You want to tell me what happened?" he asked, looking at the damaged farmhouse and surrounding woods.

"Eventually," I said, looking back at my team. "I need a pair of ambulances. I've got wounded."

Havelock looked past me to Emilia and Valerie and then nodded. "I'll put the call in."

While we waited for paramedics, Havelock and his men separated my team and interviewed us individually to find out what had happened. I looked forward one day to reading Paul and Emilia's action reports, but for now I just wanted the situation over. Mike Bowers and Sylvia Lombardo arrived about an hour later, so I repeated my story to them. And then I repeated it to a major from the state police, and then to an assistant US attorney, and finally to an attorney from the Indiana Attorney General's Office. I imagined I'd have to repeat the whole thing once more to my car insurance company when they saw my wife's VW, but that could wait. After approximately two hours, a state trooper volunteered to drive me to Martinsville, where I could get a cell phone signal. I called my wife. Captain Bowers had already let her know that I was okay, but I wanted to hear her voice. Thankfully, she didn't ask me what had happened, so I simply told her that I loved her and would be home when I could.

Everyone I had shot carried a driver's license, so we ID'd the bodies quickly. I had gotten Miguel as he ran toward the house and Jacob Valdez as he tried to kill me around the side of the house. Havelock identified the body in the woods, Miguel's partner, as Andrew Salazar, Tristan Salazar's little brother. Murder apparently ran in the family. We closed our case, but rarely did that come at such a cost. I didn't even know how many people had died.

I answered questions most of the night, but Paul Murphy drove me home at about two in the morning.

The next week went quickly. Our department's forensic accountants went through Carla's holdings and found almost two dozen properties held by half a dozen corporations. Some she used for legitimate businesses—a gym in Carmel, a strip mall in Zionsville—but we found four additional marijuana grow houses and a number of other vacant homes she could turn into grow houses with a little preparation. In addition, we found brokerage and bank accounts containing assets totaling nineteen million dollars. Since many of Carla's financial transactions involved complex financial crimes that IMPD didn't have the resources to investigate, we ended up bringing in the FBI. Given time, our departments would fight over the seized assets, but for now, they focused on building cases against the men and women who had helped Carla launder her money. Using Carla's information as a toehold, our forensic accountants would be busy for years.

As for Carla, we never found her body, but Mexican police found her head beside a *Santa Muerte* shrine in Nuevo Laredo, Mexico. Karma's a bitch, I guess.

Upon finding out that his Uncle Miguel had died in a gunfight with the police, Danny Navarra turned on his gang and gave up everybody in exchange for a plea deal for his numerous crimes. IMPD closed six homicides—two of which we knew nothing about—because of his intel, and arrested four *Barrio Sureño* members for murder. We also picked up almost every other active member of the gang on lesser charges. A couple of the youngest members—boy and girls who couldn't even drive—escaped without arrest, but hopefully they had learned a lesson. You live by the sword, you die by the sword.

With *Barrio Sureño* effectively gutted and neutered, my family and I tried moving back into our house, but with the first step inside, I knew it had stopped being home. We put it up for sale and moved in with my sister temporarily. Megan went back to school, though, and Kaden continued to surprise us every day with how much he grew and the new things he could do. My wife continued reviewing awful movies on her blog and making coffee so horrible a little part of me dies inside every time I think about it. As the days passed, and my experiences shifted into memories, I found myself less and less horrified at the prospect of civilian life. I loved being a police officer, but I didn't *need* to be a police officer. Nearly losing my job had taught me that.

Life more or less returned to normal for everyone else connected to the Santino Ramirez trial, too. Two days after being rescued from the house, Valerie Perez had a little girl. She named her Michelle, after her friend. Brian and Jasmine Alexander didn't even miss a single lunch service at their soup kitchen. Despite committing perjury in a murder trial, none of them would go to jail anytime soon, at least not for their testimony. All of them, though, would carry the guilt of their friends' deaths on their shoulders for the rest of their lives.

Santino Ramirez had a comparatively rougher go of things. The state of Indiana dropped all charges against him relating to the shooting death of Angel Hererra, but he never made it out of prison. The day before his release, the Laporte County Prosecuting Attorney charged him with attempting to hire a hit man to torture and murder his wife. I've never met two people who more deserved each other.

Throughout the week, I think I met every lawyer in the state—or at least it felt like that, as I sat through meeting after meeting, repeating the same story every time. When I wasn't sitting in meetings with lawyers, I was at the house, fixing things in the hope that would sell quicker. I also managed to reassemble my wife's rocking chair. Remarkably, that turned out okay. When I finished, it didn't squeak, it didn't wobble, and it didn't feel as if it would break as soon as I sat down. One day, maybe Megan or Kaden would rock their children in it. I hoped they would. Randy, my lawyer, called every day asking if I had decided to accept my promotion. I fended off his inquiries for a while, but by the following Monday, it became clear I couldn't anymore. First, though, I had something to do.

I put on a suit and tie and went into my office to fill out paperwork, the same thing I had done every day of the previous week, but instead of going home at lunchtime, I walked to the City-County Building and met Captain Bowers and Special Agent Havelock in the homicide unit's conference room. Both men wore suits and ties as if they planned to go to court.

"You ready for this, Ash?" asked Bowers.

"I guess I'm going to have to be," I said.

Havelock patted me on the shoulder. "You'll be fine, Lieutenant."

The three of us took the elevator to the lobby, where about a dozen reporters—local and national—and Sylvia

Lombardo awaited us. As soon as the three of us arrived, Sylvia turned the reporters.

"Thank you all for coming. We're here to discuss the events of the past week. As you know, we've had a busy week here at IMPD. Seventy-nine people died in a coordinated assault on our city seven days ago. I'm here to announce that detectives working alongside their counterparts in the FBI have officially closed that investigation. And let me be absolutely clear: it was a tragedy, but it was not terrorism. Members of a violent criminal organization smuggled men and women into our community and then subsequently murdered them when it became apparent that our detectives had discovered their illegal activities. To cover their tracks, they burned their places of business down, they shot their associates, and they murdered everyone who could identify them to the police.

"Our detectives tracked these heinous men down and attempted to arrest them. Rather than face their punishment, they opened fire on our officers, and in the ensuing fight, every suspect died. This is a tragedy all around, but it didn't have to be. These men chose to take up arms, and they chose to kill. Let me be absolutely clear, though: this is over. Thanks to the courage of our officers, this tragedy has come to a conclusion.

"For specific questions, I'll turn this over to the leaders of our team. Captain Mike Bowers, who leads IMPD's Crimes Against Persons Division and Special Agent Kevin Havelock, the agent in charge of the local FBI field office."

I waited, expecting her to say my name, but she didn't. The cameras focused on Bowers and Havelock, and I took a reluctant step back.

And so my career ends, with not a bang but a whimper.

I had hoped for more than that, but it didn't matter in the end. I counted down the minutes for the press conference to end. At almost exactly an hour, Sylvia Lombardo interrupted a reporter and drew the press conference to a close. The crowds began to disperse quickly, but before he could leave, I put a hand on Mike Bowers' elbow.

"Hey," I said. "Can we talk in your office?"

He looked at me up and down before nodding. "Sure."

We took the elevator to his floor in relative silence. Once we had arrived in his wood-paneled office, Bowers took off his coat and threw it on an empty chair while gesturing to the one beside it.

"Have a seat," he said, sitting behind his desk. Instead of sitting, I reached into my jacket for an envelope and put it on his desk.

"This is my letter of resignation. You were my last real supervisor, so I thought I should give it to you."

Bowers reached for the envelope, but he didn't open it. "Why don't you sit down? We'll talk before you do anything rash."

I shook my head. "We don't have anything to talk about. Tell Sylvia Lombardo that I appreciate the promotion, but I can't take it. Hannah and I put the house on the market, and I've put a deposit down on an office in southern Indiana, near Evansville. After shooting Dante, and the riots and the brick through my window, I'm spent. I'm hanging out my shingle and starting a small legal practice. I'll write wills and help people adopt kids."

"You don't need to do this. The riots are winding down and cooler heads are prevailing. Something good may even come out of this. Your shooting got people talking. That's a good thing."

"I'm glad Dante's death isn't in vain, but that doesn't change anything. I'm done."

Bowers squinted. "Did you read your orders?"

In fact, I had read them so often I had them practically memorized. "Yeah."

Bowers stood up, walked around his desk, and then moved his jacket so he could sit down. "Have a seat so we can talk about your new position."

"I'm done, and I'm tired. I'd rather just go home."

The humor and patience left Bowers' eyes. "Sit down, Ash."

I sighed and sat. "Fine. What now?"

Bowers leaned back in his chair. "You're not an idiot."

"Thank you," I said, crossing my arms. "I guess."

Bowers didn't blink. "Your new position pays eighty-five grand a year and has a pension. It's a good job. You've got two kids and a wife to support. You're not going to do better in the private sector."

"This isn't about money," I said, shaking my head. "I can't do this anymore. I'm tired of being mistrusted, and I'm tired of playing departmental politics."

Something I said must have been funny because Bowers smiled and snickered.

"Whatever you're doing, you've never played departmental politics. You may think you're a scalpel cutting through bureaucratic red tape, but you're more like a blowtorch glued to a can of gasoline."

"Do you have a point, or did you ask me to sit so you could insult me?"

Bowers didn't say anything for a few seconds, but then he stood, walked to his window, and stared out. "Back when I started this job, the bad guys carried revolvers and our department had its own biker task force. In your entire career, you ever investigate a biker gang?"

"No," I said, shaking my head.

"The world's changing. We don't always get along, but I trust you. You've never given me a reason to question your motives or your ability."

"Just my judgment," I said, quickly.

"Yeah. I'm not going to lie to you. You've made some bad calls," said Bowers, turning and nodding. "But you made them for the right reasons. That matters."

Funny, but it didn't seem to matter that he had tried to have me fired for those bad calls.

"What are you saying?" I asked.

Bowers walked around his desk and sat on the edge, just a foot or two from me.

"After your hearing, I talked to Dennis Parker, the point man on the review board. Leonard Wilson offered to hire his kid if he voted to fire you. He also said that Leonard offered to sponsor Frank Wong in his country club for his vote. Sandra Messenger wouldn't admit that he offered her anything, but she changed her mind about you pretty fast after a lunch appointment." Bowers paused for just a second. "Of course, Leonard didn't outright say he was buying their votes, but everybody knew. It was *quid pro quo*."

"Leonard doesn't play fair," I said. "I warned you a while ago."

Bowers looked down at his feet, put his hands in his pockets, and began to rattle his keys. "He's got a lot of supporters, but he hasn't said what he plans to do with them."

"It's not going to be good no matter what it is," I said.

"That's why I don't want you to leave," said Bowers, looking up. "This department has a lot of good people in it. We argue about how to get there, but we all want the same thing: a safe city. Sometimes, a blowtorch glued to a can of gasoline is a better tool than a scalpel."

"You're not making a very strong case for staying," I said, shaking my head.

"You've put fourteen years into this department and city. You wouldn't have done that if you didn't care about it."

I unfolded my arms and shrugged. "If you want me to stay, why'd you give me this assignment? I'm hardly even a cop."

"Leonard Wilson had us locked down pretty tight, so we gave you what we could. You'll make out of it what you can. Based on your track record, I think you can find work of your own."

I held up my index finger and then began counting off. "I don't have a staff, I don't have a budget, I don't even have a clear mandate to do anything. I've hardly got a job."

"But it is a job. You're a cop," said Bowers, his voice remaining even. "Take a couple of days off. Spend some time with your wife and kids and then come in on Monday. We'll talk more about your new assignment."

I looked back out the window, thinking. "Last week, Kevin Havelock asked me to investigate Leonard Wilson. He have any say in this?"

"I'm not alone in wanting you back at IMPD," said Bowers. "And I'd say the placement of your office one floor from Leonard Wilson's wasn't a coincidence."

I looked back at Captain Bowers. "So you really want me to stay?"

"I want you to do what's best for you and your family," he said. "I also think we both know what that is."

And I did know. I couldn't lie and say I wanted the job solely to make the world a better place. Starting a legal practice in a new city without a guaranteed income terrified me.

Maybe I had resisted my new position with the department at first because I needed to hear somebody still valued my service. Or maybe I was just being stubborn. I don't know. All I know is that I still wanted to be a cop. It felt right.

Bowers and I talked for another five minutes, but we didn't say anything of substance. I told him I'd see him on Monday, though. Afterwards, I drove to my sister's place and met my wife and kids in the kitchen. My brother-in-law and sister must have been at work. Both Kaden and Megan were drawing at the kitchen table, while my wife stood over them, her hands on their shoulders. I smiled at the scene. Sibling rivalry had only come to our house in the last few months, so if Hannah touched one of them or said something nice to one of them, she had to touch or say something equally nice to the other or a fight would break out. I liked to see them getting along.

When I walked in, Megan turned around first, but then Kaden followed. My son had seen me just a few hours earlier, but he got off his chair and ran to me anyway, his arms outstretched.

"I drew a cow," he said.

"That's great," I said, wondering what had motivated him to draw a cow of all things in the world. "What did your sister draw?"

"A unicorn," she said, holding up her picture. I took it from her outstretched hand.

"That is the best unicorn I've seen today," I said.

"Is it better than Kaden's cow?"

My son's cow drawing consisted mostly of a couple of amorphous blobs, but it was brown, a cow-like color. As much as I wanted to praise my daughter's unicorn, I had yet to see one in real life, giving me little to compare it to.

"They're both equally wonderful," I said, putting her picture in front of her. "But I especially like your unicorn's pink fur."

She smiled from ear to ear and went back to her drawing. I turned to my wife. She mouthed *hey*. I stepped close to her and felt the warmth of her torso through my shirt.

"How'd it go?" she asked.

I looked at her and then at the floor. "How would you feel about staying in Indianapolis? We'll lose the deposit I put down on that office in Evansville, but I can get out of the lease."

She put a hand on my chest and then leaned in to kiss my cheek. "I've been looking at houses. How do you feel about moving to Carmel? It's a little pricey, but they have some nice neighborhoods. The schools are good, too."

"You never thought we'd leave, did you?"

Hannah smiled and then winked. "I thought it best to consider all the possibilities. You're a police officer. That's who you are, and I didn't think you could walk away from that."

I looked at the breakfast table, and both kids looked up at me expectantly. I shook my head. Life wouldn't always work out perfectly, but no matter what happened in the future, I knew we'd survive and pull together. That's what families do.

"I choose to be a police officer. It's my job, but it's not who I am," I said, reaching out for my wife. "More than anything else, I'm a dad and your husband. And I wouldn't change that for the world."

Like Ash Rashid and Measureless Night?

Like the book you just read? I hope you did because I've got many more Ash Rashid novels planned.

If you'd like to hear more about Ash and future novels, you've got two options.

1. You can look me up on Amazon and repeatedly press the refresh button on your browser until a new book shows up. I don't recommend this as you might be pressing a button for months on end.
2. You can join my mailing list. I only send out emails when I have a major announcement, so I don't email very often. [Once a month at most.] As a bonus, you'll receive a free copy of The Abbey, my first Ash Rashid title.

You can sign up here: http://www.indiecrime.com/newsletter/

If my mailing list doesn't appeal to you, you can also connect with me on Facebook here: http://www.facebook.com/ChrisCulverbooks

Or at my webpage here: http://www.indiecrime.com

About the Author

Chris Culver is the New York Times bestselling author of the Ash Rashid series of mysteries. After graduate school, Chris taught courses in ethics and comparative religion at a small liberal arts university in southern Arkansas. While there and when he really should have been grading exams, he wrote The Abbey, which spent sixteen weeks on the New York Times bestseller's list and introduced the world to Detective Ash Rashid.

Chris has been a storyteller since he was a kid, but he decided to write crime fiction after picking up a dog-eared, coffee-stained paperback copy of Mickey Spillane's I, the Jury in a library book sale. Many years later, his wife, despite considerable effort, still can't stop him from bringing more orphan books home. The two of them, along with a labrador retriever named Roy, reside near St. Louis where Chris is hard at work on his next novel.

He can be reached by sending an email to: chris@indiecrime.com

Printed in Great Britain
by Amazon.co.uk, Ltd.,
Marston Gate.